ACCLAIM FOR *You Shall Know Our Velocity!*

A *New York Times* Notable Book

A *Village Voice, San Jose Mercury News,*
and *Minneapolis Star Tribune*
Best Book of the Year

"The bottom line that matters is this: Eggers has written a terrific novel, an entertaining and imaginative tale." —*The Boston Globe*

"*You Shall Know Our Velocity* achieves a kind of anguished, profane poetry. . . . It's so good to hear Eggers' voice." —*Newsweek*

"There are some wonderful set-pieces here, and memorable phrases tossed on the ground like unwanted pennies from the guy who runs the mint." —*The Washington Post Book World*

"If Holden Caulfield had been a child of the frequent-flyer era, he would have found fellow travelers in Will and Hand, the buddies Eggers sends ping-ponging around the globe." —*People*

"Eggers' writing really takes off—his forte is the messy, funny tirade, stuffed with convincing pain and wry observation." —*Newsday*

"Eggers can write about pretty much anything and make it glitter and somersault on the page. He can do suspense. He can do lyric description. And he can do entertaining travelogues." —*The New York Times*

"Somewhere between a winded heave and a mantric sigh. . . . Casts Eggers as an impressive first-time novelist with a stunning handle on language and a loudly beating heart." —*The Onion*

"Think of MTV's *Jackass* as scripted by Samuel Beckett. . . . Punctuated by surprising, elegant lyrics: similes, epiphanies, gorgeous writing. . . . A messy, funny book." —*New York*

ALSO BY DAVE EGGERS

A Heartbreaking Work of Staggering Genius

AS EDITOR

The Best American Nonrequired Reading:
Shiny Adidas Tracksuits and the Death of Camp,
and Other Essays from Might Magazine

Dave Eggers

You Shall Know Our Velocity!

Dave Eggers is the founder of McSweeney's, a small group that sells taxidermy equipment and also produces books, a literary quarterly and *The Believer,* a monthly review. McSweeney's, based in San Francisco, is also home to 826 Valencia, a non-profit educational center for Bay Area youth, which also sells pirate supplies. Eggers's first book was *A Heartbreaking Work of Staggering Genius,* which was a finalist for the Pulitzer Prize. This is his first novel.

You Shall Know Our Velocity!

Dave Eggers

You Shall Know Our Velocity!

[*previous retitled as* Sacrament]

VINTAGE CANADA

Published in Canada by Vintage Canada, a division of Random House of Canada Limited, and simultaneously in the United States by Vintage Books, a division of Random House, Inc., New York, in 2003. Distributed by Random House of Canada Limited, Toronto. Originally published in hardcover in the United States by McSweeney's Publishing, San Francisco, in 2002.

Vintage Canada and colophon are registered trademarks of Random House of Canada Limited.

Portions of this work were originally published in *The New Yorker*.

Previously retitled as *Sacrament*.

National Library of Canada Cataloguing in Publication

Eggers, Dave
You shall know our velocity / Dave Eggers.

ISBN 0-676-97610-7

I. Title.

PS3605.E34Y69 2003   813'.6   C2003-901957-8

www.randomhouse.ca

Printed in the United States of America

10   9   8   7   6   5   4   3   2   1

This book is dedicated to Beth

You Shall Know Our Velocity!

EVERYTHING WITHIN TAKES PLACE AFTER JACK DIED AND BEFORE MY MOM AND I DROWNED IN A BURNING FERRY IN THE COOL TANNIN-TINTED GUAVIARE RIVER, IN EAST-CENTRAL COLOMBIA, WITH FORTY-TWO LOCALS WE HADN'T YET MET. IT WAS A CLEAR AND EYEBLUE DAY, THAT DAY, AS WAS THE FIRST DAY OF THIS STORY, A FEW YEARS AGO IN JAN-UARY, ON CHICAGO'S NORTH SIDE, IN THE OPULENT SHADOW OF WRIGLEY AND WITH THE WIND COMING LOW AND SEARCHING OFF THE JAGGED HALF-FROZEN LAKE. I WAS INSIDE, VERY WARM, WALKING FROM DOOR TO DOOR.

I was talking to Hand, one of my two best friends, the one still alive, and we were planning to leave. At this point there were good days, good weeks, when we pretended that it was acceptable that Jack had lived at all, that his life had been, in its truncated way, complete. This wasn't one of those days. I was pacing and Hand knew I was pacing and knew what it meant. I paced like this when figuring or planning, and rolled my knuckles, and snapped my fingers softly and without rhythm, and walked from the western edge of the apartment, where I would lock and unlock the front door, and then east, to the back deck's glass sliding door, which I opened quickly, thrust my head through and shut again. Hand could hear the quiet roar of the door moving back and forth on its rail, but said nothing. The air was arctic and it was Friday afternoon and I was home, in the new blue flannel pajama pants I wore most days then, indoors or out. A stupid and nervous bird the color of feces fluttered to the feeder over the deck and ate the ugly mixed seeds I'd put in there for no reason and lately regretted—these birds would die in days and I didn't want to watch their flight or demise. This building warmed itself without regularity or equitable distribution to its corners, and my apartment, on the rear left upper edge, got its heat rarely and in bursts. Jack was twenty-six and died five months before and now Hand and I would leave for a while. I had my ass beaten two weeks ago by three shadows in a storage unit in Oconomowoc—it had nothing to do with Jack or anything else, really, or maybe it did, maybe it was distantly Jack's fault and immediately Hand's—and we had to leave for a while. I had scabs on my face and back and a rough pear-shaped bump on the crown of my head and I had this money that had to be disseminated and so Hand and I would leave. My head was a condemned church with a ceiling of bats but I swung from this dark mood to euphoria when I thought about leaving.

"When?" said Hand.

"A week from now," I said.

"The seventeenth?"

"Right."

"This seventeenth."

"Right."

"Jesus."

"Can you get the week off?"

"I don't know," Hand asked. "Can I ask a dumb question?"

"What?"

"Why not this summer?"

"Because."

"Or next fall?"

"Come on."

"What?"

"I'll pay for it if we go now," I said. I knew Hand would say yes because for five months we hadn't said no. There had been some difficult requests but we hadn't said no.

"And you owe me," I added.

"What? For—Oh Jesus. Fine."

"Good."

"For how long again?" he asked.

"How long can you get off?" I asked.

"Probably a week." I knew he would do it. Hand would have quit his job if they refused the time off. He had a decent arrangement now, as a security supervisor on a casino on the river under the Arch, but for a while, in high school, he'd been the Number Two–ranked swimmer in all of Wisconsin, and he expected that kind of glory going forward. He'd never focused again like he'd focused then, and now he was a dabbler, with some experience as a recording engineer, some in car alarms, some in weather futures (true, long story), some as a carpenter—we'd actually worked on one summer gig together, a porch on an enormous gingerbread-looking place on Lake Geneva—but he left any job where he wasn't learning or when his dignity, however defined, was anywhere compromised.

"Then a week," I said. "We'll do what we can in a week."

I lived in Chicago, Hand in St. Louis, though we were both from Milwaukee, or just outside. We were born there, three months apart, and our dads bowled together, before mine was gone the first time, before his started playing drums, wearing suspenders and leather vests. We didn't talk about our fathers.

We called the airlines that offered single-fare tickets with unlimited travel. The tickets allowed unrestricted flying as long as you kept going one direction, once around the globe without turning back. You usually have twelve months to complete the circuit, but we'd have to do it in a week. They cost $3,000 each, a number out of the reach of people like us under normal circumstances, in rational times, but I had gotten some money about a year before, in a windfall kind of way, and had been both grateful and constantly confused by it. And now I would get rid of it, or most of it, and believed purging would provide clarity, and that doing this in a quick global flurry would make it . . . I really don't know why we combined these two ideas. We just, blindly and without self-doubt, figured we would go all the way around, once, in a week, starting in Chicago, ideally hitting Saskatchewan first, then Mongolia, then Yemen, then Rwanda, then Madagascar—maybe those last two switched around—then Siberia, then Greenland, then home. Easy.

"This'll be good," said Hand.

"It will," I said.

"How much are we getting rid of again?"

"I think $38,000."

"Is that including the tickets?"

"Yeah."

"So we're actually giving away what—$32,000?"

"Something like that," I said.

"How are you going to bring it? Cash?"

"Traveler's checks."

"And then we give it to who?" he asked.

"I don't know yet. I think it'll be obvious when we get there."

And if we kept traveling west, we'd lose very little time. We could easily make our way around the world in a week, with maybe five stops along the way—the hours elapsed would in part be voided by the crossing, always westerly, of time zones. From Saskatchewan we'd get to Mongolia, we figured, having lost only two or three hours riding the Arctic Circle. We would oppose the turning of the planet and refuse the setting of the sun.

The itinerary changed on each of the four days we had to decide, on the phone, with me consulting a laminated pocket atlas and Hand in St. Louis with his globe, a huge thing, the size of a beach ball, which spun wildly between poles—he'd bumped into it one late night and it was no longer smooth—and which dominated his living room.

So first:

Chicago to Saskatchewan to Mongolia

Mongolia to Qatar

Qatar to Yemen

Yemen to Madagascar

Madagascar to Rwanda

Rwanda to San Francisco to Chicago.

We liked that one. But it was too warm, too concentrated in one latitude. The next one, with adjustments:

Chicago to San Francisco to Mongolia

Mongolia to Yemen

Yemen to Madagascar

Madagascar to Greenland

Greenland to Saskatchewan

Saskatchewan to San Francisco to Chicago.

We'd solved the warmth problem, but went too far the other way. We needed better contrast, more back and forth, more up and down, while always heading west. The third itinerary:

Chicago to San Francisco to Micronesia
Micronesia to Mongolia
Mongolia to Madagascar
Madagascar to Rwanda
Rwanda to Greenland
Greenland to San Francisco to Chicago.

That one had everything. Political intrigue, a climactical buffet. We began, separately at home, plugging the locations into various websites listing fares and timetables.

Hand called.

"What?"

"We're fucked."

There was something wrong with the timetable. He'd entered in the destinations, but every time we left San Francisco—we had to stop there en route from Chicago—we'd end up in Mongolia not a few hours later, but two damned *days* later.

"How can that be?"

"I figured it out," Hand said.

"What?"

"You know what it is?"

"What?"

"I'm going to lay it on you."

"Tell me."

"Ready?"

"Fuck yourself."

"The international date line," he said.

"No."

"Yes."

"The international date line!"

"Yes."

"Fuck the international date line!" I said.

"Can we do that?" he asked.

"I don't know. How does it work again?"

"Well, New Zealand is the farthest point, time-wise, in the world. They see the new year first. Which means that if we're traveling west from Chicago, we're doing pretty well in terms of saving time all the way until New Zealand. But once we get past there, we're a day ahead. A *full day* ahead."

"We lose a whole day."

"If we leave Wednesday, we land Friday."

"So it won't help to be going west," I said.

"Not much. Not at all, really."

We called an airline representative. She thought we were assholes. If we wanted to get around the world in a week, she said, we'd be in the air seventy percent of the trip. Even if we followed the sun, we'd still be hemorrhaging hours all over the Pacific.

"We have to go east," said Hand.

"Maybe we go east, then west," I said.

"We can't. We have to keep going the same direction to get the fare."

The next itinerary:

Chicago to New York to Greenland

Greenland to Rwanda

Rwanda to Madagascar

Madagascar to Mongolia

Mongolia to Saskatchewan

Saskatchewan to New York to Chicago.

"But we're losing time each flight," I said. "Each flight is basically double the time this way."

"Hell. You're right."

"We have to drop the destinations down to four maybe. Or make them shorter."

"This blows," Hand said. "We have a whole week and we have to drop Mongolia. These planes are too fucking slow. When did planes get so slow?"

Next:

Chicago to New York to Greenland
Greenland to Rwanda
Rwanda to Madagascar
Madagascar to Qatar
Qatar to Yemen
Yemen to Los Angeles to Chicago.

But there were no flights from Greenland to Rwanda. Or Rwanda to Madagascar.

"Bullshit," I said.

"I know, I know."

Or Madagascar to Qatar. There was one from Saskatchewan to New York. And one from Mongolia to Saskatchewan. But nothing from Greenland to Rwanda. We were bent. Why wouldn't there be a flight from Greenland to Rwanda? Almost everything, even Rwanda to Madagascar, had to go through someplace like Paris or London. We didn't want to be in Paris or London. Or Beijing, which is where they wanted us to stop en route to Mongolia.

"This is like the Middle Ages," Hand said.

"I had no idea," I said.

We had to scale back again. We started over.

"Let's just go," said Hand. "We get the big ticket and then make it up as we go. We don't have to plan it all out."

"Good," I said.

But no. The airline insisted on knowing the exact airports we'd visit along the way. We didn't need to provide precise dates or times, but they needed the destinations so they could calculate the taxes.

"The taxes?" Hand said.

"I didn't know they could do that."

We decided to skip the pre-planned round-the-world tickets. We'd start in Mongolia and just go from there. We'd land and then just hit the airports when we were ready to leave. Or better yet, we'd land, and while still at the airport, get our tickets out. The new plan felt good—it was more in keeping with the overall idea, anyway—that of unmitigated movement, of serving any or maybe every impulse. Once in Mongolia, we'd see what was flying out and go. It couldn't cost all that much more, we figured. How much could it cost? We had no idea. All I needed was to get around the world in a week, make it through Mongolia at some point, and be in Mexico City in eight days, for a wedding—Jeff, a friend of ours from high school, was marrying Lupe, who only Jeff called Guad, whose family lived in Cuernavaca. Huge wedding, I was told.

"You were invited?" Hand said.

"You weren't?" I said.

I don't know why Hand wasn't invited. Could I bring him? Probably not. We'd done that once before, at another friend's wedding, in Columbus—we figured maybe they just didn't have his address, so I brought him—and only once we arrived did we realize why Hand hadn't been given the nod in the first place. Hand was blond and tall and dark-eyed, I guess you'd say doe-eyed, was well-liked by women and for better and worse had a ceaseless curiosity that swung its net liberally over everything from science to even the most sensitive and trusting women. So he'd slept with too many people, including the bride's sister Sheila, soft-shouldered and romantic—and it hadn't ended well, and Hand, being Hand, had forgotten it all, the connection between Sheila and the bride and so it was awkward, that wedding, so clumsy and wrong. It was my fault, then and as it always is, in some uncanny way, every time Hand's combination of lust—for women, for arcana and conspiracy and space travel—and plain raw animal stupidity brings us, inevitably, in the path of harm and ruin.

But did we really have to get around the world? We decided that we didn't. We'd see what we could see in six, six and a half days, and then go home. We didn't know yet where exactly to start—we were leaning toward Qatar—but Hand knew where to end.

"Cairo," he said, sending the second syllable through a thin long tunnel of breath, the *o* full of melancholy and hope.

"Why?"

"We finish the trip on the top of Cheops," he said.

"They still let you climb the pyramids?"

"We bribe a guard early in the morning or at sunset. I read about this. Everyone in Giza is bribable."

"Okay," I said. "That's it then. We end at the pyramids."

"Oh man," Hand said, almost in a whisper. "I always wanted to go to Cheops. I can't believe it."

I called Cathy Wambat, my mom's high school friend, a travel agent with a name that spawned a hundred crank calls. They'd been raised in Colorado, she and my mom, in Fort Collins, which I'd never seen but always pictured with the actual fort, hewn from area lumber and still walling the pioneers from the natives. Now Cathy Wambat lived in Hawaii, where apparently all the travel agents who matter now lived. After hearing the plan, she thought we were assholes too, though in a cheerful way, and made the reservations—two one-way flights from Cairo, Hand's continuing from New York to St. Louis and mine to Mexico City.

We had to figure out where to start. Hand called again.

"We're idiots."

"What?"

"Visas," he said.

"Oh."

"Visas," he said again, now with venom.

"Fuck."

Half the destinations were thrown out. Saskatchewan was fine but Rwanda and Yemen wanted them. What was the difference between a passport and a visa? I didn't know exactly but knew there was a wait involved—three days, a week—and this was time we didn't have. Mongolia needed a visa. Qatar, in a ludicrous show of hubris for a country the shape and size of a thumb, wanted a visa that would take a week to process. We were only three days away from the time Hand had taken off work.

He called again. "Greenland doesn't want a visa."

"Okay," I said. "That's where we start."

The tickets were deadly cheap, about $400 each from O'Hare. Winter rates, said the GreenlandAir woman. We signed on and got ready. Hand would drive up from St. Louis Friday and we'd leave Sunday, for a city that we couldn't find in a dictionary or atlas. The flight stopped first in Ottawa, then at Iqaluit—on Baffin Island—before landing at Kangerlussuaq sometime around midnight. We agreed to limit the bags to one each—nothing checked, nothing awaited or lost. We'd both bring small backpacks—not back-packer backpacks, just standard ones, meant for books and beach towels.

"Coats?" asked Hand.

"No," I said. "Layers."

The cold in Chicago that January was three-dimensional, alive, predatory, so we'd head to the airport in everything we were bring-ing. We'd pack cheap disposable clothes so if we ever made it to Madagascar we could just dump the heavier stuff there. Then up to Cairo in T-shirts and empty bags.

"Okay," said Hand. "You sure you want to pay for all this?"

"Yes. I need it gone."

"You're sure."

"I am."

"Because I don't want you doing this as some weird purging bullshit thing. This doesn't have anything to do with anything—"

"No."

"Good."

"See you tomorrow."

I hung up the phone, jubilant, and threw myself into a wall,

11

then pretended to be getting electrocuted. I do this when I'm very happy.

On Saturday I had to babysit my cousin Jerry's twins, Mo and Thor, eight-year-old girls. Jerry was the only relative I had in Chicago. My mom had left Colorado to marry my father, leaving her parents, now dead, and three sisters and four brothers, all of whom stayed in or around Fort Collins. And now that Tommy— my six-years-older brother, with his own garage and mustache— was grown, my mom had moved to Memphis, to be near some old friends and take classes in anthropology. Jerry, my Aunt Terry's son, the third of five, was the family's first lawyer, with his picture in the yellow pages, and had married Melora, whose severity—she spoke only in hisses—was confounded by her small frame, that of a fourteen-year-old boy.

Jerry and Melora knew I was pretty much always around and available, so I got the nod and Hand and I brought Mo and Thor with us to get clothes and sundries. Jerry's delicate wife hated my names for her girls but I wasn't about to call two eight-year-olds, hyper kids who talked a lot, who liked to run ahead on the sidewalks and didn't mind being thrown around, goddamned Persephone and Penelope.

They were dropped off, with a honk from Melora. We found them at the door to my building. They'd met Hand three times before but didn't remember him.

"You don't look as bad," Mo said to me, her puffy pink coat swallowing her. I pulled the zipper down a few inches and she exhaled.

"It's getting better," I said.

"Now your eyes are blue," Thor added, though my eyes were always brown and were still brown. She stepped toward me and I knelt before her. "And this is new," she said, touching my nose, the red crooked stripe running down the bone.

"That was already there, idiot!" Mo said.

"Was not," Thor said.

"It was there," I said, trying to settle things, "but it's darker now. You're both right."

We walked to a nouveau-outdoors store humid with nylon and velcro, energy bars and carabiners and a climbing wall no one used. Hand and I needed pants, pants to end all pants—warm and cool, breathing and trapping in, full of pockets. I got a standard pair of khakis, though with multiple pockets—the safari-photographer kind with the big rectangular compartments with zippers and velcro, two on each leg. Hand burst from the dressing room loudly swishing—his pants were wide, shiny and synthetic, in a grey that looked silver.

"You look like a jogger," I said.

"They're comfortable," he said.

"Like a jogger with a dump in his pants."

"Yeah," Hand said, soaking his thumb in saliva and jamming it in Mo's ear, "but I feel *fast*."

The twins ran free and everything in the store looked essential. A tiny lightweight flashlight to attach to a keychain. Beef jerky. A first-aid kit. Secret pouches for money and passports. Bandannas. Mini-fans. Insect repellent. I avoided eyes, tried to save everyone the trouble of seeing me. My face wasn't as bad as it had been a few weeks ago, but it was still busted in places, and the bridge of my nose dropped blue shadows into my eye sockets, lending me a crosseyed or cycloptic look. I appeared as I was: a guy who'd been given an ass whipping by three guys in a steel box.

"You're limping still," Hand said.

"Yes," I said.

"It's not that bad," he said. "Just a little creepy is all."

Hand had ten bandannas, five for each of us. Bandannas, he said, were what every traveler came back wishing they'd had more of. "You'll thank me," he said. He said this a lot, *You'll thank me.* I don't remember actually needing to thank him all that much, ever.

Mo and Thor returned from their explorations, hair matted, sweaters tied around their waists. They wanted to leave.

"Who wants to leave?" I asked Thor. "You, Mo?"

"I'm Thor," Thor said.

"Who's Thor?" I asked.

"I am!" she said.

"I'm sorry," I said. "I can't tell you people apart."

"But we're fraternal twins!" she said.

"You're what?"

Mo rolled her eyes. "Fraternal twins! You know that, stupid."

I stroked my chin, thinking. "Well, I guess I had heard something about this, but I didn't think it was true. I guess I didn't want to believe it."

"What are you talking about?" said Mo. She was so easily annoyed, her face pinched like the tip of a tomato.

"Listen," I said, crouching down in front of them both. "Do me a favor. Don't let anyone tell you there's something wrong with you. Don't let any scientists or government researchers pull you aside and make you feel like freaks just because you're twins and you don't look alike. God made a mistake, and yes it was a very big one, because what kinds of twins don't look alike? And worse, what kind of twins look like you two, like monkeys dunked in acid—"

Thor slapped me square in the forehead.

"You were talking too fast," she said.

We took them to Walgreen's. We needed provisions for the trip. The truth is, they were easily the least identical twins I'd ever seen, and only Thor looked like the product of their parents, who were both blond and fair. Thor was Aryan and thin-boned, but Mo looked more like me, with dark straight hair, dark eyes, long black lashes. I have the sort of eyelashes, black and shaped like bats' wings, that imply I'm wearing eyeliner, and the good fortune this has occasionally wrought is nothing compared to the grief, the stares, the constant Robert Smith comparisons. Mo has been mistaken for my own kid and hates this.

I bought travel-sized toothpaste and a collapsible cup, sunglasses and two $7 sweatshirts, maroon and black. Hand had a large column of deodorant and we were at the cash register, waiting for the girls and watching the woman ahead of us assemble a small stack of coupons on the counter. Each coupon had been cut with care and the woman, tiny but with a wide purple burn scar on her thin fragile neck, had them all bundled within a wide plastic clip intended to keep chips fresh.

I hated coupons. The need for coupons. I wanted to pay this woman's difference. Two dollars she'd save and I wanted to give it to her so she could spend her time some other better way. *What better way?* I have no idea. *Maybe she likes cutting coupons?* She does not. Since I got a little money, this was a constant struggle, the frustration with people and their coupons, people and their dirty clothes, families from El Salvador living in the basement of the church around the corner—I passed them every morning, waiting at the bus stop with their daughter, on her way to school, in her white shirt, plaid skirt—and my urge to buy things for them, even just their food, and my inability, due to the imagined and impossible barrier between myself and these strangers with fumbling hands, to engage them and fix things. I never wanted a balance in a bank account, felt so much more comfortable living on the equator just above and below a zero balance, and I thought I could get rid of it some way, some way involving the coupon woman here at the Walgreen's, and the coupons, but the distance seemed limitless and deadly, I was not outgoing in this way, could bridge nothing like this, and the situation just about killed me.

"Is that it?" Hand asked.

Mo and Thor were at the Walgreen's counter now. They'd brought Valentine's cards, a package of twelve.

"Yep," Mo said.

"Do you sell stamps?" Thor asked the clerk.

"No," said the clerk.

"You should," she said.

"$23.80, please sir," the clerk said.

"You getting any sunblock?" Hand asked.

I was not there.

"Will."

I heard my name but couldn't find my way to my mouth. I'd been hearing everyone talk but was not at all present.

"Will."

I crawled back into my head.

"What?" I said.

People say I talk slowly. I talk in a way sometimes called *laconic*. The phone rings, I answer, and people ask if they've woken me up. I lose my way in the middle of sentences, leaving people hanging for minutes. I have no control over it. I'll be talking, and will be interested in what I'm saying, but then someone—I'm convinced this is what happens—someone—and I wish I knew who, because I would have words for this person—for a short time, borrows my head. Like a battery is borrowed from a calculator to power a remote control, someone, always, is borrowing my head.

"Sunblock," Hand said.

"No," I said. He added a tube to my pile.

In the parking lot we watched a trio of milk-white Broncos drive by— —and we all stopped momentarily. It was bad enough that they still made them in that color, but to see three at once seemed to bode ill. The girls were unimpressed, and I was not surprised. I'd given up trying to predict what would impress them. Just a few months before, we'd seen a grown man, older and babbling in what sounded like Russian, jogging down the street in a great blue butterfly costume, and they thought that was great. But the Broncos did nothing for them.

We passed a teenage couple in leather and studs, she with a mohawk and he with shaved head, his dented bruise-blue skull covered in messages rendered in ink the color of raw meat.

Mo got a running start and—"HiYA!" she yelled—kicked the man in the thigh. He was shocked. Hand and I were less shocked. The girls were learning karate at school, and liked to try it out on people who looked combative.

"Daaaaamn . . . freak," the skull man said, wiping the footprint off his jeans. I apologized. I gave Hand a look, making sure he didn't start talking.

"They're not well," Hand explained.

The skull man looked at me and blinked meaningfully, suggesting potential aggression. I had him by ten pounds; his outfit was apparently giving him strength. I couldn't decide if I wanted this confrontation, if I wanted to leap from it, to make something explosive and open-ended—where would it end? I could ratchet this to true conflict and find some kind of deliverance—half of me was boiling, had been boiling for weeks or months or more—

Skull-boy and his friend pretended they thought Mo's attack was funny—they didn't—and kept walking. I exhaled and we did a serpentine Chinese dragon sort of run to the next block, all four of us yelling the chorus of "Froggie Went A-Courtin'."

We dropped the twins back at Jerry's, limiting conversation with Melora to our grunts and her squinting hisses, and we sped to the UIC hospital to get shots. The nurse, Glenda, about seventy with skin like redwood, pretended to be mad at us.

"You're leaving when?" A coarse but lilting voice, half Chicago, half country.

"Tomorrow," we said.

"You're going where?"

"Greenland."

"Greenland? There's no malaria in Greenland! Why you want a malaria shot? And what happened to your face, honey?"

"Car accident," I said.

"We might go to Rwanda," Hand said.

"What? Which is it?"

"What do you mean?"

"You just said you was going to Greenland."

"Well, maybe both."

"It can't be both. Are you relief workers or something?"

Hand nodded.

"No," I said.

"You two are confused. How old are you people?"

"Twenty-seven," I said.

"And you don't have health insurance?"

"He does," I said.

"No I don't," Hand said. I thought he did.

"Well you can't get Larium today. You haven't had a consultation. What's the rush?"

"We only have a week," Hand said. "Can't you consult with us? We're all here. Let's consult."

"No, with a doctor, honey. It takes an hour. If you came back tomorrow I could arrange it."

"What can you give us without the consultation?" I asked.

"Typhoid and Hep A, B and C."

"No malaria, though."

"No. You need a consult. If you get malaria you're gonna be regretting your big rush."

"Is it fatal? Malaria?" I asked.

"Always," said Hand, junior scientist. "It's bad-ass."

"Sometimes," Glenda corrected.

"When is it not fatal?" I asked.

"You'll live, if you get to a hospital."

"Good," I said. "We'll get there."

"We can drive. We're fast," Hand said.

"Stay in at night," she said as we rubbed our arms. "You in Rwanda, any mosquito might have it."

We thanked Glenda. She sat on her steel stool, waving goodbye with both hands, like a child popping bubbles from the air.

Through the hospital lobby I was following Hand and came around a corner to find him talking to a woman in a lab coat.

It was Pilar.

"Hey," I said. She looked so slight.

"Hi," she said. We hugged and she smelled, as always, of dogs and some kind of mint. She felt weightless. In high school she was robust, an athlete with broad tennis shoulders, but now she was rangy, her eyes bigger, cheekbones shooting angrily forward from her ears like dowels bowed. She'd dated Jack years ago but I bucked against the assumption—*It has to be. It's not that easy*—that his death brought her transformation.

"What're you guys doing here?" she asked. "What happened to your face?"

We told her about the inoculations, the trip.

"You don't need that stuff for Greenland," she said.

We tried to explain—the destinations beyond, everything.

"What about your face?" she asked again.

"I fell," I said.

"Liar."

"What are you here for?" Hand asked.

"I work here. In the lab," she said, sweeping her hands down her coat, bringing Hand's attention to the obvious.

"Oh," he said.

"So why a week?" she asked. "Why not really do the trip right, like take a summer or something? You won't see anything this way."

I opened my mouth but couldn't think of any way to answer. Someone was using my head to power a coffeemaker.

Hand was looking, thoughtfully, at the ceiling, while whistling soundlessly. Pilar, olive-toned and in high school dazzling and much-coveted, had given me one night, after she and Jack were no more, though it was obvious then that it was Jack who she cared for and I was a consolation, an approximation. Between Jack and Hand, both with easier smiles and better facial structures—beaten or not—it was a feeling I'd come to know well.

"We only have a week," I said.

Pilar brought her fingers to her temples in a way one would if attempting to keep a flood within.

"Migraine?" Hand asked.

"No," she said. "I mean, yes."

"It's good to see you," he said, putting his arms around her. After a second he stepped back and I stepped forward and held her and then we all stood for a moment, waiting for someone to tell us what to do. A voice on the intercom was looking for someone. It sounded like *Dr. Doobage*. Hand laughed. We all laughed.

"That's really his name," Pilar said, then sobered.

"Well," Hand said.

Pilar made a V of her hands and set her chin between her palms. Her eyes darted between us and quickly welled.

"It's awful to see you two."

We stayed up until four, in my kitchen, trying new itineraries and reading the Greenland website. The flight was eight hours away.

"Biggest island," Hand said.

"Official language is Greenlandic," I noted.

"Not just Greenlandic—West Greenlandic. *West Greenlandic, as spoken in Sisimiut, Maniitsoq and the Nuuk area, is the official language of communication throughout Greenland. East Greenlandic is very different from West Greenlandic, but most East Greenlanders understand West Greenlandic.*"

"Total population is 53,000."

"Ice covers eighty-five percent of the landmass."

"They're desperate for tourists. They get about 8,000 a year, but they're shooting for 60,000."

"They name their winds. Listen: *East Greenland has the Piteraq, a cold katabatic wind, a well-known and much-feared wind phenomenon. The highest gusts to date in Ammassalik were recorded in 1972 and measured 72 m/sec.*"

"What's katabatic?"

"*As a visitor to Greenland, it is important to note the following: The weather can change abruptly, and technical hitches may occur. So it is always advisable to enquire with GreenlandAir the evening before—or at the latest the same day.*"

"Technical hitches. Are they talking about the weather?"

"I think so."

We fell asleep in the living room, Hand on the couch and me on the recliner, and at eight woke with two hours to gather everything and go. We had agreed not to pack before the morning, and this turned out to be easy to honor, the actual packing involving the stuffing in of two shirts, underwear, toiletries and a miniature atlas, which took three minutes. Passports, tickets, the $32,000 in travelers checks, the bandannas. Hand brought some discs, his walkman, a handful of tapes for the rental cars, some State Department travelers' advisories, and a sheaf of papers he'd printed from the Center for Disease Control website, almost entirely about ebola. He could talk forever about ebola. I threw in a Churchill biography I was reading, but after swinging the pack over my shoulders and feeling the weight of the 1,200 pages, I unpacked the book, ripped out the first 200 and last 300, and shoved it back in.

We fell back asleep on the couch. At ten-thirty, with a spasm we woke again—

TUESDAY, SHIT, LATE ALREADY

—and left and slept in the cab, each of our heads against a window, out cold; the cabbie woke us when stopped under the awning of O'Hare's international arm. The airport's quiet doors opened for us and we trotted to the desk happily, the airport tall and light, Hand whistling John Denver's relevant song, and at the desk we were told our flight was canceled; the airport in Kangerlussuaq was closed because of winds.

"It can't be," I said.

"The katabatic winds," Hand said.

"Jesus."

"We've only got one fucking week."

The woman said we could go halfway, to Iqaluit, and wait.

For how long? we asked.

"Who knows?" she said, not looking at me. She'd been talking to Hand and I realized why. My face. *"They're* waiting." She pointed to a group of people on a bench across the way. They looked like they were going to Greenland, all with parkas, backpacks and beards. We looked like we were going to play softball.

"We can't wait," I said.

"We have to go," said Hand.

So Greenland was out. Katabatic my ass. Fuck Greenland. I looked to Hand. Was that anguish or shock? The GreenlandAir woman suggested we hold onto the tickets and use them tomorrow. Hand looked like he'd burst.

"We've already lost so much time," he said.

"It's only noon," the woman said.

"Noon!" he said. I didn't know why he was so upset. It was my damned idea.

We walked out of the terminal and paced around in the cold, running through possibilities, Hand babbling. Hand has a way of talking to you, eyes staring through yours, unblinking, jaw moving that suggests either great intensity or plain country madness.

A Lincoln Towncar pulled up and from it disembarked a black family in bright dashikis. A skycap appeared and helped them with their bags. The African father paid the skycap with two bills, nodding with the placement of each upon the skycap's palm, and the skycap said, "Thank you, sir." The family walked in and through the shushing slowly closing automatic doors and I watched them glide, bright fabric swishing, to the Air Afrique desk, a few feet from GreenlandAir. I walked in after them and Hand followed.

On the small ancient screen their flight was listed in weak green light. Air Afrique, 1:50 P.M. to Dakar.

"Where's Dakar?" Hand asked.

I dug into my backpack and checked my atlas.

"Senegal."

The tickets cost us $1,600 for the pair, one-way, a price I justified by thinking—wrongly—that we'd get a refund on the Greenland two. It was the most money I'd ever spent at once. Even the two cars I'd ever bought were less—$800 and $1,400, both Corollas. We were motherfucking *bastards*. I buried the shame deep within. I burned it and danced around it, leapt over it. We were going to Senegal and I got the tickets so we'd return to O'Hare from Cairo. That way we'd fly to Dakar, would be able to get across the continent and end up at the Pyramids before flying back—and wouldn't have to see Dakar twice. Genius.

We were told to wait for a gate assignment. The floor was now full of Senegalese in dashikis, mostly men, all black, all with glasses, silver-framed, looking like a U.N. delegation or some kind of . . . some kind of group of men who liked to dress the same. After fifteen minutes an announcement was made. The flight, scheduled to leave at 1:50 P.M., would be late in taking off. We walked to the desk. How late? we asked. It was now scheduled, the woman said with a straight face, for 9 P.M. Hand fell to his knees. He was hammy that way. I waited for him to get up, which he did with a clap as punctuation, and we walked away.

"This is a joke," he said.

"The dashiki guys aren't mad," I said, pointing to their group, chatting, milling.

Hand wanted to try again, to get a refund and fish for anything else. Togo, Franz Josefland. I couldn't decide. Where were the flights that actually left the ground? All we wanted was another continent, as soon as possible. We asked if they knew anything more about the departure time, the possibilities. Were they sure it would be so late? How could they be so sure?

The Air Afrique woman had an answer: "Because the plane hasn't left Dakar yet."

The plane from Chicago to Dakar hadn't left Dakar for Chicago.

There was a shuttle bus taking the passengers to the Best Western, where we were each given a room. We had six hours. The shuttle bus filled and left and another arrived. We sat next to a young thin man, his head in his hands.

"Air Afrique. Every time," he said. He was in a grey pinstriped suit. He looked about twenty-four, probably a student. Silver-framed glasses. Senegalese, we guessed, from the accent.

"Are they a bad airline?" Hand asked. I wanted to ask why all the men going to Senegal were wearing the same glasses. Were they government-issued to men, as were pointy shoes in Italy?

"Their safety record is fine," he said, "but they take their time. Always late. Terrible. They don't care."

Next to us a white man, resembling in every way David Carradine in his latter *Kung Fu* days, was talking to another man, whom he had seemingly just met. We listened. We couldn't help but listen—Carradine was loud and they were sitting inches from us. The other man was from Ghana and was visiting Senegal for the first time. Why he was coming through Chicago to do so was unclear but Carradine was the character here, lower teeth small, fishlike and sharp, a headband around his neck, stringy hair greasing his shoulders. We caught phrases, Hand and I leaning to hear the white man speak.

"Well, God granted me abundant life . . ."

His audience, the Ghanian man, was listening respectfully.

". . . I don't know why he has done this, what I have done to deserve this . . . other than my being honest and kind . . ."

Carradine looked like a guy who would be selling handmade hemp wallets at a flea market. I was surprised Hand wasn't joining their conversation. This man was the type of guy Hand was inevitably chatting up. Hand had collected so many of these people, had so many stories, and always the stories involved someone he'd just met and instantly befriended—there are people who meet strangers and people, like me, who know only those they've known from birth—and usually Hand soon after loaned them money or, in two separate instances, allowed them to live in his garage.

"Yes, I live like a king," the white man on the bus was saying, "and can entertain my friends from around the globe. . . . Of course, I was never good at English. For three years I was in remedial English . . . my teachers didn't understand my individual needs for expression . . ."

The shuttle stopped at the hotel. Carradine had five bags, which he struggled to lift, one over his shoulder, two in his left hand, two in his right. Hand took two for him, and the burdened white man followed us out. We stepped down from the shuttle into the lobby.

"You been to Senegal before?" he asked Hand.

Hand said we hadn't.

"Well, you'll see more beggars and cripples there than in your whole life." He glanced at me. "You'll feel right at home."

We walked into the lobby. *Was that a joke about my face?* It was, I think. We were in line now, waiting to check in. The white man looked at our shoes, our backpacks, gauging their contents.

"So," he said, "you guys planning to do some drumming?"

And we were still in America. We were in Schaumburg, or Bensenville, wherever this hotel was, and were walking down a quiet hall with purple and yellow crosshatched carpeting, and were not en route to Senegal and I hadn't—I just realized—packed shorts, and wouldn't get there until morning and had wasted the day. One of seven gone.

Passing a middle-aged couple in matching jackets:

—You two need to change.

—What? Why? the middle-aged couple said, to my head, in my head.

—Because you are wearing the same jacket.

—We bought them while on vacation in Newport.

—You must be hidden from view.

—The jackets are nice.

—They are not nice. Think of the children.

I argued with strangers constantly, though only in my cloudy skull, while always I adopted this hollow admonishing tone—my grandmother's, I guess—which even I couldn't stand. The silent though decisive discussions were a hobby of my mind, debating people I knew or passed on the road while driving:

—You, driving the Lexus.

—Me?

—Yes, you. You paid too much.

—What?

—You paid too much and your soul is soiled.

—You are right. I have failed but will repent.

It helped me work through problems, solving things, reaching conclusions final, edifying and even, occasionally, mutually agreeable.

—You, on the motorcycle.

—Yes.

—It's only a matter of time.

—I know.

It would be fun, I suppose, if it wasn't constant and so *loud*. It was unavoidable and now, to tell you the truth, after many years of enjoying the debates, I wanted them to end. I wanted the voices silenced and I wanted less of my head generally. I didn't want the arguments, and I didn't want the voice that followed, the one that apologized, also silently, to the people I'd debated and dressed down.

—*Sorry!* this last voice would say, jogging after the first like a handler after a candidate. *Won't happen again! Here's a little something for your trouble!*

I wanted agreement now, I wanted synthesis and the plain truth—without the formalities of debate. There was nothing left to debate, no heated discussion that seemed to progress toward any healing solution. I wanted only *truth*, as simple as you could serve it, straight down the middle, not the product of dialectic but *sui generis:* Truth! We all knew the truth but we insisted on distorting things to make it seem like we were all, with each other, in such profound disagreement about everything—that first and foremost there are two sides to everything, when of course there were not; there was one side only, one side always: Just as this earth is round, the truth is round, not two-sided but *round* and—

Hand and I got our own rooms. On the mattress over the covers I closed my eyes and attempted sleep but instead met my head as it floated above my bed with its many nervous eyes, and my head was in a belligerent mood. *Kill the fuckers. Kill the fuckers. Kill the fuckers.* Here I was again. I shunned argument but felt close to the battle. Every day I had hours when I wanted to direct a machine gun, somewhere, anywhere, feel the falling shells tapping my instep—hours when every conflict in the world felt familiar to me—

I sat up and called my mom. I hadn't told her about the trip—I'd planned to call from Greenland—and now my reasons for waiting were confirmed.

"You're using your new money?"

"Yes."

"What did Cathy say about that?"

"She had nothing to say about it."

I knew she was livid, more at Cathy than me.

"Will, this just sounds silly."

"Well . . ."

"You're just acting out, honey."

"Well, thank you for that piece of—"

"You've had a rough year, I know, but—"

"Listen—"

"And frankly," she said, "I'm confused."

I looked across the bed, into a mirror, and saw a face so angry and wretched I turned away.

"Tell me," I said, with a level of patience that impressed even me, "why. Mom. You are confused."

"Well, wasn't it you who didn't *care* about traveling? You used to raise such a fit when I wanted to take you on trips, even up to Phelps or something."

"That was different."

"It *was* you. It *was* you who sat right there, on that stool in the kitchen, in the first house, and said that you didn't need to travel anywhere, ever. I wanted us to go somewhere exotic and you said you could do all the traveling and thinking you'd ever need without ever leaving the backyard."

I sighed as loudly and ferociously as I could.

"Yes indeedy!" she went on, "Hand was the one with the plans, who wanted to be in space and all, but you said *tra*vel was a dis*tra*ction for the uni*mag*inative. It was all very moving, your speech. I wish I had it taped."

I wondered how loudly I could hang up. Maybe this was one of those phones with the actual ringer on the base. That could make quite a sound. I would just throw the thing down and—

"Will?" she asked.

"What?" I said.

"Why don't you go home and call me tonight and we can talk more about this? I think you two are making a mistake. Think about the money! Let me talk to Hand. Is this Hand's idea?"

"It's too late. We bought the tickets."

"To where again?"

"Senegal."

She scoffed. "No one goes to Senegal!"

"We do."

"You'll get AIDS!"

I hung up. Did I mention that she might be losing her mind? The last time I visited her new condo in Memphis, she'd been using conditioner on her hands, mistaking it for softsoap. Tommy and I are terrified we'll have twenty years of angry and groping senility, as we did with Granna, who half the time you wanted to care for, whose long straight grey hair you wanted to brush—but who the other half of the time, with her barking exclamations— *Where's my baby! Where's my horse! I broke those things because they needed to be broken!*—you wanted to suffocate with a pillow.

I tried to nap, but now my head was alive, was a toddler in a room full of new guests. It jumped and squealed and threw the books off the shelves. Yes I'm one of the slowest talkers you'll ever meet but my head, when I have it and it's not asleep or being borrowed, is not slow. My mind, I know, I can prove, hovers on hummingbird wings. It hovers and it churns. And when it's operating at full thrust, the churning does not stop. The machines do not rest, the systems rarely cool. And while I can forget anything of any importance—this is why people tell me secrets—my mind has an uncanny knack for organization when it comes to pain. Nothing tormenting is lost, never even diminished in color or intensity or quality of sound. These were filed near the front.

Imagine a desk. The desk is located at the top of a green hill, about two hundred feet above a soft meadow dotted with tulips and something like cotton. Winding through the meadow is a stream, narrow and quick, which rushes with the sound of shushing and sniffing. The desk has a magnificent view, and the air around the desk and on the meadow is about seventy-two degrees. It's balmy and bright, and the sky is blue but not too blue, and in all it would seem to be the perfect place to have a desk. A desk where you could observe things and do the work that had to be done. The one catch is that the desk sits above a large structure, the entrance to which is just behind and below the desk. This building extends ten stories, down. The structure has been dug down into the whole of the hill and houses a large staff of humanoid people, oily and pale and without hair—they are moles and look like it, with huge square yellow teeth and mouths of fire—all of whom are in charge of keeping track of and retrieving its contents, a mixture of records, dossiers, quotations, historical documents, timelines, fragments, cultural studies—the most glorious and banal and bloody memories.

Let's say that I like having this structure in existence, and that I value its presence, and that I have easy access to it. If I want something, a file on something, all I need to do is summon it and one of the library's staffers, who again are all hairless, have ruby-colored eyes and wear white, will bring it to me, usually without any delay. If I'm on the phone with Hand, and he mentions the time we pushed Darren Larson over the sprinkler—we were big kids and bullies—and Darren Larson cut the shit out of his shin, all that milky white showing, and then he hid behind the fence by the lake under the sunsetting sky, mewling—then I can ask the librarian to get me all the information possible on that event, and do it quickly, so I can converse intelligently with Hand. Seconds later an eager staff member, ruby-eyed hairless and in white and with the smell of sulfur barely covered with rancid perfume, is before me, with a neat manila folder containing all the data stored within the library about that day, given that there's been, over the years, some mismanagement of the library and any number of floods and fires—so much lost but who to blame?

And as much as I value the efficiency and professional élan of the library staff, I'd begun recently to worry about a new wrinkle in their procedures. For the most part, they're supposed to act on my requests when I make requests, and to otherwise just keep an orderly file system. Part of the deal, implicitly, is that at no time should the staff members of the library *choose for me* what information I should be given. But lately I'd be sitting at my desk, trying either to work or to just admire the view and wonder about the stream, what makes it go, if there are fish inside, what their names might be, if any of them are secretly talking fish and if so what they might say—when there will suddenly be a library staff member at my side, and she will have one hand on my back, and the other will be pointing to the contents of a file she's brought me and has opened on my desk, so that I will follow her finger to where she's pointing, and when I see what she's pointing to I will gasp.

I never want to see that fucking clipping again. I was outraged at my mom for keeping it. What kind of psycho would do that?

She didn't show it to me but there it was, in the drawer where we kept the scissors and envelopes and clippings. From the local paper, a picture of the car, crushed, under the headline: YOUNG MAN DIES WHEN SEMI SPEEDS OVER CAR. I never thought I'd see a picture. I didn't know there was a picture. It had been three months and I was sleeping normally again and was visiting Mom in Memphis and found the clipping. I read the article, folded lengthwise and ripped, not cut, at first not even knowing it was Jack. For a few paragraphs it was just a chilling and pathetic story—some poor man had been killed when he'd been driving too slow. A truck traveling too fast had overcome the man's car, had driven over it, crushing it in a fraction of a second. The picture was clear, the car right there, fender to fender, but yet it was only an abstraction of a car, an angry scribble of a car, and when the clipping was unfolded there was Jack, his high school graduation picture, sportcoat over his right shoulder, the picture right next to the trucker's, like they were a team, like the quarterback who won the game and the receiver who caught the pass.

"I just thought," the librarian will say in a curt, professional way, "that you should see this."

I know this file, but I have no need to see it now. I didn't ask for this goddamn file. I tell her this.

"Yes," she says, "but I really thought you should see this again. We felt it was important for you to pore over the file right now, replaying the episode in your mind for the next few hours."

I look at the file, and its contents scream at me in a voice containing thousands of murders in unclean homes. I push it back toward the staffer.

"I looked at it. Thank you."

She leaves. I look out at the meadow and see a scattering of birds chasing each other. I can see for maybe thirty miles.

There's another tug at my sleeve. It's another staff member, a young man with eyes like animals on fire. He's leaning over the desk and he has a file. It's the same file the previous librarian had.

"I just looked at that," I say.

"Yes, but the feeling downstairs is that you haven't examined it closely enough. Especially the part with Nigel, the prick from the funeral home, and all Jack's college friends laughing and smoking out on the deck on the day of the service."

I picture what I'd say to those imbeciles if I saw them again. I wanted to act and wanted something that would cause them pain and embarrassment but wanted it to happen quietly. Everything quietly. My tolerance for anything loud had diminished every year I'd lived, and now so many things gave me a jump. The steady noise at work, drills and saws—I couldn't do it anymore, this noise. Before I quit I'd begun to ask for the quieter tasks. Painting walls and moldings, installing doors, though I maintained an option for the tearing down of ceilings—usually the acoustic tile of officed areas—and the digging up of floors. I loved doing both. So many good wood floors covered by layers and layers of indefensible surfaces—fake linoleum, particle board, rubber, carpet, cement, anything. I loved to pry under these things to find the original floor, the floor of parallel and interlocking tongue-in-groove fir planks, to uncover them, run my rough palms over their soft wood and sand them, and finish them again—to start over with this original smooth floor. And the ceilings were just as satisfying, slipping those hideous tiles, dotted like starry skies inverted, from their grids, dropping them to the floor, watching them break. Then the tearing down of the grids—so easy!—that held the tiles overhead, revealing a ceiling many feet higher, huge wooden beams old and full of the lines and curves of growth and struggle. I loved the effect when both happened in the same space: the raising of a ceiling, the lowering of a floor, exposing the wood again above and below, the space growing, the usable space and air attendant swelling within immovable walls. I thought of that painting in my boss's office, on a calendar his daughter had given him, a Callibotte, men bent over a wood floor, the sun whitening them, the men in that one painting bent over, kneeling and sanding the whitened wood floors in that second-story room in what must be Paris—

I'm on a happy thought trail, hard-won, when another young woman, hairless and white with eyes burning black and red, appears on the other side of my desk. Now there are two staffers, flanking me, both pointing to the same material. She has the same file—WHEN SEMI SPEEDS OVER CAR—I was just looking at and had managed to forget. She sees my alarm.

"What the hell is this?" I ask.

"We made copies," she says.

I turned on the TV. The State of the Union, a rebroadcast on cable. I pushed my ear into the pillow. The president had burst into the hall and everyone was so *happy*. They all seemed so genuinely mirthful, all of them. What is the president whispering to them? Most of the people just stand and clap, but some get the president whispering to them, something really great. These people, in their suits and ties, the women all wearing their bright, solid-color outfits, like a loosely distributed bunch of giant fruits and vegetables. Green and red peppers and apples and blueberries, everyone smiling such difficult smiles, not easy smiles, but smiles full of resentment and fear—

I corrected myself. I had no right to judge these people I've never met nor ever will, presuming that their smiles are forced or bitter, when there was every possibility in the world that these were happy and good people, that the senator from North Dakota for example was wholly normal and content, was someone who loved those close to him and did what he could to aid those he represented. It was entirely possible that the distinguished senator from Oklahoma was stung every time a poll indicated the public's lack of trust and admiration for those they elected. Maybe he was hurt. Maybe when results like that were conveyed to him he shook and vomited and went to his window for air and called his mother, who still lived in his childhood home and was widowed and who soothed him by using both his first and last names, and whispered them together, over and over and over and over—

Oh Jim

Oh James

Oh James honey

Oh Jimmy my dearest one

Oh Jimmy Inhofe

Jimmy, Jimmy my son

Oh Jimmy Inhofe

Jim-Jim

Jimmy Inhofe Jimmy Inhofe

—and this would work for the senator, though neither of them would know exactly why.

It was dark and the phone was ringing; the pillowcase beneath my mouth was soaked.

"You awake?"

I'd slept for two hours. It felt like minutes.

Hand came in and we ordered pizza and watched *Kingpin* on cable. The guilt was monumental. We were wasting the time allotted. We had had hours and we slept. We could have been doing something. This week was about using minutes and hours like these, taking them and holding them, polishing them, throwing them as far as we could, but at our first opportunity—all these hours free and full of infinite choice—we'd done nothing. We could have hitchhiked somewhere. We could have knocked on doors—even in this hotel—and met or groped new people. But no, nothing. We'd bought the Senegal tickets but now were waiting for pizza in an O'Hare Best Western—we wanted to be able to tell people about every hour this week, that every hour we had done something not-or-seldom-before done (at least by people like us) but instead we were watching the angry hustler guys put Woody's hand in the bowling-ball retriever machine.

"If you think about it," Hand said, tearing a slice from its crust, "the original schedule had us getting into Dakar at 1 in the morning, too late to do anything anyway. Now we get in at 9 A.M. or something. Same difference, except we sleep on the plane."

He was right. He was a titan. We were again golden.

And in an hour the phone rang again; the shuttles were coming. We jogged down to the lobby. In the lobby, what seemed to be a hundred Senegalese dignitaries milled and lined up. There were a few women among them, a pair our age, their skin so smooth and unblemished it seemed fake or too tautly stretched. I was caught staring at the full round hips of a woman in red, the color of new blood in direct sunlight.

I nudged Hand. He rolled his eyes.

He knew I liked women of heft and generous curve, 5'11" and up, as tall or taller than me—I'm maybe 6'1"—and with exuberant, exaggerated lines. It was a preference I'd developed in the past few years, after dating Charlotte, who remade me in the shade of her luxurious form. Charlotte was a plus-size model of grand sweeping landscapes, who demanded attention of sidewalks and living rooms and had a soft loud laugh like the clashing of great white clouds. We'd been together for six months or so when she announced she wanted to move to Los Angeles to do the usual things. I was invited along but passed and it was just as well. We'd begun to snap and gnaw with moods and boredom—"How could you say that when you know I can't whistle?" "How could you say that when you know my aunt is diabetic?" and besides, I'd run out of logical and erotic metaphors and in our particular coupling, with its foundation in the bedroom, this drought meant doom. She had a thing for metaphors during sex—Me: "I'm plowing your field! I'm plowing your field!" Charlotte: "Speed the plow! Speed the plow!"—and demanded new, evermore exotic images—"I'm docking my starfighter!" "I'm stuffing your burrito!" "I'm . . . I'm sinking your . . . tight, wet . . . battleship!"—and I guess at a certain point, when I found myself consulting friends for ideas—it was Hand who came up with the the starfigher/docking/Galactica analogy, which didn't do much for her—it just became too much work.

I stopped staring as a bellhop, middle-aged and white with a thin droopy mustache, spoke to us.

"You guys had a nice dinner did you?"

"I guess," I said. I had the greasy feeling he was talking to us because we were two of only three white people (Carradine, now regaling others with his tales of luck and encompassing hospitality and poor math skills) in the lobby.

"You *guess*. C'mon! I saw that pizza come through. You two had a *feast!*"

Hand and I smiled. The bellhop had what I hoped was toothpaste at the corners of his mouth.

—You moron.

—I am sorry Will.

—Wipe the spittle from your mouth.

—I am sorry Will.

I told him he was welcome to the rest of the pizza, that we'd only eaten half and the rest was still there, in the room. He said he might just do that—if Rose hadn't already gotten it. I didn't ask who Rose was. *Where was Hand?* Suddenly Hand was gone.

"So you're going to Africa too?" the bellman asked.

I nodded.

"Listen, just watch yourself," he said. "The place is a mess. They got it cut up like a pizza pie." Pizza again. He liked pizza. He stepped closer to me. "They're always killing each other! Brother against brother! You're going where again?"

"Senegal."

"Senegal. Senegal! You gotta watch out there. Remember—hey! [Grabbing my shoulder] That's the place where they shot down the Navy pilot and dragged him around by his penis!"

I told him he was thinking of Somalia. He shook his head at me, as if I were the king of chumps. Hand had returned.

"I used to send money to Africa," the bellman was saying, "but then I realized the *warlords* were taking all of it. They take the money and then when we send supplies the Russians come down and carry it away on planes. They cart it away!"

"Right," Hand said, pointing at him. "You're *right.*" I couldn't tell if Hand was being serious.

"Didn't know that, eh?" the bellhop confided to me. "The Russians get all the stuff we send—they buy it straight from the *warlords.*" He loved that word. "It's crazy. So now I don't send money."

I shook the man's hand and winced. I'd forgotten my hand was half-broken. Hand shook the man's hand.

"What is your name sir?" he asked.

"Robby." The man was easily fifty.

"Robby, we thank you." Hand did a little bow.

We got on the shuttle.

I understood the Earth's shadow on the moon. I knew that the Earth was hiding most of the moon from the light this night, leaving a curved white blade. What I didn't know was why the moon and its shadow should be so clear, the lines so clean. The sun wasn't at all clear; its outline was debatable and changing. And though I know the sun is gas and the moon is rock, still I wonder why the moon's circumference would be so clear, its edges so crisp—cut from cardboard with scissors.

The plane turned around and now the moon was behind us.

Our seats on the plane were first class and we didn't know why. We worried that we were white and in first class while the Senegalese people, better dressed and better educated and maybe even of aristocratic blood, were behind us in coach. Between Hand and me we had three years of college at UW–La Crosse and, until recently, nothing in the bank. We buried this shame in the drawer next to all the inequities, and ate. The flight attendant asked us to close our window shades; if we didn't we would disturb the people in the towns we were flying over—

"Is that really what she said?" I said.

"I think," Hand said,

—then Hand fell asleep. I did shortly afterward, but woke up hourly and moved stiffly—so stiffly *even in first class*—as if my flesh had been mixed with gravel. I got up at about 3 A.M. and remembered I had to sign the traveler's checks. At the bank they'd told me to sign them all before I traveled. I'd forgotten the directive immediately, meant to do it at home, then almost remembered in the cab, then the airport, then figured I'd have time on the plane. I turned toward the window and hid my task with my back and arm, glancing around periodically to make sure no one was watching, no one who would tell their buddies in Dakar that there were these tourists made of money—God I hated this money and this was why; it recast me and refracted my vision—on the plane who should be robbed and stabbed and later dragged around by their penises.

The signing was endless. The cashier had run out of $500 checks after the first six and so the rest were $100s, two hundred and ninety of them total, in envelopes of ten. After each check was signed I let it drop to my lap; when each set of ten was done I gathered them, neatened them, stacking—click-click on the tray table—and inserted them back into their envelope.

Out my portal the plane wing was silver and shining like it

would have fifty years earlier, carrying happier and simpler people. All of them smoking and speaking loudly—musically barking every last word—and wearing expensive hats. When did we start flying like this? So cavalier like this? I should have known, but didn't. Hand would know. Everything like that Hand knew, or pretended to know. So many questions. Did the floatation devices really float? Did planes actually float long enough for us to get out, jumping down those wide and festive yellow inflatable slides? And also: Would it be easier to kill someone who was beautiful, or someone who was ugly? What if you had to do it with your own hands, hovering above? I think there would be a difference. And why, when we see a half-broken window, do we want it *all* broken? We see the shards rising from the pane and we long to knock them out, one by one, like teeth. Questions, questions. Did Vaclav Havel have emphysema, or was I imagining that? Who had emphysema? Someone over there.

I wanted to be asleep on this flight. Too much time in my head would bring me back. To Oconomowoc and further, to that funeral home prick and what he did to Jack. Of *course* a closed-casket. What were you *thinking*, people?

My signature on each $100 meant it was mine. But otherwise the checks bore no sign of ownership; the potential for fraud and misuse seemed enormous. All of these blank things, beautiful though, their crosshatched Spartans watching as I signed, the checks bearing the colors of the sea, a Mediterranean sea, where bathers lie on rocks—everything so corruptible. But I could make them safer by signing them. Signature—mine! Blank and impersonal monies all of them until I swooped down and put my name there, swip shoosh swip, on the line. $100 after $100. My pen was so quick, and steady, and I pushed hard to make it clear and legible; the swooping was audible! Signature—mine! Signature—mine! Each ten checks a thousand, all mine in the neat envelope. *Mine!* I began to feel that all that money that had been sitting dormant in that

strange account, that godforsaken money market account set up by
Cathy Wambat—she did some minor-league financial planning on
the side—was for once almost real. What had been for so long just
a number on a line in a statement mailed monthly was now in a
stack on a tray table, made real by hundreds of names, all mine, as
hundreds of Spartans looked on.

I got sick of my signature. I couldn't do it anymore; I hated my
name. I had signed ninety checks and rubbed my tired hand like
they do on commercials for arthritis. And slowly I realized I would
have to sign again, each time I used or cashed one, in the presence
of the teller or clerk. Five hundred and eighty-six times my signature would claim this money. Mine! Mine! *Swoop! Swoop!*

A man across the aisle, broad torso under blue blanket, glanced
at me and my checks, my neat piles and busy pen, and rolled his
eyes. The money wasn't mine and he knew it. The money was lost,
someone's lost money, money that had been liberated from any
kind of logical roost and had flown, madly, to me.

So I'd been given $80,000 to screw in a lightbulb. There is
almost no way to dress it up; that's what it was. My boss has a
brochure he had his son make up on the computer, a two-fold
xeroxed thing with a list of services, past projects and pictures.
The last edition, honest to God, featured a picture of me on a
stepladder, installing a lightbulb. I have no idea why West Side
Contractors would want to so boldly advertise their lightbulb-
installing capabilities, but there it was. Was it a joke on me, Will
Chmielewski—something about Poles—sorry, *Polacks*—and their
abilities insofar as lightbulb-screwing goes? My boss insisted it
was not—Never! he said, Jesus, Will, no way!—then went back to
his trailer, muffling a guffaw. So next thing I know there's a call
from someone at Leo Burnett, the ad agency with the huge building on the river, and they want to know how I like the idea of
being immortalized on millions of packages of some kind of new
bulb.

We'd just built a sunroom for a family on Orchard, and it turns out the owner worked at this agency, was an art director of some kind, and had the brochure lying around. While putting together logo proposals for the lightbulb maker, she used a silhouette of me on my stepladder, and tried it out on the company, and the company said *That! That man is our lightbulb man!*

I knew my mom would be proud and my brother Tommy would laugh, so I did it. Here's the logo, for what it's worth, below right. In lieu of cash, they offered me stock in the lightbulb company, stock that could mature, with a stock split or two they said, into $10, $12 million—could be worth that within two years, they said, so good were these new lightbulbs. They were brilliant, I told them. Their bulbs were fucking great, I said. Then I gave them the routing number for the $80,000, their cash offer and apparently the going rate for people transformed into silhouettes to sell things. I felt briefly, mistakenly, powerful: *My outline burned into the minds of millions!* But then came back down, crashing. It was an outline, it was reductive. It was nothing.

Last year was the strangest year I'd ever been involved in, it was the most brutal and bizarre—I'd lost Jack and been given more money than I'd ever seen in one place, and I'd been fainting more, falling more. I was feeling everything much too much. Everything was pulling at my eyes. I spent hours floating in pools. I sat on terraces and stared for afternoons at mediocre views. I was feeling overjoyed for happy couples. I would see or hear about people, usually people I hardly knew or didn't even like, getting together, finding each other after so much groping, and I would feel bliss. I was being blindsided by familiar things. I was pulling over to the side of the road, my head resting on the side window, trying to understand why things could be so *green*. Songs were knocking me from wall to wall, certain songs in certain progressions strained my eyes, roughed up my throat, brought me near tears without delivering me to any kind of catharsis. I was shaking my head at how perfect some song was, and then I was in the car, on the way to Kmart to buy a lesson kit, convinced I could teach myself piano and with my exceptional taste, make an album and then I would double back and think *Fuck, I should learn to fly airplanes.* That's the thing I really want to do. *Fly planes.* But it would take years, and I needed it quicker. What I wanted to do was take a course in the bar, take it and then practice law, all without having done law school at all. It was possible. Or maybe I should just open the police souvenir store, as planned in eighth grade, or the general store in New Mexico with the local handicrafts. And marry a woman cop. She would be huge and strong and named Heather and would be such a good woman.

I'd had my ass handed to me in a storage unit in Oconomowoc and now, two full weeks after the last breaths of that wretched year, I still felt flayed, skinned and burned.

I put the checks away and went back to sleep and dreamt of a rainstorm where the drops were as big as cars. I was watching the storm, full of burgundies and blues, from a bunker and was safe, but people were getting killed, the drops perfectly and roundly reflecting and distorting the world below before crashing atop those expecting life from rain.

WEDNESDAY

The light was screaming through the windows, intent and wild, and I opened my portal's eyelid a quick few inches and we were coming at Africa at 300 mph, the ocean below striking the coast of Dakar with desperation. The neat shadow of the plane jumbled over the city's shoreline, the buildings glowing in tan and white and standing still as the water and wind came to them with all the world's fury—and then died. We were somewhere else. What were we doing here? We had no idea. Hand was awake.

"Senegal," I said.

"Senegal," Hand said.

We had pictured Senegal green but this was tan.

"West Africa I guess is tan," he said.

"I really figured on green for Senegal."

There was no gangway to the terminal, just a stairway to the tarmac. The air was warm and the wind was warm; the sky was clear, blue but bleached, and the sun hung still, bored and unchallenged. The baggage handlers, with green kneepads, watched us through their goggles, hands resting on their heads.

"We're in Africa," Hand said.

We stepped into the airport.

"This is an African airport," he said.

It was tiny, and open everywhere. It looked like a minimall. We sat on the cool linoleum floor and filled out our customs forms. When I was done, Hand rested his head on the wall.

"I can't believe I got to Africa," he said.

"I know," I said.

"How did we get to Africa?" he said. "Already I don't want to leave. Did you feel that air? It's different. It's African air. It's like mixed with the sun more. Like our air isn't mixed as well with the sun. Here they mix it perfectly. The sun's in the wind, the sun's in your breaths."

"I'm glad you could come," I said.

We passed customs and the cabbies didn't touch us because we had no bags. Carradine was talking to a young lacy white woman, Blanche on holiday, too fair-skinned and fragile to be both traveling alone and sane. What was she doing here? Hair like dead brown grass.

A large Senegalese woman in brilliant yellow appeared before us and asked us something.

"What?" we said.

"Wheech otel?"

"The Independent," Hand said, cribbing it from a huge back-lighted ad above us.

"I take you," she said, pointing to a small bus out front. We asked her if we could get some money first. "Fine," she said, with an annoyed look at her watch. We were hers already, her children, and we were holding her up.

We cashed $2,000 in traveler's checks—*swoop! swik! swoop!*—and stopped into the bathroom to hide it. I gave half the stack to Hand, who split it five times and found pockets for each portion. I buried stacks in pockets, in my backpack, in my socks, under my soles.

We stepped up into the bus. We were its only passengers. The woman sat next to the driver, and the driver never spoke.

The landscape on the way into the city was dry and dusty, the color of stripped pine. The road gave way to shoulders of sand and adobe homes, condos next to shanties, the condos given ears by hundreds of small satellite dishes. Billboard PSAs featured Sene-galese citizens frowning upon littering and public urination, and encouraged the drinking of milk. The road was busy with small blue buses and BMWs. Two cops rode by on matching scooters.

When the minibus stopped at a light our open windows were full of faces, mothers with babies walking up and down the high-way median pointing into their infants' tiny mouths.

"Bebbe! Bebbe!" they yelled. Boys below them hawked candy and mobile phones. The babies were swarmed by flies. Everything was too fast. We weren't ready.

"Give em something!" Hand yelled.

"You!"

"You!"

Cars came the other way at 50 mph. We had money and wanted to give it to them—*That's the point of all the traveler's checks, idiot!* I know!—but I was confused, everything had been too sudden, and I was preoccupied by the traffic, the babies were too close—and so managed only to smile at them apologetically, like a locksmith who'd failed to open a door. I moved in from the window and sat on the aisle, shrinking.

"Bebbe! Bebbe!"

The shuttle woman was watching us struggle. Why wasn't she telling us not to give them money? She was supposed to tell us not to give them money. We expect guides to ward off their needy countrymen. Now the driver was watching, too. I smiled more and tried to look confused, flustered. I was innocent! Hand was looking flustered with me, though he was still only half-awake and his bed-head was ridiculous but finally the shuttle lurched forward and we drove on, until the highway narrowed.

"Bebbe! Bebbe!"

"Meester! Meester!"

A gold sedan slipped in front of us, its driver on the phone and gesturing with fists. Soon the road was narrow and wound through the city, all of Dakar's citizens walking in their flat huge colors and selling small things. Men carried bike tires to repair shops. Men sold meat from carts, while others hoisted sacks of oranges to passing cars. No one was sweating, and no one was smoking. Outside a gated compound, a tousled-haired white tourist in an enormous Fubu football jersey was talking to two uniformed men with assault rifles while a group of students from Italy—Hand was sure it was Italy—in crisp white tops and black pants and skirts lightly dusted, whinnied by on mopeds. All of Dakar's residents, it seemed, were selling objects, or moving objects from one location to another—a city of small favors and short errands.

* * *

The hotel, in the left-middle of Dakar, was dark inside, the lobby low and sleek and smooth with black marble, all of it cool, safe, immaculate. The reception man was tall and wiry and wore the same silver-framed glasses as the two tall and wiry reception clerks sharing his counter. He laughed at Hand's French and gave us his English. We asked for two beds and dropped our bags in the room, the view bright and facing both the city of yellows and whites and to our left the sea, all violet and sugar.

"What time is it?" I asked.

"Ten A.M."

"How do you feel?" Hand asked.

"I feel good. You ready?"

"I'm dead but we should go."

We walked out of the lobby and into central Dakar looking for a travel agent to book a flight out. We wanted all the information on all flights leaving Senegal; we wanted Madagascar or Rwanda, tomorrow. We'd set up the flight now, then look around Senegal today and tonight, ready to fly in the morning. On the street, immediately outside the hotel parking lot, we were besieged, men stepping up and striding with us, matching our pace, walking backward, asking, "Where are you from? English?" while shaking Hand's hand. Looking at me: "Spanish?" I always get Spanish, with the dark hair, the eyelashes.

"American."

"AmeriKAHN, ah. Welcome to Dakar! You have accident! Your face! Need mask like Phantom! Ha ha! You like Dakar? How long you been in Dakar?"

"Twenty minutes."

"Oh haha. Twenty minutes! Very good. Joke! Welcome! Welcome! Do you need taxi? Tour? I—"

And we ducked into the travel agency.

Hand tried his French with the first agent but to little effect. We waited for one who spoke English.

"I thought you said you spoke French," I said.

"I do. Some."

"Your dad's French, right?"

"Not, like, *from France*. He's not *from France*."

"What are you wearing?"

"What?"

He was wearing a shirt declaring I AM PROUD OF MY BLACK HERITAGE. On a blond man with swishy pants it looked all wrong.

"Where'd you get that?"

"Thrift store."

"No one's going to get the joke here. Or whatever it is. It's not even a joke."

"No one will know. And it's not a joke. I liked the shirt. Did you see the back?"

I nodded slowly, to communicate the pain it caused me. The back said ROGERS PARK WOMEN'S VOLLEYBALL.

An English-speaker arrived and sat down at the desk opposite us. Hand leaned over her desk.

"We want to find out what airplanes are leaving Dakar today and tomorrow," he said.

"Where do you want to go?" asked the agent, a stately woman in cosmic blue.

"We are not sure," Hand said, in English. "We want to see our options. Do you have that kind of in-for-ma-tion? All of the avail-a-ble flights?"

This is when Hand started speaking with a Senegalese accent, without contractions and with breaks between syllables. It was almost a British accent, but then a slower version, with him nodding a lot. *Some kind of caveman British accent thing?* I think so. *Why does he do that?* Soon I will ask him.

"Sir, where is it you want to go?" she asked. She too thought we were assholes.

"We want to see all of the options and then to choose from them," he said.

The woman stared.

"You have to tell me where you want to go." Her English was good, her forehead high and tranquil.

"Can you not first show us the flights out?"

"No. I cannot."

We thanked her and walked out—

"Hello!" said a new man. "I see you at hotel. I also stay at the hotel. Mister has been in accident! [Now looking closely at me, too closely, examining like a med student] Mister is a toughman! You two party guys out for good time! So how long you in Dakar I know!"

—and back to the hotel and straight to one of the two auto-rental desks. We'd go back to the airport, book a flight out, and then see basically all of Senegal, by car, this afternoon. At the counter, a round and broad-smiling man. We asked for a small car. He dispatched an assistant to get one.

At the other rental desk, across the lobby delta, a man dressed for tennis was berating a different, smaller, clerk. The tennis man was smoking and talking loudly and making a show of being amazed at the prices. He was speaking English and sounded American and looked it. His socks were white and Van Horned up around his calves. We hid behind our backpacks.

With Hand watching for the car, I went into the hotel's business center to get on the web and check on flights out. A huge middle-aged Senegalese man was using the computer; there were three women around him waiting for a turn. But the man saw me and motioned me to come, that he was almost done. I smiled, trying to indicate, having no French, that he should stay and I could come back later, anytime. He waved again, emphatically.

I stepped over and smiled, hoping he'd give me English. He gave me French.

"Sorry," I said. "No parlez pat francais. Mon frer—" I said, gesturing somewhere toward the door, in a way intended to mean that I had a friend who spoke French, an old friend—from kindergarten! from birth!—but he was out in the lobby waiting for a Taurus. I'm not sure if it came across.

"English then," he said heartily. "These are my wives," he said, waving his hand over the three women surrounding him, all very pretty, all very tall. I half-laughed, in an attempt to split the difference between disbelief and courtesy. Three wives? Really? In the blush of the moment, I had to act impressed by him and respectful of them, without getting whiplash. The wives were smirking and talking to each other. They were dressed magnificently, one in the yellow of a rose, one in a rich and ancient orange, the third in a late-evening blue—three queens sitting on folding tables around an eight-year-old Macintosh SE being tapped at by their much older and heavy-sweating husband.

"It will be just a moment," he said. "Where are you from? Let me guess. Texas."

I lied. "Right! How'd you know?" I gave myself a slight twang.

"Ah, Texas. I love Texas. I have been to Midland."

"Oh," I said. "Did you meet—"

"I am so sorry," he said, not having the time to get into it. "I must finish this note." He pointed to the screen.

In a few minutes he finished and apologized and I apologized and thanked him and he and his wives left, the last wife, in yellow, floating around the corner in an ethereal way like a priest in his soutane. I wanted to go with the man and his wives. Would he take us into his grand and heavily guarded pink stucco home and leave us free to roam the grounds, to lounge by the pool as his wives or servants brought us beverages and lotion? Together we'd play squash. Maybe he played paddle tennis—

Hand came into the room with two liters of bottled water, so cold. I held the plastic bottle and it made throaty sounds of deep satisfaction.

"The car, it is coming," Hand said.

"You have to stop that."

"What is it you want I stop?"

"I'm losing my fucking mind. Use contractions, goddammit. You sound like an alien."

Online we checked planes leaving from Dakar. Nothing, almost nothing, without Paris first. We couldn't get to Rwanda without Paris. We couldn't get to Yemen without Paris. We could get to Madagascar, but only through South Africa. To get anywhere would take a full day or more. And visas. We couldn't even cross into The Gambia, the country stuck inside Senegal like a tumor, without a visa. Just getting across the continent, to Cairo, could occupy our whole week. Could we just drive from Dakar to Cairo? We couldn't. Mauritania wanted a visa, same with Mali. Neither was recommended for drivers.

"Fuck," I said.

"We're fucked."

"Yes!"

There was now a man on a computer behind us, one that had been turned off when I walked in. It was the dressed-for-tennis American man from the rental desk. It was his *Yes!* He had the computer up and he wanted us to be curious about why he was excited.

"My friend's in the Paris to Dakar rally," he said.

"The big car race thing?" Hand said.

"Yeah. He's in seventh place." His accent had something in it. He was looking at a page of results.

"Wow. Motorcycle or truck?" Hand said. Hand was interested. Hand apparently knew what this guy was talking about.

"Motorcycle," he said. "He's very good."

Hand knew things like this, and knew how many guerrilla-killed gorillas there were each year in the Congo, and how many tons of cocaine were imported weekly from Colombia, how they did it and how pure it was, and how powerful, and who ran which cartel with the help of which U.S. agencies and for how long. And how Spinoza was actually autistic—he'd read this recently but couldn't remember where—but it was true! They'd studied DNA!—and that Herbert Hoover liked little boys (this he was sure about, though it might have been McKinley, or J. Edgar), and that you could grow the bones of dwarfs by attaching external bone-growing devices that looked like Medieval torture instruments—it worked! he would yell, he'd seen a documentary and one guy had grown almost a foot, though some dwarves objected, calling him some sort of Uncle Tom. . . . On and on, for twenty years I'd heard this shit, from first grade, when he claimed you'd get worms if you touched your penis (I used plastic baggies, to pee, till I was eight)—and always this mixture of the true, the almost-true and the apocryphal—he'd veer within this emporium of anecdote like an angry drunk, but all of his stories he stood steadfastly behind, never with a twinge of doubt or even allowances for your own. If you didn't know these things, you were willfully ignorant but not without hope. He prefaced his fact spewals with "Well, you probably already know this, but the thing about zinc mining is . . ."

As Hand and this man talked, I tried more connections on the web travel sites. Dakar to Zaire: no. Dakar to Kenya: yes but wildly expensive and through Paris. Dakar to Poland: no. Dakar to Mongolia: no. This was fucked up. Why wouldn't there be planes going from Senegal to Mongolia? I'd always assumed, vaguely, that the rest of the world was even better connected than the U.S., that passage between all countries outside of America was constant and easy—that all other nations were huddled together, trading information and commiserating, like smokers outside a building.

"When does the race hit Dakar?" Hand asked.

"Tomorrow maybe," said the tennis man. "Some of the cars are here already—the ones knocked out of the race. There's one in the parking lot. You didn't see it?"

We had seen it, on the way back from our travel agency excursion, a small Japanese pickup heavily stickered and spotted with dried mud.

Dakar to Congo: no. Sudan: no. Liberia: no. Uganda: no.

"Where are you from?" Hand asked the tennis-man.

"Chile."

"Your English is very American," Hand said.

"I live in Fort Lauderdale," he said.

There were flights to Morocco. Morocco didn't require visas.

"Ah. And you're here waiting for your friend?"—Hand.

Now I kind of liked the guy. Chilean but living in Florida and now in Senegal waiting for a friend riding a bike from Paris—he was like us, I thought, flattering myself and Hand—we were all world travelers who defied God and moved and beat time in planes and rented cars. I tried to make his looks imply someone obviously South American, tried to pretend I should have known. Dark straight hair, wet brown eyes, oval face, short neat hair, good teeth, tall—

"Yes. It's very exciting. Are you here for the race?" he asked.

"No, we're here basically—" I started, but didn't know how to explain it.

"We're here," Hand jumped in, "because it was windy in Greenland." The tennis man laughed loudly, then stopped.

"I don't get it."

"We were planning to go to Greenland," I said, "then the flight was canceled because of wind."

There was a long quiet moment.

"So are you staying till tomorrow, to see the rally?" he asked.

"I don't know," Hand said, turning to me. "Maybe. We're actually trying to get find a flight out of here tomorrow."

"To where?"

"We don't know."

"But why? Why leave?"

"I don't know. We're a little jittery. It's hard to explain."

"Are you criminals?" he asked. He was serious and hopeful.

We shrugged. He accepted this. We introduced ourselves. His name was Raymond. I said I was Will, and Hand said he was Sven. They talked for a while about their jobs, Hand explaining weather futures—". . . industries affected by the weather, like energy, insurance, agriculture . . . could hedge their risk . . . one industry wants rain, the other doesn't, they share the risk . . ."—in a way I was hoping, all the way through, would depart from his usual explanation, but did not. Then they were on to soccer.

"Well," Raymond said, finally, "I have to go. But let's eat later. If you're at the hotel find me and we'll go and eat. I went to a fan-*ta*stic Italian place last night and would go back."

He stood and shook our hands and—

"Will, Sven, good to meet you"—

He left.

We checked at the counter; our rental was still twenty minutes away. It was eleven and we hadn't done anything. Planes, visas, cars. Waiting for cars! This was all so tough to take. The *slow*ness. The futility of the time in-between. Out there were the Senegalese and their sea and plains and peanuts—sorry, *ground*nuts—and beyond them The Gambia, and the sun was already finding the uppermost point of its arc, and we were still in the hotel lobby. The waiting! Every drive to every airport in the world was ugly, lined with the backsides of the most despondent of homes, and every hotel lobby underlined our sloth and mortality. This, this unmitigated slowness of moving from place to place—I had no tools to address it, no words to express the anger it forged inside me. Yes I appreciated cars and planes, and their time-squanching capabilities, but then once in them, aboard them, time slowed again, time slowed doubly, given the context. Where was teleporting, for fuck's sake? Should we not have teleporting by now? They promised us teleporting decades ago! It made all the sense in the world. *Teleporting.* Why were we spending billions on unmanned missions to Mars when we could be betting the cash on teleporting, the one advancement that would finally break us all free of our slow movement from here to there, would zip our big fat slow fleshy bodies around as fast as our minds could will them—which was as fast as they should be going: the speed of thought. Fuck regular movement. Fuck cars, rental cars, and wheels, and engineering, and great metal machines that were always too loud and used this ridiculous kind of fuel, so goddamned medieval—

"Let's at least run around outside," said Hand.

It was eleven A.M.! We'd done nothing!

"Good," I said.

The day was bright and gaudy and hot—the air like breathing through wool—so we took a path behind the hotel toward the water, twenty steps down from the hotel, past two boys walking up, carrying a lizard. Over a winding street, the path continued down. A guard at the right of the path, between street and downward stone stairs, stared at us and then closed his eyes to consent to our passage—because, we assumed, we were white. Below, an outdoor patio restaurant, next to a placid blue pool, around which lay dozens of Europeans, tanning while halving their paperbacks, in groups of two and three. We walked past, backpacks on, to the fence separating the deck from the shore of large rounded brown rocks below. There was no beach access. Over the fence and two hundred yards right, two Senegalese fishermen were bathing in the shallows by the shore, their beach crowded with small wooden fishing boats, painted recklessly in bold colors.

"I could do that," I said.

"Liar," Hand said.

"For a few years I could fish."

"I give you six months."

It was warm. We wanted to swim but we would have to find a beach. And we needed to move. We had a plan.

First, drive south along the coast to the Siné-Saloum Delta to see mangroves and crocodiles, then

Slip into The Gambia, visas be damned, then

Follow the River Gambja up to Georgetown, then

Swing back up, into southern Senegal and

Back in time for a late-evening flight to, ideally, Moscow. Easy.

When we got back to the hotel lobby the car was still missing. Hand asked the rental-car clerk, who he'd been joking with and was now our friend, how many wives he had.

"One," the clerk said.

"Only one?" said Hand.

"Soon, though, more. Soon, two." He held up a chubby finger for each wife. "Then three and four," he said, his grin growing with each wife-finger. They both laughed. I gave him a courtesy chuckle. I'd had no idea this was that kind of country.

We watched the lobby's clientele of white businessmen and wealthy Senegalese, watched the men who served them at the check-in desk, all in grey suits and with identical glasses. We'd been waiting an hour and a half. We wanted to be in a car and driving. To a beach, then swimming, then to a national park stocked with monkeys and crocodiles, then onward and back here by night to catch the flight out. Along the way, today, we planned the giving of about $2,000 to passersby.

Finally the car pulled up and as we got in two boys offered to wash our windows. We declined; they said they'd watch the car when we parked it. We pointed out that we were leaving, not parking. They laughed. We all laughed.

"Do we give some to them?" Hand asked.

"Let's just move first," I said. "Out of the city first."

"I'll drive."

"No, I better first."

We were moving, finally. It felt good to be driving. Around the square we circled four times before deciding which of the road's twelve or so offshoots to take. Hand found an American-music station on the radio and we left the center and looked for a highway. In minutes we were lost in Dakar's crowded narrow orange streets. The light was a dry white light. Seconds later we were driving the wrong way on a three-lane, one-way street, with dozens of crossing pedestrians in their unblemished long dashikis waving us back— back, idiots!—and then the car stalling, me with speedy elbows and much grunting executing a three-point turn in the middle of the road, a woman in front of us, an enormous tub balanced on her head, so many women with such things riding their skulls, all staring at us with amusement and disdain, then stall-start-lurch, stall-start-lurch, the honking ceaseless—

And then we were off again—away!—the highway in view ahead—so close! All of Senegal and beyond attainable, Senegal!— and with Huey Lewis on the local radio, coming through with stunning clarity: "Do You Believe in Love?"

Minutes later we were girding for death. What was this cop doing in our car? Or was he a soldier? He was taking us to the place where tourists were killed. If nuns could be killed in Colombia, we could be killed in Africa. Even in Senegal, which hadn't been billed as particularly dangerous, at least according to the few minutes of web research we'd done at the hotel. But what did we really know? Nothing. We knew they had an airport. We were fools and now we were driving to our deaths in a rental car. Janet Jackson was tinkling from the speakers, asking what we had done for her as of late.

The cop was sitting in the backseat, leaning forward between us, directing our turnings. He was tall, about forty-five, thin, wearing a tan uniform and what looked like Foster Grants. He had been standing in the road directing traffic when he told us to stop. We did, pulled over, and through my open window Hand's French hadn't worked at all. Hand had tried to discern our crime, but the man could not get it through Hand's head. Exasperated, finally he just opened the back door and got in.

Now he was directing us through alleys near the center of Dakar. One of us was going to be dragged around by his penis.

Hand and I needed to put together some sort of plan and were speaking in very speedy English, in case the man knew any, which we were fairly sure he didn't.

"Thisiswhentheydragyouaroundbyyourpenis," I said.

"Notfunny. Shouldwetrytobribehimnow?"

"Nonotyetwaitasec."

This guy, he was one of the bad cops. In Senegal you weren't supposed to trust the police. *Were you?* Or maybe that was Peru—

"Areyouwatchinghimclosely? Shouldweworryabouthimandthe bags?"

Our backpacks were both open on the backseat, and the cop was sitting between them. I glanced back to see his whole large hand resting disinterestedly inside my bag.

We passed small walled fortresses with driveways flanked by armed guards.

"Youthinkwe'regoingtothepolicestation?"

"Ihavenoidea."

Hand was periodically turning to the man and trying more French, grasping at some explanation for this, or a plan for the future. I prayed that Hand wouldn't blather anything stupid, though I'd never know what he was saying anyway, so I threw that worry to the wind. The man barked orders, with his big dry hand, the one not in my bag, near my ear, pointing left or right at every turn. We seemed to be circling. It was arbitrary.

"Maybethisissomekindofgame?"

He signaled for us to pull over. I did, behind a taxi, in front of a bar. The cop pointed to a street sign, just in front of the bar. This was, we quickly realized, exactly where he had stopped us in the first place. We'd made some kind of elaborate and misshapen loop to get back here. The sign was a blue circle, bordered in red, indicating that the road prohibited the traveling on it of anything but buses and taxis.

Ah. Hand and I made exaggerated sounds of understanding and approval. "Aaaahhhh!" Hand said, again and again. We were happy to be alive. We had broken a law and that's . . . oooh-kay! Now we'd pay a fine and be off. We all smiled and laughed. He had directed us around the city for twenty minutes only to bring us to the point of our crime, to demonstrate our misdeed. We laughed and nodded our heads. Stupid us! I wanted to hug the man but didn't know local custom.

We would live.

On the road, though, the one that prohibited non-buses and taxis, were dozens of non-buses and taxis. We tried to make this point but then saw no reason to bother. We would pay a fine and move on. But no. Now he told us to go again. He hadn't gotten out of the car. Hand started driving. And now we were scared. Now we would die.

"Nowhekillsus?"

"Whywouldhebotherwiththetrafficsignifhewasgoingtokillus?"

We drove on through five or six more turns. The roads were so narrow. Pedestrians wondered why this man was in the car with two white tourists, one with a face like a skidmark.

And suddenly we were in front of our hotel. We had told him at some point where we were staying and he was simply showing us the way.

"Merci," we said.

We were thankful. Our hotel. That was nice.

Then he asked for money. We offered him 10,000 francs, about ten dollars. He shook his head. We offered 20,000. No, no, he said. He finally took a 1,000 franc note from our drink-holder and smiled and got out. 1,000 francs was enough. It was about a dollar-fifty. That was, apparently, the going rate. He waved good-bye and walked in the direction of where we found him.

The car stalled. The car would not start. In the center of the city center, in the dead-middle of all Dakar's traffic, the car died. Hand jumped into the driver's seat to start it. Nothing. The honking was first insane and soon symphonic. We pushed the car the fifty feet to the hotel. Our rental man met us in the half-circle driveway, and we parked it next to the Japanese pickup truck covered in mud.

"I am so sorry," the rental man said. "I knew this might happen, but I hoped it would not be so soon."

He had known the car would die. Just not in his neighborhood. Hand finished the negotiations while I stood, unmoving, staring through a third-story window where two young white girls stood, looking out, watching us. They saw me watching them watch us and they ducked, disappearing.

In the hotel room, waiting for a new car, we both fell asleep and woke at five.

"Fuck!"

"What a waste."

"We've done nothing."

No delta, no mangroves, no Gambia.

We were hungry.

We ran into the Chilean-American tennis man in the lobby—

"What's his name again?" I whispered.

"Raymond."

"Thanks."

"Hey Raymond!" I said.

"Hello my friends!"

—and had a taxi take us all the six blocks to the Italian place he liked. The streets were narrow and dark. We opened the windows and the warm air touched us with coarse hands. The buildings looked like buildings I'd seen before—they had straight lines and neat corners and windows in between—but they seemed closer to something imagined and built by architects of another world. We flew beneath their roofs and I grinned to the wind, because we'd at least come this far and that meant we'd won.

The cabbie asked for the equivalent of fifty cents and I gave him ten dollars; he said thank you thank you, and that he'd wait until we were done to take us back, or anywhere else, anytime, while we stayed in his country, you friends!

The restaurant was empty but for four drunk and round Italians at the bar talking to the drunk Italian hostess.

"She's gorgeous, isn't she?" Raymond said. "That's why I had to come back."

Hand agreed. "She *is* nice. But I'm really starting to have a thing for Senegalese women."

"You too?" said Raymond. "I know. They are superb." Raymond raised his finger, about to make a point. "But," he said, closing his eyes slowly and raising his chin, "they are all whores."

"What do you mean?" Hand asked.

"You will see," he said.

Hand and I stared at Raymond and blinked slowly. We were stuck with this man for a while, even though it was becoming obvious that he was not of our stripe. Friendships, even temporary ones like this, were based on proximity and chance, and so rarely made any sense at all. We knew, though, that we'd part with Raymond tonight and never likely see him again, so it made it bearable.

The music piped in was a short, ever-repeating loop of Dire

Straits, Pink Floyd, Eagles and *White Album* Beatles. We had fettuccine and Senegalese beer. We learned that Raymond worked in cellphones. Something involving GPS and cellphones and how, soon enough, everyone would know—for their own safety, he insisted, with a fist softly pounding the table, in a way he'd likely done a hundred times before—where everyone else in the world was, by tracking their cellphone. But again: for good not evil. For the children. For the children. For grandparents and wives.

It was the end of an epoch, and I didn't want to be around to see it happen; we'd traded anonymity for access. I shuddered. Hand, of course, had goosebumps.

After dinner Hand asked the cabbie, who'd been waiting without radio or newspaper, to take us to see live music. "You know," said Hand, "like Youssour N'Dour." We'd read in the hotel lobby guidebook that Youssour N'Dour lived in Dakar and owned a club. The cabbie seemed to understand, began driving, and a few minutes later pulled up in front of an outdoor café.

"Here is the location of the music that is live?" asked Hand.

Raymond looked at Hand. Hand needed reining in.

"Yes, yes," said the driver, waving us out of the car. "You like, you like." We got out.

It looked fine, a French café sort of place, outdoor seating, inside warmly lit. But there was no music at all; just wrought-iron tables and a floor of white tile, a black slate bar with a bowl of Manet oranges. We walked in anyway. We'd get a drink and leave.

All eyes jumped to us. There were groups of men and groups of women. The men were tourists and the women were local. I went to the bathroom. In the cool small space, walls like a cave's wet, and brown, I washed my hands with a small piece of round scallop-shaped soap that smelled of home.

I found Raymond and Hand at a table outside, with two women, lighter than most Senegalese, both with long braided hair. Raymond stood and gave me his chair and grabbed another for himself. The girls surveyed me briefly and looked away. I wanted to tear my face off.

There were drinks for everyone. I was introduced to the two, whose names I pretended to understand and whose limp hands I held momentarily and dropped. They looked about twenty, twenty-two. They were sisters and I felt again, as so many times with Hand and Jack, like deadweight, alone.

"They're from Sierra Leone," said Raymond.

"Refugees," added Hand.

They were just short of glorious, with large dark eyes and crooked, oversized teeth. Raymond and Hand were trying to speak French with them.

"We speak little French," the older one said. "Speak English. In Sierra Leone we speak English."

"So you are liking it here in the Dakar?" Hand asked.

Raymond looked at him like he was nuts.

"What?" said the younger. The younger was taller.

"Dakar. Do you like it," Raymond said, annoyed.

"Yes. It's good."

The older one nodded. Hand ordered more drinks and then leaned toward them. He was about to dig in.

"So what's the situation like in Sierra Leone now? Is Charles Taylor still lurking around? I should know this, I guess, but it's been a while since I read about it. Have you seen any of the violence around the diamond trade?"

They looked dumbfounded, turning to Raymond for reason, as if he might translate. Hand continued:

"What did you do for a living? Are you students? When did you guys leave? I mean, are your parents still there?"

The sisters looked at each other.

"What?" the older said, smiling.

"Your parents? In Sierra Leone?"

"Yes. Live there."

"So how old are you two?" Raymond asked.

—Raymond, you're callous and cheap.

—I've seen more than you.

—That means nothing.

—It means everything.

—It's the laziest excuse of all.

"What?" the girl said.

"How old are you?" Raymond repeated.

The older one, to whom Raymond had directed the question, laughed and looked at her sister. Her sister shook her head. She didn't understand.

"How many years are you?" Hand tried.

The older held up her hands in a "Stop" sort of motion, closed them, then did it again.

"Twenty," Hand said.

She nodded.

"And her?" Hand motioned to the sister.

She did it again, with eight fingers on the second flash.

"Eighteen."

She shook her head vigorously, laughing. Then she flashed the fingers again. Eighteen.

"Eighteen."

"No!"

This went on for a while. Raymond laughed.

"Your English is not very good, is it?" Hand said.

"What?" she said.

Raymond said it in French. His French was amazing.

"Speak English!" the girl said. "We are from Sierra Leone!"

Where was this going? No one could know. I wasn't listening

anymore, and each girl began concentrating on one man—the younger on Hand, the older on Raymond.

I watched the sidewalk over the café's low hedge. The place was stocked with chubby European or American men, mostly middle-aged and cheerful, patient. Some had garnered the attentions of the available women, others waited with friends, hands cupped around tall glassed beers. By the door was a man with no legs, sitting on a mat.

Now the younger sister was laughing about something Hand said, making a point of grabbing his arm with both hands and burying her head in his shoulder to demonstrate the great mirth he'd generated. Hand rolled his eyes to me like a cat had jumped into his lap. More drinks were ordered.

"So we go to disco now?" the older said to Raymond.

Hand and Raymond looked at each other, then at me. I shrugged They reminded me of twins I'd known at La Crosse, sisters who knew their skin was more perfect than the rest of ours, and who were very forgiving of the white boys' many fumbling entreaties. These sisters, the Sierra Leonians, had the same bright but complicated smiles.

"No," said Hand, "I think we'll go home. To the hotel." It was clearly a lie. He extended his hand to his younger one. She and her sister stood up and glared at me and went back to the bar.

"Let's go," said Raymond.

When we'd been all together, and when I'd assumed Hand would ask me if it was okay to spend some time alone with one of the girls and that Raymond would follow, I'd hated them all. I'd felt for the girls, but then realized, uncharitably, that they all deserved each other. Now, though, we were leaving, Hand and Raymond were letting them off the hook, or rejecting them, and now I loved the sisters, and wanted to save them from the violence of rejection. I wanted to be with them alone. I wanted to sit with them, laugh at other people with them.

But what did I do? I gave them the tight, smarmy smile I give to homeless people when I have nothing for them, always with a slight, quick shoulder shrug, and we were gone.

I followed Hand and Raymond the two steps to the taxis and we were groped by the man without legs. He wanted money. Then an old woman, middle finger crooked through an actual tin cup, placed herself in front of us, sticking the cup a few inches from my mouth. One of the other women from the bar appeared before us—what she wanted she didn't say. We were surrounded. We backed into the cab. Raymond got in the front seat and closed his door. Hand got in the rear and I sunk in after him, but the no-legged man was now halfway in the car and the door wouldn't close. I could smell his breath, worlds contained within. Why wasn't the cabbie doing anything? He was supposed to tell us not to pay the man. He was supposed to push the man away but he was watching. Everyone in the café was watching.

"Just give him something," said Raymond, laughing. It wasn't funny. This was some kind of thing that happened in India, or the Bible.

I gave the man the coins in my pocket and while counting them he backed away long enough for us to get the door closed. The old woman appeared at the open window, thrusting her head inside. The car was moving, but her head was fully in our cab. Raymond's hand was on her shoulder, pushing her away. He shoved but too roughly—she fell back into the shrubbery with a shriek.

We were off.

"Jesus," I said.

"That was wretched," said Hand.

"These people are poor," said Raymond, without turning around, talking through the wind pouring through his window.

"Listen," Raymond continued, now turning his shoulders to us. "You're here. You came here. You left the hotel. You walk these streets, you allow your path to be chosen by me, by [jerking a thumb toward the cabbie] this driver. You invite things to happen. You open the door. You inhale. And if you inhale the chaos, you give the chaos, the chaos gives back. You know this?"

I felt my forehead tighten, indicating I was thinking—often my forehead starts thinking before I do. I committed what he'd said to memory—it was a jigsaw dumped on a rug but I was hoping I could put it back together, later.

We rode in silence for a few minutes.

"That didn't even make sense," Hand muttered.

"The imbalance is there," Raymond went on. My tolerance for Raymond was waning. "It is just that we don't acknowledge it. We know we're stronger but we ignore this. We don't know our strength. You watch *Star Trek*, how they—what's the word for their beaming up and down—"

"Teleporting," I said, shocked at this train of thought, and how it had just plowed right into my own backyard.

"Right," Raymond said. "They teleport in and out of those troubled planets?"

"Wait," Hand said, actually raising his palm to Raymond's face. "You get *Star Trek* in Chile?"

"Of course."

Hand snorted, impressed. "Okay, go on."

"So this teleporting was based on a Cold War mentality. This was the American foreign policy model then. This was based on the American strength, the American ability to move and change the worlds they touched onto."

The cabbie asked where to and we told him again: Youssour N'Dour's place. Raymond and the cabbie were arguing about something. I clenched and unclenched my fists. They tingled wildly, as if they'd just woken up. Hand noticed.

"You know," he said, "you could go to a hospital here. It'd still be anonymous. No one could track it back here."

"They could."

"C'mon. Really. You should. Get all your shit checked out."

I'd never gone to the hospital after Oconomowoc. We'd decided that if I went in, told the story and made some kind of official record of it, they'd know it was us if we went back someday and killed all three of them. But getting fixed up here, in Dakar, sounded almost feasible. The cabbie took a few more turns and pulled up in front of a club called Hollywood.

"Is this the live music?" I asked.

"Yes, yes, yes—you love it there!" he said, shooing us inside. "I wait here."

Low-ceilinged and horrible, it was a small disco, pink and purple, full of large, framed movie stills in black-and-white—the decor of an antique auto museum. Life-sized pictures of James Dean and Marilyn Monroe, two or three of each, and one each of Tom Selleck and Sandra Bullock and Charlie Sheen, but also, strangely, seven different shots of Val Kilmer in *Top Gun*. The place was empty beyond ourselves and twelve young white men with crew cuts. Sailors.

"I could do that," Hand said.

"Be a sailor? You're high," I said.

"For a year I could do that."

"Just for the pants. That's why you'd do it."

Raymond ordered drinks and began talking to the bartender, a young Senegalese woman in a lace top glowing violet-white in the black light. She came around the bar and was by his side, touching his chest. She looked at me and sniffed. I reached over for my beer and waited for Hand to get back from the bathroom. The place was confusing me. I was sick of looking like a leper.

Hand emerged from the back but was intercepted by a tall thin woman in a halter top and pleather pants. She was built like a fetishist's fantasy—her legs would reach my armpit and her rear (I can't say *ass* in this context; could never say *ass*) was so round and full it looked like it would pop if lanced. She was leading Hand to the small dance floor in the back, lit from below and facing a mirror. Debbie Harry was singing "Heart of Glass" and the world stood listless.

There was another couple dancing, a sailor and a Senegalese woman, but they were dancing with their reflections more than with each other. The man was staring at himself in a way, if directed at anyone but his own mirror image, would have to be considered lewd.

The other sailors were talking with each other, uninterested in the bartenders or dancers. Who was Hand's woman? I watched them dance, Hand doing a moonwalk and then a kind of samba, laughing. Hand is the kind of guy who has rhythm and can move, but is ashamed of this, so has to goof his way through every song. Now he was doing the sprinkler. Then the shopping cart. He was teaching his new friend the shopping cart.

"It is a shame," said Raymond, watching the sailors with half-closed eyes. "This country does not allow its women dignity."

I thought he might be overgeneralizing, but I didn't really know enough to comment either way.

"There's Burma," he continued, "there's Thailand, there is Russia. All sell their women. Their souls are sold when born. The men are mice and the women are cattle."

I drank two vodka-sodas. Soon Raymond didn't like his new friend anymore and wanted to go. Hand's date whispered something to him and he shook his head and whispered back, hand cupped around her ear. She jogged behind the bar and came back with a pen and a little notebook. He wrote something down.

I went to the bar for a shot of anything. The woman serving me was wearing a white sports bra that looked like it had been mauled by tigers—desert isle chic. I turned again. Hand was showing his friend something. A piece of paper. A picture. What was it?

I grabbed it.

"What the fuck are you doing?" I yelled. It was a picture of Jack. Hand stood and looked at me, heavy-lidded with pity.

"I told her we were looking for our friend," he said.

"What does that mean?"

He was drunk already. He couldn't be, so soon.

"You know what it means," he said.

"That doesn't even make sense," I said.

"So what the fuck?" he said.

"You're disgusting."

"I can show him to anyone I want, fucker."

"I don't know you."

He scoffed. He was such a messy drunk.

"Don't ever show that picture to some random waitress again," I said.

"I'll do whatever."

"You fucking *won't*."

"Guys!" Raymond said, with an arm between us. "Easy."

I walked out and waited in the cab. I wanted an hour alone in the cab in the cooling air but they followed me out seconds later.

Hand asked again that we be taken to the jazz club, and I wanted Hand back in St. Louis. He was the wrong guy to have brought. The picture. What kind of—? I couldn't go home, couldn't leave him, though, because we were in Dakar and only had this week.

Five minutes through deserted streets and the next place was precisely the same but worse and without Val Kilmer. "In every part of the world," explained Raymond, "cabbies are trained to bring men to clubs like this. We go in, the cabbie gets a kickback, everyone's happy. We are merely cargo. The way you guys are traveling, you're gonna be targets everywhere. You're perfect prey."

This time, immediately upon entering, we were all attacked in a very real way—women pushing each other to get closer to us, throwing jagged looks at each other, one grabbing Hand's crotch in a way less erotic than territorial. Raymond wound up next to a large woman with bursting eyes and Hand ran to the bathroom. I was being left more or less alone so ordered a drink and saw, across the bar, the two Sierra Leonian sisters, in the corner, beyond the dance floor. They saw me too and laughed a warm and commiserative laugh.

They were still on the make. The place was full—more French sailors, three dozen hungry Senegalese women, and the rest a hodgepodge of Italians and older European businessmen sitting alone, still waiting, waiting. We watched the dance floor crowd clear and change and at one point the Sierra Leonians were dancing alone and I decided then to give them the contents of my left sock, about $400, before we left.

Hand returned from the bathroom with a story. Apparently there had been a few French sailors inside and they'd asked him his nationality. American, he said. "America!" they said, "you pay for the world!" Then they both cheered and patted him on the back. He probably made it up.

"The crazy thing is," Hand said, "I think they were serious."

"You show them any pictures?" I asked.

"Fuck you," he said.

"They're young. They'll learn," said Raymond.

"Learn what?" Hand asked.

"Derision," he said.

I was impressed by Raymond. He could break out a word like *derision*, in his second language, and even better, he was an aphorism kind of man, who could conceive of such things—*We are merely cargo*—and slip them into conversation—*You give chaos, chaos gives back.* I always wanted to be a guy like that.

I watched the dance floor, full of slack shoulders and heads hung and swinging, arms reaching passively up, up. Women tucked their hair behind their ears and men pecked their heads to the beat, hands as fists.

What was wrong with Charlotte? Nothing. Every complaint now seemed ridiculous. She had long dark hairs that swirled around her nipples and I'd seen this as problematic instead of loving her indifference to them. And I'd disliked her sighs. She sighed too much, I announced to myself one day, and worse, her sighs were too sad. Too full of sorrow. When I held her she sighed, and her sighs were weary, were groaning and exhausted, the sigh of an old person who'd seen everything and couldn't believe she was now being held, at the end of a journey she could never describe. The sighs were withering, were mood-killing, and finally I complained about Charlotte's sighs, to no avail. She'd responded with another sigh and that, I know now, was the end of the end.

I was a fool. She was full of soul and now I was in this place, and the women here assumed I needed them.

"Let's go," said Hand. "This is too sad."

But I wanted to unload the cash on the Sierra Leonians. They were harmless and hopeful next to the rest of these women. I slipped past a woman, with great talons, each nail bearing a tiny painted sunset—and to the bathroom—just a hole in the floor in a room like a closet—to secretly retrieve the bills, wrapped around my ankle like a manacle. The wad stifled within my closed fist, I walked across the dance floor and found the two young women sitting on a watcher's ledge, bored, and said "Sorry" to them while stuffing the bills in the older one's hand. She didn't even look at the wad; she felt it but kept her eyes on mine. It was, I realized in a shot, the first time any of these women had really looked at me. I jogged across the dance floor, getting a running start before the throng of grabbing women at the bar.

Raymond was outside. The street was crowded and the bouncers said goodnight—that was nice, I thought—and we waited in the taxi in the dark. Hand was not with us.

"Sven's inside," Raymond explained.

Hand emerged with the Sierra Leonian sisters kissing him on

the cheeks and rubbing his chest—he'd taken credit for my gift—
and he left them on the steps. He crossed the street and strode to
the cab smiling grandly. He opened the door and got in with me
and tried to close it but jesus—a body, again!—a body stopped the
door from closing, prevented us from moving. It was my huge
clawing prostitute. She had seen me give the money to the Sierra
Leonians and wanted her share. She was enormous. I tried pushing
her back but she was strong, at least as heavy as me, and was
halfway in the car, preventing us from leaving or even closing the
door. Her hand was out and she was talking quickly, in French.
Then English: "Give me I see you! Give me I see you!"

I found a 50 dirham note and threw it to her. It fell to the
street. She picked it up and I closed the door, narrowly missing her
head. She turned around quickly and walked back into the bar,
stuffing it in her pants as we drove away.

We were exhausted and home before one. In the cool black lobby we
waited with Raymond for the elevator, watching the steel doors.

"So where to next?" he asked. "Tomorrow."

"Not sure yet," Hand said. "You?"

"I go to Portugal, with my friend. A vacation after his race.
Then back home."

"You think he'll win?" I asked.

"Win? Not a chance. But that's not the point."

I thought it was the point. "Why not?" I asked.

"The point is to offer yourself to death and see if you're chosen."

Hand turned toward him.

"He wants to make sure God wants him to live. So he spends a
lot of time asking. He brings himself close to the edge and he feels
God's breath on his back. If God wants to take him, all he needs to
do is blow."

"Jesus," I said. The elevator arrived and opened.

"Not him."

"Who?"

"I don't believe in Jesus," Raymond said. "I think He would be horrified that we called Jesus Christ His son."

He was losing me. Hand steered us back onto the main trail. "So Portugal," he said.

"That should be nice," I said. I don't know why I said this. I didn't think of Portugal as nice, though I'd never seen a picture, or couldn't remember one. When I heard the word Portugal, I thought of Madagascar, scrubby, dry, poor, the trees crowded with lemurs. I knew nothing, basically, but couldn't bear the fact that of the nations of the world, I had only ill-formed collages of social studies textbooks and quickly flipped travel magazines.

"Well," said Raymond, "I dread it, frankly. I love being here. I love wearing my clothes in these new places. Same shirt, new country! It's the only thing I love maybe—travel. I am finished with women," he said, chin jutting with a stagey defiance.

Raymond's floor rang and the doors opened.

"There is travel and there are babies," he said, stepping out. "Everything else is drudgery and death."

I glanced at Hand. *What the hell?* He held the door open.

"It's early," Raymond asked. "You guys want to have a drink?"

"Now?" I said.

"It's only 12:30! I have Scotch. Good Scotch."

I looked at my feet. I didn't want to stay up with Raymond.

"Maybe," said Hand. "Maybe we'll stop by our room first and then meet you. Which is it?"

"Seven-sixteen," he said. "This will be good. In Chile we don't end a night so soon."

"See you in a bit," said Hand.

At our floor we said hello to the teenaged security guard reading Victor Hugo by the elevator.

"You plan to go back down?" I asked.

"Doubt it," Hand said.

I brushed my teeth and Hand did his and we laid in our beds and watched a French sitcom. There was an actual maid being chased by an actual butler. The laughtrack was loving it. I wanted to tear Hand apart for the picture of Jack. I couldn't make sense of it but didn't want us to blow up after drinking so much—

"We're in Senegal," Hand said.

"Senegal."

"Yesterday we were in Chicago."

"Yeah."

"Now we're in Senegal."

The fucker.

"We came on an airplane," he said.

We'd figure everything out tomorrow. Tonight I would allow him to be an asshole.

"Senegal is in Africa," he said.

"We're in Africa," I said.

"We're alive and in Africa."

"We got here on a plane."

"Tonight we saw prostitutes."

"And a man with no legs."

"Yesterday we were in Chicago."

"How's your face?"

Fuck. "Fine."

"It still looks pretty gruesome."

"Listen Hand, just—"

"Sorry."

"I'm fine until I think about it."

"Sorry."

"You can't remind me. It's bad enough—"

"Shit. Sorry. Now I know. *Fuck man!*" He punched himself on the chest. "I really am sorry Will." But he was sorry only about mentioning it; not about causing it.

"It doesn't hurt," I lied.

"Good."

"We gotta do better tomorrow," I said. I wanted more than parking tickets and hotel lobbies.

"We will," he said, already drifting.

He was asleep in minutes, his breathing too loud, his hands between his thighs, palms together as in prayer.

Jack's mom had asked us to get the stuff, to drive up to Oconomowoc, where Jack had kept all his old things, because Jack's dad was too old, seventy something and now devastated, and she didn't think she could handle it herself. So about three weeks ago we rented a truck and drove the hour or so up from Chicago, on I-94, passing trucks carrying John Deeres, past the drug companies, Teledyne and Baxter and Abbott, beyond the Mars Cheese Castle and the Bong Recreation Area—we'd tried twice in high school to steal that sign—and flew through the crabby grey farms at the Illinois border and then over to Oconomowoc. We stopped at the Kenosha Military Museum, a rolling lawn off the highway littered with sorry-looking tanks and helicopters. We'd probably been there twenty times since we were kids, and this time got out and jumped the fence and shared the one tallboy Hand had brought. It was January and nine o'clock and the place was desolate. Even then we were talking about leaving.

"What about South Africa?" Hand asked, while touching a WWII tank someone had named Tigerbait. All the machines seemed flimsier than I remembered, and smaller.

"I don't know," I said. "Too familiar maybe."

"I always wanted to go to Turkey, too. Have you seen pictures of Turkey?"

"I think so," I said. I had no idea, actually.

Hand jumped onto a German tank and looked into its manhole. There was no way he'd fit in there now. He'd gotten a little thick in the middle, to tell the truth.

"Churchill invented the tank," I said.

"You told me that yesterday. You done with that book yet?"

"No," I said. I was reading it slowly. I was savoring it. I wanted Churchill's life. I would take every last moment.

Back on the road, Hand driving, we passed a couple sitting on their back bumper, parked on the shoulder.

"What are you doing?" I asked.

"I'm stopping. We have to."

"I'm sure they've got a cellphone, Hand."

They didn't have a cellphone. The car was an old Jetta, and they needed a push. Just forty feet, then they'd pop the clutch and be on their way. The man, in a Tina Turner sweatshirt, was round and couldn't push the car off the shoulder himself, and the woman, rounder and in overalls, didn't know how and when to pop. So the pushing would come to us.

We rocked the car until it ground the gravel. It was light. They jumped in and we pushed it onto the pavement and started running—it was so light! Within a few seconds it was going fast enough, the man popped and it caught, and Hand was standing on the bumper, riding it. What the fuck was he doing?

"Get off, dipshit," I said. He was still riding the bumper. I had stopped and was now watching as the car continued, with Hand riding it like a grocery cart. The brake lights came on and the man yelled something out the window, gesturing with a fist. I didn't blame him. Hand jumped off and the car sped away, while Hand ran after it, yelling obscenities. It had started so simply, with such good and simple intentions—

The complex was a twenty-four-hour open-air paralleled trio of long low buildings in Oconomowoc, just west of Milwaukee, twenty minutes from where we grew up. Hand and I pulled into the storage parking lot, between Industrial Avenue and Wall Street, both tiny insignificant streets of weak pavement and poor grading, full of holes.

Hand was still furious. The man with the Jetta had called him an asswipe and Hand felt that characterization unfair. We'd helped the couple and the round man couldn't allow us to enjoy the moment in our particular way.

"*Your* particular way," I said.

"That fucking guy. I can't believe people like that."

It was almost eleven and the place was empty. There were probably fifty units, positioned on a grid, each a white box of corrugated steel about the size of a small moving truck, each with a rolling door, a lock as anchor. We were alone in the complex. We parked in front of our unit and left the car running while we walked over to the Citgo market for food. There was a guy inside at the counter, Skoal circles whitening his back pocket, the frayed bill of his Blackhawks hat bent just so around his pink dry forehead. He was paying for about thirty Red Ropes.

"You gonna eat all those?" Hand said.

Hand talks to people. This is a problem. He talks to the elderly, asking them questions, and with his blond hair and clean face, his look safe but not too safe, they open themselves to him immediately. But when he's got something buzzing within him, anything can happen.

"Eat all what?" the Blackhawks guy said.

"The ropes. In your hand."

"Huh?" Blackhawks understood Hand, but just didn't know why someone at the Citgo was asking about his Red Ropes.

"*Eat,*" Hand continued. "Like, when you move your *jaws* around and—You know, like *mas*ticate . . ."

"Fucking freak," the guy said. "What the fuck are you—"

"No, what the fuck are *you?*"

Now Hand was yelling and they were standing close. Hand was taller, had two inches and twenty pounds on him. Blackhawks stepped back.

"You backing up, little friend?" Hand said.

"Fucking freak," Blackhawks said, and spit to his right.

"*I'm* the freak? You're buying the place out of Red Ropes and *I'm* the freak? Is that what people eat here in Ockah-Ockah-Nokah-Mockah . . . whatever the fuck it's called? You're like the fucking mayor of Ockah-Schmakka and you eat your fucking Red Ropes by decree?"

Hand had gone off the rails. Blackhawks turned to get his change. The clerk, about sixteen, with the distended and hopeful neck of a turtle, had been finishing the transaction, ignoring the proceedings. I was trying to ignore everything, too, and wasn't sure why. Hand was my responsibility.

"Puffer," Blackhawks said in a hiss and a fake chuckle. He was heading for the door.

"Puffer?" Hand said, but Blackhawks was walking out. "Puffer? What does that mean? That's the best you can do? Puffer? You fucking pussy—"

The guy was gone. I couldn't believe this. We were twenty-seven years old and Hand was talking smack in a convenience store with an Oco townie who couldn't have been over twenty.

"Is there a bathroom here?" Hand asked the clerk.

"Broken," the clerk said.

"Liar," Hand said.

We bought our food and outside, with the remaining half of his Butterfinger levitating from his mouth, Hand urinated on the side of the Citgo mart, while trying to figure out the meaning of "puffer."

"I'm assuming he means I'm gay, right?"

"I don't know."

"But isn't the person who gets a porn star ready a puffer, too?"

"Fluffer," I said, and wondered why I knew this.

"Oh."

Hand continued his emissions and I walked over to the storage unit. After rolling up the thundering silver door and before I turned on the light, I saw Jack Sikma. He was standing in the corner, a life-size cutout of slow-moving Sikma, totemic center for the Bucks, a huge awkward white man but not a bad player in the paint, here with a welcoming look on his face. I flipped the lightswitch and a single bulb at the back of the room went live. The place was full. Hand was now next to me, examining a stripe on his jeans where the wall had rebounded his effluvium.

"Jesus," Hand said.

The place was neat, rows of perfect boxes, stacked according to size, and to the right side were things that didn't fit, or things Jack had added at some later time. Mattresses. A net of soccer balls. A pachinko. A corner full of his old lunar maps.

The night was so cold.

"I'm gonna look around," Hand said.

"What? Where?"

"Around. There's a National Guard armory just behind here, up the hill. I'd rather not sit here with this stuff, watching you dig through it all."

"You're not gonna help pack it?"

"I am, but I know you want to look through everything first."

"You don't want to see this stuff?"

"Actually, no."

"You can't take the truck."

"I'm not. I'm walking."

"Leave the truck idling."

"I will."

"You're gonna help pack all this up."

"When you're done looking, I'll pack."

"Fine."

"I'll be back in a half hour or so. I'm going to see what's up there."

"You're really going to—"

"I'll be back."

"Fine."

And he left. He was a moron and a flake—he disappeared all the time—but I was happy for the peace. I opened a box of old school papers and drawings on construction paper, a stack of twenty, with eighteen renderings of Saturn, some with glitter. As eleven-year-olds, before I knew for sure that flying insects didn't enter rectums while you sat on the toilet and before my heart was irregular—I'll elaborate later but it was never such a big deal—Jack and I would get our posterboard and lie on our stomachs and draw our ideal future homes, the landscapes surrounding, the shape of the world in 2020. He was a better straight-line drafts-man than me, so he did that stuff, and I did the grass and animals and people, big-handed and tiny-headed, but whatever we did, however we split the duties, the pictures never looked anything like we'd envisioned. But their ambition was clear, and thus they confused our teachers, who assumed we were as dumb as we acted. Soon enough, though, everyone realized Jack was different than me and Hand, that he had calm where I had chaos and wisdom where Hand had just a huge gaping always-moving mouth. But he was not cool, though Hand and I aspired to be and occasionally achieved some level of local cool. Jack didn't have the gene, couldn't move with any kind of fluidity or fury, couldn't push his socks down the right way, wanted his hair to work for him but spent too much time keeping it in place. He was careful and kept his corners crisp—we'd assumed it was because he was asthmatic, and was for years such a tiny kid, so much smaller than the rest of us, shorter, thinner, proportionate but almost anemic. He was coordinated, a fine athlete, really, but so small, a miniature kid—even his head was smaller. Until the last year or so of high school, that is, when he shot up, hit six feet, filled out, and with his liquid eyes and chin-dimple became a favorite of mothering girls who wanted both to coddle him and teach him things they knew he'd need to know. And he'd taken the new attention with a sense of responsibility, a solemnity even, that we found infuriating.

The low rumble of our idling truck came to an end, and there were voices coming close.

THURSDAY

We woke up late. It was 9 A.M. already.

"What a waste," Hand said. "We could have slept in the car on our way somewhere."

"We'll be fine."

"We really have to move."

We were throwing our stuff in our backpacks.

"Did you get up last night?" I asked. "I woke up at 2:30 or something and you were gone."

"Yeah, I woke up. You were talking in your sleep."

"What'd I say?"

"Nothing sensical."

"So you left?"

"I went down to Raymond's."

"No."

"I did. Man, that guy—"

Someone knocked on the door. I opened it; a very small woman gestured that she'd like to clean the room. I apologized and said we'd be leaving soon. She smiled and bowed and backed out.

"Wait," I said. "What's that smell?"

"It's you. You smell."

"It's us. We smell."

I inhaled from my underarm. The smell was very strong. "We'll

have to wash these things. We'll soak through everything today."
We'd figured out long ago that it wasn't the first-time sweat that
created odor. It was the second time sweat came through once-
exposed skin or cloth. It was the *re-sweat.*

I showered with great joy. In the shower, swallowing water, the
water broke and hissed on my head, while heavy drops, after loving
my abdomen, touched, rhythmically, my insteps. I said to myself,
actually whispering out loud, that it was the greatest shower I'd
ever known.

We drove to the airport and made for the Air Afrique desk.
Behind the counter were three queens—grand, dressed in the most
florid and glorious wares, skin luminous like lanterns polished.

We asked what they had flying out.

"Where are you going?" they asked.

"What do you have flying out?" I asked.

"You do not know where you are going."

"Well, yes and no."

They had a flight to Mauritania, but Mauritania wanted a visa.

"Anything else?"

"There is a flight tomorrow to Casablanca."

Morocco required no visa. But we'd have to stay in Senegal one
more night. Which meant the diminished likelihood of us making
it around the world. We were failing in every way at the same
time.

We made sure there was room on the flight and decided to
decide later. We left the airport, heading for the coast, for Saly,
where there were beaches. First we had to swim. Then we'd see the
crocodiles and the monkeys. Then to Gambia and back. We could
make it, we figured, but we'd have to speed.

We were lost before we left the airport complex. In front of an
abandoned hangar we stopped for directions. There were about
thirty men there, half in suits, standing in the parking lot adjoining the airport. A contingent of five approached the car. We

explained where we needed to go, Saly, and instead of directing us, two of them began arguing, each with his hands on the back door handle. We asked again for directions. Directions only, we said.

Then a young man was in the back seat.

"I take you there," he said.

"What?" Hand said. Hand was driving.

"I show you the way, then you pay me, no problem."

Hand looked at me, I looked at Hand.

"I show you you pay me no problem," he said again.

His name was Abass. He was younger than us, wearing a nylon sweatsuit; he sat where the officer had sat, and I surprised myself by being glad he was there. It was good to be three.

But in a few minutes he had us on the road to Saly and had rendered himself redundant. I checked the map and noted that there were no turns for the remainder of the hour-long drive.

"Shouldntwejustdrophimoffnow?" I asked.

"Ithinkthat'dberude."

He stayed. We liked him. He liked Otis Redding and Hand had an Otis Redding tape so we played James Brown. He liked, most of all, Wu-Tang Clan, but we didn't have any Wu-Tang Clan. We had Dolly Parton.

The road was an endless marketplace—tire shops, refrigerator outlets and open-air fruit stands. Three gangly boys playing foosball at a table five feet from the road. Small buses, bright blue and painted with joy by hand, overfilled with people. When passengers wanted to get off, the bus slowed and they jumped from the bus's back door. The bus never actually stopped. The children were filthy but the Mobils and Shells were pristine, as were the adults. Everywhere were people in dashikis, long enough to brush the unpaved shoulder but still unbesmirched.

The light was the familiar dusty white. I decided that when we got to Saly we'd give Abass half of what we had left on us—about $1,400.

"You have wife?" Hand asked.

"No, no. Soon," he said.

"Kids?"

"No, no. Soon."

What would he do with the money? Start a business? Buy his way out of Senegal? I didn't have the tools to imagine.

At a stoplight, a man was selling orange juice. We flagged him over. He came to the window. But it wasn't orange juice. It was brake fluid. He was selling brake fluid and cassette tapes. Behind him, an enormous pile of fish, the shape of an anthill, lay rotting in the sun.

"We should let him get off here," I said.

Hand made the offer. Abass shook his head and smiled.

"He wants to go to Saly," Hand said.

We drove on. Hand and Abass were talking about something that prompted, from Hand, many expressions of surprise. He turned to me.

"I think he just said his father was the ambassador to Zaire."

"Tell him congratulations," I said, wondering why the son of an ambassador was in our car riding to Saly.

Hand and Abass exchanged words.

"He's dead ten years," Hand explained.

We expressed our condolences. I handed Abass a chocolate chip energy bar. He pointed out the front window, at a French army truck passing us going the other way.

"Ask him his last name," I said.

Hand asked.

"Diallo," Abass said.

"Really?" Hand said.

Another French troop truck.

"Tell him," I said, "we have a very famous Diallo in America."

Hand told him. Abass was very interested.

"Abass wants to know," Hand said, "what our Diallo did to become famous."

We drove in silence for a second. I knew we'd never be able to explain it, and we didn't want to spoil the mood.

"Tell him he's a singer," I said.

At Saly we turned off and drove under a series of canopied entranceways. This was a resort complex and the foliage quickly became more lush, the streetsides uncluttered—like entering a Floridian national park. We pulled into a hotel called Savana Saly and in the lot, stepped out and stretched.

I was getting the money ready—this particular wad drawn from my inner-waist pocket, under my belt—when he told us how much he wanted.

"What?" said Hand. Abass spoke quickly and sternly. They exchanged words. "I think he wants $80."

"Eighty dollars for getting us on the highway?"

"I guess so."

"That's too much," Hand told Abass.

He glared at Hand. Now he was not our friend. Eighty dollars for three turns and an hour on the highway.

He spit more words to Hand.

"He says he has to get a cab back to Dakar," Hand said.

There was no way he was getting a cab back to Dakar. He'd take the bus and pocket the $80. We didn't like him. He knew we'd feel awful paying him less than what he asked, but $80 was wrong. I looked up and the sky gave me no tether. We'd been driving too long and we hadn't eaten—

"Will."

I wanted a ceiling but it was too thin and porous and I went dizzy. I wanted something accountable above—

"Will."

"What? What?"

"Your pocket. The bills."

"Sorry."

I gave him the $80 but not the $1,400 I planned. He took the money and wrote his name and number on a piece of paper, urging us to call if we needed help getting back to Dakar. We said we'd be sure to call. The fucker.

He walked to the highway. Hand and I stood in the lot watching his back, my fingers tingling, my head in a half-swoon.

"That's too bad," Hand said.

In the hotel's reception desk, outside and under a thatched roof, an exhausted mélange of French tourists sat on their suitcases, waiting for deliverance. They stared at us dismissively. We checked in, dropped our things in our dark cool room. The fan overhead spun crazily. It was missing a screw, and everywhere there were pictures of parrots and peanuts.

We went to swim. At the snackbar, we bought cold orange Fantas and carried them in our shoes, which hung by their heels from our fingers. We brought one backpack between us, stuffed with towels from the room and my Churchill pages.

The beach was slim and rocky, the water a vibrating cobalt blue. The bathers were old and white, flesh melting downward, the men in bikinis, the women, half of them, topless and drooping without caution. Hand ran, jumped on and from a huge grey gumdrop rock and into the sea.

"Fuck!" he yelled. He stood waist-deep, his hands shot to his face. "It's fucking cold!"

But he stayed.

I stepped in; it was brutal. The air was about 90° and we expected the water to match this, or come close. But it was crisp, bracing. The cold of an upper-Wisconsin lake, in June.

I wanted to be hotter before I jumped in, I wanted to be soaked. I spread my towel and I lay my head on the sand and listened. A bird, fifty feet above, fell from the sky like a plane. But in a second it rose, fish in beak, and flew toward the white shore.

I rested my head deeper into the terrycloth and closed my eyes. Only on sand like this did I ever feel like I could sleep forever, did I feel that sleep could be a destination. The comfort was limitless and I knew I was mouthing the words *Fantastic, so good, fantastic, so good*, but couldn't help it. The sun had half my face, one eye, a shoulder. It pressed into me, nudging with its forefingers, into my neck, my crown, the side of my calf. *Fantastic. Fantastic*, I thought. Then thought: *You seem so content.* Yes. *Why? There are reasons why this is incongruous.* I know. *But what were they again?* I don't know. *You do.* Why are we doing this? Why are we trying to remember why this comfort is no longer possible? *Wait a second. I remember—*

I came to the answer.

Hand had turned off the rental truck's ignition. I'd told him not to. Or were we low on gas? Couldn't be. I shouldn't have left the truck running. How long had I been in here? I had lost my sense of time. There was a gas station next door so it hardly mattered.

"Hand?"

Nothing.

I heard voices outside the unit, moving closer. I put the drawings back in the box. I stood up, my back to the door. The floorboards of the unit creaked, and as I turned, something struck my jaw. An airplane made of concrete. I dropped to my knees. Instantly the same thing, or something else like it, hit me in the back.

It had been years since I'd taken a punch. Had that been a fist or a club? A bat. A fist to the jaw then a bat to the back. Not a fist;

too hard. A two-by-four, both times. I looked around for who but saw only floor. Then a pair of shoes so close, workboots, black, and behind them, a pair of white sneakers. Another pair of shoes maybe. Two guys, or three. I got on my knees and put my arms forward, bracing myself, and tried to lift my head. A corkscrew pain tore through my spine. I tried to speak but couldn't—lungs aflame. I fell forward, my hands catching me before my face hit the floor. "What the fuck?" I said. Cheek on the cool wood floor, I could make out three figures. There was blood in my mouth. It came down my chin as I spoke. *Fucking Hand.*

I tried to look up again but almost fainted from the pain. I sat up, head down, and wiped the blood with the butt of my hand. I looked around for a weapon. My back felt broken. It wasn't a dull pain; it was acute, almost sweet.

One of them laughed. A laugh like a cough.

The toe of a shoe ripped through my stomach. I lost my lungs. I spit a wad of blood on the threadbare Indian rug Jack used to have in his bedroom. I just needed a second to catch my breath. Goddamn, I just needed a second—

"Answer me!" a voice yelled. I hadn't heard the question.

On my knees but upright, I swung wildly, connecting with the metal wall of the unit. It made a small sound, quick and weak. Skin from my knuckles remained on the wall, white with red streaks. The near one laughed. And then kicked me square in the chest. My head hit the floor this time. I couldn't break its fall. I tried to stop it but my hands felt so small. Then the end of the two-by-four came down on my right hand, like a shovel.

I blacked out. When I opened my eyes it felt like hours since I'd seen life. I felt like I was sucking air out of tiny crushed lungs. Lungs the size of thumbs. I didn't see an end to it. I just needed a breath, though. Just a second. But to die this way—

I wasn't recovering. My lungs were so small and burned when I tried to yank air into them. I wanted a gun. They had the wrong guy. I tried to say something but when I tried went blind with tears. My lungs had been doused with lighter fluid and set ablaze. What did they want? Everything spun beneath me.

My breath was coming back but my hands were crushed. And if I found something and used it on one of them, the other would be there. Only a gun would work here. Two guns. A knife. I would at least do some damage. I hated the odds. They'd blindsided me and there were two of them. I had almost no options. Where the fuck was Hand? Any second he'd show up with a bat and crack open heads. I longed for the sound.

One of them yelled something. I think it was "Answer me!" again. My hearing was filtered.

I started to stand up. The close one grabbed my hair. I slapped his hand away—I had more strength than I thought. A chunk of my hair went with his fingers. I took two steps back and tripped on fragments of a table. I was down again. The close one was still laughing. I tried to yell but it retched out in a whisper. My spine was a pole jamming into the base of my skull, a broom ramming into a ceiling.

"Fuck you!" the far one roared. It was so loud in the steel box I flinched. The far one stepped inside and turned off the light. The boot came from below and connected at the right side of my head and I was out.

I woke up alone. There were only my eyes. They felt as if they'd been removed, dipped in acid and then fastened to me with pins. The planks were oak, very old, rounded on their edges. My right palm met the wood and my cheek was set upon my hand, but the other hand I couldn't place. I felt nothing in the direction I assumed it would be. I opened my eyes again. There was no dog. I thought I had heard a dog.

I tried to sit up but my head was too heavy. I could lift my cheek but not my skull. I was afraid to pull it away from the floor, for fear I would tear something. I lowered my cheek again and slept. A crash woke me and I sat up quickly with the sound of ripping. I felt my head where it had been attached to the floor. I gagged and spit. I wiped my hand on a box behind me, not looking. I didn't want to see anything white, any bone on my hands. I felt my neck, to see if blood was coming steadily, which meant I was dying, but it was not. I looked to the floor, where my head had rested, but there was only a small black pool, the edges dry. I couldn't have lost much blood. A dog's face appeared at the door and then was gone.

I was using my right hand but couldn't feel my left. I realized I was not feeling my left. Where was my left arm? I looked to where it would be and found it, hanging from my shoulder like a windchime. It was dislocated or broken. My skull was something attached but so loosely. There was a pain so active and pulsating I was fascinated by it. It was unlike common head pain, which is dim and thudding; this was a constant cracking from within, a constant chopping of the inner walls of the cranium, by pickaxes.

To see things hurt my eyes. I closed them.

There were insects in my inner ear. Something rattled lightly. Then a high-pitched sound, like a whistle, though higher and more distant. I felt my face; the right side was numb. I shook my head slightly and the pain went stratospheric.

I slept for what seemed like hours. Finally I stood and immediately fell, as a flaming burst of glass shot up my left leg. The dog was there again. He was a collie, white and khaki, and stood in front of the door to the unit. I opened my mouth and closed it. The truck was in the same place. The windshield was cracked up the middle, one large split giving way to dozens of white tributaries. I was sitting down and had no idea how I could get there.

I heard his footsteps on the gravel. Hand.

"Jesus fucking Christ!" he said. "What the fuck happened?"

I hated him. This was for him. They were here for him.

"Tell me!" he said.

"Where were you?" I breathed.

"What the fuck happened?"

I gathered my voice. "Where were you Hand?"

I raised my head and sat up. The beach was the same. Hand was farther out, swimming with his perfect stroke toward a small fishing
boat. I stood and almost collapsed. I grabbed my knees and rested
and rose again and waded in, still reeling, and the hands of the cold
calm sea held my calves then seized my knees and wrapped its thick
strong fingers around my thighs and its bony cold arms around my
waist. I dunked my head and came back wet and stronger.

I pushed my hair from my face and smoothed it in back, letting
the water exit my mouth and spread slowly down my neck. Hand
lifted himself from the water so his head peeked into the empty
boat. I couldn't see what was there. But he was often finding
things. He swam back; the boat was empty.

On the shore we dried in the sun. Far away, a fishing boat with
an old man pulling from its side a huge fish, or a part of it. It
looked like a swordfish, huge chunks torn from its sides.

"Scavenger fish," Hand said. "They bite and disappear down."

"Poor man."

"Turn around," Hand said.

"Why?"

"You didn't show me that shit. Jesus."

"What?"

"Have you looked at your back?"

"No. Sort of."

"Fuck, man. You've got a huge bruise here"—he pushed his finger into the lower part of my left lat—"and right here"—he brushed
his hand over my right shoulder—"it's all red and scratched. It's
just nasty."

"Doesn't hurt back there."

"Well, good. It's nasty-looking."

—You act like it wasn't your fault.

—We've leapt over that.

—I'm not sure I have.

A strong-shouldered woman was playing with four small children by the water. They had buried the tallest of the kids and were giggling like henchmen. Their dog walked to us and waited for our attention. It was a small white thing with short legs, trailing a leash. This one was winking at us.

"He's only got one eye," said Hand. It was true.

I scratched the dog's head. Half the animals in my life were missing an eye—growing up we'd fed nuts to a cycloptic squirrel, Terrence, that lived on our roof—and I couldn't figure out if this was good luck or bad. The dog's one eye was wide open and the other was closed tight around the vacancy. It was grinning, though—was accustomed to being appreciated. *Listen my friends, I have one eye, I'm winking at you, give me some of your love.* We scratched him everywhere, as he moved to guide our hands to his needs. When satisfied, the dog abruptly returned to his family. He had to get back to take care of some things.

As the tiny waves came to wet the sand with long hisses, I picked up my Churchill. Now he was at the Admiralty, whipping everything into shape, trying to increase the production of ships, honing his speechmaking skills, having the first of his children, writing beautiful letters to his Clementine. I'd never written a beautiful letter to anyone, and I had never fought the Boers, had never righted a derailed military train at Frere, never faced their artillery fire while loading wounded onto the cab and tender—

—Churchill what would you have done?

—When?

—In Oconomowoc.

—What? What are you talking about?

—I was beaten. They hit me with bats. I was in a storage unit, gathering Jack's stuff, just going through it, I guess I was lost a bit and Hand was gone—

—Where was Hand?

—He went off, up the hill.

—Hand should have been there.

—I know. But if I allow myself to know that I'll leave him, and I don't want that. I do want it, so often, but I'm stuck with him, worse off without him, if you can believe it.

—I can.

—So what would you have done?

—I can't say. The odds sound difficult.

—I would have fought next to you, Churchill. Anywhere. Did I tell you that? In India, I would have been there, leaping into musket fire. In Egypt, surveying the Dervish army at Surgham Hill, I would have been there. Cavalry, infantry, whatever—

"We should leave," I said.

"Right," Hand said.

We dressed quickly so we could drive through the countryside and tape money to donkeys. We'd been in Senegal for twenty hours and hadn't given away anything.

I drove. I drove fast. The road was dry, passing through scrubland and the occasional farm, the roadside spotted with small villages of huts and crooked toothpick fences. The terrain was dry, the grass amber. We passed more blue buses bursting with passengers, staring at us, at nothing.

The donkey plan was Hand's. As we drove, hair still wet, we looked for donkeys standing alone so we could tape money to their sides for their owners to find. We wondered what the donkey-owners would think. What would they think? We had no idea. Money taped to a donkey? It was a great idea, we knew this. The money would be within a pouch we'd make from the pad of graph paper we'd brought, bound with medical tape. On the paper Hand, getting Sharpie all over his fingers, wrote a note of greeting and explanation. That message:

We saw many donkeys. But each time we saw a donkey, there was someone standing nearby.

"We have to find one alone, so the owner will be surprised," Hand said.

"Right."

We drove.

"This looks like Arizona," Hand said.

"It was pretty lush in the resort, though."

"Watch it."

I had driven off the road for a second, with a whoosh of gravel and a tilt of the passenger side, then back on, level and straight.

"Dumbfuck," Hand said.

"I've got it. No problem."

"Stupid. Listen."

There was a flopping sound.

"Pull over," he said.

We had a flat.

We stopped. When we got out, all was very quiet. The earth was flat and the savannah was broken only by large leafless trees, bulbous at their trunks and muscled throughout. A bright blue crazily painted bus, full, drove by; everyone stared. The sun was directly above.

We got the spare and the tools and jacked the car up. We started on the lug nuts, but they were rusted and weren't budging. We pounded them with the wrench with no results. We sat on the highway next to the car, suddenly both very tired. The pavement was so warm I wanted to rest my face on it. I imagined what lay ahead: hitchhiking to the next town, maybe catching the bus, then finding our way to some kind of garage, then negotiations with the mechanics, a tow truck back, then, hours later, the fixing of the flat. We'd waste the day. We'd already wasted too much.

A man appeared behind the car. In a purple-black dashiki, easily seventy, with a small square jaw and eyes small and black and set deep under his brows. He said nothing.

He inserted himself between me and Hand and, without a word, took over. He first placed a rock behind the back tire, to prevent rolling. We had forgotten that. Then, crouching, with hands that hadn't, it seemed, seen moisture in decades, wrinkles white like cobwebs, he lowered the jack so the wheel rested on the road. He stood and with his sandaled old foot he kicked the wrench; the lug nut turned. He kicked again for each nut, and in a minute the tire was off.

"Leverage," Hand said to the man, touching his shoulder. He was bursting and was about to say something stupid. "You are very good man!" he said, now patting the man on the back.

I put the new tire on, and the man allowed me to tighten the lug nuts myself. When the job was done the old man turned and looked at my face and smiled and walked away. He still hadn't said anything.

"Give him something," Hand said.

"You think?"

"Of course."

The man was now across the street, heading down the embankment and into the tall grass.

"You think it's an insult?" I said.

"No. Go."

I grabbed a bunch of bills from my thigh pocket.

I ran after the man and when I descended the embankment I realized I was barefoot. The rough earth scratched my soles but I caught him fifty feet into the opposite field.

"Excuse me!" I said, knowing he wouldn't understand the word, but knowing I had to say something, and then settling on the words I would have said had he been able to understand. He turned to me.

I smiled and handed him a stack of bills. He stared at my nose. I smiled harder and rolled my eyes.

"Long story," I said.

He waved the money off. I took his hand and put the bills in his palm and closed his fingers, dry and ringed like birch twigs, around them. I smiled and nodded in an eager and anxious way, like I was taking his money, not giving him mine.

He said nothing. He took the bills and walked off. I jogged back to the car, my feet slapping the pavement in a happy way; a boy was there, about six years old, though there wasn't a house or hut in sight.

"Where'd he come from?" I asked.

"He just showed up," said Hand.

The boy, barefoot and wearing Magnum P.I. shorts, was leaning against the side of the car, looking inside, his hands cupped around his eyes and set against the window, reflecting the endless fields, newly tilled and dry, behind him.

"What's he want?"

"I think he was here to help."

"We have anything for him?"

"Money."

"No. He'll get robbed."

We gave him a package of white cream cookies and a liter of water, full and in the sun seeming heavy, like mercury.

We got in the car but the car wouldn't move. The boy, at the side of the car, yelled something, waving his tiny bony arms.

"The rock," said Hand.

"Oh," I said.

While watching us, carefully, holding his hand up in a gesture begging us not to run him over, the boy bent down and removed the rock. We thanked him and waved and honked and drove away, down the coast.

There were beaches being used as dumps. The sand was white and duned, and the water clear beyond, but the beach overwhelmed with garbage, great heaps of it, and broken boats. Periodically we'd pass through a village, the buildings, squat and of clay, abutting the road, kids running out of open doorways. We drove around more blue buses, and a few carts driven by horses nodding, but no donkeys. We couldn't find a fucking donkey. Cows would be just as good, we thought, but every time we stopped and approached a cow on foot, a car would come down the road, or a bright blue bus, or a farmer or a cart or child, and we'd abort. At one point, when we really thought we were going to do it, had the money in a pouch and the tape all around it and a cow picked out and were only a few feet away, it wasn't a car that came but a whole caravan of men, French we guessed, on four-wheel ATVs, eleven of them, in a row, half with white girlfriends strapped around their waists, all with aviator glasses, a few with scarves.

"Good lord God no," Hand said.

The image was unsettling and indelible.

We gave up on taping money to animals. We were now looking for people. Anyone to unload the money on. But choosing just who was a strange kind of task. We found a group of boys working in a field, raking hay and throwing it into a large wooden wagon attached to a mule. Five boys—

"Brothers, probably," said Hand. We stopped and parked on the side of the road.

"They're gonna see us," I said.

"Then get out and give em some money, idiot."

"Not yet. I gotta make sure."

"Here," Hand said, spreading a map between us. "This is like a fucking stakeout or something."

—working together, without pause. They were perfect. But I couldn't get my nerve up. All I had to do was get out of the car, walk a hundred feet and hand them part of the $1,400 we had left. We had to get rid of this money. Tomorrow we would cash more checks—*swoop! swoop!*—and start over. We were already so far behind. But I couldn't do it.

"That one guy looks like a dad," I said.

"No, he's just a little older than the others."

"I can't give it to them if the dad's there."

"Why?"

"Because the dad won't take it, or let them."

"Bullshit," Hand said. "Of course he'd take it."

"No he wouldn't. It's a pride thing. He won't take the money in front of his sons."

"Not here, stupid. These guys know they need it and that we can afford it. They're not taking it from a neighbor, they're taking it from people who it means, you know, next to nothing to. They know this."

"You do it."

"No, you. It's your money."

"No it's not. That's the point."

"Just go."

"I can't. Maybe we wait. The dad'll go get some water or something. Or you could create a diversion."

We sat, watching.

"This is predatory," I said.

"Yeah but it's okay."

"Let's go. We'll find someone better."

We drove, though I wasn't sure it would ever feel right. I would have given them $400, $500, but now we were gone. It was so wrong to stalk them, and even more wrong not to give them the money, a life-changing amount of money here, where the average yearly earnings were, we'd read, about $1,600. It was all so wrong and now we were a mile away and heading down the coast. To the right, beyond the fields and a thin row of trees, the Atlantic—wait; right, the Atlantic—shimmered like a dime.

The sun was low in a white-blue sky and the air was cooling. We approached a huge warehouse in a field. The place, a gallery of some kind, was immense, and shuttered, the parking lot covered in grass. There were no other buildings for miles.

We parked. We'd look around.

A flock of small black birds came across the building in a desperate way. They weren't in any kind of formation, just fifty of them, all flying in the same direction, each with its own path. Not every one with its own path, I guess, but so many of them, which struck me. I don't know why it struck me then but had never struck me before. When we see birds flying in a flock, we expect them in formation. We expect neat V's of birds. But these, they were flying in more of a swooping swarm, a group fifty feet left to right, twenty feet top to bottom. Within that area they were swerving up and down, swinging to and fro, overlapping, like a group of sixth graders riding bikes home from school. Which would imply not only free will but a sense of fun, of caprice. I mean, I want to know what this bird:

is thinking. How does he feel his flight? Does he know the difference between stasis and swooping? Birds were so much better in flight. My bird feeder, now empty in Chicago, taught me how nervous and jittery birds were when they stood and hopped and ducked their heads into the glass for their miserable little seeds. But tearing in and out of formation, there was proof of—

And then they were gone.

"This is a good place to walk around," said Hand.

I agreed to walk around.

We parked the car behind the building, hiding it from the road. Though we had no evidence of anything like it, we imagined the possibility of roaming marauders who would stop, strip our car bare and move on. So the car was hidden; we could walk through the fields and head to the ocean, less than a mile west.

"You got some sun today," I said.

"You too," Hand said.

"Let's go that way," he said, vaguely indicating a small farm in the distance, three small huts and a fence of sticks. This would be the first walking we'd done. The field was quiet. We walked toward the huts, over rough savannah breached by the huge and common bulbous leafless trees—their bark smooth and knotted. Closer now, there were figures under and around one of the farm's largest huts, and around the hut a fence and within the fence ten or twelve sheep, all a dirty grey. Four young kids ran from the fence and toward us, still very small in the distance.

"Bonjour!" one of them yelled, the word sailing to us through the thin late-afternoon air with the strong voice of a girl of eight or nine. Then another one, "Bonjour!" this time from a boy. Then they both said it as they skipped toward us: "Bonjour!"

Hand yelled back: "Bonjour!"

"Hello!" I yelled.

It had to be those kids. Only the most blessed of little people yells hello across an empty field to strangers with dirty clothes.

"We have to give them some," I said.

A man emerged from another nearby hut and faced us.

"Shit," Hand said. We only wanted the kids. This man would be suspicious.

"I liked it better when it was just the kids," I said.

"Who cares?"

"Look at him. He's carrying a scythe or something."

Hand squinted. "You're right."

"I am?" The man was standing now, hand shielding his eyes, and the kids had gone inside.

"We'll come back," Hand said. "We'll swim and come back."

We walked toward the ocean; we knew it wasn't far. We'd been watching the ocean peek between towns and trees the whole drive down. We tramped through a growing thicket and toward the weakening sun.

"Fuck," said Hand.

"What?"

"Mosquitos. That's how we get malaria."

He was right.

"You bring block?" he asked.

"No."

"Fuck. This is stupid. I don't want malaria."

"I wouldn't mind it," I said. I had a distant and untested fascination with sickness like that, that would bring you to the brink but not over, if you were strong.

We debated. Continuing on meant an unknown risk—the place could be swarmed with mosquitos any second—but going back to the car meant that we'd truly done nothing, and we would never do anything. If we couldn't pull off the road and walk through a field to the ocean then we were worth nothing.

We walked on. The ground was hard and brown and dotted with seashells. There were shells all the way back to the highway, the road lined with them, white and broken.

"You see all the shells?" Hand asked.

"I know."

"This whole area was underwater."

After a few minutes we could see the ocean. It was the lightest blue, a dry and sun-faded blue. We walked closer, a few hundred yards from the shore, and saw a group of small houses, all of the same design and standing in formation—some kind of development, between us and the water. About fifteen of them, cottage-sized and neatly arrayed, on a sort of plateau, separated from us and from the beach beyond by a moat, sixteen feet down and filled with what seemed to be—

"Sewage," Hand said.

The builders had run out of money. It was a resort-to-be, but without any sign of recent work. There were no vehicles or trailers. Only these small homes, well-built, windowless and sturdy. Each one big enough for one bedroom, a sitting room and a small porch. We got as close as we could before the moat asserted itself without solution. The water in the moat was too deep and dirty to wade through, and too wide to jump.

"There is no reason for this moat," said Hand.

There was a man. He walked into view on the other side of the moat, among the houses. He was Senegalese, bone-thin and holding in his hand some kind of electric device, black and with a long antenna. He stared our way.

"Security," Hand said. "They've got someone guarding the whole place."

"We should leave."

"No."

We were watching the man and he was watching us.

"Let's pretend we're leaving and see if he leaves," I said.

"Fine," Hand said.

We turned and shuffled away. Was he armed? He could shoot us if he wanted to and no one would ever know. We sat behind a pair of thick shrubs.

"Pilar looked thin," I said.

"She did?" Hand said, trying to balance a thin stick between his nose and upper lip. "I thought she looked normal."

"You're blind."

I dug a small hole and put a scallop-shaped shell inside, and buried it. Then I retrieved it, and set it back in the exact spot I'd found it.

"This is slower than I thought it would be," I said.

"Let's go," Hand said.

We stood and the man was gone. We walked alongside the moat, hoping to find a narrow place to cross, to get closer to the homes and then to the beach beyond. We soon saw a clothesline threaded between one porch and its adjacent tree. Shirts and pants hung from it, and on the porch towels and an Indiana University umbrella.

"Jesus," I said. "Someone's living here."

"Makes sense."

"But why does the security guy let them?"

"We could plant some money in there," Hand said. "Put it in a pair of pants."

"Yeah, on the clothesline. That'd be good."

We went around the entire moat and at the far right end found an area where we could get down the bluff, about fifty feet, and over the water. There was a rocky sort of path sloping right and after taking off our shoes, in case we landed somehow in the moat, we descended, sliding and jumping, and soon found ourselves jogging slightly, as if descending stairs in a hurry. The path was now dotted with large flat rocks, like overturned dinner plates, and we were jumping from rock to rock, and doing so at a speed that I should have found alarming but somehow didn't, and we were barefoot, which might have increased the alarm but instead made it easier, because the rocks were smooth, and cool, and my bare feet would land on the rock and kind of wrap around it, simian-like, in a way that a shoe or sneaker or sandal couldn't. I swear my toes were grabbing for me, and that my skin was attaching to the rock surface in a way that only meant collusion between natural things—in this case, feet and smooth green-grey rocks. There was no time to think, which was plenty of time—I had a few fractions of a second in midair, between rocks, to calculate the location of the next rock-landing options, the stability of each, the flattest surface among them. My brain and legs and feet all working at top speed, at the height of their respective games—it was thrilling and I was proud for them, for us. I had the thought, while running, without breaking stride, that I would like to be doing this forever, that thought occurring while I almost landed on a very sharp rock but adjusted quickly enough to avoid it in favor of a nearby and more rounded rock, and while I was congratulating myself on having made such a perfect rock-landing choice, I was also rethinking my thought about jumping on rocks forever, because that would probably not be all that fun after a while, involving as it did a certain amount of stress, probably too much— and then, I thought, how odd it was to be thinking about running forever along the rounded gray rocks of this corner of Senegal—was this Popenguine? Mbour?—while I was in fact running along them, and how strange it was that not only could I be calculating the place- ment of my feet in midrun, but also be thinking of my future as a career or eternal rock-runner, and noting the thinking about that at the same time. Then the rocks ended and the sand began and I jumped into the sand with a shhhht and my feet were thankful and I stood, watching the water and waiting for Hand.

We hopped from the middle to the side, into wet mud, the ground like wet velour. Then up the middle bluff, only twenty feet or so, and we were now amid the resort. The homes were unfin- ished inside, slate-grey adobe, dark and cool.

Hand stepped over a pile of plywood boards.

I tried to picture the complex as it was intended, in final form. The moat was an expansion of a stream that ran from the home next door, a huge compound behind a high stone wall. There would be footbridges over the water, and lush gardens would be planted, narrow paths lighted by low tasteful fixtures rising from the tended lawns. But for now it was dry, with great piles of tub- ing and cinder blocks resting unused.

"We could stay here tonight." I said.

Hand looked around. "We could."

"We'd need some netting or something."

"Get some in Saly or Mbuu."

The man appeared again. He wasn't a man. He was about seventeen. In his hand wasn't a walkie talkie, or a gun. It was a transistor radio, fuzzily broadcasting the news.

"Bonjour," said Hand.

"Bonjour," said the teenager.

They shook hands, the man's grip limp and uninterested. He looked at me quickly, squinted and his eyes returned to Hand. In French, Hand asked if he was the guard. He shook his head. He was staying at a hotel nearby, he said, waving down the shore, and was just walking. He didn't speak much French, he said. He and Hand laughed. I laughed. We stood for a moment. The man looked at his radio and tuned the dial. I watched an ant hike over my shoe.

Hand said goodbye. The man waved goodbye and we walked on, toward the beach, while the man disappeared behind the cottages. But for us there was another moat, too, a much wider and more rancid one, separating us from the beach. We turned around. Hand had an idea.

"Let's skip the beach. I want to get back to that house and see who lives there."

"We'll do the clothesline."

We went to the house with the Indiana umbrella. It didn't look like anyone was home, so we could sneak in, dump the money in the pocket of the pants on the clothesline, and leave. That was almost better, we agreed, than taping it to the donkey.

We crept around the house, past the line, our own skulking making the place seem more sinister. There was the dark and vacuumed smell of clay. This was the sort of place bodies were found. Bodies or guns. We peeked around, to the front porch. Through the open front door we could see the corner of a bed, a calendar on the wall above it.

"You go," I said.

"You."

"You."

"You."

Hand stepped around until he was peering through the front porch of the house.

"Bonjour!" he said.

A man stepped through the door and into the light. It was same transistor radio teenager we'd just met. He wasn't happy.

Hand shook the man's hand again. The man was on his porch and we were below, grinning with shame. We said sorry a few times for intruding then Hand said:

"You live here?"

The man didn't understand.

"It's nice here," Hand said. "You're smart to stay here." He gestured to the house. "It's very nice."

The man stared at Hand. Hand turned to me and I understood. I took the money from my velcro pocket, slowly like a criminal would lay down a gun before a cop. I took the stack of bills and aimed them at the man. He didn't move.

"Sorry," I said, looking down.

"Can we—" said Hand, gesturing his arms like pistons, in a give-and-take sort of way.

"We want to—" I tried.

"Will you take?" Hand said, pointing to the money as you would to a broken toy offered to a skeptical child. But this money was new. *It cannot be new.* I know. *It's never new.*

The man took the bills. We smiled. We both made gestures meaning:

Yes it's yours.

We can't use it.

Please don't worry about it.
Thank you for taking it off our hands.
You have done us the greatest of favors.

The man glanced at the stack but didn't count the money. He held it, and smiled to us grimly. He turned and with two steps was back into his house.

The sun was setting slowly and the warm wind was good. We were giddy. There was a hole in my shirt, in the left underarm, and the air darted through on tiny wings. We were walking quickly back to the car, through the low brush. We still feared the mosquitoes but hadn't yet seen any.

"There's nothing wrong with that," said Hand.

"There can't be," I said.

"We gave the guy money."

"How much was it, you figure?"

"It was most of what I had left. About $800."

"He took it, we left."

"Nothing wrong with that," said Hand.

"Not a thing. It was simple. It was good."

We believed it. We were happy. The absence of mosquitoes made us happy, as did the prospect of hearing from the kids again, running from their low fences to us.

We stood for a moment, squinting in the direction of their huts. We walked briefly toward their settlement, but the boy and girl were gone, or were being hidden from us and in a second the father appeared again, and he was holding something, a fireplace poker, a rod of some kind, a staff or walker or something more sinister.

We pressed on, retrieved the car from behind the warehouse and on the highway went the other way, Hand driving, back to the hotel.

The day had been long, and I wanted beer. I wanted four beers and many potatoes, then sleep.

And I wanted to stay in Senegal. It was the mix of sun in the air, mostly, but it was also the people, the pace, the sea.

"I want to marry this country," I said.

"It's a good country," Hand said.

"I want to spend a lifetime here."

"Yeah."

"I could do it."

"Right."

And my mind leaped ahead, skipping and whistling. In the first year I'd master French, the second year join some kind of traveling medical entourage, dressing wounds and disseminating medicine. We'd do inoculations. We'd do birth control. We'd hold the line on AIDS. After that I'd marry a Senegalese woman and we'd raise our kids while working shoulder to shoulder—all of us—at the clinic. The kids would check people in, maybe do some minimal filing—they'd do their homework in the waiting room. I'd visit America now and then, once every few years, in Senegal read the English-speaking papers once a month or so, slow my rhythm to one more in agreement with the landscape here, so slow and even, the water always nearby. We'd live on the coast.

"Sounds good," said Hand.

"But that's one lifetime."

"Yeah."

"But while doing that one I'd want to be able to have done other stuff. Whole other lives—the one where I sail—"

"I know, on a boat you made yourself."

"Yeah, for a couple years, through the Mediterranean, the Red Sea, the Caspian Sea."

"Do only seas. No oceans."

"Yeah but—"

"Can you sail? You can't sail. Your brother sails, right?"

"Yeah, Tommy sails. But that's the problem. It could take years to get good enough. And while doing that, I'm not out here with my Senegalese wife. And I'm definitely not running whitewater tours in Alaska."

"So choose one."

"That's the problem, dumbshit."

We passed two more white people on ATVs.

"You know quantum theory, right?"

This is how he started; it was always friendly enough but—

"Sure," I lied.

"Well there's this guy named Deutsch who's taken quantum theory and applied it to everything. To all life. You know quantum theory, right? Max Planck?"

"Go on," I said. He was such a prick.

"Anyway," he continued. "Quantum physics is saying that atoms aren't so hard-and-fast, just sitting there like fake fruit or something, touchable and solid. They're mercurial, on a subatomic level. They come and go. They appear and disappear. They occupy different places at once. They can be teleported. Scientists have actually done this."

"They've teleported atoms."

"Yeah. Of course."

No one tells me anything.

"I can't believe I missed that," I said.

"They also slowed the speed of light."

"I did hear that."

"Slowed it to a Sunday crawl."

"That's what I heard."

We drove as the sky went pink then barn red, passing small villages emptying in the night, people standing around small fires.

Hand went on, gesturing, driving with his knees: "So if these atoms can exist in different places at once—and I don't think any physicists argue about that—this guy Deutsch argues that everything exists in a bunch of places at once. We're all made of the same electrons and protons, right, so if they exist in many places at once, and can be teleported, then there's gotta be multiple us's, and multiple worlds, simultaneously."

"Jesus."

"That's the multiverse."

"Oh. That's a nice name for it."

A man by the road was selling two enormous fish.

"Listen," Hand said, "if you're willing to believe that there are billions of other planets, and galaxies, even ones we can't see, what makes this so different?"

We passed a clearing where a basketball court stood, without net, the backboard bent forward like a priest granting commun-ion. Two young boys, stringy at ten or eleven, healthy but rangy, one wearing red and one in blue, were scrapping under it, each ball-bounce beating a rug full of dust.

"We have to stop," I said. We were already past the court.

"Why? To watch?"

"We have to play. Haven't you ever driven past a court and—"

"Will, those kids were about twelve."

"Then we won't keep score."

Hand slowed the car and turned around and on the gravel we crunched toward them. They stopped as they saw us approach. Hand got out and called for the ball. They threw it.

Hand bounced the ball and it landed on a rock and ricocheted away. The boys laughed. Hand chased it down and returned and did some bizarre Bob Cousy layup, underhand and goofy; the ball dropped through the dented red rim. Hand shot the ball three times from the free-throw area, without luck. Now I laughed with the boys. I gave the boy in blue a handshake, making up an elabo-rate series of subshakes involving wrists and fingers and lots of snapping at the end. He thought I knew what I was doing.

I tried dribbling and lost it, like Hand, on a rock. I got the hang of the court, its concavities and dust, and soon it was a game, us against them. They weren't very good, these kids. One was barefoot and both were much shorter than us, and while I was trying to keep the game casual, Hand knocked the ball from the younger kid's hands and scored over him without apology. It was not cool.

The light kept leaking from the sky, blue ribboned by purple and then, below, thick rough strokes of rust and tangerine. Another boy showed up, bigger and more confident. He had newish sneakers and knee-length basketball shorts, a Puma T-shirt. He was serious. He smiled at first, shook our hands—another limp grip—but then he bore down and didn't look us in the eye. It was our two against their three and there was dust everywhere. The tall boy was determined to win. The game got closer. I tried to switch teams, to relieve the nationalistic tension, but the boys refused.

It was ridiculous for Hand and I to be playing like this; we weren't the players—Jack was, Jack was the best pure player our school had ever seen, rhythm and speed impossible, it seemed, in someone we knew, someone from Wisconsin whose father sold seeds. We played with Jack, were humored by him, but when he wanted to, or when we'd made his lead less comfortable and opened our mouths to make sure he knew, he turned it up and broke us like twigs.

Very soon there were ten kids watching, then twenty, all boys, half of them barefoot, most of them shirtless. Every time the ball bounced off the court and away toward the village, there were two more boys, emerging from the village and heading toward us, to reclaim it. We were holding our own, now against four of them. Hand was posting up, Hand was boxing out. Hand is tall, but Hand cannot play, and now Hand was out of control.

It went dark. We were passing the ball and it was hitting our chests before we could see it. No one could see anything. We called the game.

We walked back to the car and brought out the water we had left, took pulls and handed it to the boy in red. Red handed it to the tall one, who sipped and gave it to the blue boy, who finished it. Another boy of about thirteen pushed through the crowd around the car, arched his back and said with clarity and force: "My father is in the Army. My name is Steven."

And then he walked away, off the court and back to the village. Other than that, there hadn't been much talking.

Now the tall Puma boy spoke. He spoke some English; his name, he said, was Denis.

"Where do you live?" he asked.

"Chicago," I said.

"The Bulls!" he said. "You see Bulls?"

Hand told him we'd been to games, even while Jordan was still active. And this was almost true. We'd been to one game, with Jordan playing the first half of a blowout.

Denis's mouth formed an exaggerated oval. Was he that good? he asked. Hand grinned: Yes. Denis said he'd love to come to America, see basketball, see his cousin, who lived in New Mexico. I told him New Mexico was very pretty. *Très bien*, I said.

"But," said Hand, "Pippen is the more elegant player."

Denis smiled but said nothing. Hand said this all the time: "Pippen is the more elegant player." The rest of it: "His movements are more fluid. Pippen is McEnroe to Jordan's Lendl." It was Hand's favorite thing to say, partly, surely, because it enraged anyone in Chicago who heard it.

Denis shook his head and smiled. He didn't agree, but kept mum. Hand asked for their names. He found paper in the car and a pen and had them write their names. They all wrote them on one piece of paper.

I lost this piece of paper. I am so sorry. I can't believe I lost it.

We didn't know if we would give them money. We got in the car and debated. The kids had seemed to be expecting something. They hadn't asked, none of them had, but it seemed they knew the possibility existed, that gifts of some kind could be forthcoming. They knew we could spare it. I still had some American hundreds in my shoes, but would that spoil everything? Would it pollute something pure—a simple game between travelers and hosts—by afterward throwing money at them? But maybe they did expect money; otherwise, why would they all gather by the car after the game? Maybe this was a common occurrence: Americans pull up, grab the ball, show them what's what, drop cash on them and head back to the Saly hotels—

"Let's not," Hand said.

"Okay." The boys surrounded us, waving. We began to roll away, driving the twenty yards back to the highway, as the boys went their separate ways. I stopped the car, alongside the Bulls fan who wanted to go to New Mexico. He and two friends were crossing the highway.

I rolled down my window and said Hey to the boy. He approached the window. I reached into my sock and grabbed what I could. I handed him $300 in three American bills.

"See you there," Hand said to Denis. To me: "We should get going." We didn't have enough for everyone, and there were a lot of kids. We said goodbye to Denis, and his eyes were liquid with feeling and we loved him but there was a man in our backseat.

"This is my brother," said Denis. "He needs a ride to Mbuu."

I looked at Hand. Hand was supposed to lock the back doors.

Denis's brother was in the car and it was too late; we had no choice. Mbuu was on our way. We said hello to Denis's brother. His name might have been Pierre.

We joined the highway with Denis's brother in our backseat and his chatter neverending. We didn't like him. Mbuu was twenty minutes away, and Pierre did not stop talking, in a language Hand couldn't grasp completely and could not at first confirm was French. We got the impression, immediately, that Denis's brother had seen his brother's receipt of cash, and wanted some of his own.

Pierre used Abass's line, that he needed cab fare to get back. Hand explained his demands to me. We laughed.

"So," said Hand, turning toward him, "you want *us* [pointing to us, back and forth with his index finger] to pay to drive you [pointing to him] to Mbuu, so you can get back."

Denis's brother nodded emphatically. Denis's brother was not very good at this. He didn't know what Hand was saying. Hand laughed. "You are not such the clever guy," said Hand. "Your brother he got all the brains, eh?" Hand was getting overcon-fident; the man knew no English, but continued nodding eagerly. "But you know why," Hand continued, "we gave to your brother three hundred of the dollars American? Because he didn't ask for it. You, you are crass—you know of this word, crass?—so no money you have coming."

With that, the man began chattering again. We had no idea what he was saying, but his voice was impossible to bear—an uninterrupted belligerence to it that was sending me over the edge.

Like the police officer before him, this man had his hand in my backpack, which was still on the backseat. I reached back for it, telling him, with a tight grin, that I needed something inside. I brought it into the front seat, fished through it, found a comb and ran it through my hair in an elaborate way, demonstrating how badly I missed it, how badly in need of grooming I'd been, this night, driving in the black to Mbuu.

The man began talking again, but he had changed tacks: now he needed the money to go to Zaire. He had gleaned that we had donated to his brother's designs on Chicago, and he assumed we were providing grants to all travelers.

—You should not demand our money so coarsely.

—You freely handed it to my brother.

—That is the point. Freely. Of our volition.

—You want me to wait to be given it.

—Yes.

—You want docility. You want me to appear indifferent to the money.

—Yes.

—And as a reward I am given my share.

—Yes.

—This is shameful.

—You know it is not shameful.

He and Hand barked back and forth for a while, making little headway. When Hand had talked him away from the Zaire plan, the brother became hungry. He thrust his palm between us.

"We have any food?" Hand asked me. From my backpack I produced a granola bar. The brother accepted it, didn't open it, and did not stop talking, talking loudly, at us; he was a machine. We were approaching Mbuu, and he was getting desperate.

"Jesus," I said, "is there any way we can ask him to stop talking?"

Hand turned to him, paused, and held up his hands in a *Stop* way. The man stopped. I sighed loudly. We turned up the radio.

—You throw me, Denis's brother. You make us sad.

—My job is not to make you happy.

—Your job is to be human. First, be human.

—There is no time for being gentle.

—We disagree.

—You do more harm than good by choosing recipients this way. It cannot be fair.

—How ever is it fair?

—You want the control money provides.

—We want the opposite. We are giving up our control.

—While giving it up you are exercising power. The money is not yours.

—I know this.

—You want its power. However exercised, you want its power.

We were in Mbuu, a dark adobe village. There were no constant lines—everything was moving. The walls were moving, they were human. There were people everywhere and everyone was shifting. The homes were open storefronts. Our headlights flashed over hundreds of people, walking, watching TV—large groups or families visible through glassless windows, all in the open-air storefronts, eating their dinners, drinking at a streetside bar, everyone so close.

We stopped and said goodbye to Denis's brother. He paused in the car, waiting. We stared at him. His eyes spoke.

—You owe me.

—We don't.

—This is wrong.

—It's not wrong.

—You're not sure. You're confused.

—Yes I am confused.

—It's all wrong.

He stepped out and closed the door. We got back on the road, on our way back to Saly for dinner. We hadn't eaten all day.

"I don't feel bad about that," Hand said.

"I hated that fucker."

But nothing else in the world had changed.

*   *   *

It was early evening when we got back to the hotel. A hundred yards from the dining room we could hear the clinking of glasses and forks, the murmur of scores of people. Everything inside was white—the tablecloths, the flowers, the people. Chandeliers.

"Holy shit," said Hand. There were two hundred people seated inside, a just slightly upper-middle-class sort of crowd, older, retirees, the kind you might see at the Orlando Ramada.

We were still in our travel clothes, everywhere stained, and a good portion of the diners were staring. We were dirty and Hand looked like a snowboarder too old for the outfit. His bandanna was now around his neck like a retriever's.

We walked to the buffet and built ziggurats of chicken, rice and fruit on our clean white plates. The spread was impressive: one long table for salads, one for breads, one (particularly spectacular) table for fruits and cakes, and a meat, poultry and fish wing, staffed by three Senegalese men in chef's hats. We sat down next to an older couple, who muttered to each other while glancing our way, and in ten minutes they left, amidst more muttering. A man in white took our drink orders. Desperate and unsure of the rules, we ordered six beers for the table.

"So about the multiverse," I said.

"Oh."

"It's irrelevant. Who cares how many universes or planes there are when they don't intersect?"

Hand had a whole drumstick in his mouth. He removed the bone and it was clean, plasticine. The place was pastel-pink and devoid of joy. There was no laughter, very little movement, count-less sunburns. It had more the feel of a Florida nursing home cafe-teria, on a Monday.

"Who said they don't intersect?" he asked.

"Do they?"

"I don't know. I haven't read anything about that. But the thing you'd like is that with the multiverse, you have basically every option you want—really, every option you'll ever see or imagine—and one of your selves somewhere has taken that option. Pretty much every life you could lead would conceivably be lived by one of your shadow selves. Maybe even after you die."

He took another drumstick and removed all the meat, the veins, the gristle. He was fucking wretched.

"But it's useless," I said, "if you don't share any consciousness."

"Sure. I know. But then again, maybe we're not dying. If you combine the quantum physics paradigm with the idea of the subjectivity of time, we're basically all alive in a thousand places at once, for a neverending present."

There was one black person eating—he was French, it seemed, sitting with a white woman, apparently his wife. But otherwise the dining room was entirely white and of a strikingly similar caste and appearance.

"The thing is, it's basically immortality for atheists," Hand said, "and we don't need to wait for any sort of technology catch-up."

It did sound appealing. Consciousness or not, to be alive, always, somewhere. And what about dreams? That's got to figure in—but what I wanted, really, was every option, simultaneously. Not in some parallel and irrelevant universe, but *here*. I wanted to stop and work at the field hospital and fall in love with the local beauty, but also be home in a week so I could do so many other things, fifty life-directions all seemed equally appealing and possible—shark wrangler! *Whatever happened to training to be a goddamned shark wrangler?*

A group of six walked in, three men and three women, all white but for one woman, who was black, tall, probably Senegalese.

"Wow," said Hand, staring. She was shocking. Incredible posture, wearing a snug white dress over her astounding skin, lines drawn by the most optimistic and even hand—like the finest machines covered in polished leather. Hand had stopped eating. I stopped eating. Almost every Senegalese woman we'd seen looked like this: genetically flawless, robust, with regal bearing and skin like the smoothest stone.

"Stop staring," I said.

"I won't," Hand said.

Half the dining room was watching. It was too obvious. We were thrown back to some other time or place. Was I imagining this? Everyone was watching this woman, either because she had crossed some understood racial line or simply because—I hoped—she made the rest of us look like trolls.

"She's outstanding," said Hand.

"She's with them."

"Yeah, but why?"

I had an idea but didn't say it. The people she was with were too unimpressive for her. She was slumming. I could only imagine she'd have some other incentive, and hoped she hadn't been bought.

—What are you doing with these men?

—I have my reasons.

—You need not be with these men. We will help you.

—Your help is not welcome.

—Our help is free of obligation. You must choose us.

"Let's go," I said. "I'm done."

We left, getting a better look at her on the way out—demure but with a smile like the thrusting open of curtains—and we dodged the white spray of the sprinklers on the way back to the room. Hand showered; I called my mom.

"Hello?" It was her on the first ring.

I swallowed my gum. I didn't expect the phone to work, to reach Memphis without an operator. She was in the garden. She'd just come back from a cooking class.

"What day is it there?" I asked.

"Monday, dummy. We're only seven hours behind you."

"Eight, I think."

"Greenland is more like seven, I think."

"Oh, we're not in Greenland."

"You didn't go?"

"We're in Senegal."

"That's right. You told me that. So you caught anything yet?"

"Like what? Fish?"

"Just make sure you wear condoms. Six condoms."

I cleared my throat.

"So how is it?"

"It's good," I said. "So good." I told her what we'd been doing. I went on for a while. She had to stop me.

"I don't need every last minute, hon."

—You do.

"But that's sort of the point," I said.

"What is?"

"The every last minute part. We want you to care."

"I care. I care. How much have you given away so far?"

"I guess about $1,000."

"You're going to have to quicken your pace."

I told her about the basketball game.

"You give any to them?"

"One kid. $300 to him. He was a Bulls fan."

"What about the other kids?" she asked.

"We gave them some water."

"But what about money for them?"

"We couldn't," I said. "We couldn't really spread it out evenly. There were at least fifteen of them." I told her about Denis's brother, who got in the car and who wouldn't stop talking.

"You didn't give him money, I don't suppose."

"No."

"Honey."

"Yes."

"Why not just bring it back here and give it to a charity? There's a place Cathy Wambat works with—they help poor kids get their cleft palates fixed. She would love to—"

"There's a whole charity for cleft palates?"

"Of course."

"But what makes that better than this?"

She sighed and left the line quiet for a minute.

"Don't you think it's all a little condescending?" she said.

"What?"

"You swooping in and—"

"Giving them cash. This is condescending."

"Don't get so angry."

—It's just such a stupid fucking word to use. There's not one morsel of logic to that word, here. It's a defense you use to defend your own inaction.

"Will, who says they want it?"

"Then they can give it to someone else."

"Well, see—"

"The point is I don't want it. And we like giving it. It's a way to meet people, if nothing else."

"So," she said, "how do you decide who gets the money?"

"I don't know. It's random. It's obvious. I don't know."

She laughed loudly, hugely amused. Then sighed. "That's not really fair, is it, Will?"

"Denis's brother was a dick."

She laughed again, at me, without kindness. I couldn't believe I was paying for this kind of aggravation.

"But it's so subjective, dear," she said.

"Of course it's subjective!"

She sighed. I sighed. We waited.

—Tell me there's a better way, Mom.

—I can't. I don't know of one.

"Why are you doing this to me now?" I said.

"I'm only asking questions, hon."

—What are you saying? That we're not allowed to see their faces? You're saying that. You're the type that won't give to a street person; you'll think you're doing them harm. But who's condescending then? You withhold and you run counter to your instincts. There is disparity and our instinct is to create parity, immediately. Our instinct is to split our bank account with the person who has nothing. But you're talking behind seven layers of denial and justification. If it feels good it *is* good, and today, at the ocean, we met a man living in a half-finished hut, and he was tall and had a radio and we gave him about $700 and it was good. It can't be taken from us, and you cannot soil it with words like *condescending* and *subjective*, fey and privileged words, and you cannot pretend that you know a better way. You try it! You do it! We gave and received love! How can you deprive us of that? I'm not asking them for thanks—we're not even sticking around long enough to allow them it, and we don't speak their goddamn language, anyway. We're just wanting to see them, to touch their hands, to brush up against their arm or something. That is allowed! That cannot be explained away somehow, or turned around to make us look wrong or—

"Well," I said, "your questions aren't interesting to me."

"I see. For that I apologize."

"I just think you're overthinking it, Mom."

"I am prone to that sort of thing."

"Oh really? I'd never noti—"

"Bye bye, smart mouth."

She hung up.

Hand dressed and we scuffled back up the road. The sky was a planetarium's half-dome ceiling, full of stars but not dark enough. The trees stood black underneath and against the grey sky, shadowing the dirt road with mean quick scratches. I was pissed. For every good deed there is someone, who is not doing a good deed, who is, for instance, gardening, questioning exactly how you're doing that good deed. For every secretary giving her uneaten half-sandwich to a haggard unwashed homeless vet, there is someone to claim that act is only, somehow, *making things worse.* The inactive must justify their sloth by picking nits with those making an attempt—

"What are you muttering about?" Hand asked.

"Nothing." I didn't know I'd been muttering.

"Between that and the talking in your sleep—"

At a snack bar we bought ice cream. The woman at the counter had hair like a backup dancer and was watching dolphins on TV. Hand had an orange push-up approximation and I had a thick tongue of vanilla ice cream covered in chocolate, on a stick. I tore the thin shiny plastic and ate the chocolate first, then the white cold ice cream, so soft in the humid and darkening air, and it ran down my hand and throat at the same time.

As we walked under the infrequent streetlights we had two and three shadows, as one light cast our shadow up and the other down, sometimes overlapping. The lights didn't know what they were doing. The lights knew nothing.

The moon was yellow and ringed with a pale white halo. There were small stones in my shoes. I stopped to empty them, leaning against Hand. When we began walking my shoes filled again.

The area around the resort was crowded with discos and casinos. We went to the main casino first, a small, though plush, one-room affair with two card tables and about thirty slot machines. We recognized about a dozen people from dinner; my face parted the crowd, and they looked at us with tired eyes.

"Check it out," Hand said, pointing a finger at the clientele and casting an infinity symbol over them. "You notice anything about the men here?"

"The sweaters."

"Yeah."

"Jesus."

Every man in the room, almost—there were about twenty men in this casino, most of them young, and twelve of them qualified—was wearing a cotton sweater over his shoulders, tied loosely at the collarbone. Twelve men, and the sweaters were each and all yellow or sky-blue, and always the tying was done with the utmost delicacy. You couldn't, apparently, actually *tie* the sweater. It had to be loosely arranged, in the center of the chest, like a fur stole. It was about 85 degrees.

It hit me, again, that we were here. I'd never been farther than Nevada—with Jack and his family, for fourth-grade spring break, by car. We drove twenty-two hours, each way, leaving about seven in between, spent atop of horses that wanted us dead or in chains. Hand had been to Toronto, which was closer, actually, to Milwaukee, but he didn't see it that way.

There were postcards near the door, not of the ocean but of the resorts on the ocean, and I bought one—the first postcard I'd ever even pretended to plan on sending. If I had someone to write to, a Clementine, I could document this, could shape it into some sense. If I wrote to the twins, even on this napkin here and with this ballpoint pen borrowed from the Senegalese bartender with the birthmark like an Ash Wednesday smudge, they would keep the letters and always know I thought of them—

Dear Mo, Dear Thor,

Senegal! Can you believe it? It is something here. Something like some other place. The people . . . there was this man . . . Then again, at this point I really don't know if we're seeing anything or missing everything. . . . The air here, though, is different enough, so that's something

"That's good so far."

Hand was over my shoulder.

"You really captured it, Will. All those blank spaces, too—"

"Fuck you."

We stood outside in the cooling black night, and wondered if we could do anything extraordinary. If we could live up to our responsibility here: We had traveled 4,200 miles or whatever and thus were obligated to create something. We had to take the available materials and make something worthy.

"You call home yet?" I asked Hand.

"No. You?"

"Yeah."

"Mine won't care. You know them."

I did and I didn't. Hand's father was a tall man who bent over, had been bending to talk to his much-shorter wife for so long that his head seemed permanently tilted, chin in his sternum. With the face of a shovel and the eyes of a wolf, he worked for a law firm but I'm not sure he was a lawyer; he might have been a lawyer but somehow I suspect he was not; he was one of those distant small-eyed men about whom anything could have been possible—molestation, murder, tax evasion, bigamy. Hand's mom was a nurse who worked, for most of our growing up, at the hospital, though later just in one dying man's house, for two years—a grand marble-laden house that became more or less hers, with her own bedroom, her own parking space in the garage, everything.

Which was fine but also wrong, because then Hand had to be jealous of this new home and his mother's effortless way of seeming its matriarch. Hand had two older brothers, much older. I had seen them only a few times each, knew them more from their graduation pictures; for some reason they had graduated on the same day, even though one, I think Steve, the one who was almost cross-eyed, was a year older than Eddie, who had Shaun Cassidy hair and eyes that didn't blink and had come up with Hand's nickname—first it was *Hands*, because as a toddler he'd catch any ball thrown to him—and was later shortened to Hand, to sound less like someone who would want time alone with your children.

We decided we'd head into town and find someone's home and walk into it with flowers. It was something we'd talked about doing in the last few years—I have no idea when the idea originated or why. We would knock, we imagined, or maybe come through a back door, the porch, and either way we would bring wine or flowers. It was our firm belief that we could walk into any office or home, anywhere in the world, with flowers, and be taken in. Shock would be softened by blind confusion then affectionate bewilderment, and soon we'd be family.

The road was busy with vacationers walking to Saly's main strip, about three blocks of restaurants, clubs and bars, and the occasional car weaving slowly around the potholes, looking for parking. We bought a small loud bouquet of daisies and violets and something local, red and wet like meat.

Two young girls, barefoot and without saddles, rode by on horses the color of gravel. Hand made a gesture indicating he was going to run after them, jump onto a car and from there onto the back of one of the horses. I shook my head vigorously. He pouted.

From a right-leaning building with a second-story balcony, a cat spoke, and we stopped. There were two mailboxes by the doorway and we, with me holding the flowers, gripping too tightly, took it as a sign.

"This is it," I said. "We have to go up."

"And we ring the bell, or what?"

"What time is it?"

"Ten maybe," Hand said. "Is that too late?"

We decided to go up first and survey. The steps took our footsteps, knocks of knuckles against wood, and we were soon at the upper landing, between doors.

"Which one?" Hand asked.

One was ajar. "This one," I said.

With a handle in place of a knob, it looked like a door to another hallway, so we pushed through. But it wasn't a hallway. We were in an apartment. We gave each other looks of alarm. We were in someone's apartment already.

But neither of us made a move to leave.

We took off our shoes, and I set the flowers down atop them. We stepped into the home and closed the door behind us, so quiet it confused me. A large portrait of a man in uniform, a political portrait, hung over the doorway. A table, a dinner table, stood on tip-toes in the middle of the small main room. Four place-settings, the remains of dinner. No sounds yet. The painted walls a faded olive, stained with fingerprints. Pictures torn from magazines pinned to the walls—three or four of professional motorcross riders, and next to them a series of postcards of women in ornate and bulbous Easter outfits. Above them, a large studio picture of a family of four, the family who lived here, we guessed, all wearing soccer uniforms. Hand raised his eyebrows at me as if to say: *Look at this! Look at us! Holy shit!*

The apartment was tight, tidy and empty of anything of objective value. The kitchen was just off the main room, a cramped nook with a blue tile counter. The kitchen gave way to another room, a kind of den, with a couch and a small, upright lawn chair on either side. There was a small mountain of stuffed animals in one corner—Yosemite Sam on top—and a neat row of four plastic soccer balls. A TV pulsed, but without sound.

There was no movement in the house, no noise, but I expected something at any second. A man in a robe with a shotgun. It would almost be a relief.

Hand was across the room already, looking for the bedrooms.

There were two doors. He opened one, a closet. His head was then in the other, and quickly he jerked it back. He tiptoed back to me—I was hiding in the kitchen by now—and opened his mouth to speak. I made the angriest face I could, as quickly as I could, to thwart his attempt to talk. He stopped in time, making an elaborate gesture of surrender.

We stood for a few seconds, calming down, watching the TV across the kitchen table, in the next room. A desert scene, an ancient village in dry pink. Then a close-up shot of a gaunt man. Then Ernest Borgnine in Roman soldier gear. Then the gaunt man again, someone's hands entering the frame—Borgnine's?—and placing onto the gaunt man's head a bird's nest sort of thing—Oh. Crown of thorns.

Hand pointed to the bedroom, and held up four fingers, then made a sleeping gesture, indicating that the family, the four of them, was sleeping in the room, in one bed. We were in their house and they were sleeping in one bed in the next room. It was only then that I began to wonder so many questions: Why was the apartment door ajar? What would we do now? We'd wanted to come in, with our flowers, and then sit with them, be welcomed in, fed, and we'd leave with new friends in Saly, and they'd be left with a gift commensurate to our appreciation. But where I'd pictured loud conversation and joking in broken English and bad French, we were instead skulking in the dark, making no sounds. At least we could unload some currency.

The home was clean and comfortable and small. People lived here, even with the sound of the bars and clubs below and down the sandy street. The kids had places where they put their things, and the—I would never have something like this. I didn't want a kitchen table or pictures on the wall. I wanted to leave.

Every time there was a close-up of the apostles, they were staring off in a way that appeared drug-induced. Saints did not have to stare so glassily, did not have to move with slow graceful gestures. Did they? I wanted a clumsy saint—or a fast one. A saint that liked to run like a sprinter, in little silky shorts. Anne Bancroft. She was there, as mother Mary. And then, just below her, wailing, the woman from Zefferelli's *Romeo and Juliet*. She looked the same. Borgnine, watching his comrades hoist Christ up onto his cross, was having a hard time. He felt terrible about what was happening but was, it seemed, powerless to stop it.

Hand stepped over and turned the TV off.

I looked in the cabinets above the sink for a vase, or large glass, or jar. There was a short stack of plastic NFL cups. None would support the weight of the flowers. Hand gave me an urgent look. Now he wanted to leave. I shrugged with great force, needing more time. There was a bucket in the corner, full of sand and ciga-rette butts. I brought it to the center of the kitchen table and jammed the stems of the flowers into it. Hand rolled his eyes. The flowers would be dead, dead, dead by the morning.

We sat in our car thinking.

"We can go looking for more donkeys," Hand said.

We left the town and were quickly leaving the sphere of lights and people. We drove through black fields, miles and miles.

There was someone behind us.

"Jesus," I said.

The headlights were coming quickly.

"How is that possible?" I said. "We're going too fast."

There was a roar from behind. The headlights engulfed us. They were coming from above, from a truck. It was inches from us. I was sure it was closing in.

—Jack.

—

—Jack will you—

I swerved to the side of the road. The truck screamed by.

"What happened?" Hand asked.

"That fucker was going 200 miles an hour," I said.

Hand looked at me, not with me.

"Will, it wasn't—"

"What?" I said.

"Nothing."

The highway was dark and the air was cooling.

We got out, and sat for a while on the hood, throwing pieces of the road at the road. I had the idea that we should lay our heads on the road. It was a vision that had occurred to me, and we'd decided to follow through on these ideas, pretty much all of them, so we did it. The pavement was hot, but we heard nothing.

"Let's do the money-taping," said Hand, getting up.

"Where?"

"We'll find a place."

We drove on, stopping at a small square adobe home with a thatched roof. We jumped out; a goat bayed. It was a big goat, about five feet to the top of its head, white with grey crawling from its underside.

"We could drop it through their window," I said.

"No," Hand said.

"Why?"

"Let's do the goat."

We had to. Hand got the pouch and applied new tape to its sides. We were ready.

"You come at him from the front," Hand said, "and I'll sneak up the side. You distract him."

"With what?"

"Make some hand movements."

The goat was watching me now. He was on a long leash.

"Like shadow puppets?"

"Whatever. Sure."

Jesus. Hand had the pouch, and was walking slowly toward the goat, hands outstretched, the pouch ready to be attached.

"Hey goat," I said, wanting badly to make it feel at ease.

The goat bayed again.

"Be careful," Hand said, "goats can be really nasty."

"How? What makes them mad? You fucker."

"I don't know. Your eyes. Don't stare at him."

"You just—"

"Don't stare! He's growling or something. Are you staring?"

"No!"

"And don't yell. They hate that."

I hated Hand. I turned my head away from the goat while walking sideways toward it, a Ben Vereen kind of thing.

"You close yet?" I asked.

"Almost there. He looking at me? He see me?"

"I don't know. I can't see either, dumbshit."

"Well glance at him at least."

Glance at him.

"You!"

"Shh. I'm almost there," Hand said.

"Got it?"

"I'm scared to touch him. Grab his head."

"What? Grab his head?"

"Get his horns."

"No."

"Uh oh."

"What?"

"Look!" Hand yelled.

The goat was coming at me. But sideways. Its head was down and it was jumping at me, in great and bizarre lateral leaps. It was unnatural, the way it moved. For every few feet it propelled itself forward, it threw itself eight feet to the side. I backed up a few steps, then turned and ran.

"Not that way!" Hand yelled.

"What?"

"Run this way! His eyes are bad!"

"Where?"

"Serpentine! Serpentine!"

I ran toward Hand but to the side of the goat, getting within five feet of it, hearing its snarling and coughing. Hand was behind a low wall near the hut.

"Come here!" he yelled.

I jumped over the wall, huddling next to Hand. The goat was on the other side of its pen, standing still, staring into the black night like the stupid rank animal it was.

"Now what?" I asked.

"Do the hut," Hand said.

"We're not going in," I said. I could never do that again, go into a home like that. Any home.

We took the pouch and taped it to the outer wall of the hut. It barely stuck, but Hand smoothed it as much as we could.

We had taped money to the outer wall of the hut.

"How much you figure?" I asked.

"About $300."

"That's a weird thing to find, money taped to your house."

Maybe it was too peculiar. Maybe they wouldn't open it, given the circumstances. There was no time to debate it. Any second we'd awaken everyone inside, and we didn't want that. The package still bore Hand's message—

7 HERE I AM 7 ROCK YOU LIKE 7 A HURRICANE

—and would have to speak for itself.

We ran from the hut, almost skipping.

"Man," said Hand, "we really should be here tomorrow morning to see what happens. I have to see."

"They'd know it was us. They'd see us."

"We could get binoculars and watch from a—"

"A what?"

"A nearby ridge. Or a safehouse. A safehouse!"

Now I wanted to meet the family. I wanted to watch them find the pouch, to see their surprise, their joy. I wanted to watch them sitting around their dining table, all four of them, mother, father, brother, sister, trying to figure out where the money came from, what it meant, who left it, and who in hell they could find to translate the words on the face of the pouch. Maybe they'd buy more goats. How many goats would that kind of money buy? At least a couple. Maybe a dozen? I assumed they were a family of great beauty. Why would we not visit them? Because we were flying out in the morning, or early afternoon, and because meeting them would—Well, I wanted to meet them, would kill to meet them, would want to spend a day with them, a month, have them build a lean-to beside their house for us, share meals with us, show us the land, the care of their goats. But we wouldn't meet them because it was an invasion, and because I could not leap this gap. I could hope for good things for them, and tape a pouch of money to their wall, but I could not shake their hands, and could not show them my face.

I was driving. I asked Hand to find me food. He threw a chocolate chip granola bar into my lap.

With the first bite something broke. The sensation of having broken through gristle, or cartilage. Something harder. The chewing of rocks.

"Drive for a second," I said.

Hand reached over and took the wheel. I spit out the contents of my mouth—a loose mass of granola and blood and small white stones. A tooth. A molar. I was confused why it didn't hurt.

"What is it?" said Hand. "I can't see."

I presented my palm to him.

"Oh. Man."

I knew why it had broken. My whole mouth had felt loose and reconstructed since Oconomowoc. Three teeth were unsteady or chipped, this the largest of them.

I pulled over.

"Sorry," Hand said.

I threw the whole mouthful out the window. The tooth fragments made a *tickety* sound on the roughly paved road.

"Listen," he said, in a low tone, implying serious information was forthcoming. I listened. But Hand hadn't thought of what to say once he had my attention. We sat there for a long half-minute.

"It's the first tooth I've lost in so long," I said.

Hand turned off the radio.

"Will. I'm sorry," he said.

"I know. You've said that before."

"I know. But—"

He exhaled loudly through his nose, leaned his head back against the seat and closed his eyes.

We rolled from the gravel to the highway and I feared my head once I went to bed. For many months, sleep without alcoholic or masturbatory help had been elusive, and tonight I knew I would fight my way down.

"Let's go back and swim," he said.

I wanted this.

At the hotel we found our way to the water and left our clothes on the large grey stone Hand had jumped from earlier. We waded in wearing boxers and were blue under the moon. The water was warmer now. We had been loud before but the water, black and oily, made us quiet. We cut through the surface slowly, embarrassed to break the calm. We kept our shoulders under the water and it was much warmer. Hand's head came toward me without any sign of motion, a head sliding on glass.

"You look bad," he said.

"Sorry."

"Fucked up look on your face."

"I know."

I sunk under. I held my knees and fell.

The water hissed in my ears but didn't enter and fill me. I was still falling, in my ball, underwater. It was cloudy here, it was tumult. I fell more. It occurred to me that I might be in a part of the bay where there was a hole, a hole through the bay's floor that went miles down, and I could be sinking forever. I could sink into a sort of watery wormhole, and fall thousands of feet, only to come up again somewhere else entirely. I would come up in a different sort of world, one run by hyperintelligent fish, or—

For no reason I pictured raccoons, that under the water and through the wormhole there would be a society of talking raccoons, who smoked pipes and laughed at the happenings on what they called The Upper World, meaning my world. I would live with them for a while, and the queen, older but not too old, imperious but not unkind, would fall for me, and insist on my being her male concubine, and all in that regard would be just fine, the perks impressive and life in general very good—until she tired of me one day when another prospect arrived, a Jordanian man via a Dead Sea passageway—

But why doesn't this water fill us up—why doesn't the water come through our ears and drown us? *The hissing is the ocean's rage at not being able to drown us.* But what prevents our overflowing? Are we so pressure-packed? *I believe that we are.* Oh, shut up.

When I broke into the air again there was a woman with us. She stood near Hand. She was the woman from dinner. The miraculous woman from dinner.

She was laughing at something Hand had said. She wore a one-piece bathing suit, white. Her skin looked more perfect in the dim light, and her teeth shone as she laughed.

We were standing in water waist high.

"Hello," she said to me.

"Hi," I said.

"Your friend, he says you were hiding from me."

Hand was grinning. I told her I wasn't hiding from her.

"You're ashamed your face," she said.

"No," I said. "He is, though." I nodded to Hand. He bit his upper lip with his row of lower teeth. *"He's* ashamed of my face."

I was shaking. I didn't know how she could be here with us.

"You two are very far from home," she said.

"I guess," I said.

She fell to her knees and soaked her head.

"You are, too," Hand said.

She was Annette and from Paris. She was with her family, she said, two young boys and her husband. They'd been here for six months, since her husband was sent here by their doctor to cure a persistent strain of bronchitis. I didn't know people still did that kind of thing, had the time and money to move for so long to a climate softer on one's trachea. She imitated his cough, a deep hacking thing, and then laughed. This was a European thing, I thought—at once decadent and loving and weary, this laughing about your husband's cough.

It was too cold to stand, so we all dropped to our knees. Only our heads rose above the surface and we were warm.

"You two are gay?" Annette asked.

She was serious. We told her no. She smiled.

"It's good to meet you," she said.

We nodded.

"Look at us. We're a bunch of heads!" she said. "Just our heads. Frightening!" Her voice was full but coarse at its edges, honey sprinkled with sand. Her eyes, when she faced me straight-on, were wrong. They leaned left and right, strained outward, slightly, so that only when you looked directly at her and she at you, could you notice that she couldn't focus on whatever was directly before her. Her vision parted around you like wind.

Hand dove forward and away, showing Annette his stroke. We watched and I told her I sometimes thought about swimming without any legs. Which I did.

"Swimming without the legs," she said, tipping her head back to wet her hair. "I like that. That would be spectacular."

I sunk under again, to soak my head. While under, water hissing, I debated whether I should come back up, and if so, in the same place. I could grab her legs. I could bury my face between her legs. I could push my way underwater far away, and surprise her. But while debating I ran out of breath and came up in the same place.

"So we are part of the club," she said, nodding to each of us, Hand and then me.

"Yeah," Hand said. "We're in room four-fifteen."

"No," she said. "Not *this* club." She laughed. "Not this hotel. Out here is our club." She darted her eyes left and right.

"Oh right," Hand said. "Like the Polar Bear Club."

"No, no. You shush," she said, pointing to Hand. "You keep jumping to the answers! I am saying I came out here and you came out here to be alone. Or where the other people are not. They are inside sleeping and we are here."

"We really wanted to swim," I said.

Annette looked at me for a long moment and then threw her head back into the water, soaking it again. She was not human in the way we were human. We were real, of skin and hair, uneven and unfinished, but she had been carved and sanded and—

"My mother," she said, "this is what she called the Fourth World."

"What? Senegal?" Hand asked.

"No, no. Not *Senegal*," she said, her head gliding toward his. She stopped when about a foot from his face. "You are one so misunderstanding easy!"

"Fine," Hand said. I was grinning and Hand saw me grinning. We didn't know this woman, but she knew things about us.

"Not the *first* world," she continued, "the world we are from, not the second or *third* world, so many people treading water. This is *dif*ferent. The fourth world is voluntary. It is quick small steps from the other worlds."

I ducked my head into the bay again. Underwater, I couldn't get a grip on her accent. Her syntax was off but her vocabulary was impressive. I tried to remember how much I'd drank at dinner. I half expected her to be gone when I rose again. I broke through and she was still there, her silhouette like a teardrop inverted.

"Everyone is sleeping and we are here, in the sea. *That* is the fourth world. The fourth world is present and available. It's this close. But it's different. It's passive. We are make the action here. We come and then we create things that will happen. The fourth world is half thought, half actual. It's a staging ground."

I moved closer to the two of them. Now our three heads were within a few feet of each other. She could tell we were confused.

"Okay. For instance, what brought you to Senegal?" she asked.

"It was windy in Greenland," I said.

A small school of fish threaded between our underwater torsos.

"The main point is," she said, trying to contain her frustration, "that we have to cut from hope of continuity. Momentum. We must to see each setting and moment as whole. Different, independent. A staging ground."

Why does she keep saying "staging ground"? I will ask her. *No, don't.* Why does someone whose English is imperfect know a term like this "staging ground"? *Because her mom made such a big deal out of it.* Oh, right. *Where is her mother? Should we ask?* We should not. Women of this age lose their mothers.

Hand opened his mouth to speak, but only water came out, dribbling down his chin and then neck before rejoining its source.

"How old are your kids?" I asked. I didn't know where else to start. A cruise ship, full of buttery light, was moving along the horizon, much more quickly than I expected.

"Seven and twelve," she said. The whites of her eyes were much too white in the dark. I looked away.

"Those are good ages," I said.

From the ship came a flare, or a single arcing firework.

"That is a decision," she said, nodding her chin at the ship. "To get on the boat is a decision. But the decisions after that choice are limited. My mother she urges me to have a chance for the fourth world at all time. You have to forget about momentum and start again, and again, and again, and again." She said again about twelve times. She was a little batty. "And from here you can go all into Africa!"

She dove into the water and swam a few perfect strokes away from us, toward the shore, her shape clean and unresistant. She stopped, unfolded herself and stood. "Now I join my babies again," she said, then shushed to the sand and buried her face in a towel bearing the pattern and texture of a gazelle, faded.

"It was good to meet you," Hand said, his voice carrying to her quickly and loudly over the hard still water.

"I will see you again, I am sure," she said. "Our world, the one you love now, is not so big." She turned and jogged up the steps, her nimble feet leaping and striking the sand like a match. She ducked through palm fronds and was gone.

Hand and I floated on our backs, letting the water hiss in our ears and come over our faces. You could see all the stars. You could feel, under us, huge fish wanting to eat things, maybe us. Far off, across the water, someone was kayaking. It was well past one in the morning.

At that moment I was sure. That I belonged in my skin. That my organs were mine and my eyes were mine and my ears, which could only hear the silence of this night and my faint breathing, were mine, and I loved them and what they could do. There was so much water in so many places, rushing everywhere, up and down, the water on top moving so much faster than the water below it. Under the water was sand, then rocks, miles of rocks, then fire.

But I was getting tired. We needed to get out of the water before we mistook it for a bed. I was sure that was how people drowned; not with a fight, not with thrashing but with thoughts of rest.

Hand was asleep in seconds. The room was split-leveled, his bed in a nook above mine. I could hear his breathing, uneven but distant, like an insect fighting a screen door. The fan overhead spun wildly.

There was bustling in my library. I felt the staircases shake with the running of feet, librarian feet, hooved and carrying files. I closed doors, I shut off the elevator. I climbed my own stairs and ran across my valley, escaping the coming information—

I forced my thoughts away from Oconomowoc, plugged my fingers in the dike. I jumped from Wisconsin, from North America, and summoned Africa. I moved through Africa, imagining rivers crowded with small skiffs transporting food. People in the most brazen colors unloading goods from boats. I wanted to count the packages. I concentrated on the details of the vision. I needed to focus on the scene, counting things, noting things, living in this scene and not going back. The river was smooth. The river was straight. The river was brown. Then red. The river was soaked in blood. There were bodies floating, bodies jamming the river like logs. This was Rwanda. Why had Hand and I wanted to go to Rwanda? To see. We had a responsibility to see. To see what could be done. Were we them? Or were the Rwandans really someone else? Their backs facing the sun in the thin brown water. Church to church, under nave and pew. Fuck them. That we wanted to end their slaughters but had to know the number, 800,000, and have no ability whatsoever to take back that number. Fuck them for giving that to us.

We wanted him to speed but Jack would not speed. He drove with his hands perfectly at ten and two, which was fine and afforded him the most control, especially in time of danger, but still it blocked, completely, his view of the speedometer. So every few seconds he would have to raise his thumbs, as if giving a double—thumbs up, granting himself a view of the gauge. It drove us nuts. Hand and I wanted to go at least seven miles over the limit, because everyone knew you could do at least that without getting caught. We would say, "Jack, when are you gonna open this baby up? You got a V-8 here, my man!" And he did, even if it was in a station wagon, the same one his mom drove and then his sister Molly drove, and now he drove, stopping at every stop sign, a full stop even if there wasn't a soul for miles.

So when I first heard, heard it was a car accident, for a second I was relieved because I knew it was a mistake, because Jack could never have been driving fast enough for that. I pictured car crashes involving only cars going very fast, two cars colliding, both at top speed. But it was not that with Jack. He was driving in the right lane and had been going the speed limit, or below. The truck came from behind doing 80, downhill, sees Jack's car, moving too slowly, a speed which would be, to the truck, as if it were standing still—as if Jack and his car were immobile objects. The truck hits the car but doesn't bump it; the momentum drives the wheels up and over Jack's, grinding it flat as it passes, twelve wheels at once practically, all of it happening in half a second, then the truck runs off, veering right, it jackknifes, falls into the median, driver is thrown against his side window, giving him a concussion and nothing more.

—I know your name, trucker fuckhead.

—I was forgiven by your friend's family.

—I forgave nothing.

The smell in the storage cell was a cold smell, cold wood, cold aluminum. I was on the ground, before I went out for good, and I thought an explanation would come. I was there, on the cold wood planks, already bleeding from the mouth and with my ribs throbbing, wondering if they'd punctured my skin, and I was thinking of an explanation. I was so *curious*. I had to have the answer. Was it something among his things they wanted? I had to know. I wanted to kill them and soak in their blood but first I wanted to know why.

—Why did this happen?

—We were there, you were there.

—Give me an answer.

Hand was gone, upstairs asleep. How could he be asleep in Senegal? I wanted to wake him but didn't. It was his fault. It was partly his fault. Everything was partly his fault. The world was partly his fault. I stood and found another blanket high in the closet and put it over me and closed my eyes again.

—Shit, Hand.

—Sleep, friend.

—Fuck. I want out of this fucking head.

—Have something to drink.

—What? Where?

—Relax. Breathe.

—Why didn't we kill those fuckers?

—We tried. We waited. We looked. Then you didn't want to go back. You didn't want to call the cops and then you didn't want us to go back.

—My heart's been jumping since, fluttering up and sinking down—that's no goddamned way to exist.

—It isn't.

—Nothing cures it.

—Time will.

—I can't wait.

—Will, this happens.

—I can't be alone with my head, Hand. I fear it. My own head! There was a time when I wanted and loved time alone with my mind. Now I dread it. I used to do gardening—

—I know. Mrs. Yorro. I worked for her, too. We were thirteen.

—When she left me to myself in the pakasandra I would sit on the mat she would give me—an old car floormat—and I would see the pakasandra and see the weeds among them and I would drift. My hands would reach for the neck of a weed and I would pull, slowly, feeling the base, taking the soil with it, the gentlest of pulls, causing the faint snipping sound of the roots breaking; then it would come completely, I would fall back the smallest amount, the weed would bring soil with it, and shower the pakasandra with black as I shook clean its roots. Then I'd toss it into the pile and move to the next weed. Some required two hands. Sometimes I could do two at once. I was being paid by the hour and wanted to be in the pakasandra indefinitely. I was more thorough than I needed to be. By the end I was spending five minutes hunting for weeds remaining. I parted the pakasandra leaves to see if there were weeds beginning underneath. The dirt was so black and moist. She watered it often. And all the while I was caressing every wall of my head. I was wandering around my head, teary with joy, wistful even, loving the surfaces, the many rooms, the old rooms and empty rooms.

—Listen, Will . . .

—But slowly these empty rooms are filled. Filled with things so wretched and brutal that you could not have conceived of them at thirteen. And soon you find there are too many rooms, too many occupied rooms, too few empty ones. I walk through my corridors and I open doors and now it's so hard to find a room unoccupied or not full of screaming clouds.

—Oh cut the shit.

—They live in these rooms. They breathe there, I hear their laughter. I try to keep them in the rooms I don't enter, but they move, and I forget where they are, and when we're in a room together I vibrate, I have too much within me, I cannot contain my desire—death for them and even me, I will tie my blood to theirs, a line to anchor, whatever it takes, they make me want to end my brain.

—I can't listen.

—Don't you see that as we've traveled, nearly every minute, they have been with me, they have been with me always? I have given you a small insignificant indication of their presence with me. When you shake my hand you shake theirs. When I place my elbows on tables to eat, to look across a table and talk with you, they eat with me, they talk through me.

—I didn't know.

—The only times they are not with me are those times when speed overwhelms, when the action of moments supersedes and crowds out. When my movements stop they come. When my eyes are fixed they come.

—Hand you will help me avenge and then I will rest.

—Who? Who are you after?

—The fuckers at Oconomowoc. Them first.

—There are others?

—Of course there are.

—Who?

—The trucker.

—Stop.

—The fucker at the funeral home, the one who did that to Jack.

—He did his job. And we closed the casket.

—You want it too. You want to throw that man around.

—No.

—You said you did!

Out my window and beyond the sprinklers, there was the sound of giggling, a small voice emitting tiny laughs. Then a door closed. I put my hands between my legs.

—I brought all this upon us, Hand.

—Don't start.

—We beat up kids. We pushed them down ravines. We ran by the retarded girl, Jenny Ferguson, and we tore her dress on purpose. Remember that, asshole? We did that and this is retribution. There is balance. Everything lives in perfect Newtonian opposition.

—You are fucked.

—I will have more coming. I acted too often with unprovoked

aggression and now it is enacted upon me. I have done other things. Things you don't know about.

—Your father started this.

—Let's wipe these fuckers away.

—Who?

—These pigs. From Oconomowoc. They have eclipsed all my years. I've tried too long to grow again into the world and now I'm being sent back. I don't want to remove myself again. I spent so long away and finally rejoined the world and now I can't be here. It's too much to walk around with this skin and this blood—it all hisses at me. I sink into my blood and it hisses at me.

—Stop.

—You remember how I was.

—We called you Robotman. You withdrew. It didn't make sense. Your dad had left so long before.

—This was unrelated.

—This is when your heart went offbeat.

—Irregular. I'd been passing out, and at first the doctors called it something else, something common in teenagers—you stand up quickly, you black out, a byproduct of quick growth—but it was happening too often, I was finding myself on the laundry room floor with broken recyclables under my back, a shard of Schweppes stuck three inches into my shoulder blade.

—I remember that.

—Six stitches. It was that time at the emergency room, when we did the first tests with a tall beautiful doctor, Dr. Hilliard, who reinvented me, gave birth to the me with Wolff-Parkinson-White Syndrome, a very specific heart irregularity condition involving electricity and valves, or the dysfunction of these valves and their electricity, dubbed WPW. Most of the people who get it, she said, are—

"Wrestlers," my mom said, wanting to make the doctor laugh. Hilliard sat down and covered the basics of the condition, an arrhythmia that was not common but not rare. But I didn't want all the details. I wanted to know what I could and couldn't physically do, what I could and couldn't eat—dry foods? wet foods? only soup?—and leave it at that. Dr. Hilliard—she was something, her steady unblinking eyes, the serene but determined face of an Egyptian sarcophagus—told us that almost no one died of WPW, but some did—some did, she said while looking up from my knee, which she was squeezing like a grapefruit. Almost everyone with WPW, she said, led normal lives, outside of the occasional attack, spell, fainting or minor stroke. It concerned me in a distant way; at the very least, it would provide some suspense. There were certain cures, open heart surgery, a way to get through the obstruction—ablation, they called the procedure—but it was only necessary in the most extreme of cases. Mine was not one. Until recently, my spells were twice a year and minor, and easy to work around. But this past year has been one of slow tightening, and shock, of flash floods and mudslides—

—I remember when they told you about the WPW. You got so weird for a while. Your dad had left again—

—I decided at age twelve, after first getting the whole thing explained to me, that I would no longer express or be party to any human emotion. I watched the TV news and wanted to disassociate myself. I renounced my membership. I would be a better human by stripping myself of human weaknesses. I would be a better human by not raising my voice, by not crying, by not being angry, or sad, or annoyed, or excited. I was tired of staying up at nights waiting for dawn, wondering what would happen if I slept, who would come to kill me.

—I remember you sleeping in school.

—The idea was to solve the problems of the world via removal, withdrawal, starting with me. There was no order in the world but there would be order in how I moved through the world. I wanted to remove those elements of human behavior that led to trouble—

the trouble I had seen with Mr. Einhorn, who I had known as the guy who ran the pool over the summer but who had recently been courting and touching my mother, his two fat hands on her shoulders in the kitchen in a way that did not look gentle.

—I can't believe she dated him.

—Twice.

—You had evolved over the rest of us.

—It was easy to become a better human. First, I spoke in a monotone. I could not be excited and could not be upset. I was a visitor from elsewhere, Russia maybe, and found everything amusing, interesting, but only slightly and even then, solely from an anthropological standpoint. I was not sullen; I was predictable. I walked at a normal human pace. I rode my bicycle at an optimum speed, a practical speed, without standing up on the pedals, because to do so would imply urgency. At school events I would clap when others would clap but I would not cheer or yell. My phone calls were brief and to the point. I set the receiver down gently; I walked the stairs not quickly, not slowly; I brushed my teeth for fifteen minutes because that was what my dentist, who I admit now was not sane, suggested; I kept my head level because tilting seemed to imply too much interest; I did not pass gas or pick my nose; I washed myself thoroughly in the morning and at night. I thought of the least emotional walk I could engineer, and decided that it required minimal arm movement and long even strides.

—Are you sure this wasn't all after the thing when your dad fell on your mom?

—That happened after.

—But it did happen, right?

—I know that I was in the middle of the living room. The carpet was shag, yellow or white. He looked like he was sleeping when he fell. I was sitting there, or standing there, and it was night. I know it was night because I saw my reflection in the black window. I looked like me, only my eyes seemed more hollow, my flesh papery.

—And?

—And then he fell on her. She was standing under the mini-balcony in the middle of the room, holding a bowl of apples. I think she was asking if anyone wanted them because they were old and bruised. And then she was under him. He fell from the balcony and landed on her. His drink crashed on the carpet and splashed. She started wailing.

—How was that possible? In the house on Oak?

—No, the house before that. There was a railing at the top of the stairs. The balcony was about nine feet up. It was a split-level house, and he was at the top of the stairs, at the railing, looking down at us both, and then he was falling down and landing on her. She shrieked and then wailed. They were a tangle on the floor. He seemed so heavy while falling.

—I still don't understand how a man can land on a woman without breaking every bone in her body.

—She wasn't hurt much at all, outside of a hairline fracture on her wrist. She had a cast on her arm for a little while, a cast I still have. She doesn't know this.

—It's amazing he didn't kill her.

—Yes.

—And how long after that were they divorced?

—They were already divorced. They'd been divorced for years.

—How did that work? I don't get it.

—I don't either. I just know they were already divorced. But I don't know why he was there.

—They were back together.

—I felt nothing when he left again. "Oh," I said when she told me. I half-closed my eyes. I watched her weep on the kitchen floor. I watched the drool come down her chin. Tommy was in Alaska at the cannery so it was us. She came at me and hugged me and I let my arms drop to my sides. She could hold me if she wanted because she was that type, a loose weak human chaos of emotion, and from that I had graduated. She was sweating. I watched her cry again each time she told a different friend, on the phone sitting at the kitchen table, hand spiked through her matted hair. I watched as she breathed like people birthing babies breathe, in narrow streams with wide eyes. She cried again when she was throwing out all his food, from the fridge and pantry, his frozen waffles and apricots and venison still marinating.

—I didn't like you then. But you came back.

—I know but Hand, there's just too much of this. It's all a jumble. It comes out at once. The librarians swarm and multiply. Why all of this? I want this cleared away. I have no use for this shit anymore. It's sending me back.

—Replace it. Fill yourself with new things. Better things. Gold, pictures, cobwebbed feet.

—It won't work.

—This is about your dad.

—Jesus, no.

—Where is he now, anyway?

—Still in Milwaukee.

—When was the last time you saw him?

—Seven years. More.

—You don't know him.

—I remember only how he peels an orange with a knife, quickly, with the blade meeting his thumb, kissing his calloused thumb as he turns the orange around. He did this when I was small and he did it when I saw him last. He attacks the orange like a trapper skins an animal. He's so good with a knife. He knows how sharp the knife needs to be.

—That's what you know of him?

—I remember his Old Testament recitations. I was too young to know those stories from Grimm's, but I remember the language,

I know the wrath in those pages. I don't know if he was a God-fearing man or not but I know he loved those pages. We didn't go to church but he read the Old Testament and knew it well. He would read from his version, underlined in red and marked in its margins; he would read from it on our screened porch, while in the yard Tommy and I caught frogs and fireflies. From the end of the yard, in the moist tall grass, we could see his silhouette, could hear his murmuring, his occasional bursts of volume. He read his Isaiah whether or not we or anyone was there to listen—aloud he read it, swatting mosquitoes against his neck.

—That's all you know of him.

—That's all.

—This is about him. All this. Your rage.

—It's not, fucker! Not everything is about something else. This is about retribution! This is about balance!

—For Jack.

—Yes for Jack.

—You want a head for Jack.

—Yes. For Jack I wanted a head. I wanted the trucker's head. I knew the trucker's face, his long snaking hair. My red-eyed librarians brought me his picture on the hour and on him I imagined revenge in a thousand ways. But not necessarily death. I would remove things—one leg, three fingers, an ear—I would do it slowly while reciting laws of traffic and manslaughter but I know how long I had him with me, how long it took for his face to fade and my fists to uncurl. I know how long it takes! And now I am here again. I have years of this ahead of me and I cannot do it this time. I fought my father's ugly fucking head for ten years, his long bony arms, his wrinkled forehead, his constant winking, and then Randall Winston Jr. of United Van Lines and his oily unrepentant soul and now there is this and I cannot do it again. I need sections of my head removed. I need less memory. No memory. I need—

—You're confusing these fuckers with—

—I'm confusing nothing.

—Will, I understand your rage but this is all about Jack. But it'll be years before we get any kind of grip on this and—

—Fuck your head. You don't need your head. Remove your head from its casing and throw it to the world.

—I want that.

—Throw your head to the world!

—I want that.

—Then throw! Throw your head to the world!

—Lord I tremble before you my lord—look what they have done to me, the thoughts that ride with me down the canals toward sleep, that walk with me as I walk each day—if I could I would raise their bodies to you, my Lord, for your wrath or mercy. Please pick wrath!

—Who are you talking to?

—Never before have I wanted such harm rent upon another, but here I am and this is what I want. Oh grant me this! I know forever they will be in my house, the rooms of my mind, I know this and have accepted this but while I know they will be there I want them dead there. I cannot have them breathing there! I want them in the floorboards of the basement of my soul. Can you not will you not grant me only this? For this I will forever be your servant, resolute, your tool here among the wretched. I will do for you deeds sinister or noble, in public or private, whatever the cost. Let me dear Lord bring these men to you, allow me to make them available to your rage. I will hold them upright as they are struck down. I will collect their remains if you choose to tear them asunder. I will bleach their bones if you strip them of their flesh and muscle. Out here under this sky of stone I feel I can know your rage. Oh please tell me you know rage! I want now your storms to converge, I await the blackening of your skies and the cracking of bones as you prepare for—

I opened my eyes. I could hear Hand's even breathing. Outside humidity and crickets, the shikka shikka of sprinklers shooting through hedges and ferns.

FRIDAY

I woke up angry at Hand, though he couldn't know why.

"I can't do another night like that," I said.

"What? The disco? Why?"

"I don't know what to do."

"What are you talking about?"

"Let's go."

"We're going. Look at us. We're going."

He was shoving his stuff in his backpack. He zipped it and stood ready.

"We have to go," I said.

Hand paused. He looked at me like a father would, when a father knows his son needs a mother.

"We'll keep moving," he said as we crossed the white gravel parking lot. "I'll make sure. Let's go."

"I can't go to bed tonight," I said.

We threw our bags in the backseat.

"Fine. We'll stay awake, find something to do."

"Good."

"We won't sleep," he said. "That's the plan. We shouldn't be sleeping anyway."

We had to get out of Dakar by noon. It was our second day. We'd left Chicago thirty-six hours ago. The road was clear for us and Hand swung the radio volume right and we were delirious. The air soothed me and we bought oranges from a boy on the road-side, and pastries in Mbuu, afraid we'd see Denis's brother. We didn't. We ate and my hands were sticky from all the juice.

"I have a surprise," Hand said.

We were on the coast and he turned off at one of the beaches loaded with garbage. We parked by the road, among a group of young men, all wearing light shirts and jeans.

"What is this?" I asked.

"Hold on," Hand said, jumping from the car.

He spoke to the group for a second, and one man directed him down the beach to an older man, painting a large white sign protruding from the beach. They discussed something, and Hand walked back to the car.

"We're going for a ride," he said. "Quick, but it'll be nice."

Hand had contracted this man, Thione, to take us up and down the coast for half an hour. We had to see things from this side, he said, and there was no speed, he said, like water speed.

We set off from the beach, helping with two other men to push the boat off a narrow sandbar near the shore. I sat at the front, Hand in the middle. A teenager jumped on just before we took off. He was the navigator.

We were in a small white motorboat–water taxi steered by an older man and guided by a teenager who stood on the bow as the boat bounced, holding a rope tied to the point, standing as if riding a white and featherheaded circus horse. At our feet, the water sloshing to and fro. I leaned over the boat's edge, watched the same point as the froth blurred by, white and blue—and I wanted to have my arm in the water. To have it lazily running through the water, like I did that day, with Helen Peters, at Phelps Lake, on that boat, both of us naked—But here it wouldn't really be water like that, not here so fast, this wouldn't feel like water at all but more like fast-moving pavement. The foliage went right to the water and then went up, furry and dense, squiggly with dementia.

The sea was not smooth, the ride was thunderous, as if the boat had been thrown and was skipping along the surface. Tick-tick-tick—*WHAP!* When the boat jumped and its flat bottom struck the hard water, my spine compressed, briefly, between expectations of flight and the boat's great desire to come down and pound the surface, to slap it like you slap a shoe on a summit table— *WHACK*—and it rose and struck again, and the water blurred by and I saw it all, the white beaches, the small cottages along the shore, the miles of rocky beach, and then I knew that all I wanted evermore was *WHAP! WHAP!* The boat was skipping and then there would be a larger wave, or we would hit a regular wave a certain way, and the pause between when we became airborne

Y.S.K.O.V.

159

and *WHACK* when we landed we landed like a cannon and I clenched my teeth—*BAMBAMBAM*—for the aftershocks and I looked to Hand and the old man for a commiserative glance—*what the fufu-fuck?*—but no one wanted to share. They were busy, devoting their attentions to traveling, to watching the progress of the boat—instrumental in traveling is the participation in it, the belief in progress, the witnessing of passage. And I was traveling, too, I was serious about it. In a low hard motorboat one had to be serious. *WHAP!* There was urgency about a boat like this, riding the coast, banging against the surface—three little waves coming: *BAP-PITY!* We were going somewhere. And not just moving, but moving quickly—past things that were moving slowly or not moving at all. *WHAP!* The only motion I knew was relative motion, the only speed that truly felt like speed was when I was speeding past things. *WHAP! WHAP!* A sudden veering of the boat.

—Hand you've saved me today, but what about later?

—I will continue to move us.

—What about tomorrow?

—I'll move us tomorrow.

We sped through the savannah and suburbs—we'd tipped the boat man and boat boy like kings—and made it to the airport by eleven. We dropped the car in front of the rental office, gave the keys and a $50 tip to the attendant, and ran into the airport. At the Air Afrique desk, the three stunning queens, again splendid in blue and yellow and green, wanted $400, in cash, for each of the tickets to Casablanca, so I put my name on more traveler's checks at the money-change desk—*me! me! swoop! swoop!*—and came back and presented the money, two inches thick, to the eldest of the three.

"Ah, so you the big boss?" she asked.

"The what?" I said.

"The big boss! You!" she repeated.

"Yes, the big boss, this one!" said another of the women.

"But it was you who wanted of the cash," I said, in Handspeak. I was confused. I didn't want to be the big boss.

"Some man hit the big boss," said the third, gesturing at her face with loose fists.

Then they all laughed. For a long time.

On the plane I flipped through a magazine called *African Business,* featuring a profile of Sierra Leone's Charles Taylor; in one picture, he was wearing Keds and a visor. We descended into Morocco. Which was green. As far as we could see, from the air, it was green.

"Isn't this a desert—the whole country?" Hand asked, leaning over the aisle and toward me. Everywhere, squares of farmland stitched together with orange thread. That Hand didn't know more about Morocco—that it was green, for starters—demonstrated the great gaps in knowledge that occur when one gets most of one's information from the Internet.

"I thought so," I said. "But the same thing happened with Houston. I always figured Houston was all dry and brown, but it's trees in every direction, for a hundred miles."

"We thought Senegal would be green."

"We got it backwards. Or they did. Senegal should be green, Morocco brown."

"It's gorgeous down there," Hand said.

"It really is."

"Man, I hope we meet some Tuareg guys."

"What guys?"

"The Tuareg? You know the Tuareg."

"No."

"The Tuareg? They're the blue men?"

I wanted to throw rocks at his head.

"Tell me," I said.

"Blue men. I think that's what the word means. Blue men. These guys were badasses. They're like nomadic trader-thieves, who would spring out from the Sahara and rob caravans. They were insane. Blue eyes, blue skin and everything. Scariest people ever. Twelve feet tall."

I squinted at him, wondering how I'd get along if I ditched him in Casablanca.

"You don't believe me?" he asked, offended. "Ask anyone in Morocco about the Tuareg. Or the blue men. Say *blue men* and watch them run in terror."

* * *

A train brought us to the city. The passing country was an electric green and studded with grey jagged rock outcroppings. Crumbling stone everywhere; children dressed like medieval peasants ran along the tracks and threw rocks at dogs and each other. Shanties and tents and broken brick homes tied in place with clotheslines.

"Jesus," said Hand. "This isn't what I expected. I expected Tunisia, desert, that kind of thing. This looks like the Balkans."

We watched, from our window on a passing train, one boy throw a rock at the head of another, hitting him.

"What do you think the Balkans look like?"

"This. Right? The crumbly buildings, the people with the earthtone garb, everyone walking around, the fires everywhere? This is cold-weather poverty; it looks like it was hit by tanks."

But it was so green. Was the country as poor as it looked? On the plane we'd been afraid this was a too-middle-class sort of country, that we'd be giving money to people like us, but now, here, the women in shawls, the boys and their rocks, the tent-cities—

Hand turned to ask, in French, a young guy behind us on the train, how much longer to Casablanca.

"Where are you from?" the man asked Hand, in English.

"Chicago," Hand answered.

"Oh Chicago! Is it very dangerous?"

I waited for the inevitable:

"Oh yes—very," Hand said.

I laughed. Every Chicagoan uses this. The man was sitting with two friends, backs to us, who now turned.

"Smashing Pumpkins—from Chicago, right?" the man said.

"Right," said Hand.

"I am their greatest fan! I'm in the music business. I produce rap records. French rap."

He and Hand talked music. Apparently French rap was huge in

Morocco. The greatest! said the man. Out the window the country receded and the buildings became larger, neater and more square. To the right, across the aisle, the Atlantic appeared, rough and dark, whitecaps rushing at the walls of Casablanca. To the left, the city grew in view and gleamed; the buildings, so much glass, were glowing afternoon-golden in a hazy, perfectly somnambulant Los Angeles way. We passed into the trainyard and to the right, now, within the outer corridor's walls was a series of tents, twenty in a row, circular, fires adjoining, the hides of the tents stitched and patched.

Behind me Hand and the record company man were talking about Falco (though hadn't he died?), and Right Said Fred, and Run-DMC, and the possibility of a comeback for one or all of them, at once or, better yet, sequentially.

"What about the Tuareg?" I asked, over the seat, interrupting them. I figured these guys were as good as any to prove Hand's inability to leave any fact unbent, any truth unmolested. "Do they exist?"

The man's eyes hardened. "You're not looking for the Tuareg, are you? I must advise you to run from this mission. Is this indeed your mission?"

"Yes," Hand whispered with urgency and intrigue. "Are they killers? I have heard word of this—they are the blue men and are slaughterers, with none of the love of humanity."

"Well," the man said, leaning forward, "they have been known to kill everything, anyone who sees them. No one has returned after seeing them face to face. Only rumors live. They reside in the desert, the lower Sahara, and are legion in number, and are without mercy. They are smarter than us, but stronger. Some say they are eight feet tall, and have hands with six fingers—"

Hand turned to me, smug like crazy.

"Tell me more," he said to our new friend, while looking at me. Then he turned to the man. "Is this all true?"

"Of course not," the man said, roaring. "I am yanking on you, stupid person!" Two of his friends were cackling. The third was not an English speaker, was just watching.

I was dying. I couldn't believe how good this guy was. He was a monster. Hand was rolling his eyes, his tongue tight between his teeth, bobbing his head around like a marionette. "Nice," he said. "Are you finished?"

The Moroccans were still laughing.

"Not yet?" Hand asked.

They couldn't speak. They shook their heads. Not yet.

At the hotel's smooth chest-level desk, mahogany and older than us, a trio of American girls, all about twenty-four. They were sighing and scoffing. There was some problem with something, many problems with all kinds of things. They could not *believe* they were in Morocco and there was this *prob*lem. A credit card was not being accepted. The card company had to be called and this was just the *worst*. Yes they would sign the fax to authorize the transferral of information, if that's what it *takes*. By all means, whatever it takes to get things *done* around here! Next they'll want a note, ha ha, from my *mother*! Things were im*pos*sible and travel so very *di*fficult.

They were the first tourists we'd seen in Casablanca. We hated them. They had their organizers on the counter and were blowing their bangs from their foreheads. They made phone calls using the reception's phone. They begged to be despised.

We asked the desk people, while they awaited the results of the American girls' fax, about renting a car. Hand and I had decided that the plan would be to rent a car, from this hotel, go to the shantytown near the train station and give cash to the men in the tents, then sweep around Casablanca, eat dinner quickly, and drive to Marrakesh, getting there by midnight. Then a day in Marrakesh tomorrow, but with the idea to leave at six the next morning, for Moscow, then on to Siberia.

The hotel people were not helpful, as hard as they tried to help us. The hotel didn't have a car-rental agency, and the two desk women didn't understand why we wanted to drive to Marrakesh tonight. "Why tonight?" the older one asked. She was big. Next to her a smaller, thinner, younger and glowing one shot a smile to Hand and looked down. Her English was shy so she let the large one talk. The large one was large but not my type.

We tried to explain the need for us to move. Hand made motions with his hands implying lots of movement, circling, spinning. They stared at him. We borrowed their phone book. There was a Hertz listed and we called but they were closed. Outside it was already gone black and I couldn't believe how quickly the night dropped around us. We asked if there was a train that left for Marrakesh tonight. They didn't know; they suggested we go back to the station and find out. We were trapped.

Some don't know, and those who do always forget that there's electricity firing within us. I'm too dumb to know why it's electricity and not some other kind of power source—why not nuclear fission on a submolecular level?—but there you have it. Electricity firing synapses, electricity triggering motions of the heart. And mine's somehow not right. I've got some extra muscle there, and apparently we with WPW have an extra pathway, and while normally the signals are sent through something called the *Bundle of His*, our extra pathway picks up electrical impulses in the ventricles and sends them abnormally back upward to the atria. I saw a movie about it once, in Dr. Hilliard's office, and it made sense then, but never since. I've come to love the idea, though, of the necessity of electricity to the heart, and its unreliability, its outages and surges.

I was remembering an experiment I did when I was younger, involving an old battery and two of Tommy's roach clips—I have no idea why I was remembering this. There's this very old and strange payphone in the lobby of the hotel and it brought me to the battery and—

We walked out and down the street and debated.

"Do we want to stay here?" Hand asked.

Men in the next door café were watching soccer on TV. All in tweed, browns and tans, smoke above shifting like water.

"I don't think so," I said. "Even the guys on the train recommended going to Fez or Marrakesh."

We kept walking. Another café, more men in tweed watching soccer on TV, vague in umber smoke.

"It must be a big game," Hand said.

"We should leave."

"We can't go."

"We could go back to the airport and find something leaving."

"But why did we come here?"

"To spend a few hours and move, right?"

"I'm exhausted."

With great shame, we checked into the Hotel Casablanca. The room had a linoleum floor and no towels. Hand reached up to turn on the TV. There was coverage of a skiing competition in Aspen. Then:

"Holy shit. Look," said Hand.

The race, the Paris to Dakar road rally.

"I can't believe it—it's on TV here."

"Morocco. Wow."

We watched as the SUVs cut through the Senegalese savannah at 90 mph, bouncing on their huge tires like kittens pouncing on yarn. The camera, above on a helicopter, implied that someone else was remote-controlling these cars—but who?—as they dusted through settlements and fields. But who? There were shots of villagers watching while drawing water from a well, shots of villagers crowding around a car that had lost its left rear wheel. The driver of the car was apoplectic—the camera swirls from the helicopter above, soundless, as the man tore his helmet from his head and threw it on the ground; it bounced high through the golden grass. A boy ran to pick it up.

In the room there was no soap. The room was cold. In the race, on the screen, motorcycles were flying through the desert like wasps. We were in Casablanca, and the TV hung from the corner, and Hand was standing below it, immobile, fists in his pants.

I showered and put the same clothes on, hiding cash, folding, rolling and crinkling in the same pockets and socks. We'd both been alternating our two T-shirts, and now both were unwearable. I filled the sink and lathered shampoo on my spare shirt, leaving it in the grey water. When I stepped out into the cold room, Hand still had his hands in his pants, watching the rally.

"Can you smell me?" I asked.

"From here?"

"I guess."

"No."

I could smell me. Not a bad smell, not yet, but a distinct one, one with something to say. On the street we looked for food. We passed a streetside butcher presenting passersby three whole cows, hanging from hooks, behind which whimpered, under glass, an array of meats and sausages, crowned by a row of small brains, perfectly intact, the color of purple popsicle juice. We walked on.

A man, squeezed into an undersized sportcoat, caught pace with us and assured us he saw us in the hotel and that he wanted to ww-wel-w-wel-elcome us to Casablanca did we l-l-li-like it. A hustler with a stutter.

We told him we liked Casablanca, but not some of the people. Some of the people, said Hand, were kind of pushy. The man agreed readily and kept with us.

Where were we g-g-g-oing? he wanted to know. I had never heard someone stutter in another language, much less stutter in his second language. It was kind of great.

To eat, we answered. "G-g-go to disco later?" he asked.

"No thanks."

"You like the disco! Very good the disco!"

"Thanks though."

—You have a choice, stuttering man.

—I do not.

—Then we have a choice.

He changed tactics.

"You you have to look out around here," he said, "boys will come and grab from your pockets," he said, and while he said this, he pulled on Hand's pockets in a way unnecessarily graphic.

A car full of teenagers passed us yelling something lewd about the French; they thought we were French, which we didn't know how to take. We lost the stuttering hustler and passed empty Chinese restaurants and more cafés full of men and their coffee and tweed and soccer and smoke.

We ate in a diner with a door open to the street and a TV yelling the game. Morocco vs. Egypt.

"Jesus," said Hand. "No wonder."

We pretended that people cared we were in the diner, but they did not. We ate some kind of chicken and rice dish we guessed at on the menu, which was printed in Arabic. The city, here, looked like Chicago's North Side, in the oblique angles of the intersecting streets, the neighborhood bars, the homogeneity, both comforting and discomfiting. It was cool, about fifty degrees, and the food was good. We'd forgotten to eat all day and here we were. It was my first meal without my left back second molar and the vacancy was chasmic and wet and thrilling. Across the aisle from us, two boys, brothers of ten and twelve, had their mouths open, tongues bobbing, showing each other their half-chewed food.

I've done stucco, a little bit of it in my job, applying the goop to a bathroom or two and once in a tall hall with a ceiling of apple-cinnamon, and I pitied those who had to live within it. Why we'd want walls that broke skin when scraped—these people, of the apple-cinnamon hall, had kids!—is beyond me. But these Moroccans like their stucco, their textured wall surfaces. Everything is given some pronounced epidermis, something that comes back at you, and it was starting to get to me.

Ten blocks away we passed through a door of beads and into the darkest of bars, long and narrow, full of men and more tweed, more soccer—a kind of Moroccan sports pub. We ordered beers, small and in green bottles. Everyone was drinking from the small green bottles.

We stood and glanced at the jukebox; everything in Arabic.

"Bonjour," said a man at a table by my waist.

I said bonjour. Next to him were nine empty green bottles, neatly arranged in two rows. I looked around and this was custom—the bottles drunk were kept and arranged, as proof.

"You are not French," he said.

"No," I said.

"American," Hand said.

"Ah, AmeriCAHN," he said, grinning. "AmeriCAHN pop music, yes yes! Eagles!" he said, then went into a credible version of the guitar part from "Hotel California."

Hand clapped and the man smiled.

"And Pink Floyd! I like! *We dunneed . . . no eddjoo . . . kayshun!*" He was really going now. "Yeah! *Wedun needno eddukayshen!*" He was banging the table. Then another guitar solo, but not, unfortunately, one found in that song.

—I want you to come with us.

—I'd like that.

—You'll come with us to Cairo.

—Sounds like a dream.

—But we won't. We don't have that kind of courage.

"You still want to go?" I asked Hand. We were walking through the quiet city, along a park, dark and extending forever. He said he did. We could get our stuff from the hotel and leave.

"Where?" I said.

"Somewhere. Marrakesh."

"Now?" It was 11:30.

"There's got to be an overnight train going somewhere." He paused and while we were standing, at a stoplight in a large intersection, a car flew by, there was yelling, and someone threw a half-empty plastic bottle of Sprite. It grazed my leg.

"What'd they say?" I asked.

"Something nasty, I think. Anti-French. Maybe we should go."

"Yeah. We're not moving fast enough. And we haven't gotten rid of much. How much you think?"

"Maybe $8,200 or so."

"We have to be quicker."

We walked toward the hotel, planning to pack and leave.

We passed a woman, a baby in her arms and toddler sleeping on her lap, sitting in front of a movie theater offering Schwarzenegger in *End of Days*. Above the entrance was a huge poster of *Casablanca*, the first sign of that movie we'd seen in the entire town. The woman held out her hand and we passed. I hated mothers who brought their children to the streets.

—You should not bring them here.

—What would you have us do?

—There must be homes. What did you do to your family that they won't bring you in?

—You will not know.

—You are using these children.

—You are ignorant.

—Then I will walk by.

—But anyone who asks for money needs it. Your mother said that. Your mother said anyone who begs must need. That is why there is the word *beg*.

—At least wash their faces somewhere.

—I will try.

I ran back and gave her all the American cash I had—maybe $350—though I couldn't look at her as I did it. I leaned down to her and her baby wrapped in brown plaid, and found her hand and stuffed the money in, my eyes closed as if reaching into a crevice to catch a salamander. I jogged back to Hand.

"Let's get off this street," I said.

"Why?"

"She can still see us."

He looked at me and squinted.

"Please. Hand. I want to walk away and turn the corner somewhere. I don't want her coming after me, saying thanks or being confused or anything. Run with me."

We ran a block and turned down a quieter street.

"That was so hard," I said. I was leaning my back against a window. I looked back to make sure she wasn't following us.

"The giving it away?"

"Yeah. God was that hard."

"I know," he said.

"It's shaming, don't you think?"

"Why?"

"I don't know."

—When you give them the bills, Hand, you feel so filthy.

"You think she's okay?" I asked. "I was afraid someone would see me give her the money and then come and take it from her."

"I'm sure she's fine."

"Someone's going to take it from her," I said.

"She's smart."

"We should stay with her."

"She looked tough," Hand said.

"I'm so confused," I said.

"I know."

"Why the *fuck* is that so weird? Why is it so hard?"

We had no idea.

We walked to the hotel and knew I was getting close. We'd promised not to sleep but here we were. I feared the bed. The bed tonight would break me.

—Hand let's not sleep.

I could drink to pass out and keep from thinking. That would be the plan. I could make it sound fun, have Hand and I drink from the minibar, if there was one, or buy a bottle of something on the way home, act like it was part of the trip's grand design. *The grand design was movement and the opposition of time, not drinking, hiding, sleeping.* Too late. I haven't won yet. *You won't win.* I don't want even two minutes with my head. I don't know where it would go tonight but knew that the funeral home fucker was there somewhere. He was getting closer, he was somewhere in the basement of my mind and he was pacing and getting ready to climb my hollow stairs—

"We could go to the mosque," Hand offered.

I loved him for taking me back into the air.

"Which?" I asked.

"That one there."

"That's not a mosque. Look at it. It's a church."

We walked closer to the huge white structure, ghostly in the dark shooting upward. A sign gripped the wrought-iron fence separating the park from the sidewalk: Cathédrale du Sacré Coeur.

"That's odd," Hand said.

"Let's get something to drink and head back to the hotel," I said.

"Boring. You tired?"

"Yes."

Jack's mom asked us to come to the service early. She and Jack's dad, who could barely stand and had spent the day before the service in a wheelchair, weak beyond hope, hadn't settled on whether it would be an open or closed casket, and wanted us to help decide, once we saw Jack.

"Then we'll sleep tonight but not again," he said.

"Good. Fine."

We got to the church at two for the three o'clock service, and waited, in the lobby, fanning ourselves with paperback psalm books. It was almost one hundred degrees, and the church wouldn't turn on the air conditioning until ten minutes before three. Jack's dad was outside, on the bright bleached patio between the church and the rectory, in his wheelchair, staring at the flowerbed, full of cheap daisies and dying groundcover. I hadn't had that much to say to him for ten years or so, since he sent Jack to Culver Military Academy for a year. He'd been caught stealing a six-pack of Coors from their basement fridge and that was that. Jack's sister Molly wasn't there, hadn't been heard from in three years; there'd been the distant fear she would show up, but it was not to be.

Jack's mom left to get candles; the priest had realized they were short on white ones and was about to use red. Jack's mom wailed *No* and, out of something like madness, insisted on white, hissed to the priest that it had to be white, and drove off to find two tall slender white candles.

She asked us to stay, to look first at Jack, and if he looked okay, she and her husband would then decide.

The funeral home man, Nigel, emerged from the back twenty minutes before three. He was only a few years older than us, with glasses held within thick black rims. His eyes were vibrating and his heavily gelled hair thrust from his head with cold competence, like dewy plastic grass.

"He's ready, if you want to take a look," he said. We hated him.

We followed him into the church and from the back I knew it was wrong. The casket was half-open and it was wrong. From so far away Jack was grey, or blue. The color was wrong.

"Jesus," I said, and stopped.

"What?" Hand said. "You don't know yet."

"I do know."

"I know he looks bad from here but it's the light, probably. These people know what they're doing."

"Who says?"

"People do this all the time. Everyone has open caskets."

"It's so wrong."

"We have to get closer."

Nigel was waiting for us, a few feet down the aisle, his head slightly bowed, deferential to our discussion. Hearing that we would get closer, he lifted his chin, gave a tight smile and nodded. We followed him. My legs felt asleep. They felt so light. They were hollow and being moved by someone else.

Ten steps further it was obvious. They'd fucked it all up. Jesus Christ. He was grey. His face was huge and wide. They'd added feet of flesh to his face. There was too much flesh. It flowed down from his nose like drapery. There was no color on his skin—there was a dull hue, like house paint, and there was blush on the hollows of his cheeks, as if applied by young girls with paintbrushes. He looked fifty. His hair was parted, but on the wrong side.

"So fucked up," I said.

"I know," Hand whispered.

We'd stopped again, about twenty feet from the casket. The lining of the casket was silver and was too shiny. He looked sixty.

"Please," Nigel said, with his arm extended toward Jack's body, hand open, asking us to get closer.

"Please no," Hand said. "Please fuck off."

They'd messed it all up. I'd never seen anyone before like this, never an open casket, and it was wrong. These people were imbeciles. Who wanted this? This was criminal. Where had they gotten all the extra flesh? It hung from him, it swam down into his starched white shirtcollar. His chin was loose, liquid. Who wanted this?

"Justin, William, you should really examine the work we've done. If you're worried about the accident, you should know that we took great care to obscure the puncture to his left temple—" Nigel was interrupted by Hand, who grabbed him at the bend of his arm and turned violently toward him.

"If you don't fucking leave us, fucker, I will break everything in you that can be broken."

Nigel exhaled through his nose, and left. Jack's mom returned a few minutes later. Hand and I were sitting across the aisle from each other, on pews at the back, and the casket was closed. She raised her eyebrows to us and we shook our heads.

"Good," she said, and sat down, legs straight in front of her, on the floor of the aisle between us. "Good. Good."

Hand and I were in the Marrakesh hotel room and we'd bought a bottle of wine and he was letting me drink it because he knew. I filled and drank six glasses and was out cold, blissful and stupid.

SATURDAY

In the morning we found an Avis and a man, inside, round and wearing the red jacket. That same red jacket. It was good to see him. We filled out the forms and on a phone he called for a car and soon was screaming at the man on the other end. He was doing so while banging on the desk with each syllable. "Ack [*pound*] nek [*pound*] rek [*pound-pound*]." He was so mad about something.

In ten minutes, a different flustered round man arrived in our car and we drove off; the car never stopped running. The little car had no tape deck or radio but we took it anyway, driving around the coast. It was Saturday and everyone was out and the light was Californian. All around the Palace of King Hassan II—an enormous and glorious temple hanging over the ocean like a beachhouse— there were men pushing daughters on bikes, and teenagers fishing over the guardrails. Farther down the shore, along the Boulevard de la Corniche and thousands more, boys mostly, playing soccer and swimming, though the day was not warm—sixty degrees on the upper end. We got out briefly, finally, for the first time, knowing we were in Casablanca, examining its air, which was different than Senegal's—denser, lighter, brighter, dimmer—we had no idea. You couldn't go wrong with a name like Casablanca, we figured, and wondered if it carried such a tune in every language. A group of kids rode their bikes by us, boogie boards balanced above. This was suddenly Redondo Beach; they called it 'Ain Diab and it bore no resemblance to anything I'd pictured possible in Morocco. We thought briefly about staying and spending the day at the beach, helping small children search for crabs in the cracks of the huge rocks licked by waves. But we didn't because we had to move.

We drove through and on to Marrakesh.

Out of the city and past the dozen enormous gas stations, perfect and clean like lacquered boxes, and the country went flat and green. Marrakesh was a few hours' drive from Casablanca, we were told. The roadside was all farms, dotted with small crooked adobe homes. I was driving and was driving fast.

We were passing cars like they were parked, or being pedaled, propelled by feet to the sound of xylophones.

"You will call me Ronin," I said. I'd probably never driven this fast. The speedometer said 130 kph.

"I will not call you Ronin."

"I drive like Ronin, you call me Ronin."

"I can't have you doing that anymore."

"You kind of—"

"Will. Stop."

"You kind of rev the first R, like rrrrrRonin."

The roadside was an expansive and ripe kind of green and the soil was orange; it was exactly what we'd seen from above. We had about $4,000 in Moroccan money we'd changed in Casablanca.

The poverty was incongruous. Rural poverty is always incongruous, amid all this space and air, these crippled homes, all half-broken, most without roofs, standing on this gorgeous, lush farmland. It wasn't clear who owned the farms, or why these crumbled houses stood on these well-kept farms, and why none of the homes had roofs. Clotheslines, chickens, dogs, garbage. We rushed past families, bundled and huddling though the day was warm, on carts driven by mules. We passed, still going at least 80 mph, a group of women just off the road, bent over in the embankment, dressed in layers, heads covered with dull rags, large women hunched and gathering hay—

I pulled over. I gave Hand a stack of bills.

"What are you going to say?" I asked.

"I don't know. What should I say?"

"Ask them for directions."

Hand started getting out but was wearing huge silver sunglasses, shiny and with a series of round holes in the arms.

"Hand. Can you do it without the sunglasses?"

"No."

"If you get out in your nylon pants and Top Gun Liberace sunglasses, then it sends a weird message—"

Now the women, including the one with the scythe, were watching us as we sat in the car arguing. I grabbed a map and spread it in front of me.

"And just what is the message we're sending, Will? Are we sending a normal message otherwise?"

"Forget it."

"Can you just take them off? Please?"

He did, then threw them at my chest. I caught them but broke one of the glasses' arms, on purpose.

He walked down the highway shoulder to the women and up the embankment. Once within fifteen feet, and once they'd all paused in their work and assembled around him, he asked them something. Directions to Marrakesh maybe. Graciously, they all pointed the way we were already going. He then made an elaborate gesture of gratitude, and offered the stack of bills to them, about $500.

They took it and as he backed away, they stared, then waved, and he waved. I waved. We drove off as they gathered around the woman he'd handed the bills to.

"Were they nice?" I asked.

"What do you mean?"

"Did they smile? Were they nice?"

"I couldn't talk to them. They didn't speak French."

"But they smiled?"

"Sure. Nice ladies. Big. Burly. They were happy. You saw them. They were happy to help."

The sun was everywhere and the landscape went curvy. Green hills, red hills, then hills covered in thin-trunked mop-topped trees.

Then a huge red city, to the left of the road, Benguérir, red like barns, of clay and stone, ancient, unchanged and terrifying, low-lying and endless. A few miles later the land sprouted hills, olive trees—it was so green! Soft curves and such green. I had never lived anywhere with this kind of drama. Cities are billed as drama-filled but are in fact almost totally safe, are so like being constantly indoors—too many small lights and heavy windows and perfect corners. Yes there is danger from other humans hiding in dark tri-angles but here! Here there is swooping. Here there are falling rocks. Here you picture tidal waves or quickly moving glaciers. Or dragons. I grew up obsessed with dragons, knew everything, knew that scientists or people posing as scientists had calculated how dragons might have actually flown, that to fly and breathe fire they'd have to be full of hydrogen, at levels so dangerous and in such tremulous balance that—I wondered quickly if I'd give my life so that a dragon could live. If someone offered me that deal, your life for the existence of dragons. I thought maybe yes, maybe no.

Then over a river, the Rbia, and the roadside now punctuated with men standing, selling fish, offering them to drivers, long wet fish on hooks. Then men and boys selling asparagus, holding a bunch in one hand and waving to cars with the other. Men selling small bundles of sticks.

I knew Hand wouldn't resist.

"Look at those. . . ." he said.

"Don't," I said.

The taxis, out here, were Mercedes-Benzes, all of them char-treuse. Then it was the southwest again. The dirt went redder and bloodier as we approached Marrakesh, laid wide and flat below a mountain range that spread left and right. Churchill had loved these mountains, the High Atlas; it was the only landscape he'd painted during WWII. "The most lovely spot in the world," he'd said to Roosevelt when they'd met here in '38, planning the assault on Normandy.

—Mr. Churchill you were given a mission.

—Yes.

—I want to have been given your mission. I want your place in world events, the centrality of it. You were born in the cradle of a catapult!

—You are wrong. I found my mission.

—I disagree.

—If you must.

—Tell me: where is my mission? Where are my bunkers and trenches, my goddamn Gallipoli?

Now, on the approach, see the increasingly green hills, the preponderance of tall dark green pointy trees, see the sloping rivers, everything so lush. See the red soil. See the winery colors. See so many colors, working in perfect concert. We had no idea it would be this lush. A man on the roadside held up something, but not a fish—something bulbous and furry. As we passed it became not fur but feathers—a group of chickens hung on a hook. The man wearing a hooded brown dashiki. See us ten miles later stopped on the shoulder, Hand running across the road and across a field to a family with a horse, traveling, all with packs. See Hand ask directions, pop his palm on his head—*Aha!*—and then give them a stack of bills. See them offer him some figs, which once in the car he will take and chew and spit out and throw. See Hand give to a boy selling fish, and see the boy insist we take one, which Hand puts in the trunk, grinning and squinting at the boy, who looks like he expected us to eat it then and there. Hear Hand afterward:

"There is nothing bad about what we're doing! Nothing!"

"Right," I said.

"That one was fun. Good kid."

I sped up. We were at 120 kph.

"You need to call me Ronin," I said.

"You need me to thump you."

We debated briefly whether we were giving people false hope. That now the common belief around these parts, on this country-side, among the rural poor, would be that if one waits by the side of the road long enough, Americans in airtight rental cars and wearing pants that swish will hand out wads of cash. That we pay extravagantly to be told where to go.

The road was empty in the midafternoon. Only the occasional luminous Mercedes taxi, or BMW, or tour bus. There didn't seem to be any mass commuter transport in Morocco. Most of the people on the road, and on the roadside, were men, and most of them were wearing suits, dust-powdered and threadbare suits. Men in pin-striped suits tending flocks of sheep. Men in worn tuxedos holding bouquets of asparagus inches away from careening cars.

In a small city full of banks we stopped for something to drink. Nattily dressed men at café tables nodded to us and we walked into a dark cool restaurant and at the takeout counter we bought oranges and sodas. The sunlight over the clerk's shoulder was white and planed, and when he poured us glasses of water it was clearer than any water I'd ever seen. It was the unadulterated soul of the world.

Ahead, the mountains clarified themselves; their tops were white-capped. As we descended into Marrakesh, the billboards appeared, each for one of various resorts, for golf courses and cellphones. The road went from two lanes to four and there were scooters every-where, whining when revving and jabbering while shifting. Condos left and right—so far it could be Arizona—and at the first travel agency we saw we stopped. Inside, there was a single employee and he told us, when we asked where we could go from Marrakesh, that night, that he handles only cruises and package tours for Danes and Swedes.

The city was so red! The walls, which were everywhere, were everywhere red, the precise color of the scab bisecting my nose, a dull but somehow sweet maroon, soothing but vital. Minarets and medinas jostled with Parisian cafés, buildings of seven stories and iron balconies, the sidewalks bustling with fashionable people, and we sped to the airport as the sun was lowering and wrapping the city and desert in fine pink gauze.

Around the airport was a park, dirt and small trees, where dozens of families were picnicking, kids playing some version of duck-duck-goose.

Inside, in the cool white linoleum airport and at the airline desk: "What flights do you have leaving tonight?" Hand asked.

A friendly and smooth man in a blue uniform: "Sir, where do you want to go?"

"We'll know once you tell us where your planes are going."

"Sir, we first need to know where you want to go."

"Just tell us where *you're* going."

"Just tell *me* where *you* are going."

The man had quickly jumped from amusement to something approaching rage.

"I asked you first," Hand added.

This went on for a while. It hasn't worked anywhere and never will. We learned that a plane is leaving for Moscow, via Paris, in three hours. If we could get to Moscow we could get to Irktusk, Siberia—we checked before, on the web with Raymond in Dakar, and those flights were constant and affordable—and if we could get to Siberia we can get to Mongolia, because surely there were shuttles between Irkusk and Ulan Bator!

We decided we'd be on the flight to Moscow. By morning we'd be there. The airline desk wanted cash, almost $1,100 for the two tickets. We were grinning. Flying! We would do this!

At the currency exchange desk, I added my name, swooping like mad, to twelve $100 traveler's checks and handed them under the glass wall to a glowering man with a thick and uncompromising moustache, a brush to sweep a pool table. The man, squat and angry about the wrongness of his flesh, the things he's seen, all the air in the world, wouldn't take them; my signature did not, he said, match my passport. He pushed them back under the window and grunted and waved us away.

I said please. I told him, yes, I changed my signature not that long ago, thus the mismatch. But he wasn't listening.

"I am allowed to change my signature!" I said.

He spoke no English. Hand tried French, without success. Hand lost it.

"You can *not* do that! You must change the money!"

The currency man sat behind the glass, completely satisfied.

"You take these checks and you cash them!" Hand was now spitting on the glass. People were watching us. The man said nothing. Hand started again, now in French. Then reverted to his other English. "You are bad man!" he yells. "We have flight! Flight to Russia! We need this! You are bad man!"

Hand's eruption was sudden, bizarre, and not productive. Another man, behind us, told us to go to a bank, in the center of town—that they'd cash the checks. We had no choice and just enough time. As we were leaving, Hand yelled, pointing, shaking: "We come back to get you, bad man! You will see Americans again!"

We sped through the city, slowing, stopping, jumping, continuing. All the banks were closed. I got $500 from an ATM—all I could retrieve at one time—and then remembered another $800, in American cash, taped inside my backpack.

We now had twenty-five minutes to catch the flight; all we had to do was change the U.S. bills.

"Shit," I said.

"What?"

"We'll have to go back to that squat fucker."

"Right. But this'll show him. We've won!"

I agreed. He'd have to change the cash, and we'd beat him, we'd roll over his body, laid in our path, and he'd have to go home to his wife, he slump-shouldered and weak, unable as he was to make us unhappy—unable, today, to thwart the plans of innocents abroad. We had seven minutes to get there.

We drove around a turnabout in the center of town, almost cut off a scooter and were immediately stopped by a foot-cop in a yellow raincoat. He waved us to park on the side of the street. He was tall and also wore a thick black mustache. His skin was olive but cheeks ruddy from the sun. He was like the other man; he would thwart us.

He took my license and examined it.

"Chicago!" he said.

"Right," I said. He was different.

"Nice?" he asked.

"Very nice."

"Tommy Lloyd Wright!"

"Very pretty there," I said. "Big buildings. Lots of Tommy Lloyd Wright, right."

"I study architecture. Like Wright very much. You see?"

"Yes, much. The Robie house? Very nice it is." Now I was doing the Hand talk. "Very pretty there," I added. "Also very pretty in Morocco." I smiled confidently, strong in my love for his country and my belief in its future.

—If you stand in our way you're our enemy.

—See it as you will.

—It's inhuman to impede another's progress.

Leaning over me, Hand tried to tell him about the plane we wanted to catch.

"Sir, we must to catch a plane! At airport! We can go?"

Hand was making airplane gestures, his hand flying around the interior of the car, with sound effects. While Hand was having the plane take off amid various whooshes, the officer rolled his eyes and waved us off. We loved him.

At the airport, we abandoned the rental in the lot—we'd call the agency from Paris—and ran to the check-in desk, which was empty. In the airline office, adjoining, they were surprised to see us again.

"You're back! Where are you going?"

"Moscow! We have the money now."

I spread the money on the counter. It was obscene.

"Oh no, no," he said. "It's too late. See?" The agent pointed to window. The plane, a large AirFrance jet, was on the runway, visible, right there. People were still walking up the rolling stairway.

"Can you call them?" Hand asked.

They did. They wouldn't let us on. We were fifteen minutes early, but ten minutes too late.

"I am sorry," said the Moroccan man helping us. "They don't want you. Security reasons, they say."

"Call them!" yelled Hand.

"I cannot. They are French," the man said.

We paused long enough to realize we didn't understand.

We were stunned. Two hours we'd rushed around and now we would have to stay in Marrakesh for the night. It broke us. We couldn't get on the plane, which was right there, not two hundred feet away. There were people still climbing the staircase, from tarmac to jet, people still turning and waving to loved ones inside.

One man had three golf clubs with him in one hand, a stuffed Goofy in the other. But we couldn't get on. This was an abomination. We couldn't stay in Marrakesh! We'd already seen it, and we'd been in Morocco for a *full day*, in Africa *two days* already, almost *three*, and here we were, grounded, stagnant. There were seven continents and we'd spent almost half our time on one.

I sat on the smooth cold airport floor outside the office as Hand continued to argue inside. He whined, and pretended to cry, then offered them vodka that he didn't have, Cuban cigars he'd never possessed or even seen—"I assure you sir these are of the highest quality, made by Castro's personal tobacconists"—and finally, having failed completely, asked about flights the next day. The floor beneath me was cold but it was still and clean. The airport was immaculate. I tilted my head and squinted across the floor, thinking I could make my sight travel the floor like a low-flying bird. The floor shone in a dull lifeless way. I had a brief sensation that I was at O'Hare again, trying to leave for Senegal. I was alternately enraged and spread wide with great peace. Any thwarted movement was an affront, was almost impossible to understand. It was so hard to understand *No*. But with every untaken step a part of the soul sighs in relief.

Mo & Thor—

Everyone's got their own money. It's the first thing a new country does, it prints money. The money here's beautiful, as almost all money is everywhere outside the U.S.—even Canada's is better than ours. Hand (you remember Hand. He told you how the hunters trap meercats, and demonstrated on you, Thor) says that in New Zealand, the money has little plastic see-through windows. Money is really the only tangible communication device we have, if you

"Let's go, dipshit."

Hand had emerged, laughing with the Moroccan airline man, who was dressed like a pilot and carried a similar suitcase. I put away the postcard and while outside our plane rolled away to Paris, we passed through the hissing airport doors and into the darkened clear cool night of Marrakesh.

We regained our car, feeling like we were stealing it—it was still there, we had the keys, but it was so odd—and drove back to the city to find a hotel. We'd check in and then head to the mountains, where we planned to find people, dwelling in the hills, living in huts, and to them we would come in the night—in the blackening sky there were already stars and a low moon climbing—and we would throw small bundles of bills through their open glassless windows and then drive off.

First, though, we would see the Djemaa el-Fna; we'd driven past it on the way to the bank and it was already insanity, thousands massing and growing, countless locals and tourists milling around outdoor shops and food kiosks in dashikis and Dockers, all eyes overwhelmed and ears dulled by the roaring murmurs. We checked into a bland hotel of glass and silver and for ten minutes watched, again, the Paris to Dakar race on TV. They now had a camera in one of the cars, and the driver passed village after village, all blurry homes and faces, leaving all behind, very literally, in his dust.

Hand, magazine in hand, stepped into the bathroom. "I'm goin' in," he said, meaning half an hour at least—twenty minutes for the bowel movement, ten for the after-shower. Hand has to shower every time he dumps; I have no idea why.

I called my mom.

"So who got it today?" she asked. "More basketball players?"

"No, now we're asking for directions."

"Where?"

"To wherever we're going."

"Don't you have maps?"

"Of course."

"So you know where you're going."

"Oh yeah, always."

"So it's all pretend."

Hand burst from the bathroom like he'd been feeding bears and they'd turned on him. His own stink had overtaken him and now threw itself around the room.

"I don't know," I said.

We had a beer in the hotel bar, called Timofey's. The bartender was a young woman who looked at my face and gave me a commiserative pout. I accepted this and smiled. We were alone in the room, except a very old woman, white with hair pulled back into a neat ponytail, at a table overlooking the lobby, with a glass of something clear before her, her small hands cupped around it.

"We should sit down with her," Hand said.

I knew he was right. But I didn't know people of her age. She could hate us. She was easily seventy-five.

Hand was already halfway there. I followed. By the time I made it to her table, Hand was sitting, leg crossed, ankle on his knee. I don't know what he'd used as an opening line. She held her hand to me. I shook its fingers, which were cold and the skin loose, a small leather bag full of delicate tools. She was French. We introduced ourselves; her last name (she gave us both) sounded like *Ingres*. Hand sat to her right and I across from her. She was a beautiful woman. Up close she looked younger, maybe sixty. Her nose was still aquiline, her eyes beaming. She sipped her drink through its tiny red straw.

"You two are lovers," she said.

Hand laughed. My eyebrows skimmed my hairline.

"Well, thank you," Hand said. "We take that as a compliment. But no."

She cocked her head and looked between us.

"You are brothers. One is adopted."

"No," I said. I realized I was grinning. I wanted her to keep guessing.

"I know nothing anymore," she said, pursing her lips in a dissatisfied sort of way. "I pretend at wisdom."

She was the oldest person I'd spoken to in probably five or six years, since my Mom's uncle Jarvis died, who she loved because he'd taught her to ride horses and tan hides. But Jarvis had never spoken like this. She was scanning my face now, her head pivoting like she was trying to see around me.

"Accident," I said.

"I think so," she said. "Something to forget, I think."

"I'm trying," I said. "Maybe, yes."

Hand asked why she was here. She said she'd come here with her husband just after they were married, and had come back with him every so often thereafter. He was dead five years now.

"This is our fiftieth anniversary," she said, smiling in an exhausted way. Her sentences trailed off, the last words like hats taken by a sudden gust. "What brings you to Marrakesh?" she asked. "Golf?" She looked at our clothes. "You do not look like golfers."

"We're botanists," said Hand. God Almighty.

"You're lying," she said, then sipped her drink with her eyes still upon him. Ella Fitzgerald was singing from a small speaker over our heads. Maybe Sarah Vaughan. I worried briefly that they, Sarah and Ella, knew I didn't know the difference, and were angry.

"You lived through WWII," Hand said.

She laughed.

"Where were you?" he asked.

"Cernay," she said. And they were off, together.

"Was that Occupied or Vichy?"

"Occupied."

He was leaning in. The more I watched her the more I thought she might be younger. Her cheeks were tight and full of color. Her features were delicate but strong, like a face of blown glass.

"We helped," she said. "My mother and I ran the farm."

"You helped the *maquis*."

"How do you know all this?"

"Am I right? You were near Switzerland maybe?"

"You're a fan of the war," she said, pointing at him with her tiny finger, wrapped in skin as with a loose bandage.

"I've studied it," Hand said. "Not a fan, a student."

"Me too," I said, thinking that my current reading of Churchill somehow qualified.

"Did your father fight?" Hand asked.

"He was killed in the first month of the war," she said. "He wasn't army. He was a truck driver, killed near Abbeville."

"Sorry," I said.

"His brother, my uncle, went to the hills," she said. "There was a forest above our farm, in a valley. He stayed there for years. With three Hungarians."

"Anti-fascists."

"Yes."

"Was your uncle a Communist?"

"No. Not at that time. No."

"How old were you?" I asked.

"When?"

"When what?"

"When they invaded France."

I could never say the word *Nazi*.

"Nineteen," she said.

She and her mother had sheltered escaped POWs crossing over to Switzerland. They'd underreported farm production to the Germans and gave the surplus to those passing through and fighting from the hills. She had married one of the Hungarian soldiers.

"We're not botanists," I said. "We're just here."

"He's on a lightbulb," Hand said.

She looked at me, smiling politely.

"He was the Number Two swimmer in all of Wisconsin," I said. We were such jerks.

"What did you two do after the war?" Hand asked.

"We left," she said. "We left France. My uncle was killed in the town square by French Nazis. He had poisoned their food, had killed six, so they flayed him and then shot him. It was a time . . . It was not very real after some time. Or perhaps it was . . ."

She was trailing off again.

"You don't have to, you know." I said.

"I know," she said. "But it is so rare to be able to . . ." she laughed a little and wiped her mouth with her napkin. "To educate a few young Americans."

She sipped her drink.

"I remember it like a week . . . it was like you remember a time in bed, sick. When your head is . . ." She was throwing her hands around her head as if directing tiny winds, or weaving.

"The next year," she continued, "my mother died in 1944 of complications during labor," she said, and, registering our surprise, said, "she was forty-two and it was a priest, of all things. But that is another story. We had to leave the town. We could not stay."

They had moved to Amsterdam, where her husband, who she was calling Pipi, I think, resumed his work as an engineer. They never had children. Hand was staring at her watch, a simple gold-trimmed piece held by a wide black band. A man's watch.

It was getting late and we had to go. We told her where.

"You should come with us," Hand said, in his magnanimous host sort of way. Then, realizing the quality of his notion, he blurted: "You should!"

"You won't find the people you want up there," she said.

"Why?" I asked.

"Maybe you will. I shouldn't discourage you."

"Come with us!" Hand repeated.

"To the mountains? It's 9:30."

"We're going to the Djemaa el-Fna first."

"Oh please," she said, her hand resting on Hand's. "You two will do your adventure without me. I've seen the mountains during the day. I can't imagine that could be improved upon."

—Hand, we should stay here with her. We will be her companions on this night. And her stories! They will be worth more than anything we could find in the mountains.

—But this is history.

—Exactly.

—This is not what you were talking about. We had agreed on speeding, not sitting and listening.

—I thought you would want to stay.

—I've heard enough.

"We need you, though," I found myself saying to her. "We really want you to come."

She looked taken aback. My urgency had reminded her of something else. We were no longer harmless.

"No," she said. "Say hello to the mountains for me." Her last words trailed off again, in a way that sounded like we were hearing them from far away, downriver and upwind.

We stood.

"Can we buy you another drink before we go?" Hand asked.

She nodded.

I strode to the bar and ordered another of whatever she was having. It looked like gin. I brought it to her and set it between her thin bony fingers. Hand bowed before her and took her small hand into his and kissed it, on the thin silver band around her finger. I bowed too, but my back cracked in a new way and I couldn't go further, and couldn't look at her again. I turned with my eyes closed and we jogged down three flights to the night air.

* * *

On the street it was still warm and at the car, our back left tire was flat. We both stood, mouths open, for half a minute. We had not been in a country without blowing a tire.

This time Hand and I could handle it, remembering the tricks of the savannah man with the obsidian cobweb feet. We left the car resting on four wheels as we loosened the bolts. In a few minutes a man's legs appeared in my peripheral vision.

He was about forty, successful seeming or pretending, wearing a white scarf. He shooed me from the wrench. I stood and handed it to him. I didn't know what he wanted. Finding the bolts already removed, he got to work on the jack, turning it around with great urgency.

"Whoisthisguy?" I asked.

"Ihavenoidea," Hand said.

Another man came and shooed the first man from the jack. The first man stepped aside and left the second man to finish it. We had no idea what was happening. We were perfectly capable of changing the tire, but now, including us, there were four men working on the tire, and two more were now watching. It was an American highway construction project.

"Thisiswhathappenshere," I said. "Everyonewantstochangethe-tire. Thisistheirfavoritething."

"Thisiseveryone'sfavoritething," Hand corrected.

Everyone wanted to help. Everyone wanted to help or be ready if their help was needed. This was the way of the world.

We were done the tire was new and we were worthy and we ate a Pizza Hut meal and felt at once shame and great joy with our pizza. The place was empty; the day had been so long; the food was real and warm. The Pizza Hut man brought our soft drinks to us, and then refills, for free. We looked like hell. We were tired, but there were only five days left, now. We had started with seven days and now we had five, four and a half, and had we used them well so far?

"I really have to get to Cairo," Hand said.

"I know."

"But if we head north, to Moscow—"

"We can do both," I said, not knowing a thing. The rest of the trip in my mind sped by with airplane speed and hovercraft grace. More water, more air—a balloon! A zeppelin! More boats, and monkeys and where was that wall again? the one the millions touched, set in the center of that golden square—

We drove to the Djemaa el-Fna. Past the interlocking streams of pedestrians in silhouette, we saw the crowd, a great low mountain moving against the darkening horizon: the heads of intermingling thousands. We didn't know, exactly, around what they were gathered. Some kind of flea market? We had not been told.

We parked and two boys on one bike offered to sell us hashish. We said no thanks. They begged us to buy some. We passed. Hand patted one on the back to wish them well.

"Faggots," said the boy.

We walked through the square, but already, while we were looking for a parking spot, the crowd had thinned. It was about 10. All the women were gone and the men were hungrier. In grumbles and whispers ten different sellers of hash made their presence known. We passed through them and around the monkeys handstanding by lanternlight—the crowds were for the street performers—and into the halls of shops.

We entered and shuffled through an ever-narrowing thicket of proprietorships, separated by makeshift walls and rugs hung, vendors barking, selling sneakers, backpacks, scarves, CD players, cameras, crafts, carpets, jewels and vases and anything one can make from silver- or gold-painted tin. We stopped in a tiny enclave, manned by a small quick-moving man with fast small sad eyes and great animal eyebrows. Every object we picked up or glanced at prompted a flurry of proposals and urgings. He called us his friends, and offered us student rates, and put his hand on Hand's back, patting it nervously.

"My friend," he said to me, grabbing my shoulder, "you had something happen to you so I have the thing." He retrieved a long sword, almost three feet long, curved and sheathed in an ornate case. "See how nice?"

"How much?" I asked. I liked the sword.

"For you one hundred dollars."

Hand laughed in a great burst. I moved onto smaller models.

The salesman kept talking. At first, we laughed when he spoke, while he did the *My friend, My friend I help you out* part, and then we tried to let him know that he didn't need to do the act with *us*, we knew better, we had the blue book and knew the real value, etc., but he continued, and we had to laugh more. We bargained with him halfheartedly. We wanted a couple silly things, a pair of knives, a small jewelry box, oval and studded with fake emeralds, which broke apart and became a bracelet, and we pretended to leave when he would not take our offer. He sighed. He looked around left and right and behind a burgundy curtain, to make clear that if he gave us this price, he had to do so out of earshot of his boss and God. Out of appreciation for his efforts and great comaraderie and fortitude, we bought from him five things—two decorative knives, two of the small jewelry boxes and finally a small tin plate, engraved.

"See you my friends!" he said to our backs when he realized we were leaving. "You want nice chess set? For you beautiful student rate!"

But we were gone and had more elaborate plans.

We walked back into the square and looked for a new merchant-alley. But we had wasted too much time. Most of the shops were now closed. Their metal gates had come down, or their proprietors were packing up.

"Fuck."

"No, there's one."

On the outskirts of the square, a large shop was still open, just an open garage really, but bright and full to the ceiling, sixteen feet up. In front of it, a stray dog foraged through an enormous pile of garbage and human waste.

We greeted the portly store owner as we stepped up and among the bright overcrowded shelves of dishes and rugs and boxes, platters and knives. It was, this store, in its tins and brasses, blues and reds so bright, enamel on tin toys, more ravishing than almost any painting I'd ever seen or had likely ever been made—it was an intricate medieval tapestry and a hundred perfect Dutch still-lifes together melded but brighter lit—the accumulated care and craft put into these objects, each bauble, was surely equal to almost anything more celebrated artists had done or could do, as is any aisle in any grocery store, as is any decent toy shop—but these places would never be recognized as such, nor would a casino so—

Among the tea sets and chess sets and tiny chests for special things, I looked for and found the smallest, cheapest and least desirable item the store held. It was a keychain anchored to a small white animal, probably a sheep, crudely carved from a smooth milky material looking like lucite. I held it, I caressed it, I presented it to Hand, posing as my knowledgeable dealer in precious objects, with a rumble of approval. He came to me and touched it and purred his interest.

"It's incredible?" I said.

"It's almost painful," he said.

Our interest was made clear. We turned to the portly man and asked him, in French, how much.

He spoke no French. He scurried to a desk in the back and returned with a lined piece of paper, folded to a fourth. On it he wrote:

60DH.

Sixty dirham, about $3.

I looked at the paper, then at the keychain. I frowned. I shook my head slowly. This is where the trick would come in. I asked for the paper and pen. He handed them to me and on his paper, under his 60DH I wrote:

150DH.

Then I gave it back.

"Okay!" he said, grimacing. It was a deal. We had taxed his patience, but a hard bargain had been won; he was a fair man.

Hand stepped closer. I showed Hand the paper, and indicated that this good man had agreed to my hard-driven terms. Hand, though, was not to be so easily satisfied. He asked to hold the sheep keychain. I put it in his palm. He held it and weighed it in his hand. He ran a finger along its length. He examined, closely, the keyring, clicking it open and shut as if fidgeting with a carabiner. Then he shook his head and took the pen and the paper and under the 60DH and under the 150DH he wrote:

250DH.

Here I thought we might have gone too far.

Not a chance. Instead, again, the man took a long hard look at the proposal, fist to chin . . . and slowly agreed with a slow nod. My knees were shaking.

I took the sheep again. Now I held it to my face and rubbed it. I kissed it softly, and looked into its tiny black eyes. The price was not right.

"Two-fifty?" I said to Hand. "That's an insult."

I took the paper from Hand and wrote under it:

1800DH.

I handed it back to the salesman, at this point truly expecting him to throw up his hands and laugh. We were insisting on paying about $120 for a keychain priced at $3.

But the man didn't flinch. He was a titan. He touched a finger to his mouth, either gauging our sanity or pretending to mull our newest offer, and after a long perfect pause . . . again acquiesced. I was having probably the best time I could remember ever having.

But Hand turned to the man, shook his hand, said "Good," and paid him. It was over.

We left. The square was almost empty.

"How come you didn't keep going?" I asked. I was pissed. "We were just getting started."

We passed two men disassembling their food booth, dumping the ice back into a rolling cooler, packing their fish.

"How far do you really want to go with this?" Hand asked.

"Till the end."

"*Seri*ously."

"I am serious, fucker. That's what we're here for."

We stood. A small crowd near us roared about something. A monkey had done a trick.

"C'mon. Really. We've got about $14,000 left. Why not just get rid of $2,000 or $3,000 more and call it even?"

"That wasn't the original idea, Hand. Jesus. What about the staging ground? You remember? We were there, we had perfect control over that moment. We were creating art there—"

"Are you talking about that woman in Saly, the head lady?"

"Annette."

"She was insane. Staging ground? Fuck you. The problem with that idea is that you have to see these other people as—well, how do they figure in? How does that guy in the shop figure in? Is he part of it, or part of the scenery?"

I thought for a second.

"He's in the chorus," I said.

"Right. In the chorus."

A tall man strode by, face dark under a hood the color of bark. "*Hashish*," he whispered. Then "*Crystal*," and was gone.

"Listen," Hand said, "fuck the original idea. I could use that money."

"Why are you doing this now? You didn't say anything about this earlier."

"I just didn't think you were that serious. I figured you'd get your shit together at some point and we'd save the rest."

"You don't have a right to do this, especially now."

We stopped. We stood in the middle of the Djemaa el-Fna. There was a hotel on the far end of the square, and on a balcony a man seemed to be watching us.

"Maybe we should go home," Hand said.

He didn't mean it.

"I'm not going home," I said. "You can."

His hands were on his hips, his head hung.

"I just don't want to——" he started. "I just think this has something to do with everything else, and that's fine, but you're not telling me why, and then I have to be reminded constantly, because every time we give some away I think it means something to you——But even then I don't get it."

"There's no connection," I said.

Hand's head was slung to one side, defiant.

"There isn't," I said.

"Well why the fuck not?" he said.

"You want there to be some connection, but there isn't. We're here. We were in Senegal now we're here. Let's go."

"I'm not going," he said.

"Good," I said, "Jesus," and sat down. The ground was cold.

Now I didn't want to go. I wanted to make Hand cry. I couldn't make that fucker cry.

Hand stood, hands on his hips, watching the people leave the square. He sighed. He closed his eyes. He opened them after a moment, looking like he would say something——his eyes again had that unblinking and wild stare and I expected his jaw to start churning—but he closed his mouth and eyes again and now tilted his head so his ear met the roof. He whistled a few notes of nothing.

I leaned back until I was lying flat, staring up. The smoke from the grills striped the black starless sky. I couldn't see Hand, but his shadow dimmed my right eye's view. My body became heavier the longer I lay. I felt huge, sluggish, limitless in mass. It would take me hours to get up. I might never move again. I could become this landscape. I could fade into this pavement. I could watch as a mountain would watch, as a man on a balcony would watch, the people and their transactions, their hissed offers and threats, myself amused and without obligation. From a balcony, even twelve feet up, there was enough distance. There is movement below but it's not your movement.

My eyes were hot and full with water. The water ran down either side of my face, into my ears, cooling in the black air.

"Will."

"Oh fuck," I breathed.

He was standing near my shoes.

"Oh fuck oh fuck oh fuck."

"What? Will, talk."

"Oh fuck oh fuck oh fuck."

The tears made the smoke overhead into crystal, surging and bursting. I dragged the mucus back into my nose and closed my eyes and pushed the water there out, spreading it down over my bones and to the ground.

"Oh fuck oh fuck oh fuck."

Hand's shadow threw itself over me. He was sitting now, arms holding his knees.

"Holy shit," I said. "Holy shit holy shit."

I was hiccuping now. I could sense people walking by, slowing, walking on. I was the only person lying on the pavement of the Djemaa el-Fna.

"Slow down," Hand said.

My eyes hurt. The water was being pulled from me and the strain was incredible. My forehead was tight, a pressure above my nose. My throat jerked and coughed. I couldn't remember crying this way. It was pathetic.

"Fuck," I said.

"I know."

"Six months holy fuck."

Hand breathed out.

Six months meant it was in the past. We'd lived all these months since and we didn't know why. Had we decided to do it, had we decided that this was what we wanted, to wake up and work, as I'd been doing, in my pajama bottoms? Who had told me that I should, as I had just a month ago, spend a full week sitting in the SRO section of Wrigley, watching the maintenance men replace broken seats? That I should, as I had, bring Mo and Thor a half-dozen times to the lake in November and December, showing them where the boats would be if it were warmer, showing them the tall twin buildings that looked like flasks, running through the slush by the dead fountain, hoping my feet would freeze. I couldn't think of anything I'd done in six months that brought me anywhere new or proved in any way I'd been there, that I'd been taking air from the world and using it to any justifiable end.

We just hadn't decided yet, any of us. I know Jack's dad hadn't decided. We hadn't yet made a conscious decision about what we would and wouldn't do. We were standing and blinking and waiting to be told.

There was a tapping from within me, something tapping my breastplate from within. I was hyperventilating. Extra firings, a surge in the *Bundle of His*. A man stopped and said something to Hand in French. Hand stood and thanked the man and sat back down again.

"I knew what he'd look like when he was fifty."

Hand said nothing.

"You know he'd get fat," I said. "He'd look like his dad, bald and with that big fat ass. You know he was headed there. Fuck."

Hand said nothing. I could hear someone nearby dunking something in water, removing it and tapping the excess on something made of wood or plastic, a table or bucket.

"I was always serious about that valley," I said.

"I know you were."

When Jack had moved to D.C. and Hand was in St. Louis, I'd gotten the idea that even if we lived in different states for a while, eventually we'd buy land together, maybe near Phelps if Jack could telecommute, since he was the only one with a more permanent sort of job. We were very serious. Or I was serious, and the other two said *We'll see*, but you could tell they wanted it, too, especially if I did the work. Our kids could be playing with Uncle Jack's kids, Uncle Will's, Uncle—

We were planning some kind of less sinister name for Hand.

The land would be on the lake, but if not, a valley. A small valley, unpopulated, wooded, not too steep. We'd get a few acres each, and I was sure we could afford it, the land up near Phelps wasn't priced too bad, and I'd do the plans for each, and Hand and I would guide the construction and hire local crews, and Jack and Hand would help, and we'd get all three built in one summer.

We'd have a motherfucking shitload of dogs! Horses. Peacocks. Oh to live among peacocks. I'd seen them once in person and they defied so many laws of color and gravity that they had to be mad geniuses waiting to take over everything. Mudskippers, ocelots, tree sloths and hanumans—we'd have all the most ridiculous animals. And it made sense that we'd stay together, and have this valley, and it made sense that our kids would feel at home in any house, and know every inch of that valley, would roll down the sides in the fall when the leaves had fallen and were brittle and red. We'd hear their yelps from our third-story windows, where we were building skylights and painting old furniture new.

The smoke of the market cleared over us and a few weak stars were visible. They did nothing and meant nothing.

"It hit me about a month ago," Hand said.

A dog, rangy and shaking, was sniffing my feet.

"The permanence of it," he said. "I know you're supposed to know it's permanent, but then you're walking down the street—I was walking on a Sunday morning, past a church I think, everyone outside afterward, and I just stopped in the middle of the sidewalk and I said Holy shit. Holy shit." He hissed the words.

"I know." I was trying to slow down my breathing.

"There's the time right after," Hand said, "when you're shocked and putting on your suit, and borrowing the right shoes and putting gas in your car on the way to the fucking funeral, getting the gas on your hands, using the gas station bathroom to wash it off, worrying—You know how worried I was of showing up smelling of gasoline? At a funeral like that, with everyone thinking about cars and everything?"

"I know."

"But then there's these months, when you live half-thinking it'll be corrected. I had to renew the goddamned registration on my car a few weeks ago and I'm sitting there in the place and I started thinking that all I had to do was pay a fine on Jack. Like we were just overdue on payments on him and they'd towed him or something. I jumped a little in the line, because I was like, Fuck, I gotta go get the papers for Jack! Maybe they're in the car! I get these thoughts all the time. Did you keep answering-machine tapes?"

"I couldn't. Voice mail."

"Well I saved a tape with a long message from him. He was drunk and was calling, just describing going down to the Lincoln

Memorial with this woman he worked with. I guess there was some kind of youth chorus singing there at midnight, and he had this crazy night there, in the Lincoln Memorial, with some older woman he worked with."

"Who was it?"

"Older woman. She's separated. But I guess they went out to dinner and then drinks one night when her ex-husband or whatever was calling a lot. She didn't want to go home so she and Jack went out."

"He didn't tell me that."

"He did the whole story into my answering machine. I'll play it for you when we get back. They ended up at the Lincoln Memorial and there were about a hundred teenagers singing gospel songs. 'If I Could Just Touch the Hem of His Garment,' right there at the feet of Lincoln. Will, shit. Your chest is going crazy."

I tried to breathe in and slowly. A pair of sandals appeared beside my head and I was in the shadow of a man crouching.

"No, merci," Hand said.

The man's fingers were on my temples.

"No, no!" Hand said.

I shook my head free. The man stood and walked away.

—We're so weak, Hand. We haven't done anything.

—It's too soon.

—We haven't done anything.

"How does something like that happen?" I said. "I don't know."

"No one's ever heard of something like that happening. Jesus, has that ever happened before? No one said that was going to happen. That wasn't on the list of things that can happen, a truck just—"

"Wipe your nose again."

I was still on the ground, my legs folded under me like I'd fallen.

"You ever think of his last seconds?" he asked.

"I don't know," I said.

—I know his last seconds, Hand.

"It was quick, you know," Hand said.

"I know. We've talked about this—"

"If you have to have something like that happen, at least it wasn't drawn out—"

"Hand. It's not like that."

"It was."

"It's not. I know we said he was at peace and everything, but Jesus, I don't think of him that way. I don't at all. Everything I see is different."

"I know."

"I lost grandparents before, and an uncle, but with them I actually pictured rest for them. I think of them dead and I picture them lying down. In the grass, in long grass, deep green. Infinitely comfortable. But Jack—"

"I know."

"Jack I picture frozen under ice. He's still awake, and he's frozen there, under the ice. Somewhere else, fucking shocked under the ice, and he's there alone. He's always alone and that's the hardest thing about it. That's the fucking part that makes me murderous. That's why I want that trucker's head, because he's alone under the glass or ice or whatever. He's waiting."

"Listen. Just—I don't want that picture in my head, Will."

"It's not just that we won't do the valley, all that shit," I said, "it's that there's nothing like that anymore. It's just not possible, anything like that anymore—"

"Meaning what?"

"You think I want to be here? I don't want to be here. This fucking place is wrong, Hand."

"Where? Here? Marrakesh? How?"

"It's all wrong. You know it's wrong. Everyone knows it's

wrong. This fucking place! It's all wrong. We're all here and we're pretending it's not wrong because we're too fucking polite."

We were at the car. Hand had dragged me off the ground and now he rested his palms on the roof, and his chin on the backs of his hands, atop one another.

"I'll drive," he said.

"No, that's okay," I said.

"I want to. Just tell me for real that you want none of this money when we're done."

"None."

"Because I believe that you'd do it. If that's what you're proving—that you'd do it—then I believe you."

"Not the point."

"Fine."

"I'll drive," I said.

"No," Hand said. "I have another idea first."

In a few seconds Hand was in a cab. There was a long line of cabs waiting for straggling tourists, and Hand had gotten into one. I followed him in.

Hand directed the driver around the cul-de-sac and back to our car. The ride took about eleven seconds. We stopped.

"Here?" the cabbie said.

"Yes."

"Yes? Here?"

"Yes."

The cabbie laughed. We gave him an American fifty.

As my face dried and cooled and my breath evened, we did this three more times. He got in another cab immediately and had him drive us around the cul-de-sac and gave him $80 in dirham. It was great. Once we went around the square, once the length of three cars. Each time we paid them extravagantly, each time they took it knowing we knew what we were doing. The cabbies, in contrast to the merchant, knew what was what, knew that none of it really meant anything, or meant everything but in a way we wouldn't ever really understand. Each drove off grinning. Comrades!

The bike boys rode by again.

"Faggots," they said.

We agreed to go to the mountains. We took one more cab, about a block this time, to our car, and headed in the direction we'd last seen the mountains. Where were the mountains? They weren't visible from the city anymore; I drove us in the direction we thought them to be, past the buildings and the tall red walls separating the street from the compounds and castles and soon we were in a rural area, but we were lost.

It was midnight and we were lost in the wide flat land around the city. The air was cooling and the night was quiet. We drove back to the city, and soon found a cabbie, sitting on his yellow Mercedes hood in an alleyway, at a café's outdoor checkered table, next to a group of men playing dominos.

We proposed paying him to lead us, he in his car and we in ours, to the mountains. He was skeptical. Hand grabbed a wad of bills from his thigh pocket and waved it near his ear. Idiot. The man raised a finger to us, asking us to wait, as he walked back to his table, where he conferred with the three men, all heavy-set and moustachioed. They looked over to us, all at once and then one at a time, then stared down at their hands, as the man continued.

"What are they talking about?" I asked.

"Directions maybe," Hand said, sitting on our hood.

The men went on, their discussions more heated now, staccato bursts of whispers hissed. One man pointed to another, who pointed angrily back at him. The first went through a doorway behind them, an eye on us, and emerged a minute later with a different jacket on. He walked down a side alley, without looking back, while our cabbie approached us, nodded, and got in his car and we in ours. I looked at Hand and he at me, and we both understood that something seemed not right.

Marrakesh is full of tiny alleys no wider than an elephant's ass, and through those we drove, I drove, much too quickly. The walls were no more than six inches from the car. Our rims scraped twice against curbs, planters. It was like driving through the halls of an apartment building. Dozens of times I doubted we'd fit through this or that entranceway, that we'd get stuck like a truck in a tunnel too tight. We guessed and hoped and prayed for deliverance through the labyrinth, narrow and crumbling. Our car whined around the tightest of turns and squeezed through impossible corridors.

Residents stared from windows and doorways—did they? were those faces or?—and those on the street stepped out of our way. We didn't see any other cars, this fact making our passage easier but more unsettling. Were we supposed to be here at all? We were the only two vehicles active in this part of the city, at this time of night.

Through the alleys we sped and then under an arch and suddenly we bled into a large square, high-walled but open. It was a hundred yards left and right, and there—holy shit—was a soccer game going on and we were driving through the middle of it, fifteen young men yelling, thin and high-socked, right in front of us, after midnight. We were in the game. Our car was driving through their midfield, straight through, our car following his.

"Did you see that?" Hand asked.

I did.

"We just drove through a fucking soccer game."

"At one in the morning."

"You are Ronin."

"I am Ronin."

Through a maze of high red walled avenues, precisely as through a maze, and—hell, this went on for half an hour, all this, the alleys, the narrow black stone streets with the men pushing carts, the men sitting on stoops, our two cars buzzing by, no more than two feet from their toes. It was exhilarating though I expected at any moment to be stopped and the car taken and both of us throttled or examined or both—

And now there was a car behind us.

"You see that?" I asked.

"The guy behind us? Shit. Yes."

"Why would there be a car behind us?"

"No idea."

"How many guys inside? Don't look."

"Two."

"Who is it? Don't look."

Hand turned.

"One looks like the guy from the café."

"Which guy?"

"The guy with the jacket. The one who went in and—"

"Okay. Fuck!"

"This is bad."

—You fucking imbecile, Hand.

—I know. I know.

"They're definitely following us," he said.

They were. We were following one car and being followed by another. There were two men in the car behind us, and they were allowing about twelve feet between them and us. The car in front took half a dozen turns, and we took them with him, and the car behind followed. There was no mistake, no coincidence.

"Still there," Hand said.

"I know!"

"They're in it together," said Hand.

"Who?"

"All of them. They're taking us somewhere. To a dead end. We won't be able to back up."

"Shut the fuck up."

My stomach felt grabbed and compressed. I had a fleeting stupid sense of relief that our French resister hadn't decided to join us. Because the future now seemed set: at some point, in a narrow alley, the car in front of us would stop and the car behind would close in and we'd be trapped and killed and disappeared.

It had been many minutes now. Maybe twenty turns. The men behind, barely recognizable in the dark, made no gestures, gave no hints. This was business.

"I can't believe this is happening," Hand said.

"Maybe it's not happening."

"Of course it is. We're the only three cars in this whole city. You see any other traffic?"

It was true. These two cars were here for us.

Hand rolled up his windows and pushed the car's automatic door lock, the resulting sound a gun being cocked.

"Take a left somewhere. Get away," Hand said.

"I know, fucker," I said.

There was nowhere to turn. For all the choices we seemed to have, or the car ahead had, there were no choices at all. Every side street was a dead end.

"Wait till the last second and then—"

"Shut up, Hand."

He grunted, and then was sticking his lower jaw out, rotating it like he was trying to get it back into place. I'd never see him do that. "Are you going to do it? I think we—"

"Let me think!" I said.

"Fuck it, man."

"No, fuck *you*! You're the stupid fuck who waved all the money in front of the guy."

This registered with Hand. He had no answer.

"I didn't say fuck *you*, I said fuck *it*."

"Well fuck yourself anyway," I said.

My hands gripped and regripped the wheel. My knuckles were not white, but red. I checked the mirror; they were there. I couldn't decide it if it would be easier or harder to die with your closest friend. I wanted to die first, that much I knew—

There were other men on the street, walking in pairs and alone. Some pushing carts. I worried about running over their feet—we were that close. We passed a crack of an alley, oozing with mustard light, where two men were embracing, with others watching, twenty men, at least—

No, it was a fight. One with a knife to the other's throat—

"You see that?" I asked.

"Fuck yeah I saw it."

Everything was wrong all at once.

"Just keep going."

The car behind hadn't let up. There was no way to even slow down without them hitting us. But where were we being taken? The street opened up. Then narrowed again. I couldn't deal anymore. My heart was humming, shaking. I almost wanted to stop, give it up. I began wondering if I was ready.

"Fuck," Hand said. "I can't believe this. You know what, though—I have to say, this is a pretty glamorous way to die. I mean—But will they shoot us or what?"

"Shut the fuck up."

"I swear I'll take one of them with me. What do they want? Our money, or the car? Both, I guess. Fuck!"

"Maybe we should turn off."

"We'd be dead if Jack was driving."

"That's nice."

Maybe I was ready to go.

I was so tired.

Maybe I wanted to be crushed, too. To be ready you need to be tired, and you need to have seen a great deal, or what you consider to have been a great deal—we all have such different capacities, are able to absorb and sustain vastly different quantities of visions and pain—and at that moment I started thinking that I *had* seen enough, that in general I'd had my fill and that in terms of visual stimulation the week thus far had shown me enough and that I was sated. The rock-running in Senegal was enough, the kids and their bonjours—that alone would prepare me for the end; if I couldn't be thankful enough having been there I was sick and ungrateful, and I would not be ungrateful, not ever, I would always know the gifts given me, I would count them and keep them safe! I had had so much so I would be able to face the knife in the alley and accept it all, smiling serenely, thankful that I'd be taken while riding the very crest of everything. I had been on a plane! A tiny percentage of all those who'd ever lived would ever be on an airplane—and had seen Africa rushing at me like something alive and furious. I could be taken and eaten by these wet alleyways without protest.

The car behind seemed ready to ram us. It was so close we could hear its engine roaring over ours.

Suddenly Hand was yelling, almost crying.

"I *hate* this. [Hitting side window] I *hate* this! I feel closed in! I *hate* having no options!"

The turns were increasing.

—Jack I need—

—

"I hate being followed like this! I fucking hate it." Hand was hitting the dash now.

"Easy," I said.

"Fuck you, easy!"

—Jack.

—

"We could stop and get out and just run for it," I said.

Hand mulled this.

"Okay," he said, calming. "That's an option. I like that. We could always just bang on the door to some house and get help."

"Right."

"How close are they now?"

"Still right behind us." I looked into their faces, both with mustaches, both expressionless. I turned quickly back. This was very real. This was our lives, the whole of our relatively straight-forward lives, concluding savagely on this bizarre note, someone splicing onto our happy safe Wisconsin lives the wrong, bloody ending. This is Hand's fault. *How?* I don't know. *You'll fight together.* We'll be led into some pitch-black alley, some warehouse. We'll be stripped, robbed, beaten, flayed—*You will disappear. You're not afraid.* I know. Why? *You used to fear death so tangibly. When you were Robotman you would wait till dawn to ensure no one took you while you were asleep. You cried during the astronomy unit when Mr. Geoghan talked about how brief our lives were comparatively, how brief was all mankind.* I know. I couldn't hear it. When they talked about the imminent death of our sun, I lost it. *And remember what he said, the first day of class?* I do.

"Will."

He said: "The only infallible truth of our lives is that everything we love in life will be taken from us." He had just lost his wife. *That was it.* It was. He had lost his wife and came to class each day in a sweatsuit, royal blue with white stripes. He was a marathoner.

"Will."

I remember. I remember it being somehow soothing.

"Will, motherfucker."

"What? What?"

We had to slow past a group of men, and one pounded the car.

"I hate this shit! The not knowing! Why the fuck are they banging?"

There were a lot of butchers for some reason, men in white bloody aprons, pushing tin carts, knives and cleavers hanging from the cart's handle.

"This just makes no sense," Hand said.

"I know."

"The fact that we're not already dead is the most totally illogical thing. We should have been dead by now."

"If there was any sense to anything, we wouldn't be here at all. We have to just wait."

Hand snorted.

"I'm not here to wait," he said. "Where are they now?"

"You look."

Hand turned around.

"They're gone!"

"What?" I looked in his rearview mirror. "Holy shit." I looked again. "They're gone. That is amazing. Why are they gone?"

We were out of the narrow road, the walls spread; we were again on the open road, the sky open and proud.

"I really thought we were in trouble there," Hand said.

"You know, I actually think we were."

Seconds later the cabbie stopped his car. We pulled up to him. I was still jittery, half-expecting some kind of ambush. He didn't get out. He just pointed up, with his whole arm, like semaphore—*this road*, he indicated, *all the way*.

Hand paid him $100, even while we wondered if he'd intended to kill or rob us moments before. We drove a mile in silence and finally stopped on the shoulder. I rested my head on the side window. The car wheezed. I turned it off.

"Sorry," I said. "I thought—"

He stared out for a minute.

"Forget it," he said.

"You still want to go?"

"We should. I'll drive."

We got out and the air was cold and the hood hummed. We switched seats and Hand drove. Toward the mountain another ten minutes. No people anywhere, no movement.

"What did you think would happen?" Hand asked.

"I thought we'd watch each other die," I said.

The air was cooling more. The road inclined.

"I'd want to die first," he said.

"Let's not do this," I said. I must have killed those men a hundred times in those minutes. "I'm worn out."

We went on, in a few minutes stopping for gas at a brilliantly lighted station staffed by a huge blue-overalled black man—the first and only black man we'd seen or would see in Morocco—and with his mustache he very much looked like a walrus, a walrus wearing a blue jumpsuit. I went in to use the restroom and inside were three men watching TV. One said something as I left.

"What'd he say?" Hand asked.

"I heard the words 'America' and 'whore.' I think. Add a predicate and I think he insulted us."

"This is just a weird thing, this night."

"You still want to go?"

"We should."

So we went up the mountain.

We switched seats, Hand driving now, but this wasn't the poor part of town. We kept thinking it would get poor but instead the road—as much as we could see in the unlighted road—was lined for twenty miles with perfect trees planted neatly, and high walls just beyond, left and right. Gated compound after gated compound, a few clearly marked as resorts, and dozens more that were either immense private homes or military bases or huge hidden dens of intrigue—sex camps or subversive training centers or fantastic new labs where humans were being made from stem cells and extractions from ice-age holdovers. It wasn't clear to us, none of it, while speeding past, on the other side of their high and endless walls.

Then we were climbing, the road was and we with it, our path winding and without guardrails. We knew we were in the mountains when the air went cold and when our headlights illuminated the tops of trees, their brittle leaves peaking from below road level, grey photographs of branches in our passing flashes.

In the quiet dark hollow of our car, Hand was talking about the origin of AIDS, something about a truck route in Zaire. It all started with truckers, he said. The truck drivers were delivering some kind of cloth, terry cloth, he thought, up and down Zaire, and were stopping in brothels, as truckers do, thus facilitating the spread of the virus. We found ourselves over a bridge and knew we were very high above whatever we were crossing—water or dry chasm, we'd never know.

At the other side of the bridge, at one in the morning in these frozen black mountains we came upon two men in uniform, thumbs outstretched, hitchhiking. Their uniforms, different but familial, looked like military.

"Should we?" I asked.

"Man, I don't know. We've had too much tonight."

We passed them full of conflict and shame and drove up around six or seven more bends, the air getting so cool the car's windows seemed to stiffen and the sky tightened and shrank. But we saw no one. There were no shanties, no tents or tiny crumbling adobe homes. There was no one up here. There was no one living here at all, really—no one, at least, visible in the black taut overnight— no weak fires warming peasants, no clotheslines strung between hovels.

We parked on the shoulder and got out. It was twenty degrees colder up here, maybe forty degrees, and we had no jackets. With fifteen feet between us, we could barely see each other. Hand stood, fists in his pants, warming them. I stood, fingers entwined and resting on my head. We had no idea why we were here. There was no moon, no stars.

"We could drive over the side," Hand said.

"I thought of that," I said.

"If we picked the right place," he said, "the worst that would happen is we'd wreck the car."

"I know."

"It would be something to do. We'd run down a ways, hit a tree, get out, maybe meet up with those military guys and hitch back with them."

We stood for a minute and I noted that there was no sound. There were no animals, no people, not even wind pushing through trees. We stood on the mountain, what we figured might be the top of the mountain, and for a second I thought I heard water, but then didn't. There was nothing. We got back in the car.

We turned around and descended and drove quickly, back over the bridge high over the river canyon, past the military men again, still standing where we'd passed them, on the cusp of the bridge, and we rolled down and down and they stayed there and we didn't know how they could stand the cold.

In fifteen minutes we reached level ground again and were blowing through a flat road lined with trees straight perfectly spaced.

"There's a guy," said Hand.

I slowed down.

"Where?"

"Back there, a guy walking with a huge staff in his hand."

I backed up for a few hundred yards until I could see him. A man in the snug wool clothes of someone who lives outdoors and hikes constantly—completely self-sufficient, but carrying next to nothing. His backpack, leather, was small, mall-girl decorative. We stopped. The man stopped.

Hand got out, carrying about $500 in Moroccan cash. He approached the man and asked directions to Marrakesh. The man looked at Hand like he was mad, or an apparition. There was only one road to Marrakesh from whence we came, and we were on it; we were obviously heading straight for Marrakesh. Hand did the thing where he pointed down the road, as if to say, *If I understand you right—and I think I do—we just follow this road and we'll hit Marrakesh, like you say.* The man nodded again and made a javelin of his arm, aiming it toward Marrakesh.

Hand pulled out the bills. For some reason—the dark?—he held them up in front of the man's face, as if the man had never seen money before, or was far-sighted. The man refused the bills and tried to walk away. Hand stepped in front of him and insisted. The man took the wad like he'd been asked to carry someone's trash. Then he continued walking.

Hand jogged back to the warm car.

"That seemed weird," I said.

"Yeah, he didn't even count it or anything. He just put it in his pocket and kept walking."

"He'll use it."

"I don't know. I don't think he'll keep it. He seems like the kind of guy who'd give it to someone else. He was like someone out of Middle Earth—a man and his staff, walking through the countryside in the middle of the night."

I thought of the man's brain, of the uninterrupted hours of time inside his head, without distraction, without dialogue.

—I don't know how you do it, sir.

—Will, you had this peace of mind and you might again.

—That much I know is not true.

"We're almost back," I said. "What time is it?"

It was a little after two. We'd started the day in Casablanca sixteen hours before and we'd almost died—we were almost butchered in the alleys of Marrakesh—or possibly not. But it felt so real. It was the closest I'd ever come to feeling so near to the end. No seizure or flurry or fainting had come so near.

We were parked now, in town, on the main strip. The road was wide and stray cars sped past with groans and whinnies and shushes. Hand's head was resting on the side window, and he was looking up at the moon.

"Is that full or almost full?"

"Almost full."

I was ready for sleep. It was 2:30. We drove toward the hotel and stopped at a light; the hotel's vertical sign, neon, was visible two intersections ahead.

A car pulled alongside us. Four people in their midtwenties, three women and a man, were crowded into a silver compact. The light went green and we drove. At the next light they stopped next to us, on the left of our car. The woman in the passenger seat leaned out, urging Hand to roll down his window. He did.

"Bonjour," she said. She was Moroccan, magnificent. Next to skin like that, ours seemed so rough, like burlap woven with straw.

"Bonjour," Hand said.

"You're English," she said.

"American."

"Oh! Good. Where are you going?" Her English was seamless. Everyone's was. I had sixty words of Spanish and Hand had maybe twice that in French, and that was it. How had this happened? Everyone in the world knew more than us, about everything, and this I hated then found hugely comforting.

The eight eyes in their car were watching, faces close to the windows. It was a small car. The light turned green. No one moved.

"Home," Hand said. "We just came from the mountains."

"The mountains? Why?"

We were talking in the middle of the road.

"Long story," Hand said.

"What?"

"Never mind."

The light was red again.

"So what are you doing now?"

"I dunno. What are you doing?"

"You should come out!"

"What? Where? Where are you going?" Hand was leaning out now, arms draped out the window. I think my mouth was wide open. This was unbelievable.

The woman ducked her head back into the car. Inside there was a quick and animated debate. She re-emerged.

"Club Millennium," she said.

Hand turned to me. I had a surge. It felt good. We told them we'd follow. We knew we had to. We'd been up for twenty hours maybe but it felt so good to say yes. Where had they come from? In all my life I'd never been approached this way, the car pulling up, the *Where you going?* It was something I wish had happened hundreds of times. I was a looker—someone who looked over at every car at every traffic light, hoping something would happen, and almost never finding anyone looking back—always everyone looking forward, and every time I felt stupid. *Why should people look over at you? Why would they care?*

But these people do. They threw out a line and I felt like I was living a third or fourth life, someone else's life. It felt like regaining, in the morning while slowly waking, the ability to make a fist. I'd been so close and ready for the end—closer and more ready than

I'd ever been before—and now I wanted this, all this, I wanted everything that would happen:

We would meet them there, and get out, and would be happy to be out of the car.

We would be ashamed of our clothes, of our Walgreen's sweat-shirts, of our strong personal smells.

We would pay for everyone, $100 in cover charges, while knowing—really being electrically conscious of the fact—that that money could perhaps be better spent.

We would walk down a slow dark burgundy flight of stairs, everything rounded—the inside of an aorta—and at the bottom, get assaulted by a flood of mirrors, glass, chrome.

The place would still be busy, the clientele half Moroccan and half European, all of a powerful but lightly worn sort of wealth, the place dripping with what I guessed—I'd never seen it in person—to be decadence.

While I would wait for the drinks everyone, all five of them including Hand, would bound off to the dance floor, holding hands, like a string of kids connected, cut from folded construction paper.

I would want to dance. I would be too sober, and would be watching the purses. I would sink into the booth, grinning for them, soul scraping me from inside.

I would note that I was often too sober, watching the purses.

When they would rest, I would try to talk to the Moroccans, but the music would overwhelm us, like talking through wind and rain. Two of the women would be in law school, wanting to be judges.

I would try to explain how we had been in the mountains, look-ing for people to give money to—and where are your poor, by the way? Why none in the mountains?—but they wouldn't hear me, or would maybe just pretend at incoherence.

Hand would dance with one of them, in silver snakeskin pants and radiant in shape, while the other three would leave, smiling and shrugging at me, as I worked on a fifth vodka-soda.

Hand would do the shopping cart.

Hand would do the sprinkler.

Hand would do the worm. Hand could do the worm.

I would know that in any city, at an hour like this, there are people sleeping. That most people are sleeping. But that in any city, in any cluster of people, there are a few people who are awake at this hour, who are both awake and dancing, and it's here that we need to be. That if we are living as we were this week, that we had to be awake with the people who were still dancing.

Even if I couldn't loosen my head enough to dance myself.

After an hour we would find ourselves in a booth with half a dozen Germans—four men, three women, all in their midthirties, on a company retreat, we would learn. "We are here to reep it up!" one would say, then snuff a lit match with her tongue.

Hand would look over at me.

"You okay?" he would say.

"I'm good," I would say.

"You look better," he would say.

And I would know I was different for a while. We had beaten death yet again and we were now beating sleep and it would seem like we could do without either forever. And I then would have the idea, seeming gloriously true for a flickering moment, that we all should have a near-death experience weekly, twice weekly—how much we'd get done! The clarity we'd know!

"I want to keep going," Hand said. It was four o'clock, and we'd left, dropped off the last two women we'd danced with, at their home, a condo complex looking like grad-student housing. He was driving, and had stopped the car a block away.

"No," I said. "Where?"

"Fez. It's only four hours. Less maybe."

"We can't. We fly tomorrow. Later today."

"I know. Still."

I had come crashing down. My eyes hurt.

"Let's sleep," I said, letting us both down.

"Sleep is boring. We go to Fez and come back in time."

He was right but I couldn't let him know this. I could barely talk I was so wrecked. "We have to sleep," I whispered.

"You don't know that. Not for sure."

"I do. Right now I do. I can't even see."

"We could keep doing this. Stretch it out. We still have $10,000. That would last us a month maybe, at least. Two."

The car was clouding with our words.

"That girl tonight, the first one—she was the most ridiculous woman I've ever been that close to."

"I want to stay so badly."

"You just said you wanted to move."

"I do. Maybe we go to Siberia but come back."

"We'll never come back," I said.

We found a parking spot in front of the hotel.

"I know," he said.

"You see the rest of the world, then you come back."

"I know. Okay."

We slept.

SUNDAY

We woke at ten and went to the airport to see what they had. We knew there were flights to Paris and London. In the airline office, the manager spotted us and he opened his arms. "Where will it be today, friends? Mozambique? China?"

We laughed. Funny man.

"Wait," said Hand. "What flight to Mozambique? When?"

The man flinched, like we'd had taken a swing at him.

"No, friend," no longer meaning the word, "we don't go to Mozambique."

A plane to London left at three o'clock; another, to Paris, at six. We wanted to speak English again. "We want that flight to London," I said. We knew now that to get anywhere north and cold we'd have to first hit a hub. At Heathrow we'd figure out where to go.

"This time you'll wait for the plane?" the man asked us.

"We'll stay here."

Hand got us sodas and we sat. The airport soon filled with white people, tanned, most with golf clubs. Where had they come from? We hadn't seen any of these people in town, in the mountains, at the disco. We hadn't even seen a golf course. *We* hadn't gotten tan. Who were these people, all of them young couples, a few fabulous ones, tall thin-haired blondes with toned men in perfectly pressed jeans—neither fearing the loss of the other.

There were two hours, 120 minutes, before the flight left. We still had about $400 in Moroccan bills.

"We have to leave," I said. "We can't fly with this."

"We told them we wouldn't leave."

We left.

We drove to the resort walls. Not far from the airport was a string of hotels, with long driveways and gates of iron, and we sped to one, called Temptation, and parked across the road from its grand pink-flowered entrance. The resort was walled in on all sides, parapets of twelve fuschia feet, and just beyond the walls, on the right side, a small shanty community stood, in the shadow of the barriers and the small overhead trees.

"You go," I said.

"How much?"

I gave him what I had, saving a few sample bills for Mo and Thor. Hand approached the closest structure, a yellow box of wood and sheetrock, big enough for two people, no bigger than a large camping tent. He was—moron—still carrying his soda. His sunglasses, mended with eight adhesive postage stamps, were atop his skull, staring at the sun. He peeked around the doorway. A woman stepped out, wiping her hands on something like a dishrag, red and heavy with water.

Hand waved. She nodded to him and looked immediately to me. I waved. She nodded again, this time to me.

His left hand holding his soda, Hand dug into his right pocket to retrieve the bills. The woman looked at me again. I smiled apologetically, but with an expression that said *Just you wait.*

Something was stuck. Now Hand was reaching to the pocket with two hands. He'd wedged the soda between his arm and torso, and when he finally pulled the bills free, the soda jumped and spilled, in a small geyser of brown liquid, a foot upward and three feet down, onto the woman's legs and bare feet.

I turned around. I couldn't watch. I walked a few steps toward the car, wanting nothing to do with Hand. What kind of person brings his soda? You're giving $300 to people in a shack and you bring your soda? Nothing we did ever resembled in any way what we'd envisioned. Maybe we couldn't help but make a mess everywhere we went—

I had to see what was happening. I turned around again. Now Hand was on his knees. The woman was holding the money but Hand was using the woman's dishrag on her legs and feet. He was dabbing and wiping, quickly but gently, and she was watching him, astounded and unmoving. He stroked the rag down her left calf, washed her right knee, rubbed her right dusty foot and then her left. Then he did it all again. It was unwatchable.

She touched his head, asking him to stop, to stand, and after giving her legs one more good look, he stood.

* * *

Hand's garage, with fresh shingles still the color of stripped pine, was sturdy but not too high. My own was low enough but full of holes; Tommy and his friends, years before, had tried to build an addition, on the roof, with plywood and tar paper, and things had gone south when they realized the beams had termites and couldn't hold even their own weight. Hand's garage, though, was strong and sloped downward and it was his we'd planned to jump from. The idea was simple, and was logical for three boys who wanted to be stuntmen: we had to jump from a garage roof to a moving truck below.

We were thirteen and Hand's dad had a blue pickup he backed into the garage every night because he liked the rush—he called it a rush; it was the first time I'd heard the word used that way—of being in the truck, facing forward, receiving the sun, when the garage door rose and he could bolt out onto the highway without looking back. He was a strange man but his enthusiasms had come down through Hand, obvious and undiminished.

One morning before school Hand, Jack and I waited. We'd put blankets in the truck bed the night before, dark ones to match the truck's blue, cobalt and metallic, so Hand's dad wouldn't notice in the dim garage light. We were ready but Jack didn't want to jump. He wanted to watch us jump. He'd planned to be a stuntman, too—he claimed he did when we asked him; we'd asked him pointedly, to make sure, after he declined to try out our homemade grappling hooks and roused suspicion—but though his commitment seemed real enough, he didn't want to do this jump.

"Pussy," we said.

"Fine," he said.

But he didn't see the point. Why not wait till we're older, when we'll get trained by actual *certified stuntmen*? What? we asked. He thought he was making sense but we were stunned. Certified? Stuntmen? We argued him into submission. We wouldn't get that chance, we insisted, we wouldn't get the chance to even *try out* to be stuntmen, unless we could prove we had what it takes. Fine, he said, and promised to jump when we jumped.

The garage door rumbled open below us, and we saw the roof of the pickup slowly emerge and collect the light of the rising sun, still cool and blue. We hadn't prepared the timing. We hadn't prepared a signal and hadn't planned to count—

Jack jumped. We watched his back descend toward the steel of the truck, watched him land on his feet, then tumble forward onto hands and knees, then roll onto his back. The truck wasn't moving. Hand's dad had stopped immediately—120 pounds had landed in his bed—and was opening the door as Jack, on his back, on the blankets we'd laid down, looked up and saw us both, mouths agape, still on the roof. He didn't seem surprised.

Dear Mo, Dear Thor,

We've been in Morocco for two days, I think, and I just want to plant the idea in your head now: You know nothing until you're there. Nothing. Nothing nothing nothing. You know nothing of another person, nothing of another place. Nothing nothing nothing. With this knowledge—that you know nothing but what you see—things get more complicated. People want it easy, so they guess. And guessing is when the shi

"Can we go now? We should go."

"Hold on," I said. I was determined to get this postcard out. We were parked near the airport.

"Did you just say shit in a postcard? You can't do that. They'll confiscate it."

"Who?"

"The censors! Moroccans won't put up with that. Who's it to?"

"The—Forget it."

I folded the postcard in half and started another one.

Mo. Thor.

I'm writing to you just before Hand (you remember him. At the batting cages, he threw the ball that hit Mo in the stomach) will jump from a moving car (ours) to a moving horse-drawn cart. Wait until you're older to try

*something like this—a lot older, I think—but then don't wait much
longer. I can't believe we waited so long ourselves. This will be great. I'll
finish the postcard when we're done.*

Today we would do it.

"Okay," he said.

Hand would jump from our rental car to the back of the cart,
while we were moving, and then give the driver the money we had
remaining. We would pull our car alongside, doing maybe 15
mph, and Hand would jump from his window onto the cart, a big
enough target, as big as the bed of a large pickup truck. Easy.

"Maybe too easy," Hand said.

We drove up and down the airport road seven times, trying to
time it with a series of different carts. Here's one:

They were all perfectly shaped and traveling slowly enough,
but every time we were close, something went awry. A cop behind
us or coming from the opposite way; a man on a scooter pulling up
and asking if we needed directions; another man on a scooter offering hashish. Kids on bikes looking too curious. The road was too
crowded. Where were they all going? They were like extras, paid
to drive to and fro—

Hand was sitting on the door, his torso out the window.

"This won't work," he said, ducking his head into the car.

He got back inside. I asked why it wouldn't work.

"Torque," he said.

I pulled over. I stared forward. I wasn't going to ask him what torque had to do with jumping on a horse-drawn cart.

"Let's switch," I said.

"You can't do it. You can barely walk."

"Let's go. I'll do it."

—I have to follow through, Hand.

—We've already followed through.

—We have to follow through every time.

Hand drove and I sat on the doorframe and we turned around to catch up with a man in a cart. We found one near the entrance to the airport. This would work; I'd jump, give him the money, then jump off, onto the road, and we'd fly off to Moscow.

We pulled alongside the same cart. Was it the same cart? It was. Hand slowed the car to match the cart's speed, about 12 mph. The man, at first not paying us any mind, suddenly turned his head and watched us, confused, concerned. We were looking at each other, he and I. I was trying to see a way that I could get myself onto his cart and he seemed to know this. I looked at the back of his cart, and then at him, and at his donkey, then back at him. He didn't want me jumping on his cart. With a *Hah!* directed to his donkey, he sped up his cart.

This was stupid. *This would be great if you made it work.* Stupid. *Completely spectacular!* I set one foot on the armrest on the inside of the door. With my right hand I grabbed a ridge between the door and the car roof. It was only three or four feet to the cart. *This is an easy one.* Shut the fuck up. *A breeze.*

"Get back in here, idiot," Hand said.

"This is easy," I said, though too quietly for him to hear.

"We'll get arrested," Hand yelled.

My foot was on the doorframe and I jumped. The cart came at me and I could see the grain of the wood of the side panels. I could see the asparagus, or whatever it was. The shoulder and elbow of the man. Then a gap in his cargo, a gap where I would land, grey wooden planks. I felt them, my hands smacked against them, my chest, but my legs were below. My chin hit the wood and then I saw the quick swirl of sky then wailed backward and my back struck the pavement and I saw the sun and was still.

I'd missed. Or I had hit it, but hadn't jumped far enough. I didn't have enough thrust. *Torque*. It's not torque. *It could be torque.* My spine was a tunnel and there was crushed glass shooting through. I could see the underside of the cart and the legs of the donkey. The donkey's legs were patchy with stiff steel-blue hair, resembling a threadbare stuffed toy. The light down here was forgiving and soft. It was cool in the shadow of the cart, a perfect temperature. I had the immediate sensation of comfort and contentment. The cart's dark undercarriage reminded me of a barn.

"Speak!" It was Hand. "Speak, dumbshit."

"What?" I mumbled.

The cart driver was now bent over me, too. These two faces. They were so different. The cart driver's face was crooked. His jaw jutted to the right. His teeth were headed in so many directions.

The pain in my spine began to know parameters. Soon it would dull again. I sat up.

"That looked fucking awful," Hand said.

The man next to him, crouched down now, said nothing. He looked at me like I was a neighborhood child who no one understood but had to be dealt with daily, the kid who chased cats and spied on elderly women.

"Does it hurt somewhere in particular?" Hand asked.

I got my legs under me and stood. The man was short and now looked up to me. I closed my eyes and stumbled a few steps to my left. I was losing equilibrium. Was I? I didn't know. The damage at this point could be anywhere. Nothing would surprise me.

"You want to get in or stay here?" Hand said. "You fell like a bag of sand."

"Sorry," I said. My lungs hurt. "I thought that was a sure thing." I noticed that the donkey was watching me, too. Of the driver, Hand and himself, he seemed to be the most sympathetic.

Hand and I stood, he waiting for me to walk or fall, me waiting for a sign. The man from the cart started toward his donkey.

"Wait," said Hand. Then to me: "We might as well."

I got the bills from my sock and gave them to Hand, who delivered them to the man. The man shook his head, bewildered, but took the money. He climbed back onto his cart and urged his donkey on, before we could change our minds. My back was raw, dented by a hundred pieces of gravel. We got back in the car.

"We should stay and see a doctor," Hand said.

"In Morocco? No."

"You look around this city? There's money here. They must be good."

"Let's make the flight."

Hand sighed and started the car.

"I don't want this on me," he said.

"You won't. I'm good."

"You're a fucking wreck."

We returned the car and and saw the currency exchange bastard, who refused my right to change my signature, who threw himself in our path. We changed the money we needed to change—the fucker did so without incident, and we walked away, walked backwards, glaring, shaking our fingers silently. I was done with the man. Hand was not. When I was at the door, Hand strode quickly back to his window.

"You are bad man!" he yelled.

The man watched Hand, unmoved.

"We are here giving your people money and you try to stop us! You are the wall! Everywhere there are people like you! People who get in the way. You are a constipation! A constipation!"

Everyone was staring.

"You see what you do to my friend?" He was pointing at me. "You make him fall off cart! All is your fault! All in world is fault of people like you!"

The man registered no emotion whatsoever. This sent Hand over the edge.

"You know what they do to you in Bible? They throw you out! You are lost in the flood of Noah! You are cast out of the temple! Cast out! You read the Bible, rude man? Do you?"

I was grabbing him now. I yanked his shirt from behind and he turned to walk with me.

"Cast out of the Bible!" he yelled one more time, as we left the room and stepped out into the light.

The in-flight magazine offered an article about a man who was building a single-person commuter plane.

"Holy crap," I said to Hand. "You see this?"

"I'm reading it at the same time." He had his own copy.

The plane would be small, affordable and able to take anyone anywhere. A plane for one person, fit to travel to any destination in the world, more or less—some details needed sorting. It seemed to be the solution to really every problem there was, especially mine. There would be no real restrictions, and no one to wait for, no one on whom to rely. I thought I might swoon. The only issue was the timeline. The inventor had been working on the plane for about twenty years and now he had a prototype—it was ravishing; they had a picture and everything—but, they said, it would likely be twenty years longer, best-case scenario, before the planes would be available to civilians, another ten years before they'd be the least bit common. I'd be in my late forties or more likely dead. And the plane, like any perfect idea, any perfect idea dreamed and built by one person acting alone, had its legion of doubters. Why, they wondered, would someone design a perfect machine that could travel anywhere to anywhere, but build it to accommodate only one?

Hand put his magazine down.

"You were like a flying squirrel," he said, turned to me. "I wish you could have seen it. Your hands were out and everything. And your shirt sort of caught some wind—it was cool there for a second, it looked like you had that extra flesh or whatever, like a sail. But then you didn't get a grip on the cart. You just kind of hit it and bounced off."

At Heathrow we made straight for the information desk. A middle-aged woman, with curly iron-colored hair and the happy tired face of a third-grade teacher in her last year, asked if she could help us and we said she could. We needed, we said, to know if there were any flights leaving within the next two hours to countries in Eastern Europe where no visa was required for entry.

She didn't even laugh. Let's see, she said, finding under the counter a huge book, a kind of phonebook, full of comprehensive visa information for the world's nation-states. We grinned at the woman, at each other. This woman, she was something. I thought of gifts we could send her once we'd gotten home. We were happy to be in London among these people, in this airy and sparkling air-port full of exotic space-age persons in well-cut and thoughtful and understated clothes, walking purposefully, striding even, confident in their futures, sure of their loves.

Belarus required a visa. Kazakhstan needed a visa. There was a flight to Moscow but a visa would take two days minimum, the woman guessed, chewing the inside of her mouth. Why Eastern Europe? she asked. We didn't know. We wanted to be cold. For a day or two, Hand added. "A day or two," she repeated, looking down through her small glasses and onto the flipping grey pages of her phonebook of nations.

"Estonia?" she said. "They don't require a visa."

Hand slapped the counter. I feared he would whoop. "Estonia!" Wait.

"So is there a flight to Estonia?" I asked.

She checked her monitor. There was. In two hours, to Tallinn, via Helsinki, on FinnAir. The woman had all the information in the world.

"Can we take you with us?" Hand asked. She giggled and touched his hand. We said goodbye and soon we also loved the woman at the money exchange desk, who cashed my traveler's checks, my name written—*swoop!*—another twelve times—*mine mine mine mine mine mine mine mine mine mine mine mine!*—and though she had no Estonian currency, she gave us British pounds and German marks, both of which were accepted in Tallinn, and which she counted and recounted, this young freckled woman, a face wide like a sail full of wind.

I bought a book about Estonia and Latvia and mints and gum and batteries from a tall Pakistani—I think Pakistani but know I shouldn't guess—clerk who smiled for no reason weirdly at Hand and we ate dinner at an Irish diner staffed internationally—Dutch waitress, Swedish busboy, Korean bartender (we asked them all)—and while two were rude to us we didn't mind because the book said Estonia was full of natural wonders and that Tallinn was a gleaming jewel in Eastern Europe—

"It says it's like a suburb of Helsinki," Hand said.

"So it's not poor?"

"No. Says here everyone has cellphones."

"Shit," I said. "We'll have to leave the city then. We'll leave and find some people."

"Huh," Hand said, scratching his ribs, still reading, "I'd thought it would be like Sarajevo or something, full of crumbling walls and bulletholes."

The plane was all white blond businessmen under forty—a Scandinavian young entrepreneurs' club. We sat at the back and read British tabloids, their pages bloodthirsty, bewildered, pious and drooling. The flight attendant needed help getting a mini-vacuum out of the overhead above us. Hand obliged, and we had free wine the whole way there.

We toasted each other repeatedly and at midnight we were drunk in the bone-quiet empty and dirtless Helsinki airport, wandering through the long-closed brushed-steel shops while airport employees were gliding past—"Jesus Christ," "You're kidding"— on folding silver-gleaming push-scooters. Then forty minutes in the air to Tallinn and through customs and blasted by the frigid angry glass air and into a cab where the driver, with his neat hair and heavy jowls, looked like the guy who ran our community pool back home. That man, Mr. Einhorn, had exposed himself, they said, not to the kids but to their grandmothers, one of whom finally objected. Our cabbie spoke English cheerfully and took us to the only place where people would still be awake.

It was one in the morning and the night's black was flat. We were close to the Arctic Circle but we couldn't see a thing. Were we close to the Arctic Circle? I thought so. The air was mixed with night, the air sucking your breath from you. The landscape was soaked in a grey-black wash from which streetlights stared with a dull intensity. I pretended briefly we were on the moon, and the homes were labs for surveyors. Estonia could be the moon, I decided—it was one of ten or twelve countries I'd never remotely planned to see, had never heard of anyone seeing, but which now seemed to contain everything we wanted—

"I always felt like Estonia would be the coolest of the Baltics," said Hand.

"What?" I said.

Hand leaned forward and spoke loudly to the driver. "I always am thinking Estonia is the most great of the Baltic nations!"

"Thank you," said the driver, turning to examine Hand. "You are from the United States?"

"Morocco," Hand said.

"No!" the driver said, again turning to look at Hand.

"Today we come from Morocco!" Hand continued, "tomorrow we come from Estonia!"

They both laughed. Where did he get this shit?

What we saw of Tallinn was ancient and dark, but we saw very little on the way. We arrived at the Hotel Metropol and dropped our bags in the simple clean room and then fell back down to the bar, which acted also or primarily as a casino, everything burgundy and bright Kentucky green, with all of the tables, maybe seven of them and one in the back, occupied. We drank burnt umber beer at the bar, Hand closely watching the unabashedly implanted and low-cut woman, blond and with a bright strong face of sturdy opposition, serving our drinks.

"So," Hand said, "Estonia."

"We're in a casino in Tallinn."

I was exhausted. *You should sleep. Wake up early.* That's not the way. *It's the same.* It means less that way. We sleep when we fall. We only sleep when we can't move anymore. *That's juvenile.* But it means everything. *It's the illusion of progress. Staying awake isn't progress.* The illusion is enough.

There was a man next to us, greasy, showy with a silk handkerchief waving from his suit, chatting with a younger woman in blue velvet. Beyond them, two men with coats on, skirting around the bar, toward us.

One was tall and burly and sweating heavily under the burden of his coat, his backfat, his small overworking heart. The smaller was wiry and thin-faced, like the bassist for a British Invasion band. They asked us our nationality. We told them American. The bigger swayed toward me, spittle at the corners of his mouth, his eyes unfocused, about to say something.

He said nothing. He lost interest and turned to the silk hand-kerchief man with the leggy woman. He asked the man a question in Estonian. The man answered something inaudible and to that the large heavy man saluted him with a loud *Heil Hitler!*

All eyes darted toward us, to the bar area in general. Had I ever heard someone say that? No. Not in person. But because the man was close to us, and we were newly arrived, it looked like we were with the man. Or that we were responsible, complicit.

I backed off and smiled apologetically to the room while Hand said *Whoa whoa* to the large one, who then took Hand's beer, poured a third of it into his mouth, and gave it back. He turned back to the silk man and did it again: the salute, the *Heil Hitler*. Then he and his bassist friend left. It was clear I was missing some subtext. Had the Nazis ever gotten this far? Why didn't I know this? There was so much that Gilbert's biography of Churchill hadn't said, and so much that had to be condensed. D-Day, the cornerstone of all American accounts of the war, is summed up in a page or two. Hiroshima gets a paragraph, Nagasaki one sentence. We knew nothing; the gaps in our knowledge were random and annoying. They were potholes—they could be patched but they multiplied without pattern or remorse. And even if we knew something, had read something, were almost sure of something, we wouldn't ever know the truth, or come anywhere close to it.

The truth had to be seen. Anything else was a story, entertaining but more embroidered fib than crude, shapeless fact.

Hand played poker while we pieced it together. The silk handkerchief man was German, we guessed, and the Estonians still resented the Germans for their role in the Soviet takeover? Hand was sure that Germany had taken Estonia—he knew they took Latvia—and this was reason enough. We settled on this explanation and I watched as Hand lost $100 of my money. It confused me for a minute, the money-losing. It was becoming less clear what was happening with this money. How much had we given away? No idea. It had seemed like a lot but it couldn't have been over $7,500. We had a long way to go. And only three days, or actually less—sixty hours. How would we do it? And to whom would we give it? Was the point to give it to people who needed it, or just to get rid of it? I knew the answer, of course, but had to remind Hand. Didn't we figure this out before, in Marrakesh? Always we learned things and forgot them. Almost nothing could be learned for good. Hand wanted to lose money, now, here. We could lose it all here, certainly, easily, and would we be more free? In a way, sure, but—

"Let's go," I said.

The casino workers, matching in number the patrons one to one, were busy watching, touching their fingers lightly to the felt, the leather, the burgundy walls.

"Fine," said Hand. And with that, he was done. I had vague fears that Hand was a secret gambling addict and was now relieved. We were still mobile.

We stepped outside—the cold whipped our bare faces—and asked the cabbie, the same one, still sitting in his Mercedes reading Günter Grass—that was weird, that kind of callback—to take us to Old Town, the cultural center, and he started the car, while warning us that nothing was still open.

It was two now and Sunday and everything was dead. We had been traveling all day, a waste. We'd done nothing.

The cabbie rolled us through Old Town, windows open, the car moseying over the cobblestones, as he pointed out various landmarks—churches and places of assembly, all presumably older than even the beaches of our own country. I was yawning, eyes tearing from the frozen air, when finally we pulled up alongside a small sign, bearing the silhouette of a curvy and naked woman.

Hand pointed to the sign. "We have to go. Is it open?"

The cabbie said it was; it was the only place open in Tallinn at two on a Sunday night. Do we really want to go to another gentleman's club? *It's all that's open.* But we've been to too many of these places. *I know.* We travel thousands of miles east, then thousands north, and always these places where girls and boys pretend to be women and men. *We have no choice. We need the communion of souls and only here are they awake.*

We paid the man and walked down a narrow alleyway and through a medieval wooden round-topped door and then down. Down a low-ceilinged hallway and down again and then through a swinging double-door and finally we were in a sort of basement den, the basement of an ancient building, almost surely once this structure's dungeon or crypt, where hay would be stacked in one corner and men tortured in the other. In one corner sat two men in suits, separate and each alone, and in front of us, beyond the clear plastic column of water, bubbly and lit green and full of fake flat zebrafish jerking up and down, a topless shiny woman with Barbarella's boots was swinging wildly around a gleaming golden pole.

We sat down. A booth around a silver table.

With new drinks we watched the woman dance. She was tall, with barn-red hair, petal-white skin and blue eyes. She was not such a great dancer, but she was loving this pole.

"Always the pole," Hand said.

These dancers love those poles, and they go around and around on the poles, and sometimes they get so acrobatic on the poles, and it's always lost on me. Upside-down on the pole, twirling on the pole, back against the pole, front against the pole, climbing the pole. The pole is fine, I think but I think maybe the pole is not worth so much concerted attention.

—Hand, people like this can teach us nothing.

—Maybe, but they're awake and we're awake. That's enough.

Or it could be that I wanted a pole myself. These women were doing some impressive maneuvers, but with the pole as home base, as pillar and facilitator. I had no such pole. Could I do more and better things with a golden pole? I had no pole.

She finished and while Hand went to get us more drinks she came to me. A second earlier she had been the dancer on the mini-stage, with the boots and the pole, and now she was here over me, her knee, next to my thigh, on the upholstered bench, her heat on me, the smell of garlic, her shampoo, strawberry-scented and strong, her long hair tickling my nose. She touched my chin, tsk-tsking while scanning the various flaws and scabs, and I smiled politely, in shock.

Her name was Olga. She was Russian, but wanted to go to Sweden to make more money. "This is my last day here," she announced. After tonight, she would go to Sweden to become a bartender. We asked if she knew how to bartend. She said no.

—You're not going to Sweden tomorrow.

—I know.

—We are to overpay you to help you on your trip.

—Yes.

—But you will stay.

—Maybe.

—I can't even begin to know how you got here in the first place.

—You're more like me than you think.

She had a warm snaggletoothed smile. She looked like a neighbor I once had, Angela Tomaso. It struck me for a second that this might in fact *be* Angela Tomaso. The idea seemed tantalizingly possible. Why not Angela Tomaso dancing in Estonia? I hadn't seen Angela for sixteen years, since the summer her brother—

This was not Angela Tomaso. She smiled into my eyes and then turned. Hand had returned—where were the drinks? He'd forgotten the drinks—and now she was on Hand and things were much less polite. She seemed to genuinely like him. She preferred him to me. Even in a transaction like this, she got to choose. He was grinning like mad. Every act of charity has choice at its core. My head was still talking to her.

—I think you do have love for Hand.

—It's impossible to fake this all the time.

She was straddling him, her hand between his thighs, her other hand in his hair.

—Olga I agree. You can't fake it all.

—There's no way to pretend. I have an irregular and bursting heart and that's why I'm here. It erupts so many times every night and I can't help it. I know this is a strange way to express it but I feel real love for your friend, and for you. For you it's more general, it's my love surveying you from above, approving, you as part of a landscape I love, a human one, while with your friend it's more specific. It's his smell, his thick neck—

—Fine. Enough.

Hand was trying to get something—what? Oh, money—from his sock. I was looking at her dimpled and thong-bisected rear as it rose and descended on his crotch.

—But see how we are the same? You and I, Will? We both see strangers and we react. We don't like to walk by people without nodding. We're broken when people are rude. We're broken when people can't meet us halfway. We can't accept the limits of normal human relations—chilly, clothed, circumscribed. Our hearts pull against their leashes, Will!

But as suddenly as she'd come to us, she was back to the dance floor and engaged in more spinning around the gold glimmering pole. Maybe someone else was liking the pole. Maybe I was missing something. I looked around, at the other patrons, half-expecting to find some guy grinning and clapping, going nuts for the pole. No such men were here.

There was a payphone near the bar so I called my mom.

"You're where?" she said. "I can't hear anything."

I pressed my finger into my free ear.

"I'm at a bar in Estonia. What time is it there?"

"Three. I'm staining a footstool."

"You're what?"

"A footstool."

"You're aiming it? At what?"

"*Stain*ing. Staining."

"In the garage?"

"I'm outside—"

"Make sure it's ventil—Oh."

There was a delay in our connection and it made us tentative. We waited to speak and then spoke at the same time.

The dancer had two fingers in her mouth. Now her ankles held the pole, and she was upside down. The link between the acrobatics and anything erotic was tenuous and slipping. I turned to face the phone, to concentrate.

"You're where again?" she said, almost yelling.

"Estonia. Tallinn."

I situated it for her. No one knows where Tallinn is.

"Hey honey," she said, not caring about Tallinn anymore, "you would tell me if you'd broken something here, wouldn't you?"

"Broke something? Like what?"

"A plate, a glass, anything."

"I don't get it."

"You know I walk barefoot sometimes."

"Right. But did you step on some glass? What are you talking about?"

"You would tell me, wouldn't you?"

"Of course. But I haven't been there in months, Mom."

—Jesus, Mom. What is going on?

"I just wanted to make sure you'd tell me. I woke up this morning and was afraid to walk in there—I was sure it was covered in glass. And you know how hard it is to see that glass, Will."

"Okay."

"I can't have the glass everywhere, hon. I can't have the broken glass underfoot."

"Okay," I said.

"So why Estonia?"

"I don't know. They didn't need a visa."

"I almost went to Denmark once."

"When?"

"With your father of course. We wanted to honeymoon there. All the tulips."

"Oh." I hated it when she mentioned him without malice.

"Get away!" she yelled.

"What?"

"The dog next door. He's brushing up against my stool."

—Mom. Bring it together.

"Honey."

"What?"

"I should let you go."

"I have time."

"I don't."

"You should see this place. They've got these tall fishtanks full of fake fish, and they're bubbling up to the top, flying up there. Like embers from a campfire. Or like when you try to burn newspaper in the fire, and it gets so light and starts floating around, when it all goes up around your head—"

"Will."

"Or the embers go up too. Remember that? The one time on the Wolf River, remember that, when you took us for my birthday? And there was that fake open grave along the path, with the shroud on it? With the bloodstain in the middle—"

"I have to go, Will. Have a nice strip bar."

She was the one who'd wanted to go to Great America. This was only three years ago, in the middle of a June everyone was marveling about—so blue and clear, the heavy May rains giving the greens unknown depths, underwater hues—and so many were home for a wedding—Teddy, from high school, was marrying a woman seven years older and twenty pounds heavier, and there was much talk, before and during, especially when she chain-smoked through the reception and its many speeches—and my mom wanted to go to Great America, and Jack and Hand and I with her. We were twenty-four or -five, Jack, Hand and I, and we all followed my mom—oh shit, Pilar was there too, for some reason—all day, letting my mom pay for things, letting her choose the rides. This was the day they rode the Demon—I wouldn't ride anything that brought me upside-down, and the smell of the bar across my chest brought memories of bike accidents, so I waited and watched—and afterward I watched the three of them, arm in arm in arm, legs almost linked, walking toward me. It was stupid and embarrassing and funny and stupid. This was the day Hand announced, while eating fries and mayonnaise for lunch, that in his opinion, a great shit was better than bad sex, a view that was seconded by my mom, which just about killed Jack. On this day Jack mentioned that he wouldn't mind staying at his current job, in his current position, for "twenty or thirty more years." He was content. When he finished enumerating the pleasures of his work, we were quiet. This day ended when we left at six, but began again when in the parking lot we learned that Mom had left her lights on. It was foggy in the morning and her lights were on then and now the car was dead and we had to start over.

We played backgammon on the hood while we waited for a Triple-A jump and when that was done the day ended again but began once more when we stopped for dinner and afterward the engine wouldn't turn. Triple-A again but this time we waited inside, at the bar—the first time I'd ever had a drink with my mom, anywhere—and Jack and Hand acted like it was natural and good—better here than in Hand's basement, where we used to shot-gun Old Milwaukees before going out looking to steal Melinda Aghani's Cabriolet. But for me, with my mom here, and them here, it was the collision of worlds and every sip confused me. Jack told his story about how his sister Molly said, at thirteen, that she'd never have sex, ever. Why? *Because do you know what makes a penis erect that way? Blood! A penis full of blood!* Jack did her voice perfectly, the deafening shrillness, the indignance of a matron offended. My mom was loving it, not only because she didn't like Molly much—no one did—but because Jack and Hand knew my mom wanted to be treated without deference and they obliged, they didn't change a word for her. Her hair was so short then. She'd gone the way of a few of her friends and gotten the middle-aged short cut, the Liza Minelli, a helmet with curls licking her temples. It made her look too intense, her eyes too big, cheekbones too strong. But she was in love with this day and it was obvious she didn't want the jump, didn't want to leave the bar. She listened to Hand's tale of hiding his dead cat in his room, when he was seven, to prevent it from being buried. He couldn't stand the idea of burying anything, and so first put the cat in an old Lego box, but ants took over swarming, so he later cut open the belly of a stuffed bear and kept the cat's stiff decomposing body inside the bear's stomach, above his dresser, until the smell, in August, was too dense and he was found out. My mom listened and her eyes were so wide and so full of glee that with the hair she seemed bordering on madness. We didn't get home until twelve, but she was up all night, talking to Cathy Wambat in Hawaii, recounting every moment, her periodic shrieks of laughter keeping me up, though I'd never let her know.

"I can't feel my ankles."

"Ankles? Really?"

"That happens to me. Can we sit down?"

"In this cold? We're better off walking."

We were walking through the city, across a frozen park, toward the hotel, and something was thundering from within my chest, a beating on my breastplate. This was new. "You're right," I said. We kept walking. I scanned the roads that bordered the grass, for cabs.

"You okay?" he asked.

"Why?"

"You're holding your stomach. Was it dinner?"

"No, no. I'm good."

"Cramp?"

"No."

He gave me a untrusting look. "We should just keep heading this way. I can see the church next to the hotel."

"Good," I said. "I need to lie down."

We walked toward the steeple. There was such a weird tightness, a new kind of grip, lower in my chest. I was just starting to really examine the pain, map it—

I dropped. I landed under a bench at the edge of the park and was flooded with warmth. It was so warm, so many creeping-quickly vines spreading throughout my limbs and torso and all so hot, such a liquid heat within me—I dreamt of my face in dirt. My head was burrowing through soft black soil, was pushing its way through, twisting and clawing, without fingers. The dirt felt so warm. I opened my eyes. I was on my back.

It was snowing! It was so gorgeous. They were the biggest flakes I'd ever seen. Wow they were big, the size of birds, and they were falling at me, spinning, but too fast. Too fast—they were falling as if leaden, without their usual caprice. They were falling straight, like rain. I could barely breathe. I was sucking air out of tiny crushed lungs. Lungs the size of thumbs. My lids shut and I went out again. I saw myself on the back of a dragon, as he was scorching forests and countrysides—Or maybe I was the dragon. *I was the dragon!* I was flying so fast, swooping and breathing fire upon the roads, all the filthy trucks—*I was the goddamn dragon!*

Jesus, what were we supposed to do that night? Jack died ten minutes before noon.

After silently eating curly fries and gyros, watching a boy play an old Galaga machine, we went to a movie, *Antz*—the only thing playing at the right time. There and on the way between dinner and the theater, we were feigning interest in the world. I was touching all the glass I saw. I was touching the windows of the shops. I touched the windows of the cars. I touched the glass of the elementary school near my house. Hand would stay at my house that night and the next two, through the funeral, before going back to St. Louis.

After the movie, which was too dark for our mood, we got popsicles from the 7-Eleven and stood in the parking lot, waiting. Soon we were done with our popsicles and were chewing on the sticks. We had nowhere to go. The next day was not possible yet.

There was a man on the outdoor payphone, lit blue under the malfunctioning awning light. His palm rested on the brick wall of the building above the phone, his hand gripping the receiver like a barbell. He kept hanging up, dialing again, hanging up, swearing, dialing. We watched, chewing, quiet.

A police car, huge and roaring, swung into the small parking lot like a whale thrown on a beach. A khaki-clad officer, wearing black boots over his calves, over his pants, walked slowly to the man, took the phone from his hand and hung it up. They began talking. Soon another police car arrived, this one an SUV. There were three cops, and they were all talking to the man, who we guessed was making obscene phone calls, or hassling an ex-girlfriend. Minutes later there were five cops—two talking to him, one on a radio—calling for more cops?—the other two watching the talking two.

Hand and I made each other laugh, putting words in the cops' mouths. We were knocking each other out and the cops didn't seem to care. They periodically glanced at us, two men standing under the awning, watching them, giggling, and I worried then hoped they might hassle us, too—it would give a new direction to the night and we had no idea how to use these hours, any hours anymore—but they only glared, sneered and finally handcuffed the man and drove away with him.

The blood was draining to my head. I was upside down and my stomach was being jabbed. I opened my eyes and was floating above the ground, watching the sidewalk and the frozen grass from five feet above. Oh shit this could be—

No.

"Put me down," I said. Hand had me over his shoulder.

"You're awake."

"You're fucking killing me."

"You want to stand or—"

"Just put me down."

He swung me down to my feet and I stood.

"Where were you going?" I asked.

"I wasn't sure yet."

"Dumbshit."

"Your face," he said, pointing to my nose. I touched it and felt the blood. The scab had opened.

"Hey!" Hand yelled. He was running away now. There was a taxi gliding slowly along the perimeter of the park and Hand was waving his arms at it, sprinting.

The cabbie, dark-haired and with a goatee, shared the front seat with his wife and their baby. We sat in the back and argued about hospitals. Hand insisted and I insisted. Hand worried and I worried a little bit, but we agreed that we'd see how I felt in the morning. The episode was brief and I felt good again. The blood still tickled through me, filling me again, but it was the cold, I decided. I thought about calling Dr. Hilliard but didn't want to do the time-zone math and didn't want to bother her anyway. It was the cold. The pressure of the cold air, the pumping of cold blood, all of it too much work. Why were we in Estonia anyway? It was all so much work. The air, the high-pressure air. I needed warmth. I wanted Cairo. The sun in Cairo would be so giving.

At the hotel, the man at the desk gave us a sour look and the casino was closed. We went to our room, Hand droning on about infant mortality in South Africa, Mandela's role—

I think Hand was still talking when I fell away. I slept and dreamt a dream almost only aural—hours, it seemed, of someone, huge but distant, cackling in a pained, choking way, and the room this time looked precisely like my mom's, with that painting of the boat up on sawhorses, the ground beneath roped with drought. Then Olga and my mom were the same person and they were both telling me to buy a gun to shoot the sick frothing dogs.

AN INTERRUPTION

by Francis R. "Hand" Wisneiwski

MONDAY, A DIFFERENT ONE

I MIGHT AS WELL start here. This is Hand, writing almost two years after the action taking place in this book. I sit on the second floor of a house much too big for one. The house is in New Zealand, in the Coromandel peninsula, and its occupant, thirty-one years old, of strong body but a mind that swerves and sputters, is alone. There is rain here, in a village called Matarangi, in a valley facing a bay, surrounded by green hills, under a ceiling of rain.

At first there was no rain. I arrived on a cloudless Tuesday and expected the best for my stay. I have rented this place, old, leaning left, on the end of a wide beach, for just over two weeks, so finally I can do what for around two years now—since the initial appearance of the book you've been reading—I've wanted to do. It's appropriate, I hope, that I add my contribution here, at about the point when I personally found the plot, or whatever it was, to begin waning. There will be corrections here, and explanations. I'll try to keep my rage and bewilderment in check.

Here in New Zealand, I sat down with the book sooner than I'd expected; I'd planned at least a few weeks of swimming and drunken evenings, fuzzy and full of rugby on TV, but instead I was given rain. So I got started. Here, until I'm done, I'm going to correct, delete and elaborate upon Will's text, which tells half the story it seeks to tell, and makes all kinds of things up, and, I think, does a rather half-assed job of all of it. Earlier readers of this book, I feel, read a diluted version of the week Will and I spent, a version afraid to speak, one which found solace in innuendo and gesture, as opposed to simple and declarative speech—one that left unspoken some of the most essential motivations and implications, and was built in large part upon at least three enormous and unjustifiable lies. I have never been one for outright untruths or so-assumed subtlety if it comes at the expense of the message, or realization of potential impact. See, just now, I came out and said something that Will, or those who convey things in the way he would choose, would find some fey, twee, or sublimated way of communicating. There is a time for twee, and a time for just fucking opening your mouth and giving it to you plain.

So I'm here to fix things, and this house seemed the perfect setting. I know no one here in Matarangi, so my distractions were likely to be minimal. I have only this book, the one you're reading, and my own more accurate notes and memories, and the photos I took, which I'll sprinkle throughout. There is a grocery store not far from this house, within walking distance if I'm feeling robust, and in it—a small place, no bigger than a living room—they sell all I would need, and the proprietor wears no shoes.

No one seems to wear shoes in New Zealand. On the drive from the airport, I stopped at two different malls, looking for pens, paper, scotch tape—things I knew I needed but couldn't carry on the plane from Phuket, where I'd spent the last eight months trying, as part of a fledgling pseudo-missionary (nondenominational) outfit, to convince teenage Thai boys not to sell themselves to German pedophiles, that they had alternatives—though my colleagues and I haven't completely figured out what those are, quite yet. For those who couldn't or wouldn't leave the sex trade, we tried to educate them about STDs and other perils of their occupation, which include the simple over-enthusiasm of many of their clients from Berlin's suburbs. Anyway, in both Auckland-area malls I entered—the first didn't have a stationery store or anything approximating or inclusive of one—there were barefoot shoppers. Whole families of barefoot shoppers! It was fucked up. I was jubilant but perplexed. I'm all for this kind of thing, get me right, the shrugging off of refutable or plainly uncomfortable habits, but it was a shock, all the bare feet indoors, as is any national custom of which you haven't heard but should have. Did you know this? The guidebook said nothing about this, though it did make clear why the residents of New Zealand are known as Kiwis; it has nothing to do with the fruit, which is what I'd assumed, with no evidence that that sort of fruit is native here. The kiwi is also a flightless bird no bigger than a robin, somewhat endangered here, with a long curved beak. I haven't seen one of the birds yet, though signs about the preservation of their habitat are everywhere, as are their images on logos, restaurant signage, and on the national currency, which is, with its clear acetate windows and bright colors, easily the most beautiful money in the world.

I have now been here, in my rented house, for three days, this being the fourth, and after a few hours of clarity that first day, there has been only rain. Sixty-three hours of rain so far. I've been counting, when I haven't been pacing, and doing push-ups, and re-reading Giambattista Vico's *New Science*, which I assume you've read and so won't get into much beyond recommending your revisiting the section on Poetic Wisdom and then trying to reconcile it with American foreign policy toward Khadafy in the late 70s and 80s. Seems impossible, though so many—far too many!—have tried.

But the rain has not stopped, that's my current point to make, and this rain is keeping me from my present task. It's gotten me to re-read the book, which is a good thing, something I didn't think I'd do so soon after arriving, but at the same time the rain has impeded my ability to dig into my revisions, to amend and edify. When I chose this spot, on this island and on this thumb-like peninsula and on this bay and in this house, built like a wooden jungle-gym with boldly colored Danish accents, I pictured myself much like Ernest H., swimming in the morning, writing a few hundred words just after that, then allowing the afternoon to drift on the slow river of five or six strong cocktails.

But without the swimming—which is impossible in this rain, for the water is already colder than I expected or would be desirous to anyone, my day is without a beginning—I flounder. I sit for long stretches with my hand in my pubic hair. I have picked my nose so much it bleeds. I wake up to rain and can't even walk outside. I have no car. I dropped it off in Whitianga, because I thought that would be distracting, to have a car here, a car making possible escape from the work at hand. So no car, but without one and without sun, things here are wretched and I'm losing my holy damned mind.

TUESDAY, WITHOUT MERCY

Of course I'm mimicking the structural device of the book as a whole, and I'm finding it a comfortable enough contrivance to live within. It shapes my words and circumscribes my task. Today I've decided that I'm going to spend seven days, while the rain continues, illuminating this manuscript, and will do so in as orderly a fashion as I can manage, given that this is not my bag, this reworking of text, within red borders, in the midst of a book. I'm a scientist, really, not recognized as such by the Obeyers with their degrees and lab coats, but I have ideas, and provable theses, and I believe and many have noted my ability to see connections that no one else can (including Brian Greene, who I met once at an airport and who told me, and I quote, "you've got some interesting ideas there, buddy." Beautiful man).

At the moment I'm typing onto standard printer paper, in green ink, to make as clear as possible the separation between my words and his, with the hope that if I send my pages to the book's publisher, they'll see fit to include my comments somewhere— ideally where I've placed them myself, between Will's Sunday and Monday, well before the assumption mentioned on the book's original cover.

Sweet people, I want to mention, tangentially but relevantly, before I get too involved here, that this is my fifth day here, and it's still raining. I call you sweet people because it's not your fault. The rain is not your responsibility. The rain! It's not always a downpour kind of rain, no, but often it is, at least once a day it is, and otherwise it's just constant. However unsettled I was before, I am twenty-six and one-third hours further along now. It's been almost a hundred hours of rain, and I wonder about their drainage ability inland, and what it's doing to the rivers. (On the news are reports of motorists stranded and houses drifting away, but the instances seem isolated, which is odd, considering that where we grew up, the troubles would be far worse, I fear.) I want to also apologize for my tone, when there is a tone to my tone, which I blame on De Profundis, which I was reading on the plane, when I wanted to be reading Teirno's microbe-hunter book, which I heard was definitive.

All the food I bought that first day is gone, everything but the beans, which I don't know why I got in the first place. I don't eat canned beans and never have. I would go get more food but I'd be soaked and then would catch something and lord knows where the closest hospital is, and will the doctors there be wearing shoes? I can't take that chance.

And I can't get the washing machine working, so I'm wearing the same pair of underwear I came with, which was not my plan.

True, I only brought two pair, and true, I usually wear a pair three days before rotating, but still this overuse was not my hope, and is always inadvisable for a man of my active lifestyle and fur-inclusive back end. Do you hear that accursed ocean? I have a few of the doors and windows open, anything to relieve the pressure in this place, so I hear it all day and all night. I'm supposed to be comforted by the sound, that unstoppable and wide white distant slow soft car-crashing, but it's starting to warp me. There's just too much weather here. I feel like I'm on a ship, surrounded by indifferent and relentlessly unsubtle forces of nature. I can close the door or the windows but at this point I'd still hear it; I can feel it, like you can feel bass in your heart or your mother's footsteps on the floors above.

This morning a really disturbing thing happened. I looked out the window of this home, at the ocean, which was grey like slush, and before it, on the sand, directly in line with this house I'm renting for almost nothing, was a black lump. It was long and bulbous in the middle, and immediately I knew it was a body of some sort, or a garbage bag filled with something, shaped like a body. It was not a log, or anything plastic or man-made. I could tell it was once alive. It's still there now, a few hours later. Damned if I'm going out there to see what it is. Usually I would, I suppose, but these three days of rain have done something to my sense of movement and my access to courage. It's like I'm carrying on a long-distance relationship now to these aspects of myself, previously so close at hand.

Even on the TV, the people are a little surprised by all the rain—uncharacteristic in February, they keep saying—but I don't believe them. They knew it would rain and knew I'd be driven halfway around the corner and down, the fuckers. I'm sure it rains like mad like this every February, that every February they have a wet season, but they don't want to lose all the tourist money, so they lie through their teeth, or call it the Green Season or some shit. Lord I'm going soft and weird. I haven't swum in so long, haven't seen the sun in a week—it's been so long since I've walked out of the ocean licking the wet salt from my mustache and beard while the sun dries the water on my back. It's just wrong. I need these things. The storm has apparently dredged up all this seaweed, the beach covered in it, and in the shallows you'd be enveloped in it, so I don't swim—from what I hear this part of the world is plagued with lyngba, the hair-thin seaweed that causes stinging seaweed disease, which I've had once—like poison oak but a thousand times worse, itching with the power of speech, a baboon's screeching kind of speech—and refuse to live with again. I have no taste for the seasons anymore. Nothing is worth seeing in the rain, and all I really want to do these days is see things.

Well, what happened to us, to Will and me? Everyone asks that. You know he died, and that much is true. But there's much more you don't know, or that he fibbed about, for reasons justifiable and otherwise. This is our task, to untangle the cords. But right now I need sleep, because I've had a bottle and a half of Pinot Grigio and it was bad stuff, too dry, with the finish of a day-old salmon dinner, and I'm going upstairs now, to do better tomorrow.

WEDNESDAY, TO WORK AT LAST

Day Six here, Day Three of my attempt at correction, and still I haven't begun. I will soon begin. But let me tell you first that it's rained without interruption for nearly my entire time here, all of the godforsaken hours since I last saw you, and the air in this rented house is humid with my own stench. A man has smells, I'm told, and though I'm not usually sensitive to them myself, or even cognizant of them, by this point, I am acknowledging that the place smells of me and my habits and my food and my habits with my food. There has been no time for the air to replace itself, to wipe itself clean. The rain comes from the sky and is crushing us slowly. On the TV they show images of people paddling to work, and someone's house has floated away, to sea. Elsewhere, in a small burg where the streets leaving town were closed, a young childless woman stabbed her husband out of rage born of confinement (my theory, not that of the authorities).

And the black shape on the beach is still there.

It's been there two full days now, and I haven't had the interest, or inclination, or maybe courage, to go see what it is. I suppose I know it's a body and I just don't want to be the one to find it, to name it. Normally I'd be running out there to see it, poke and prod it, but there's something about this shape that's unsettling. Its size maybe. It's most definitely a person, but because it's a very large person, I'm held back from investigating. From here it seems to be about eight feet tall, which would make it almost as big as Robert Pershing Wadlow, the tallest man ever, born in Alton, Illinois—I knew a guy from Alton at UW-Lacrosse, named Denny Catfish, honest to God—and grew to be almost nine feet. But this body is rounder, blacker. Why is no one else finding it? The beach, on this remote bay on the North Island, is not crowded, ever, and has been desolate during this downpour, but still I wonder why no one else has claimed this body. It's so obvious there, and it needs to be removed.

And it's moved up the beach. It's farther into the sand today, closer to the house. Before it was on the break of the shore, pushed inches to and fro by the surf, which was gentle despite the rain and the winds. But now it's closer. It's moved fifteen feet inland, and now the water only kisses its black shape with its most far-reaching waves. If I were a superstitious man I'd think the shape was heading for me, slowly, to bring me some kind of message. But I choose instead to believe that the ocean will retake the body while I sleep.

There are so many things that are not true in Will's account of this trip, but his death is not among them. He is gone, almost three years now, I guess, and it's a stupid thing. No one should find it romantic, because there's never any romance in death. There would have to be at least commensurate romance in life, and there isn't—it can be beautiful but it's plodding—so in death there can only be a succession of ever-quieting minor notes. Anyone who's witnessed a death knows how unromantic it is. The man who falls on his sword bleeds for hours, and still ends up choking on his own blood. Will, I suspect, died in an unspeakably horrific way, surrounded by underwater screams. That it was plastered on the cover—written by a ghostwriter, if you'll forgive that dual-sided pun—is a disgrace. (I'll get to that ghostwriter soon enough, and will explain how it is that a dead man seems to be writing from the grave.)

But first, I need to give you a better picture of Will at this point. Maybe you don't want to trust me because he's been dead so long and I've been open about the fact that I'm losing my mind, but I don't see the point in your reading too much about this story when you know next to nothing about the man. He didn't describe his looks, but they're easy: he resembled very closely a young Martin Landau, though I'm not sure how helpful that is. Will was a handsome enough guy, with a large mouth area, but maybe too long in the head—he always looked more adult than the rest of us. There were those in high school who called him Munster, because there was a distant resemblance to Herman, but the nickname was too cruel, and he made it clear it pained him to hear it. Besides, the guy was handsome enough; his looks were not an aid, but they were rarely an impediment. His hair was black and his nose Roman. He did okay romantically, though it's telling that you don't yet know anything about how much he used to masturbate. Which was a lot, holy shit it was. It's hard to imagine just how often he was doing it as a teenager, when he discovered the idea, when we were seventeen, late in our junior year. Before that, as often as the rest of us would mention it or joke about jerking off in one way or another, Will—honest to God—didn't think it was possible. He thought, and this is so hard to prove but you must believe me that it's true, that it was some kind of urban myth, like queifing or the existence of women possessing three nipples or men with three testicles. I don't know how he kept himself so ignorant of so many things. But someone must have walked him through the process at some point, because Will comes to school one Monday with this new and desperate look on his face, like the second he gets to school he can't wait to get home. Peter Moorehouse had the same look for a month or so, when his cousin Annette came from Norway for a month and used to sunbathe topless in the backyard drinking white wine. Will was pretty average in a lot of ways, in the ways you glance at—he didn't stand out in a group of strangers. But he had a haunted thing about him that everyone recognized, and some thought affected, but all wondered about, and it was something, contrary to the implications of the account he's written, that he's always had. He was always the sort who you'd expect to be having long and vicious arguments with his head, or with others, inside his head. You'd almost find him, occasionally but demonstrably, moving his lips while walking alone; still far from a self-talker or a screamer of obscenities on the city sidewalk, but nevertheless someone who wasn't moving through our world with a brain unequipped with the appropriate shock-absorbing equipment.

Which brings us to his imagination. He always dabbled in writing, as a lot of us did and do—I have three screenplays at the ready, if you're interested. Their titles:

"Humiliation Nation"

"A War Between the People of the Future and Today's Smallest Fears"

"The Less-Known Life of Louis Pasteur"

—but I have to say that I was impressed, perhaps most of all, by Will's account of the beating in Oconomowoc, which is pretty realistic for being completely fabricated. In terms of dispelling the largest and most unjustifiable fictions, it's good to start here. Will wasn't beaten by anyone, ever. The kid was never in a fight in his life. Nothing like that at least. I did some fighting in junior high, but Will was never that way. He was an athletic enough kid, but he really didn't have the outward-facing rage you need to fight; you just plain need some rage, some simmering zig-zag blood somewhere in there, blood that's either constantly at a boil or is prone to boiling, and Will had neither. You couldn't get the kid mad—outwardly—about anything, really, unless you took his hat off and threw it into the river. I did that once and he punched me in the stomach. I admit that he did that, and that it hurt, a lot, and that I was impressed by how hard he could hit. I took off the hat for no reason, and meant it to be—well, I didn't think much about it either way. I saw the hat and was convinced that it needed to be removed and thrown into the river. And looking back, I still get a chuckle out of it—the hat! in the river! oh lord the comedy!—but Will was afraid the girls would see his bed-head, I think, and that he'd always be called Bed-Head, and thus he'd never have love, so he punched me in the stomach, tears in his eyes. The kid was frustrated, and he hit me hard.

When I first read this part, about getting his *ass handed to him* in Oconomowoc, I was deeply confused, and at first thought there was something I didn't know. Had this really happened? I forget things every so often, and so wondered if. . . . The scene is so vivid, so I asked around, to other people who knew him, and no dice. No one beat up Will; Will went to Africa with a face as clear as could be, while still bearing a distant resemblance to Herman Munster.

Thus, this beating nonsense is one of two major devices he's used—the other one concerning Jack—to, I guess, thicken the plot a bit, to give it some kind of pseudo-emotional gravitas. But why would he find it necessary to have himself, the narrator, get beaten up? And by three men in Wisconsin, no less. It makes no sense. I've been thinking about this, and a few times in the last year I've understood why he might do this, why he'd have himself beaten up, traveling the world with a face showing pain in the most obvious way, all bruises and scabs.

I read Will's account of his trip to the storage unit shortly before I had to do the very same thing—only in this case, I was retrieving Will's stuff, after his own death. I had never done that kind of thing before, but there was no one else to do it. Will was an only child, and his dad was never around, and with his mom gone, too, it fell to me. (Another piece of news I have to unceremoniously dump in your lap, for lack of time and suspense: Will has no brother named Tommy. The name was likely taken from a mutual friend of ours, Tommy Wells, a year older, who we'd both liked but who moved away just before sixth grade. Will always wanted a brother, though, and envied those with larger families, and I suppose then it's natural that he, when creating this semi-fictional backdrop, would throw in—unnecessarily, I think—an older brother, a Tommy, a guy who likes cars and mustaches. It wasn't the only wishful fabrication in the book.)

It was up to me to clear out Will's things, most of which had been there for a long while, though he updated its contents once or twice a year. I did the drive, which I'd done of course a thousand times before, on a good day, clear and bracing. It was March. I got there to find that the place does sit between Wall and Industrial streets, a fact I'm sure Will relished mentioning in a book in part about economic disparity (for it was, aha!, an area in great need of repair). The place was really just a decrepit parking lot cut by three parallel buildings set into the uneven pavement. I pulled in, my tires licked puddles and then gravel, and I stopped next to the Citgo.

When the door of No. 503 rolled upward, I saw boxes. They

were crooked, all of them, because Will was organized but never neat. I've never seen so many bent boxes, leaning every way, for some reason evoking a forest of mushrooms. There was moisture in there, and the cardboard was soft. I thought of graham crackers left outside, at a picnic, half-spoiled, chewy.

Will never expressed to me any sort of idea that when he was leaving for South America—I think he started in Guatemala— that he would not be coming back. And his storing of his possessions leaves the question open. On the one hand, I know that before he left, he did give up his apartment. On the other hand, the range of things he decided to store, and the recent visit he'd obviously made to the unit, would indicate that he was storing things not for my probing afterward, but for safekeeping until he could get back and better edit his belongings. I knew that I couldn't leave anything in this unit. I stood before everything Will had left, knowing I couldn't leave until this steel container was empty. I was hoping that there was enough that could be remorselessly thrown away, and that the rest would fit in my car. I went to work, though my heart had moved up eight inches and was thrumming against my chest. This was sorrow.

There is a sensation when you're looking at the physical remnants of a person's memory when you are sure that you shouldn't be there. I'm of the opinion that secrets kept in life should be honored in death, that nothing changes simply because you're not there to defend yourself. So I decided quickly that I would not read or open anything looking private—would only sort between those things I should dispose of, and those I would bring back to Chicago with me, to be stored in my basement. I wasn't thinking far ahead, really, though I vaguely recognized how strange it would be to be keeping his possessions, and to be storing them in my own place, and had no idea what would eventually become of them—the best I could hope for them, I acknowledged, was that they would be kept safe and dry for a few more years, but that when next I moved,

I would dispose of a few more boxes, until eventually there was very little left of his things, and that someday, far in the future, they would either be confused with my own things by my own decedents, or be sold at estate sales or thrown away by strangers. There is no dignity to these things, and their destiny is invariably grotesque. Memory, perhaps, should have no physical shape.

Thankfully, the first boxes I opened were the easiest—anonymous and disposable. There was a dumpster beside the building, and I knew great satisfaction in heaving boxes over the green steel wall and inside the empty container, where they thumped or clattered.

There were three boxes of coat-hangers. Clatter.

There was a box of blankets. Thump.

A box of very old and unusable sheets and pillowcases. Thump.

There was a box of plates and glasses and cutlery. Clatter.

I should stop here and tell you that everything, absolutely everything, was covered in mouse droppings. I assume that's what they were, though I saw no mice. I thought for a second that the tiny hard pellets, smooth like Tic-Tacs but black, could be the result of bats, but then remembered guano, and guano doesn't come in pellet form.

Every box I picked up, to move or inspect, rattled. Sometimes there were thousands of pellets in one box. I knew there was no food in any of the boxes, so I was baffled as to why the mice not only chewed their way into each and every one of forty-one boxes in that storage unit, but why they stayed there, perhaps *lived* there. There was nothing to live on in that room.

But let me back up. Opening the door to the storage unit gave me that immediate acidic taste on my tongue—I last got it when I saw a man on Navy Pier kick another man in the head; it appeared in the nanosecond between when I knew the fight was getting out of control and when I knew the victor was going to

throw his foot into the back of the man's skull. The door was pad-
locked, and fittingly enough, the guy on duty had to break it open;
the metaphorical clarity of the action didn't escape me. Immediately after the broken lock dropped to the floor, the door rose up,
rolling into the roof of the room, and I cried immediately and
didn't stop for five minutes. What a strange fucker he was. There
was a box full of bathroom and shower things—shampoo, conditioner, scrub brushes, a loofa, a six-pack of Dove soap, more shampoo, two empty bottles of some kind of body wash. In the same
box, combs, a pair of brushes, an electric razor, a bunch of brand-
new hand towels. Three boxes of books, paperbacks mostly, some
legal textbooks, from when he thought he could pass the bar without law school. His few college textbooks. Mattresses, a bedframe,
end tables, lamps, posters, and yes, a giant cardboard cutout of
Jack Sikma. An antique globe, before Israel, with a lightbulb
inside.

I began throwing the clothes into garbage bags I'd brought.
For some lucky reason I didn't recognize a lot of them, and this
made it easier; I didn't need to stop. But every so often, something
would come up, a CB jacket or a woven belt, and for a second Will
would inhabit that thing. His old backpack, still with the word
FLAMER written and crossed out in Sharpie, sat flattened at the
bottom of one soft brown box, and when I took it up I could see it
moving on his shoulders, could see it sitting under his desk, could
see him throwing it into the backseat of my car, could see his
strange grimacing smile and his dark eyes, his dark lashes. He had
scars all over his knuckles. Did he ever mention that?

I was trying to get the task done, but was fighting too many
fronts. I was all too aware of the strangeness of actually doing
something that Will had described, fictionally, in the book about
us, and it was scaring me. I felt like I was being watched, like it
was all too neat and circular to be happening randomly, unplanned.

And he'd gotten it right, in the strangest way, that feeling of being attacked by shadows, on every side, of breathlessness, of being beaten. I stuffed the clothes in four black garbage bags, and tossed the books, but I took a number of breaks, walking over to the Citgo for snacks, hiking around the area, up to the National Guard building, which indeed exists, just where he said it did.

There was a small box of maps and tickets and money from our trip, and I kept that.

There was a bass guitar, with no strings strung.

There was a box of puppets, all of them ancient, certainly something he'd inherited himself. Their heads were large, the size of a cat's, and their clothes were made of silk, harlequinned but filthy. I'd never seen them or heard anything about them. I put them in my car, the box of them.

I was there for three and a half hours, but I don't know why. There wasn't any reason for me to stay, really. I came to the conclusion that this was just punishment, that no good was being accomplished. I had my memories of Will already—I had a hundred pictures, easily, and a thousand objects that brought him back—and this was just unnecessary. I should have left everything there, should have allowed the owners of the storage facility to empty the room; no one could have objected. My going up there was doing nothing for anyone; it was a suffocating afternoon for me, when I felt the air become thinner, the breathing more difficult; I didn't trust my hands, and wanted to become an animal. I didn't like being a human, and thinking this was something humans should do, and though part of me had wrapped this up somehow in the idea of fairness and rightness and dignity, it was more correct to see this as the opposite, as playing in the slop of a dead man's past. Dignity would be to incinerate this stuff without a look, and to then rely on my own memories to do Will justice. I just hate all this work in the physical—the funerals, the clothes, the caskets and makeup and pulling of flesh! The writing of checks to those who handle the dead! I refuse. I will not do it again.

Will's possessions filled my car. The dumpster next to the unit was full, too, of mattresses and frames, Jack Sikma, pillows and cardboard. I would recycle some other day. I drove off, feeling a hollow around my eyes, knowing my hands were fists, wanting to swim, wanting to watch a lot of TV, wanting to masturbate for days, wanting to watch basketball on cable while drinking from a mug, wanting to have someone waiting for me at home, wanting a dog at the very least, wanting to go deep-sea diving, wanting to be seventeen again, before we left a time when our hands didn't know how to pack up the possessions of the dead, wanting Will to rise, to refind human form in the thicket of his things in my backseat, to speak again so I could knock his fucking head off.

On the way home that day I thought about the perfect parallel of Will's experience at Oconomowoc and mine, his fictional and metaphorical, mine so mundane and worthless. It's my guess that what Will was describing was his packing up of his original house, the one he and his mother lived in until her death. I'm not sure there was a storage unit involved, but my guess is that he was extrapolating, using his own unit as a model, and because he couldn't describe the shame in the disposal or sale of his own family's heirlooms and incidentals, he created a stand-in setting, and for his mother, another stand-in: Jack.

For there was no Jack. As long as I have known Will, there was no Jack. Throughout the book Will talks of Jack, and the death of Jack, a death that in some circuitous way leads to both the beating at Oconomowoc and to this trip. But both of those things are fictions. I have addressed the second fiction, and now will address the first.

I can't tell you how confused I was when I read that first paragraph, with all that shit about Jack. He's in the first sentence, and he's a lie. I thought at first that it was another cute little device by the ghostwriter,* like the implication that Will is writing from the grave, but then found all the references to Jack within, and was shaken to my core. Will and I had always been a duo—there is comfort in a mutually acknowledged and exclusive duo—so you can imagine my frustration when I see this manuscript and throughout there is this third person, missing but present, named Jack, who is painted on glass, with the sun forever shooting through. He's a saint of some kind, better at everything—basketball, drafting, romance—and why the fuck why? I can't understand it. He is, like any creation of friend-fiction, an amalgam of a bunch of people we know, and then an idealization of that amalgam. Worse, Will gives him more than a few of his own Will-characteristics, like the tendency to drive slowly, checking the speedometer by giving a double thumbs-up.

I don't know why he would begin the book with such a premise, with the death of this third friend—or rather, I understand it all too well, and I'm disappointed in him. It's my opinion that the book didn't need the lies. This is something Mark Twain wrote, or Samuel Clemens wrote, or whatever: "To string incongruities and absurdities together in a wandering and sometimes purposeless way, and seem innocently unaware that they are absurdities, is the basis of the American art." And I like that—it invites Will to have just put the truth down, in order, and let the facts underline the absurdity in the situation, our motives, the results, everything. But Will chose instead to set things up in a more conventional way, and I guess it makes more sense, to some, to provide this kind of motivation for our trip, it thus seeming like a kind of fleeing.

---

* Though the text as printed before and after my interlude is as Will wrote it, there's no way, of course, he could have written that first page, being no longer with us, and therefore not close to a word processor. His manuscript was sent to the publisher before his second departure, for South America, and after his death there, they shopped the task of writing a neat opening paragraph to a writer of semi-fictions with a tendency toward the clever setup. The result speaks for itself.

But the fact is that it wasn't. There is no correlation between the trip we took and any particular death, I don't think, but then again something must have given him that sense of urgency about things, and probably inspired the idea of such a quick but potent trip, with such tight parameters but with the outward gestures of his inner mix of confusion and love, the outward expression of an inward grace . . . but that's another issue, the issue of the sacrament. More on that later.

I just want you to understand, though, how much it could piss a person off to have him supplanted by a fictional dead person. It's already bad enough that Will's cartooned me to the point where I'm half-insane and half-insufferable and always puerile, but it's so much worse to have the object of his fraternal affections be some imaginary deceased person, who's apparently so soft and saintly that he couldn't survive in this world (the run-over by a truck seems to me a little heavy-handed, but whatever). It's a comfort, a small one, that at least you few people who will read my comments will know that there were always just two of us, and our motivations were self-made and without tragic source.

It's dark now and still raining. I forgot to even step outside today; I've scarcely left the couch. Living this way makes you feel both captive and complicit in your captivity. I could certainly walk outside, into the rain, and take some air in me. I could walk a bit on the porch, with its greasy-wet surface, with the rain still coming in vast armies never tiring. I could step from the porch onto the sand and continue, down to the water, and within a few hundred feet, walking straight to the ocean, I would come upon the body on the sand, which as I look out the window from the kitchen, I see has moved even closer, and now is equidistant between the house and the water, and now there's no chance it's there by chance.

*   *   *

THURSDAY

You don't want to believe this, but it's still raining here. You're sick of hearing about it, I know, but still, isn't it kind of weird? Are you with me now, believing that this country is promoting some vast tourism-hoax, pretending to all the world that their winters are inhabitable? These Kiwis are becoming ever-more mysterious, ever-more intriguing, ever-more likely, I'm thinking, to be the small nation probably hiding other secrets, like perhaps human clones, alien life-form tissue, cave paintings pre-dating those in France, whatever. It's now been eight days, I think, and in that time we've had only six or seven damned daylight hours where the skies cleared. This morning the rain slowed for about twenty minutes, and in the mist and drizzle, blinking and shuddering, I took a walk.

I stepped down over the dunes, heading to the shore, and stopped. It was still there. It was closer this day than ever before— no more than fifty yards—but still I couldn't make out just what it was. It looked, to me, like a human form, wearing something black, a black uniform, a jumpsuit maybe, with his back turned to me. It was a man, or a large woman. Its back was fleshy and wide, and so I assumed it was a man but now am thinking it's just as likely a woman. It would be more likely, wouldn't it, for a woman to be wearing a unitard of some kind? I went inside, and stayed inside while the sky remained dry for another few minutes, still swallowed by the interminable grey.

This morning, when I cracked from my bed and opened the curtain, first I laughed. I knew it would rain, and there it was again, rain. So I guess I'm a little surprised. Surprised that I'm right that it's raining again. So I guess I actually figured it would stop. Then I wonder how the fuck I'll spend the day, when there's really nothing to see but some body on the beach, dead and getting soaked. But I have country music here—music kept by the owners

of the house, who are gone indefinitely. I have Glen Campbell here; have you heard that "Galveston" song? It's incredible. This stanza:

Galveston, oh Galveston
I am so afraid of dying
Before I dry the tears she's crying
Before I watch your seabirds flying
In the sun, at Galveston, at Galveston

The song itself is very sad but somehow soars. Otherwise there's some very early Johnny Cash here, and lots of Dolly Parton, and Roger Whittaker, and some Emmylou and Tammy. And then some Billy Joel, some Lionel Richie, a good deal of Tom Jones. The people who own this house, for the most part, know the good stuff, and the fact that Kiwis are listening to this much American country music is a comfort to me.

Today I want to talk about the idea of the trip in general. I will return to why and how Will's many fibs fit in soon enough. I mentioned before that the germ of the notion of the trip wasn't a result of any recent death. It wasn't even a result of some recent cash influx. That money he'd had for eight years, and I'll explain how later. The fact is, since he'd run into the money, he'd never touched it, not a cent, it was in some kind of mutual fund plan, unchanging, really, even while every other fund in the world was making 15 to 20 percent a year. He had about $82,000 and wanted to get rid of roughly half of it. How he came up with the number $32k I have no idea, but it still seemed insane, at first. Insane that he should feel so strongly about ridding himself of so much cash in such a strange way, and insane also because it was my opinion that if you're going to do it, to make a statement like that, sweeping and bold, why not go the entire way and give away every last penny? But maybe I'm picking nits here.

I do want to say that though the trip wasn't remotely my idea, I never objected to it. Later in this text, just before Will supposedly collapses on the pavement of the Djemaa el-Fna—didn't happen—I am made to object to the whole concept, or at least the carrying through of it. But this never occurred. I knew, when Will first called me about this notion, the idea of this week, that he was serious, and I knew that he would go through with it, to the end, or further. We had been talking about something like this for a few years, about taking a week, starting on a plane, traveling incessantly but randomly, pushing every button we could, acting on every impulse. For Will, part of the point of the trip was a means to break through the many social boundaries he lived within, or felt he lived within. He'd been born Catholic, as I had, and I guess that mattered in some way to him, actively or subliminally. His mother had been protective of him, and thus he'd been protective of him, too. That is, because his mother sheltered him from the cruelties and unpleasantnesses of the world—everything from the nightly news to coarse words at home—he did the opposite of what we're inclined to believe a kid might do. Instead of rebelling, and seeking out the things kept from him, he kept himself from them. That's a long way of saying that Will was shy and leaned not toward the dark but toward the light.

When the trip begins, he'd never been to a strip club, he'd never seen a violent act in person, he'd scarcely left the Midwest. And so his idea of trying to get around the world in a week, while acting on impulses along the way, was quite a big deal, and achievable, I think, only because he could gather and compartmentalize his courage—and he did act courageously—within this one week. Because for him, approaching strangers, or interacting with them much at all, took some good measure of strength. He was absolutely shy—without being strange, or agoraphobic—and he didn't like this about himself. He longed to be more like I used to be, when I could walk into any room and ask anyone any question, would approach any woman anywhere and try anything in the way of conversation, without any sort of fear of rejection, likely as it was. But Will feared rejection of any kind, and would never purposely put himself in the path of the word No. He feared bouncers, and low-level gatekeepers of any kind, and I know for a fact that he avoided everyone of the kind with great success. That's why—well, one of the reasons—why he was a reasonably happy person, at least on a day-to-day basis, at least on a person-to-person basis. He was friendly. He smiled a lot. He looked you in the eye when he shook your hand. He patted you on the back when there was fun being had. He knew how to relish something that was going well. And things had been going well for him, for a number of reasons, in a number of ways, and thus this trip was born not from tragedy—or rather, from a death—but from what I would like to call the shame of contentment.

I knew generally why he wanted to do this, and knew that he'd eventually write about it, even though, again, all the fictions were a surprise to me. Yes, I do object to much of this original text, because frankly I just don't know why the little bastard—and he was shorter than the 6'1" he claims—didn't just tell the damned story the way it was. I want to find and slap around the people who told him—and it must have been someone; he never would have found it insufficient himself—that the story needed embellishment, needed all this background, all this Jack and Oconomowoc, a mother with Alzheimer's, all of it as fictional as the day is long and drenched with grey filthy rain. It is and has been my vocal opinion for twenty-two months now, since the book first made its way into a semi-circulated final form, that a story about two friends leaving Milwaukee for Senegal to give away $32,000 would be good enough, back story be damned. I thought the story, as it unfolded, was, for one thing, a rather neat and tidy allegory for any sort of intervention, whether by governments or neighbors—but mostly the idea of humanitarian aid, on whatever scale, micro or macro—from NGOs to panhandlers and passersby. The story, when we lived it, was about economics, and about desperation, and about inequity brought to levels that are untenable. And more than that, as I will come to reveal, it was about what we called, in Sunday school, a sacrament. But more on that later.

On the surface the story is ludicrous, and all of its terms are absurd. It's absurd, I believe, that humans can travel around the world in a matter of days. It's absurd that some have the funds—as we did—to do so, while thousands go without necessities every day. It's ridiculous that we still would go on such a trip, thinking it justifiable that if we gave back along the way, all would be somehow rectified. And of course it's without logic or any sense of rightness that Will and I would be in a position to do this, given our unremarkableness in so many ways. That we would have this idea, and be able to act on it, simply because of the location of our birth, is itself absurd. In the face of this absurdity, there is Will, who not only turns to face it, but dives into it, with his $32,000, and with the intention of personally addressing the inequity, not from a distance, but from the nearest possible proximity—by handing large and random sums of money to as many people as possible.

But in telling about the dissemination, Will disappoints. If he was going to do it, and write about it, why fictionalize so many things? The odd thing is that I know for a fact that Will wanted more than anything, at the outset at least, that everyone should know that we actually did this, did precisely what is described in the book—stopped alongside the roads of West Africa and Eastern Europe, unloading $32,000 in cash, in local currency. He wanted to indicate that it could be done, and that it could be good. But even while we traveled he began to have misgivings about writing about this in a nonfictional format. He feared what people would say, to tell you the truth—he feared that people would accuse him of being reckless, misguided, stupid, showy, preachy, whatever. There were a thousand pitfalls to writing it as fact, because quite frankly, from a distance, it appears to be a monumentally silly idea.

But the strange thing about this business is that nonfiction, when written well, is unequivocally more powerful than fiction, because if all details and evocations are equal—meaning, if the writing brings alive the people and places described with equal skill, then the story that is true will evoke a stronger response in the reader, for the same reasons that we feel stronger about a real person than a fictional person, or a person we've met in person, versus a person we haven't. I am a fan and reader of the occasional fiction, but a real book, like *Guns and Germs and Steel*, describing the movements of actual people, and their deaths, just has to hit us at a more visceral level. I am here to express the opinion, no one's but mine—not Will's, not this publisher's, not the wretched ghost-writer's—that those who prefer fiction to nonfiction prefer game shows to the news. It's a decadent mind, a mind that has known ennui and passed through it to something more dangerous, that wants fictional contraptions over the more difficult—sometimes more obvious and clear, other times utterly incomprehensible—truth of fact. But this is the opinion of a man who knows nothing, and it's an opinion that I throw at you to make you angry. Anyway, I read news and look for and collect facts because so far they haven't added up to anything. I had pictured, as a younger man, that the things I knew and would know were bricks in something that would, effortlessly, eventually, shape itself into something recognizable, meaningful. A massive and spiritual sort of geometry—a ziggurat, a pyramid. But here I am now, so many years on, and if there is a shape to all this, it hasn't revealed itself. But no, thus far the things I know grow out, not up, and what might connect all these things, connective tissue or synapses, or just some sense of order, doesn't exist, or isn't functioning, and what I knew at twenty-seven can't be found now.

I miss the things he left out.

I miss the time in Senegal, near Saly, when a group of young men, twelve or so of them, converged on us, as we did a tight three-point turn at a dead-end. We will have no idea what they

were looking for, and I know why Will left the episode out, but it would have underlined how often things were genuinely fraught.

I miss the fact that we actually trounced those boys near Mbuu; we could both play basketball, Will and I, and we wiped that dusty court with eight of them at a time.

I don't miss the old woman in Marrakech, the Resistance survivor, who was fabricated. We were alone in that bar, and nothing happened. Nothing much happens in bars, and we will not make that mistake again.

I miss the time in Riga when we watched the street performers, two young dancers, no older than eight, do some kind of samba on the street, in the dead of winter. We gave them about $100.

I miss the time, on the flight from Dakar to Casablanca, when a pair of siblings, sitting next to me—Will was on the other side of the aisle—asked to borrow my walkman, which I lent to them. They were wealthy, each studying English in Morocco, and they loved my CDs: Air and Tricky, but not Reverend Horton Heat, which the woman described with a twirl of her finger around her ear. I didn't know they did that in Africa, too. At some point, while her brother closed his eyes while wearing my headphones, I had this conversation with the woman, who was young and allowed me to flirt with her.

"Where are you from?" I asked.

"Kinshasa Congo. You know where this is?"

"Of course," I said.

The woman was still smiling. Her teeth were startlingly white and without flaws or gaps.

"Your teeth," I said, "they are remarkable."

She thanked me.

"Did you ever hear," I said, "about Mobuto, how he wanted to export an 'all-natural toothpaste' because the Congolese teeth were so superior to the rest of the world?"

She had heard this. She was a fan of Mobuto, which was disconcerting, so I changed the subject. She asked if I was married, and I said no. She asked if she could buy my walkman from me, and I said yes. Which she did, after customs, and after I kissed her cheek, which smelled like simple powder.

A few small corrections:

Mo and Thor: There were twin girls in Will's life, but they were babies when this trip took place—no more than two years old. Did he mention them on this trip? He didn't once. Did he write notes or postcards to anyone? He didn't. When we were traveling, he was entirely there, in Africa, in Latvia, because there was little time to think backward, to think of anyone at home. That's the simple and unvarnished truth. I would venture to say that even if Will had kids himself, a wife and twin daughters he'd nicknamed Mo and Thor, or Thor and Odin, for this one week his mind would be seeing, doing and seeing, and might not rest upon them more than once or twice. This is the truth, and it's either unromantic or infinitely more romantic than you can imagine.

Raymond: His name was Sean.

$80: When Abass asked for $80 after accompanying us to Saly, we gave him the $80, and we thought it was too bad, because we wanted to give him more. I didn't want to give him anything. As he walked away, though, Will chased after him and gave him another $500 or so. "You can't penalize him for being unsubtle," he said.

You Shall Know Our Velocity: I really loathe that title, and that's why I've changed it. I'm sure Will didn't come up with it, because his notebooks weren't labeled as such. I've retitled the book in accordance with a theory that I will lay down as soon as I get a chance.

Good people, everywhere we went our plans were compromised. We were limited to our access to Will's money by the banks and their hours, by what we could and couldn't travel with on planes, by our own fatigue. At the same time, our urges were sometimes the wrong urges. Driving between Casablanca and Marrakech, we wanted more than anything to pull off the highway and explore the red city of Benguérir, and we did pull off, momentarily. The place hadn't changed in a thousand years, it seemed, and we really thought we'd be seeing something new there; we'd be swallowed up in a good way. We sat at the roadside, watching as a man selling asparagus was about two hundred yards ahead of us, on the gravelly shoulder. We had a few minutes to debate, because the man was walking toward us, and would soon enough be upon us, wanting us to buy his rancid asparagus or something. I was in the driver's seat.

"I want to go into the city," I said.

"Like, walk around and everything?" Will said.

"Yeah, walk around, meet people, get invited into someone's house for dinner, sleep on someone's floor in exchange for some pens and batteries. Something like that."

"But then it'll be a day before we get to Marrakech. Two days till we leave Morocco—"

You know where this conversation went. I just peeled and drove into Marrakech, where eventually Will has his most pronounced breakdown, on the floor of the Djemaa el-Fna, which did not happen, unless he did it while I was watching this one monkey-performer steal hats from members of the audience. People like us just don't emote in the way he describes. I have never seen Will cry, though I know he has, and I have never been near him when he's done anything like this, and if there were ever someone who would not bawl in public, on the ground, in front of strangers—especially not in front of strangers, for it was their judgment he worried about most—it was Will.

Really, why do we disguise these true things, why do we take the actual events of a life, which I would expect to be transcribed with art but without fabrication, and distort and dilute and obscure them? Why this blurry fiction? I don't, I should say, find his book blurry, or even vague—for it tells the plain truth eighty-five percent of the time, day to day, of what we did. But when pressed to explain just what about the trip made it so worthy of transcription and dissemination, instead of breathing life into the story, he simply diverted attention, threw in random cookie-cutter background tragedy, and embellished. I find the technique kind of cheap. And given Will's enormous sense of urgency, his awkward but buoyant spirit, that he fell back on this is, to my eyes, a shame, and an uncourageous way to leave this earth. I realize how difficult the world makes it for those who want to lead and talk about unusual lives in a candid way, in a first-person way. I understand that to sublimate a life in fictions, to spread the ashes of one's life over a number of stories and books, is considerably better-accepted, and protects one greatly from certain perils—notably, the rousing of the anger or scorn of all the bitches of the world (more often male than female). But then again, I don't know—maybe he wasn't afraid of that sort of thing. Maybe he just wanted to fictionalize for his own entertainment. Maybe he found it artful. I don't know. But I do know that while we traveled, his idea was this would be an experiment and would make its way onto the page unadorned.

That was why we didn't sleep! We were, goddamnit, trying to live a week that would be worth documenting, worth writing down, minute by minute, so for him to embellish is counter to our aims, and I think a great betrayal of what might have been a great thing. The idea we came up with, well before we left, was something we coined Performance Literature. Excuse the use of that second word, because I realize it's presumptuous. Also, excuse the first word, and the term in general. I know better than you how fatuous it is. But it is accurate, and concise, in that what we had planned was a book conceived, then acted out, then transcribed, then ostensibly made into art. Thus, our actions in Africa and onward were predetermined to be transferred to the page, and we were therefore actors performing in a book not yet written. And we found this to be a new sort of concept. I can't guarantee that it hasn't been done a hundred times before, but I haven't personally seen it.

But then again, there are a number of ways one can take personal experience and make it into nonfiction. (For now we'll ignore the semi-autobiographical stuff.) The first is to decide, years after the lived life, to write it down. If I am eighty and decide to write about a summer when I was sixty, that's what I'm talking about. It's far after the fact, and not premeditated. Second is the travelogue, where one goes somewhere, intending to take notes, to later write something coherent about a place. But in this case, the observer is, more often than not, passive, writing chiefly about his or her surroundings, and the people he or she meets. The writer reacts, instead of acts. Well, I suppose they do act, in that they have to do the traveling, choose the destinations, and so forth, but again, largely they are observant cargo, being shuttled from place to place, notebook in hand.

We weren't passive observers, we were active characters. It was our motivations that drove the story. It was our actions that would be of equal or greater interest than our surroundings, and the two would no doubt play off each other constantly, essentially. And lest you think that doing so, traveling and interacting with the intent to write it down, would, via Heisenberg, necessarily influence the very interactions we were documenting, well, then you're missing the point. Here's why: Because we had the stated intent of documenting our trip, and because our minute-to-minute motivations were to act in a way that would deserve documenting, it's therefore not accidental but essential that our presence influence the outcome of events, and that our knowledge of such so-called perils were at the forefront of our minds, not buried within.

That said, we didn't think as often as we'd expected to about the transferability to the page of what we were doing. We tried to be exciting, but knowing what's interesting while you're doing it is sometimes very difficult, and in the event that you find yourself hours from anyone or anything, in the middle of the Latvian countryside, for example, you have no choice but to do something stupid, like driving with your tongue. Which we did on more than one occasion.

The other term we coined was Conceptual Life, which I guess isn't all that different from Performance Literature, with the one chief distinction being that Conceptual Life doesn't depend on the participants planning to write about the experience afterward. The liver of a Conceptual Life sets forward, ahead of time, certain goals and a framework within which he or she will live. Much like the artist who pledges to spend a month on a platform atop a telephone pole, for one example. The act of living, of eating and sleeping and defecating, is all included in the larger concept set forward—in this case, of living an elevated and observed life. As long as the liver doesn't leave the pole, all of his actions are still small marks upon the canvas he's sized and stretched.

Now I'll stop. I've been drinking vodka and Orangina, trying to put myself to sleep, and now it's working. I guess the last thing I'll say on this subject is that whatever you take away from this book, his text and mine—and I have no idea what you're taking away—please take away this one thing about the trip:

It happened, and it was good. It was good because it happened.

FRIDAY

Today was a day without rain and I walked out onto the deck at dawn and it was magnificent. The sun popped whole at seven and kept rising, faster than I could track. At about noon, after I read some local paper on the deck, feet up and face tanning slowly, I heard a voice, a woman's. I turned to see a woman with a bountiful head of hair, colored somewhere between blond and ivory, racing away from a face that looked familiar in the way that classically beautiful faces look. You feel you've seen them before, but what seems familiar is the demonstration of perfect symmetry. She was talking but I had missed the first few sentences and so gambled.

"Hello!" I roared, to make up with enthusiasm any error I'd made in response. Had she asked to borrow a rake or bag of rice? It didn't matter. A hearty hello would break through and at least color me friendly, if hard of hearing.

"Hello yourself," she said. And then I noticed that she was holding a hose. "Is this yours?"

I looked at the hose. I had never seen it before. It was brown.

"I have no idea," I said.

She owned the house next door, or rather she and her husband did, but she frankly didn't know where her husband was. Were they divorced? No, she laughed. Separated? No, no, she said. But he is a strange man. He disappears for many months at a time, she said.

She was lovely. Lovely is a word I usually use when commenting on my nieces, dressed as bridesmaids or for proms—it's a word for a young flower, or a view of rolling hills gauzed with mist. But I looked over at Sonje—that was her name, and I was thrilled that I'd caught it and pocketed it in time to lock it—and I thought of the word *lovely*. She was about forty, wearing overalls and a gardening hat of straw, and had those kneepads on, for enthusiastic gardeners with bad knees. Everything she wore was blue, except for a scarf around her neck, the color of margarine.

I explained my presence, going a little vague on the details, calling myself a researcher working on a very demanding project, due in two weeks. She was intrigued but respectful of my privacy. That, or she was bored silly and was glad to leave the details alone. She smiled at me in a way I hadn't been smiled upon a while. It was a sympathetic smile, which I'll take in a pinch.

"How long are you out at the house this time?"

"Just a few days," she said. "I have work back in the city. I have to get back late Sunday."

"To Auckland?"

"Yes."

I was trying to get a grip on her accent. It was not British, but it sounded more British than it did New Zealand . . . ish.

"What day is it today?" I asked, and hated myself for asking.

"Thursday. Don't tell me you're one of those."

What did that mean? I didn't know. I said:

"If I was, I wouldn't tell you," and confused myself more. I didn't know what she'd meant, and I have no idea what I meant in response. It was a wash, and we moved on. When the sun had appeared today I felt awake again, felt locked in battle with the sun, and felt good about that. I'd felt strong, and when I'd seen Sonje I felt so much stronger, but what was coming out of my mouth?

"Have you seen that thing out there?" I said, pointing to the black shape on the beach. Sonje was lovely, but already I was back to the shape. I couldn't help it. She turned and cupped her hand over her eyes.

"I thought it was a log, but I suppose you know better," she said.

She brought to mind English actresses. She had a straight back, was thin without being shapeless, and had a nose that I associate with aristocracy in film—straight, small, but strong. Her voice projected like an actress's, an actress who was also a wit, who could tell stories, who could make a group of children laugh but who also knew dozens of filthy limericks.

"We'll have to investigate it together," she said and I almost flew. I was so shaky in the head that I blurted something about dinner and she accepted, as long, she said, as we ate early, around five in fact, because she was expecting a phone call, from Amsterdam, at eight. Then she went back to her hose, and waved, though I hadn't moved.

I went back inside, determined to get as much down as possible, in the five hours before I'd knock on her door and we'd drive around the bay, and through the twenty or so turns, all coastal, to Whitianga—the closest town for a good dinner out. And now I'm here, and what I want to talk about is the idea of the sacrament. I want to explain why I've retitled this formerly mistitled book, and the explanation starts in Copenhagen, at the airport chapel.

There was a priest there, an Episcopal priest, heavy-set, with a neat beard of black and grey, and wire-rimmed glasses. Around him were a group of travelers, mostly businessmen, and one family of six, all Indian. Will and I walked in, having time to kill; neither of us had ever been to an airport chapel. The priest, who was American for no apparent reason, was talking to them about the uselessness of what he was doing. He was noting, and I paraphrase: "What I'm doing here, and what the church is doing here, and to some degree what you're doing here, is not of much utility. But you do not need me to tell you, while here, what to do. You are doing what your soul tells you to do, without my help or the help of God. The Bible, in some part, is a handbook for those who might forget our obligations to each other. And those obligations are obvious, and constant, even though they become more obvious, more pronounced and more urgent and immediate at a time such as this. [His voice carried, and was a beautiful voice, I should add. It was obvious that he was a singer of some kind, and one who sang from deep in his chest, his core.] What we are doing is much like the sacrament I will be handing to you shortly. For what is the sacrament? It is not in itself nourishment; it is, rather, an outward symbolic act of an inward grace. It is the external, social demonstration of how we feel within. It is not practical and without it we would feel the same way; it is a reminder only, and a relatively unnecessary one at that. But that does not mean it is dispensable, nor does it mean it is unbeautiful."

This was the first time I'd ever heard this word, *unbeautiful*, though since hearing it I have stolen it and now it is mine. It was clear he was a theologian, a scholar, but one with a taste for the irreverent. Will and I knew, with a brief glance out of the corners of our eyes, that our own Catholic priests wouldn't agree with his assessment of this particular sacrament as in some way unnecessary, but we liked his style. We always loved going to the Presbyterian church Youth Night, wherein we were given the run of the church basement, full of pool tables, Ping-Pong, pinball machines and couches, in exchange for listening to twenty minutes of the minister's thoughts, which were, we always had to admit, a lot more applicable and comprehensible than what we got at our own church. And as I was listening to the airport priest, I was loving the notion of the sacrament, or rather was quickly forming my own version of it, a secular version of the sacrament, because the only way I ever could make it through any Mass, or any Youth Night, was to take whatever message they were sending and bend it, sometimes beyond reason, to give some holy weight to the things I was already doing or already believed. In that airport chapel, I nudged Will, and he smiled. I want to think he knew what I was thinking about, but we never had a chance, afterward, to talk about it, because he was late for his flight to Mexico City, and afterward all we had a chance to do was shake hands and say good-bye. (He nodded a few times at me, like he was taking my picture, mapping my body, and then backed away. It was the last time we saw each other.) But what I was doing was connecting the idea of the sacrament to what we were doing that week, on the road, with those strangers. First, what we did was intensely ritualistic, in that the procedure was very similar each time, and involved the observance of certain rules, namely that the recipients should seem needing of the funds, and that, whenever possible, they should be asked for directions, given them, or should have helped to take us along our journey. Second, the exchange of the money was much, if

I may be so bold, like the exchange of the Holy Eucharist, in that in each case it is preceded by a brief and seldom-changing dialogue. In the case of the Holy Eucharist, the recipient is told of the symbolism of the communion wafer, and accepts this symbolism and reinforces his or her Catholic faith, by ingesting the wafer. In our case, we asked directions, and were pointed where we were already headed, and the recipient, by acknowledging the significance of the funds, accepts the symbolism of the money, and the symbolism of our giving it to them, and perhaps even reinforces his or her faith a little, too, in this case a humanistic faith, which I personally find even more difficult to keep . . .

I am being called away. It's Sonje. She's knocking on the glass—it's five already, gah—that separates this home from the air outside, and I am going to answer that door.

SATURDAY

Before I make some notes on the preceding passage, let me first say that Sonje makes an extraordinary bundt cake. When I left you last, she was knocking, wholly unannounced, on my sliding porch door of tempered glass. I was surprised but not all that surprised, because when you're one of a pair at the cusp of something brief but strong you know when someone might arrive. Her hair was down, and her hair is a thing of such extravagance that I sucked in a quick breath. I hadn't seen her with it down yet, and it was like something painted by a Wyeth, any of them—I thought first of Helga, because wasn't she Andrew's neighbor, and wasn't her hair, though rust-colored, rendered strand by strand?

She drove us to Whitianga, her Volvo tight around the coast. She drove like a lunatic; she knew the road and its many turns, and even in the rain she slowed for nothing. We ate on the second floor of a casual place, tables without cloths, where we both had sea bass, after I confirmed—I had to make sure with the manager because the waiter couldn't verify anything—that it wasn't Chilean.

At dinner, in the soft light from the room's corners, Sonje looked older. Her eyes, when she smiled, pulled a dozen tiny lines from her temples, I liked her more and though the food was plain it tasted fantastic. Her mouth was still full-lipped and while a baby downstairs wailed I wanted to be alone with her in her house, to see how she arranged her pillows. She was a banker, she said, or used to be. She'd also been a lawyer, almost a judge, and once worked in Connecticut for the World Wrestling Federation. She liked professional wrestling a lot.

"We have to go see it," she said. We were now talking about the shape on the beach.

I didn't want to.

"I can't understand why," she said. "You don't seem like someone who'd be afraid of a shape on a beach."

Back in her house, with all the lights turned on, she gave me a tour; the house was full of outsider art, much of it American, and African sculpture, which always looks the same to me, indistinguishable from anything you'd get at a flea market, but again, I know nothing. We walked in and quickly out of her bedroom and I understood but by the time we were in the second guest room, and she was pointing out the view from the shower, I couldn't hold back and from behind I wrapped my arms around her and sucked on her neck.

This morning we walked over the dunes and down to where the beach was flat. The shape was no more than fifty yards away. I stopped and squinted at the shape. Sonje waited for me.

"You notice the colors in this country are so bright?" she said. "I was in Massachusetts last year, in February. There weren't any colors. It's not that there was snow, because there wasn't. But it was monochromatic anyway. Just a kind of grey-brown everywhere. And I know it was winter and all, but I still missed New Zealand.

It's a kind of cartoon palette down here, wouldn't you say? The ocean is blue and the hills are green. They keep the good colors handy."

"You don't think it's a body, do you?" I asked.

She smiled and shook her head.

She hadn't let me stay long the night before. We groped each other while standing in the shower, and for a time with her sitting on the sink, but she'd wrapped things up.

"That was needed," she said, and led me to the door.

I couldn't concentrate when I woke up, knowing she'd come over after breakfast to take me down to the shape. She had her theories about it, which she wouldn't divulge, and she wanted to prove herself right. I hadn't slept much; I fell asleep after getting home, but already the bed was stupid with just me in it, and I had to use the vodka and Orangina trick again, which brought me awake at six, before the sunrise, which came without rain.

Sonje was wearing shorts, blue plastic sandals, a long-billed baseball hat and her margarine scarf. We walked to the shape. It was bigger as we walked closer. If it was a person, it was a very large person, at least three hundred pounds. Still the body was laying on its side, but now perhaps a third of it was beneath the sand, and as we walked closer, the smooth blackness of the shape became dotted with sand, and what seemed to be hair. The shape was wearing black everywhere. I stopped again.

"Hand, you're being irrational now," Sonje said, and she took my fingers in hers and continued.

Within seconds we were upon it, and the smell was upon us. A farm smell, thick and meaty.

"I had a hunch," she said. "There's the snout."

"I didn't know pigs got that big," I said. The thing was enormous, the size of a cow.

"Beautiful thing, though. Look at that coat. It's still in good shape."

"Don't touch it!" I yelled. She was leaning down to touch the damned thing.

"I'll wash up afterward," she said.

And she did, and I was there.

SUNDAY

Sonje has a great walk. It's slinky, in that her feet precede her shoulders, and she has a fluidity that's reassuring. We played Hide and Seek last night, we really did, and it was one of the most oddly intense things I've ever done. We took it very seriously, and because neither of us knew my rented house too well, there were many places to hide. Afterward, still walking around the house, we drank most of a bottle of red wine the owners had left in the pantry, and eventually were laying on the couch, where we were temporarily too tired to move.

I'd been telling her about my work on Will's book, and about that trip, and about Will generally. She asked if I missed him and I said yes, reflexively.

"That's normal," she said, and finished the wine. We were drinking from the bottle.

"I don't miss my brother," she said.

I hadn't known that she'd lost a brother.

"He drowned two years ago," she said, taking off her socks and placing them in a bowl of oranges I'd arranged earlier in the day, to impress her.

"I'm sorry," I said.

"I think I'll miss him eventually," she said, "but I'm not going to force it."

It seemed like a perfectly logical answer that would have horrified most people. It was an answer that freed me, completely, too, because I haven't missed Will in any familiar way yet. Will's own account of his tears over Jack were a mystery to me, because I hadn't shed many over Will. Maybe it hasn't been long enough. There were times during our friendship when we didn't talk for months, even six months at a time, and so far it hasn't felt any different. Or maybe I just always figured he'd die young. That's the most true I can be, but I have no idea why that's the case.

"But it's awful, I think, to die like that, in a dirty river," Sonje said.

"Where did your brother die?"

"Out on that bay," she said, and pointed through the dark window, past our reflections, where we could make out the pink horizontal line of the breaking surf.

"Jesus," I said. If I had lost a brother here I would not return to this beach. I didn't tell her this.

"I don't come here for any ghoulish reason," she said. "But I must say that it just doesn't really move me one way or another. I don't look out into that water and see Adam. He's not some body for me anymore. Even if a body like his did wash up someday, I wouldn't see that body as Adam. Does that sound strange?"

I shook my head and kissed her shoulder, half-hoping that she would adjust it. Where it was, it was digging into my sternum but I hadn't wanted to interrupt her.

"My point," she said, "is that for me there's a difference between drowning alone, while sailing, on a clear bay, and dying in a brown river full of people. And with your mother! It's so much worse."

"Oh lord, that didn't happen," I said, blurted really, and it occurred to me that I haven't told you this, either.

Will's mom had been gone eight years when we left for Dakar. This is a fiction that I can't be angry about, and one of which admittedly I could have relieved this text long ago. I have been writing this, as promised, in order, no looking back, and though I'd meant, time and again, to explain this part to you, I didn't, and now I wonder if I'm somehow complicit in this particular fiction. Will's mother was never available for phone calls while we were traveling. My shock at reading the first lines of this book, those giving birth to the fictional Jack, was only matched by my surprise and then sympathy when, in a few years, it's implied that Will's mom was alive and present at the point when Will was lost in Colombia. It's my guess that even the ghostwriter was fooled at this point, because I have no doubt that Will wrote every last word, throughout this text, of the passages that render various conversations with his mother. I remember where I was—riding the Northwestern community train from the city to Milwaukee, on the upper level, trying not to touch the window, which was frozen—when I read the first conversation between Will and his mom, dead ten or so years. I dropped the book and my throat went coarse. I didn't know, for so many years, that he was still so close to the grief. Or perhaps he wasn't; perhaps he had to have the distance he did to feel comfortable rendering her again, resurrecting her in this form. But I couldn't help picturing him, writing the story, with a pen on a series of spiral-bound unruled pages, and wanting to be able, as he did so, to tell his mother about the trip. She would have loved it all. She was a great lady; the story about Great America is true, though of course it was just the three of us, without Jack. She was a woman that always teetered close to the sort of parent who tries too hard to be liked by the young, though she never went over that line. She was comfortable with her age, with her role, and I came to understand that she went to arcades and Lasertag with us not because she had to prove her understanding of us, but because she plain liked that kind of shit. And so there she is, sort of, in these brief conversations, while her son traveled through Africa and while she was slowly slipping into senility. (Another fabrication: in life, she died of complications from surgery on a lymph node.) But even when she was scolding or harping, Will would have found solace in hearing her voice again, and it does sound like her, precisely so, even though I could hear little of her as I read, so preoccupied was I with this new insight into Will, and how badly, it was obvious, it was breathtaking, he wanted her back.

As would any mother's son, especially if that son was the only child. His journal from his days after Cuernavaca, in Colombia, etc., incomplete as it is, also includes his mother as his constant companion. I don't want to think that Will was losing himself or his mind; I prefer to believe that he was fictionalizing different things for different reasons, but anyway, only broken men and dictators can be made from the separation from their sole parent, and if that only parent is his mother, the extremes would seem more likely. So of all of Will's fabrications, I want to emphasize that it's this one that I understand the most, as much as it slashes my heart diagonally. We do know this: Jack is there so Will could write about pain. I see his mother every time he mentions Jack, and every time he lies awake, mouthing the words of a silent debate, he's giving voice to his outrage that he's still separated from his mom, and that they were picked on, singled out, when they had no one but each other to begin with. But this is just a guess. Another: I think the book as a whole is a sacrament of sorts, a physical representation, of too many things otherwise ephemeral—a social demonstration of a partly unknowable internal state, a messy combination of Twain's shapeless string of absurdities, and something like that state of secular grace I was talking about earlier. Maybe all books are sacraments. Do we achieve a state of elevation, as we read and write? That's probably a stretch.

There are things I probably won't and can't understand about him, and why he did what he did. You'll continue to read now, knowing what I knew, what is true and what is less true, and I hope that his account still holds the power he intended. I'm of the opinion that its power might be increased, and am of the view that had he stayed straight from the beginning . . . well, you know my opinion about that. I believe in fact, and I believe in the plain truth told wholly—that the truth retold can be a net thrown around life at a certain time and place, encompassing all within, and that people can go out there, live as actors, work within their staging ground, do so with a soft heart; I want others to go out in the world with an idea, with intentions and means, and come back with a story about how their actions affected the world and how they themselves were shaped by the results. I have a belief that such endeavors can improve the world, however recklessly, especially when these people go forward and interact, give, solve, change the situations they encounter—and also, even those with no intentions of recording their actions. There's nothing to be gained from passive observance, the simple documenting of conditions, because, at its core, it sets a bad example. Every time something is observed and not fixed, or when one has a chance to give in some way and does not, there is a lie being told, the same lie we all know by heart but which needn't be reiterated. Friends, I urge you to find us hopeful. I urge you to find that we tried something, knowing nothing of the results. I remind you that we did freeze on a Latvian beach, which is pictured somewhere in these pages, we froze our fingers and knees and ears, in order to tape almost a thousand dollars in a rubber tire. And there is a chance that this money will not find the right new owner, and there is a chance that it's still there, full of mold or now the home for some disease-carrying insect, and there is a chance that everything we did was incorrect, but stasis is itself criminal for those with the means to move, and the means to weave communion between people.

MONDAY

Sonje went back to Auckland yesterday, to the house she shares with her husband, who she hasn't seen in two and a half months. I leave today and have things to do in Phuket when I get there. I will be good.

The pig is gone, the one that washed ashore behind this house. Today the morning was dry and clear again, and I stepped onto the deck, and where the pig was, there was just a low mound. I'm not sure if someone buried it there, or if the sand just built up around it.

The pig symbolizes nothing.

MONDAY

I felt good and strong so we packed and left.

"You're good?"

"I think so. I feel good."

We rented a car from two young blond women in red jackets—we knew such comfort from those red jackets—and we told them we would drop it off in Riga, Latvia, the next day. We didn't know if we could feel good about the day before.

"Your first trip," the one on the left said, "should be to buy some coats." She was frisky and correct. It was a dull but intense cold, and snow flurried through the city, changing direction in midflight, flakes swarming, losing their way, then finding a new paths.

We were going to three or four hours south, looking for poor on the way. We'd spend the night in Riga, and in the morning visit the Liv. Our guidebook mentioned the Liv, a Finno-Ugric fishing tribe five thousand years old, the descendants of which still lived on the west coast of the Gulf of Riga. There were only a handful of elders who could still speak the Livonian tongue, and we figured we'd go there, find them, give them the rest of the money—about $11,000. Then we'd swing back down, drop the car in Riga, catch a flight to Cairo, bribe a guard at the pyramids to let us climb to the top of Cheops and from there watch the sunrise come over the Sahara. Perfect.

At the café next door, as we waited for the car, we shared a local newspaper—on the front page a picture of a man, a hunter, standing above three dead animals, lynx or snow cats—and watched a meeting of three young businesspeople, all speaking English to each other with similar Eastern-European accents. We ate toast and jam. At the nearby bank, looking precisely like every bank in America, glass and steel and expensive signage, I cashed more traveler's checks. I was so sick of my name it pained me. I wrote it on each one, my signature more and more deranged each time. The teller counted my money three times, quickly like a dealer, and handed it to me slowly, implying it meant more to me than her, which I wasn't sure was true.

We left the city and turned on the heat. We still had no coats.

On the side of the road, in the trees, we began to see men. Every five or ten miles a man in the forest on a stump, sitting. They weren't doing anything in particular. Certainly not ice-fishing—there was no water under their feet, just the forest floor. But otherwise it did seem to be an ice-fishing pose. We saw three or four and then a man of maybe seventy, closer to the road than the others, sitting on a box before a small but robust fire. A dirt road beside him led from the highway through the tall straight trees. I was driving. Hand was still watching them as we passed.

"There's a little girl with him," Hand said.

"Where?"

"Look."

"I can't. The road's icy," I said.

"They're perfect. Turn around."

"Really?"

"We should. You'll see."

I turned around and parked on the gravel shoulder.

Hand got out and talked to the man, asking directions to Pärnu, a smaller city on the way to Riga. The little girl, about six, was in a pink snowsuit and dragged a sled, plastic and also pink, up to Hand and the man. Hand held a stack of bills to the man. The man looked at the money and then led Hand over to a pile of sticks near the road. Hand examined the sticks for a second and then seemed to register the man's intent. The sticks were for sale, and the man was offering them to Hand. Hand waved them off, smiling, and shoved the money into the man's palm. Then Hand walked back to the car. The man stood, unmoving, watching him get in. I waved. He waved back.

"Hmm," Hand said, buckling his seat belt.

"What?"

"I really hope that little girl was his granddaughter."

"Oh—"

"Otherwise we just bought a pedophile a new dungeon."

"How much was it?" I asked.

"I don't know. I gave him what you gave me."

"About 3,000 kroon, I think."

"Enough for the dungeon and a pool, too."

"She's fine," I said, wanting to believe it. "She looked happy. She was smiling in a pink snowsuit. With a sled. She's fine."

"I guess. But that guy was in bad shape."

—Every story, Hand, is sadder than ours.

—Every last one.

.

We were both tired of talking. We drove in silence for miles. The road was barren. The ground was white and the treeline was low. Estonia could look like Nebraska and Nebraska could look like Kansas. Kansas like Morocco. Morocco like Arles. On and on. Growing up I thought all countries looked, were required to look, completely different—Congo was all jungle, robust and wet and green, Germany was all black forests, Russia was white, all of it Siberian. But every country now seemed to offer a little of every other country, and every given landscape, I finally realized, existed somewhere in the U.S.

Which took some of the fun out of it. It made little sense to leave one's country if all you're looking for is scenery and poor people, just as it wouldn't make sense, really, to cheat on someone you're cheating with. Hell. What were we doing here? It felt like we'd been gone for months, as if we'd been in Estonia for weeks. But it felt so strange. To travel is selfish—that money could be used for hungry stomachs and you're using it for your hungry eyes, and the needs of the former must trump the latter, right? And *are* there individual needs? How much disbelief, collectively, must be suspended, to allow for tourism?

Hand lunged for the radio dial and turned it up.

"Hear this?" he said. It was "Up Where We Belong," the Joe Cocker song. "This was the main Champagne Snowcone song. Remember that?"

"Snowball. Champagne Snow*ball*."

"What did I say?"

"Snowcone."

"Man, I have never stopped thinking about those fucking dances. That was junior high, right? Junior high dances and that's like my favorite time on Earth. I've never reached that level of bliss again."

We had a feature at our junior high dances called Champagne Snowball. Champagne Snowball happened first at the dances sponsored by the local recreation center, and these dances everyone came to; we weren't yet too jaded to enjoy that kind of thing sober. We would all go, everyone would go, to these dances in the gym of the Rec Center. We'd get a ride from our parents, or (much better) our older siblings, and from eight to ten o'clock in that square huge gym, chaos reigned. I don't remember ever seeing a chaperone, or really any representative of the Center, or anyone in any position of oversight or restraint. It was just three hundred of us and the deejay—

"What was the deejay's name again?" Hand asked.

"B.J. McGriff."

"Right. Exactly! Holy shit."

—and no one knew if that was his real name, or if he had changed it for hopeful but misdirected professional reasons. B.J. was in high school, but not at the one in town. And he didn't look like someone from our town. He was a New Wave kind of guy far before our town got cable. His hair was short and dyed orange, he wore small sturdy gold hoops in both ears, and had his velour pants tucked into the neat and curvy boots of a delicate man.

We were in seventh grade, and it was 8:15 when Hand, Jack and I got in Jack's family's red wood-paneled Grand Caravan, driven by his sister Molly. Eight minutes later, when we pulled into the Rec Center driveway and as we scooted across the backseat for the car door, she turned to us.

"Dances are for assmunchers," she said.

"What's an assmuncher?" I asked. Even at thirteen, I could tell she had just heard the word and didn't know what it meant.

"*You* should know," she said, and laughed in a big, fake way. She was such a bitch.

We opened the doors. I had an idea.

"See ya, assmuncher," I said, and we ran off laughing. For about two years that would be the biggest burn I'd ever pulled off.

Even though Molly was not so cool at the high school, we looked good getting out of the old beater. She peeled away while flicking us off, as the other kids were standing at their parents' passenger windows, leaning in, nodding as their fathers gave them instructions for when and where, outlining issues of money and caution and restraint.

"Molly—she was so troubled," I said.

"I remember," said Hand, as the song ended and Starship followed. This was an 80s station in Estonia. "Molly. Wow."

We walked from the car to the light. Inside the gym was pandemonium. Rough-surfaced red kickballs were thrown at newcomers dumb enough to enter through the gym's main double-door. The lights were out save a few small spotlights on B.J., which he apparently brought himself. Otherwise the only illumination came from the open doors at the gym's four corners. The whole social portion of the school was there, as were the kids who wanted in. There was Meredith Shannon in her tight blue pants with the words DO NOT BEND printed and stretched across her rear. She wore those every Tuesday. There was sneering Terri Glenn, who had just acquired, and managed to use, the word *omnipresent* in every fourth or fifth sentence. And Larry and Dan, the two huge round boys, not twins or brothers and thus scarier, who everyone liked but who came to dances wearing helmets. We walked through the dark human garble, looking for people we liked and people we wanted to tongue, because that was the improbable and glorious thing: here you could not only tongue people, but here the tonguing of your classmates was sanctioned, was commanded.

"I can't believe they let us do that," Hand said, rolling down his window and throwing out an apple core.

This is the way of Champagne Snowball: First, a slow song. "Open Arms," "(Here I Am) The One That You Love," anything by Spandau Ballet. You scope, you choose, you find someone, you say these words: "Will you dance?" and then lead them to a spot crowded enough where you won't be easily seen. Put your skinny worthless arms, arms you've vowed to work on, around her waist, while she puts her arms around your wet neck. Everyone is already soaked from the fast songs, from Dean and Hand initiating an elaborate group-dance routine to the 5-4-3-2-1 Major Tom song, so expect your partner's back will be moist. She will smell of Sea Breeze. Her temples will drip onto your shoulder. Feel the heat of her chest against yours. Feel the *heave*. You will never know heaving like that again so soak in that heave. Put that heave into a small velcro pocket in the parachute pants of your soul. If she's as tall as you, and she probably is, move closer and set your face upon her hot cheek. When it gets too hot switch cheeks. Hope she won't ask you if you have a pen in your pocket while knowing it's not a pencil. Hope you don't pee. *Why would you pee?* You don't know. She will blow her face cool with her lower lip outstretched, her bangs floating briefly upward like banners tied to balconies. Know her hot chin on your hot shoulder, know her chest breathing into your chest. Wonder if she likes you in a making-out way. Wonder if you should (sexy!) or shouldn't (queer!) rub your woody against her inner thigh. Wonder where your friends are. Wonder what time it is. How much time is left—you needed more time! See Jack dancing with Annmarie and roll your eyes. Watch him act offended and start to fake-cry. Laugh and when your partner asks what's funny say "Oh, the comedy of life." Feel the cooling of the sweat on your partner's back. Let your hands drop a little. Wonder if she'll be a good kisser. Finally, a minute or so into the song, it will come, the B.J.'s decree: "Champaaaaagne."

He will say it in a sultry and drawn-out sort of way, doing his seventeen-year-old best to simulate a baritone by wrapping his lips around the cold black dimpled microphone. And with this word, you are mandated to kiss your partner.

"Can you turn the stereo down?" Hand asked.

I did. Hand was curled toward his door.

"I could never sleep after those dances," said Hand. He activated the car's windshield defrost.

And after the dance, at home and on my bed, bent toward the wall and trying to sleep but completely unable, we knew we had been given this, a point on the sun where it burst for us—

"But I'm so tired now," Hand said. "I just got hit by it."

"You're gonna sleep now?"

"I just have to close my eyes for a second."

"Okay," I said.

Maybe ten seconds after the uttering of "Champaaaaaagne," as
we were just starting to know the shape of the partner's mouth,
would come "Snooooowwball," at which point we were supposed
to switch dance partners, mid-song, giving us a chance to meet and
enjoy the next partner. But we only really had to trade if it suited
us, if our current partner no longer held appeal or if there was
someone better, freer. Did B.J. enforce the partner-switching sug-
gestion? He did not. And almost half the night's songs were slow
songs, meaning that if you wanted to, and I did, some did, most
did, all did, you could dance with twelve different people, kissing
each for two, two and a half minutes—and more if one of the songs
was "Stairway to Heaven," in which case, though, hell, you'd have
to kind of try to dance again when it got fast at the end. No one
knew just how to dance to "Stairway to Heaven." Some continued to
hobble slowly, ignoring the quickened pace, the sudden urgency,
all that screaming, while most people started bouncing a little,
jumping in place, maybe a little air guitar, anything. It's just the
wrong song for dancing; that's the lesson there.

But when the word *Champagne* arrived, we pulled our heads off
each others' shoulders, same height we were, and her mouth was
upon me, a black hole approaching. Our teeth clicked at each
other, and she breathed into me. There was so much moisture! I
found myself flying quickly around her mouth, a bat scanning the
walls. As food stuck between molars makes explorers of tongues,
the tongue becoming topographer and every canker sore a ridge of
saw-toothed mountains, so did my tongue become the mapmaking
conquistador of Mary-Kate's dark wet mouth. I knew its crevices,
its stalactites and stalagmites, the smooth runs of the tops of her flat
back teeth. I fought for dominion with her tongue, which probed
my mouth while guarding her own. After thirty seconds, having
explored her mouth's offered worlds, I went farther and soon could

feel the extremities of her brain, could tickle its smooth underside. I scuttled around the back of her skull, was rushing through her, pinballing between cartilage and capillary, then up again, devouring and searching, her eyes like marbles in my mouth. That reminded me: I opened my lids to see if hers were open too but they were not, they were closed but just barely, lips resting softly atop mine, and so I closed my lids too and went farther into her, into her center, and there, finally, I found her landscape. It was dark where she was and I could see almost nothing, doubted what I knew, but I did make out her winding river, a thin and clear one, warm from the day's sun, and then her cluster of a dozen or so small hills, and at their base was her tall white home, clean and fair in the spotlight of a three-quarter moon, illuminated within by a hundred tall thin candles.

I opened my eyes and Jack was watching me. He was there, arms around Jenny Erdmann, watching me, smiling his old man's wise and benevolent smile. It was this time, more than any other, that I noticed how far his ears stuck out. He really was a jug-eared bastard. I gave him the finger.

"Hand."

He slept.

"Hand."

After the dance we waited for Molly but not very long. We knew she wouldn't pick us up, after I called her an assmuncher. Shirts wet with sweat now cooling in the night, we started home. It was 2.2 miles to our neighborhood; we knew this because Hand had made his father measure it with their car's odometer.

We walked through the woods first, behind the rec center, then across two fairways of the county golf course. There was a new berm built between the highway and the new housing development, so we climbed that and walked atop its rounded ridge, only half-sodded then, past the pond the developers had made into a lake.

Hand wanted to stay out and I wanted to stay out. We stood on the top of the berm, the highway busy below, the air cooling, the wind gusting. Jack wanted to go home.

"Why?" we asked. The electrical wires howled.

Jack looked perplexed. Because we have to go home, he said. Because we lived at home and we had curfews.

We argued for a while, though Jack didn't really know the terms of debate. He didn't understand exactly what would be gained by staying out. What would we do? he asked. We'll be tired all day tomorrow, he said.

We couldn't think of anything to do. But it felt good to be out on the berm, above the new lake.

—Hand, we shouldn't have brought him with us.

—He was fine.

"Hand, we shouldn't have."

Hand continued to sleep.

—He didn't want to come. He never really wanted to come. He wanted to be with us but he never saw the point in the things we decided to do.

—He wanted to come.

—I have had visions of that cow for ten years now, twelve. I see its eye, I see it just burning and its eye seemed awake, alive for so long. That black liquid eye.

—Stop.

—Hand, it's what we did to that cow.

—Will. It's not the cow.

—Hand we burned that cow alive.

—The cow was dying.

—We poured gasoline on that cow and we burned it.

—We were young. We don't talk about the cow.

—We knew this was an affront to the world.

—The cow would be eaten. We were thirteen and we had to react violently to the world. We'd seen its rules and the demons it allows to live among us. We killed the cow to express our outrage.

—Jack didn't want to do it but didn't want to leave us.

—He stayed because he wanted to.

—We walked from the dance through the golf course and into that one small farm with the six cows. We went into the shed by the barn and we found gasoline and we burned that cow. We didn't doubt what we were doing, not for a second. We didn't doubt it for so many years afterward, right? It felt right at the time, to pour gasoline on a cow and set it aflame.

—We're allowed to grow up.

—We are not allowed this reaction. Only some are allowed to pollute the world. We were sober and we planned it. We hated that cow. We three rode by that cow every weekend on our bikes and we planned to kill it. I had a vision of a cow on fire and we decided we had to make that vision real. We had no right.

—Doesn't matter.

—The cow didn't move as we doused it. Then it felt the burn as the gasoline soaked into its hide. It rolled on the ground. And then we threw the match. We had no right.

—We did it and it was done.

—We had no right. This was the same year we first wanted to kiss all the girls. We were darkhearted boys. We should have been jailed or drugged or killed. I remember watching that cow burn with total detachment. It barely made a sound, that cow. It was all so quiet, and the night was so bright, so clear and the stars were in brilliant clumps, and we stood by the fence, leaning on it afterward, watching, the flames blue and red, and the body beneath darkening from white to grey to black.

—Fucking stop it. Now you're just dredging for the sake of dredging. There's no point.

—This is my head, asshole! *This is how it works.* It jumps from one wretched episode to the next.

—Leave me out of it.

—We polluted Jack, Hand. All the bad ideas were our ideas.

And we had no right. We were given things others have not been given. We had a clean 7-Eleven within walking distance—we had—this is the reason they took Jack. And why my face is mangled. This is simple and deserved retribution.

—From whom?

—I don't know.

—From God?

—From whomever settles scores. Someone settles scores. Someone keeps the balance.

—No one keeps the balance, Will.

—Balance is at the foundation of the world.

—If there was balance, Will, we wouldn't be here. If there's balance, there's logic, and if there's logic, you're not on a lightbulb package and we're not here.

—There's balance enough.

—Don't flatter yourself to think this is your doing. Your problem is that you think things have happened for the first time to you, and that you're the fulcrum from which all people and the current world pivot.

—But still there will be retribution. I have had mine. And we all are punished. It happens first within our minds and then in the physical world.

—No. There is no balance, and no retribution, and no rules. The rules and balances you blather about are hopeful creations of a man fearing death.

—There is so much more. I have seen this and you will see it when they have beaten you in your own head. I sat and read from our past and they beat me near death. This is our punishment for our hubris, for our brutality.

—Don't bring me into this. I am no victim of anything.

—If there were no limitations we would be able to make real our visions. But we cannot.

—We can. Champagne Snowball.

—Oh lord no.

—Yes. It was one of few perfect instances where every impulse was followed through, every desire fulfilled. We showed up at the dance and our pants were bursting with confusion but we were clear in our desires. There were all those thighs in tight corduroy and nothing looks better on full thighs than tight corduroy, and all we wanted was to hold those people, and sway with them, and then open our mouths to them. We wanted to feel their heaving and we did. We wanted their mouths upon ours and we wanted to see their lights within and we did.

—And that was fourteen years ago. Junior high, stupid. Everything else has been chaos.

—Well now you're contradicting yourself. With balance there cannot be chaos. With randomness there can be no punishment. You're pleading for punishment in hopes that you'll see your God. Without punishment there is no God. If there is balance then there is your Lord. If balance then afterlife.

—I have thought of leaving you.

—When? Why?

—I have thought in my dimmest moments of leaving you as you left me. As you left me in Oconomowoc. When we were in Marrakesh and being followed through the labyrinth one of my first thoughts was *Wow, this would be something. I could leave him out here.* I thought of *Kingpin*—

—You were thinking of *Kingpin* when we were almost dead in those alleys?

—I cannot tell you how quickly my head moves.

—Fine.

—I thought of Bill Murray tricking Woody into getting out of the car when the bowling alley guys wanted to kill them, and then Murray drives off, leaving Woody alone and—

—What's your point?

—There were times these past weeks when I wanted it to have been you.

—What? What to be me? The beating? I wanted it to be me, too, asshole! I've told you that a thousand times! I would take that beating and ten more for you, dipshit.

—I wanted Jack to have been you.

—Jack wouldn't have come here with you. Jack was too cautious. Jack—

—No, no. Before this.

—Not the truck.

—I had the blackest thoughts, Hand. Those days after Oconomowoc. I slept and when awake I boiled. I didn't want to be awake. The librarians swarmed. They catalogued and duplicated. They filed everything carefully in deep storage, while keeping copies at hand. I didn't know if I should keep my eyes open or closed. Closed I was at their mercy; they had no competition for my attention. Open I saw my face, my body. I kept them open and watched TV. I didn't answer the phone. I wanted another day to make sure it had happened. How much had happened? I charted the pain but wouldn't check everything. I didn't want all the answers yet. I was full. I'd swallowed a dozen grenades. My spine smoldered. I could stand, but had to hunch over to walk. My jaw wasn't broken and felt better than I'd expected, but was blue on the right side and growing blacker, with a small bruise of green expanding.

—I know all this.

—My eyes were getting darker, the left one at least would go blue. There was a scratch, thick as a pencil, on the bridge of my nose, and I couldn't remember when I'd gotten it. My left temple was cut and looked to be dented. I took a bath and the water quickly went grey then pink. I couldn't raise myself from the tub and had to slither over the side and crawl to the toilet, which I used to hoist myself up. I drank all the beer in my fridge, seven bottles. I lay on the couch and went in and out of a shallow sleep. I needed the voices and laughter from the TV.

—Will.

—I found myself watching some cable-access comedy improv show and loving it. It was ten in the morning then four in the afternoon, and five beers later—warm from the pantry—it was eleven. I watched people walk their dogs outside and wanted them to come to me and share their animal with me. I wanted Mo and Thor there to complain about everything, to play catch with my old records. Seven more—cans now, from my neighbor's stash in the basement—and it was almost six in the morning and then I'd know if this was real. My right hand was fractured somewhere; I couldn't make a fist and this more than anything enraged me.

—Shut the fuck up.

—And somewhere in there I wondered what would have happened if it was you in that car. If the truck had crushed you. I wished for a second it was you. I wished that it was you, and that Jack and I were in the storage unit because he wouldn't have left me. He wouldn't have been gone. He would have been there. But I will never say this to you. And I don't wish it or believe it or wonder about it anymore.

—Thank you.

—Sure.

—But Will, your life has been lived a hundred times. A thousand times. It's not all that great, really. Don't take it so seriously. Don't handle it so delicately.

—I'm too fucking fragile. I hate being fragile. My hand, I think I broke it. I swung and missed and hit the steel wall and I can barely make a fist, and every time I shake hands I wince. I'm no use now. Everything makes me flinch. I see boxing on TV and I have to turn it off. I hear loud voices and I jump. On a cop show I see three men beating one man and I need a drink to calm me.

Hand, nobody told me about the weight. Why didn't our parents tell us about the weight?

—What weight?

—The *fucking weight, Hand.* How does the woman Ingres live? The one from Marrakesh? If we're vessels, and we are, then we, you and I, are overfull, and that means she's at the bottom of a deep cold lake. How can she stand the hissing of all that water?

—We are not vessels; we are missiles.

—We're static and we're empty. We are overfull and leaden.

—We are airtight and we are missiles and all-powerful.

"Hand."

He continued to sleep. I turned up the radio.

"Hand."

—Oconomowoc was my limit. Until then I was full to my brim but Oconomowoc was overflow. I couldn't hold it. I can't hold it.

—It wasn't Oconomowoc. Oconomowoc was nothing. Jack was it. Jack broke you but you have to—I don't want my own thoughts anymore. I want my head to be only a part of something else. A small part of a thinking organism. What's that plant they found in Minnesota? The largest continuously living organism—some underwater plant or something that's miles around? That's what I want. Make me part of that, make my brain just part of that operation. I want none of my own thoughts anymore. I want to donate my head.

—Then fine. Throw it.

—Jesus, Hand, we're only twenty-seven. Doesn't it seem like someone's fucking with us here? The weight! I can't do—It'll only get worse. I'll have a baby and that baby will die. What if I have a baby that dies? I've been cut to the bone. They've cut me too many times. My limbs hang from tatters. If you could feel what it's like to live in this body—everything screams, my hands I can't even tighten into fists—

—Don't you understand? Leap over this.

—Hand I am ready. I am tingling for the world. But I was already raw. I didn't realize how raw. Then we planned this trip and I thought I could do more, that I could do better. But now I want to see the end. When you know when the weight will be lifted you can bear it in the meantime. You know this?

—You have to give everything.

—This is what I'm doing.

—We are creating it. We are conjuring it.

—Every time we do it it's a new world. I live again. Love is implicit in every connection. It should be. Thus when absent it makes us insane. It breaks our equilibrium and we have to flounder for reasons. When we pass by another person without telling them we love them it's cruel and wrong and we all know this. We live in a constant state of denial and imbalance.

—Well, I wouldn't go so far—

—Everyone must embrace us.

—They have embraced us.

—Hand, did you notice that that one boy in Senegal looked like Jack? The one who moved the stone under our car? The first time we blew a tire? He looked just like Jack.

—That boy was black, Will.

—But he—

—Jack had red hair and freckles, Will.

—But in his eyes there was something. The way he sort of bowed when he was backing away with the rock. I don't know. Something in the give of his eyes. Shit. I see Jack's face a lot. I see the back of his head, or his profile—I see his profile next to me, in the backyard, with him bent over a piece of posterboard, with him holding the marker in his retarded way, in his fist like he did then, his knees all wet from the soil under the grass, and the way he would run when he ran the 440, with his chin all the way out, not just at the finish line but all the way through—

"Hand."

—Oh fuck we tried.

I pulled the car over. I needed him awake.

"Hand."

—Oh fuck we tried.

He continued to sleep. I turned up the radio.

"Hand."

"What? Why are we stopped?"

We were stopped. I'd pulled over because I couldn't see.

"Will, Jesus. Wipe your nose," Hand said. He gave me a sock.

"Holy fuck," I said. I tried to move all the shit out of my eyes and off my face. There was all this shit there.

"Holy fuck," I said.

"Holy fuck," Hand said.

The car was grey inside, the windows fogged, and I was ready to go. We'd been stopped for ten minutes and that was enough.

"Let's go," I said. "Let's do the next thing."

We stopped a few miles up the road, at another clean unfriendly gas station–café. Inside we bought candy and while walking back to the car agreed we had to bury a treasure. On the way to Riga we would take a stack of bills, bury it somewhere, make a map and let someone, a kid, find it.

We stopped in a small suburban town and in the clean suburban bank, with Hand across the street buying new socks for us— the odor from ours was newly unendurable—I changed another $1,000 in traveler's checks. I signed the Mediterranean papers angrily. They had to figure out an easier way to do this. I would have to change my signature after this.

We met back at the car, put on our new socks—warm, clean, dry—and we left the town, looking for an offroad where we could walk into the woods unnoticed, bury the treasure, and afterward find kids nearby. We pulled off and drove down a long scraggly country road looking for people. We needed a small village near the forest. But the woods thinned and soon it was farms only, blank, gothic, with no sign of its residents. We stumbled into some kind of logging operation, enormous trucks being loaded with timber of equal proportion. But no kids. I thought of something.

"It's only one o'clock. They're still in school."

Hand exhaled in dim recognition. "Right."

On the side of the road, a hitchhiker stood, a man of about twenty, in jeans and black leather jacket, weathered grey.

"We should," I said.

"Why?"

"It's fucking cold."

We stopped and he got in and ducked into the backseat, head between us, smiling. We drove.

"Where are you guys from?" he asked.

We said Anchorage. He thought that was cool.

His jacket, an enormous black leather thing, had a large Nirvana patch on the breast. Below it, one for Pantera. His wrist bore one of those thick black leather steel-studded bracelets worn by bulldogs. His head, which I put together in the rearview mirror: unwashed hair, the whitest skin, a redness around his eyes and on the corners of his mouth, as if he'd been licking skin rubbed raw by fierce and constant winds.

"Cold out there yes?" Hand said.

"Not so bad," said the hitchhiker.

It was about ten degrees.

"How long you been out there?" I asked. His eyes widened when I asked and I realized it was because of my face. But he didn't turn away.

"Two hours, three hours. I guess," he said.

We asked him his name and he told us. Taavi Mets. Taavi was in a band. He played drums. He and Hand talked details for a while, brands and years. Hand used to play guitar in a band called Tomorrow's Past. Taavi asked for the name again. Hand told him: Tomorrow's Past. Taavi didn't get it and it was just as well.

Did Taavi's band have a tape out? Yes. A CD? Too expensive.

We asked the name of the band. He took the piece of paper back and wrote both his name and the band's:

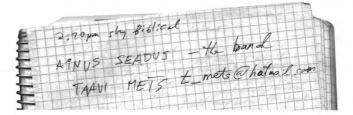

We wanted to please Taavi so we put in the Foo Fighters—the best we could do. Taavi was a student at a vocational school in Tallinn, on his way home. It was good to have him in the car. Three felt good. Three felt right. He was studying mechanical engineering and lived in Parnü.

"So listen," said Hand, turning in his seat to face Taavi. I assumed he'd start asking about the current economic situation in Estonia, the conversion to the free market, the privatization of industries, but something else was on Hand's mind.

"I have question about this the fighting of bears and dogs."

I laughed in one quick grunt.

"Excuse me?" said Taavi.

"Why do they fight bears against dogs?"

Hand was being very serious. Taavi didn't understand. Hand elaborated.

"You know, they take the bear, yank his teeth out, chain him to a post and sic dogs on him."

"Who?"

"Estonians!"

Taavi shook his head. "Where do you see this?"

"On the TV."

"When?"

"Actually, a friend sees it. A friend sees it on TV for real."

"A bear fighting dogs?" said Taavi, "I have not seen this."

"They do not do this?"

"No," Taavi said, with a little chuckle.

"They take the [long *e*] bear, and take its claws out?"

"Bears? I have not seen this."

"Not popular in Estonia?"

"No, I have not seen this."

I was relieved, but it was obvious Hand still suspected or even hoped that the Russian dancer, Olga, was right and that Taavi, the Estonian drumming engineer, was wrong. Hand wanted it true that they fought bears against dogs. To be deprived of this was cruel—it would have become part of his fascinating fact library, a cherished and much-polished object in his grand wing of animal cruelty anecdotes, though he had too many already.

We asked Taavi what he did for fun and he told a long story about him and his buddies drinking illegal vodka—not stronger, he said, but cheaper—out in the forest the week before—

"We call it moonshine," I said.

"Moo-shy?" Taavi said.

"No, mooooon-shine."

—around a fire. It sounded like fun; it sounded like Wisconsin, we said. Only certain people drink outside in the winter: people from the Midwest and people from Estonia.

"I think I like Wisconsin," he said, grinning.

"You miss the Soviets?" Hand asked.

He laughed. "No. Not so much."

He told us how he and his friends, as kids, would throw rocks at the army convoys. We told him how we'd thrown acorns at cops. He thought for a second. He stuck his lips out in an elaborate thinker's pucker. It was good to have Taavi with us, but awful, too.

The landscape around us, wooded and dusted with snow, was too familiar. Taavi was too familiar.

"You like it much better now? Since 1989?" Hand asked.

"Yes, yes," he smiled.

—It's your mouth maybe, Taavi.

"Estonia, the economy is very good?" Hand asked.

"[With chuckle] Starting to be good."

—It's the laugh.

—What about it?

"But it's doing well, in a short time, no?" Hand asked.

"Yes. I think so."

"But Tallinn is wealthy town, no? We hear everyone has the cell phone."

"Who says this?"

"The book." Hand showed him the guidebook. Taavi scanned the page, his fingers touching the paper like you would a crystal ball.

"[Chuckling] Oh no, not me, not me."

Nothing was true. Nothing in the guidebook was true but the maps. Are maps true? Nothing else was true. The word *fact* could not exist. All facts changed on the way to the printer.

Taavi pointed to a small factory, up ahead a half mile.

"I used to work there, during the summer." His English was better than Hand's.

"Right there?"

"Yes. I was . . . we build bridges."

"Right here?" I said. "They build the bridges there?"

"Yes."

The place didn't seem big enough.

"Like a factory? You did welding?"

"A little."

"So there's a big factory there?"

"Eet's not very big. Small bridges."

If this was true—that there were factories that built big bridges and others that built small ones—I knew my life would be richer and more intense in its pleasures. Hand was filing away this information, too.

"You want to see?" Taavi said, gesturing with his hand like a paddle, in a way that meant we could pull off at the next exit. Could we do this? *We could! We should.* It'll take too long. *Where else are you going?* Riga. We're going to Riga. *But what's in Riga?* Riga is in Riga, and we decided we'd see Riga.

"We better just keep going," I said.

"So tell us," said Hand, now in the booming voice of a generous host, "you want to be the engineer, or the drummer?"

The answer was quick: "A drummer, drummer!"

We all laughed. Hand and Taavi talked about studio time, what it cost in Estonia, where they had their tapes made, about how Metallica came to play Tallinn and drew over 30,000 people—the biggest-ever concert in Estonia. We liked Taavi and he liked us. I wanted to ask so many questions—I wanted him to tell us about Soviets with tanks stationed in Tallinn—to paint us that picture. And were there ever mini-revolts, mini-riots, an organized underground resistance? Did he have friends in the Soviet army, and if so had that created conflict—had any of them been punished or killed after Estonia was liberated—were there reprisals?

But we talked mostly about music and drinking. Hand had been to New York and that's where Taavi wanted to be. Hand had seen both the Who and the Sex Pistols reunion tours, both in Milwaukee, and that just about killed Taavi. That Taavi Mets seemed in every way someone we knew in high school was a natural thing and a reductive and unfortunate thing—Or maybe this was good. What did we want? We want the world smaller and bigger and just the same but advancing. We don't know what we want. I wondered if Taavi would want to come with us to Cairo and thought of asking him but thought against it. There was something so familiar about Taavi, maybe just something in the way he listened, or his little snorty chuckle, or probably it was the way he listened. His presence had begun to unsettle me. I liked Taavi but having him there, in that space between the front seats—it wasn't right, really. I was afraid someone would see him there. He would know—

This landscape was so familiar. The pine, the birch, the frosted road, the crows—

Oh fuck we tried. We could have gotten there sooner. He was still alive when we got there. When we got up to that godforsaken hospital in Fond du Lac, he was still alive. When I first knew and believed he'd been in the accident, that a truck had crushed his car, I thought he was gone but then Pilar said he was alive, he was hanging on, on respirators, and I gasped. Hand and I drove up at 8 P.M. and got to the hospital at ten.

Jack's mom was there, but his father was in the car getting a blanket. Why was he getting a blanket? Hand asked. "He gets cold so easily," she said. We couldn't see Jack. We weren't family and it was too soon. The room was crowded with doctors. Most of Jack's vertebrae had been crushed and his spine had been nearly severed. There was almost no chance of repairing it. But was there or wasn't there, for fuck's sake? We stood in the hall. We sat in the hall. I rested my head on the floor. Was there or wasn't there? The floor beneath me was cold but it was still and clean. The hospital was immaculate. I tilted my head and squinted across the floor, thinking I could make my sight travel the floor like a low-flying bird. The floor shone in a dull stupid way. *Was there or wasn't there?*

Jack's mom asked Hand to check on her husband—he'd been gone twenty minutes. Hand did and came back with him and whispered to me that he'd found Jack's dad kneeling by the trunk of the car, his hands over his head, on the hood, and Hand had stood above him for a minute or two before Jack's dad had noticed he was there. Hand was telling me this and I was listening but was

looking at a picture over his shoulder, one of a hundred in the hallway, all from the local arts center, watercolors by amateurs. The
one behind Hand was a blood orange with a knife through it.

Jack had been conscious when they brought him in. It was
midnight and we were alone with Jack's mom in the cafeteria and
she told us. She was eating a banana and told us while chewing.
She had such small eyes, lidless, slits cut from her face. Her forehead was lined heavily, the skin thick, the wrinkles like knife-cuts
into clay. We loved her but now felt betrayed. She hadn't told us
this sooner and she wasn't doing anything about anything. I was
jealous of the paramedics. I wanted to punch them in the stomach
and then stand over them, with my feet on their chests, and
demand to know what he said. What did he say? Jack's mom didn't
know. He was incoherent. Which was it, conscious or incoherent?
Idiot mom. She was gone. Useless. Everyone had already given up.
Jesus Christ, no one knew what they were doing. She went back
upstairs.

"She's worthless," Hand said. He was right. The father was
huddled in a blanket in the waiting room and the mother was eating a banana.

He was conscious when he came in. Goddammit, people, no
one's conscious when they come in and then—You can't let go
when someone's conscious when they motherfucking come in.
What were the chances that the doctors of Fond du Lac had any
idea what they were doing? No chance. Jack's parents were waiting
for the doctors to do something. There was no time to wait. What
the fuck were they doing?

"We should find those guys," Hand said. Outside the cafeteria,
we used the payphone and yellow pages to call the private ambu-
lance companies. No one would tell us anything, the fuckers—
wouldn't tell us if they had or hadn't picked him up. We decided
we didn't need to know what he'd said. We'd find out later but for
now it didn't matter. We had secret meetings in the parking lot,

Hand and I, kicking rocks and pulling branches from trees. Back in the hospital, Hand chased a doctor into the elevator and grilled her. Hand wanted to know more about the prognosis and treatment. No one would talk to us. "They fucked up," he said to me. "They fucked up and they're hiding something." "What'd she say?" "Nothing. Which proves it." The doctors knew more than they were telling us, and Hand was sure they could be doing more. They'd messed up and were covering it up. If he was conscious when he came in, he should be fine, Hand said. I agreed. He was conscious! They'd done something wrong.

Hand went to the twenty-four-hour Walgreen's and came back, walking briskly down the corridor, nodding, squinting, ready. "What is that?" I asked. "You know what it is," he said, pulling from the bag a minicassette recorder. I knew what he wanted to do. "You're not gonna get anything if they know they're being taped," I said. "I know that," he said, and then showed me the rest of the contents of the bag—a notebook, a bunch of bags of peanuts, a roll of white serrated medical tape and an ace bandage. "They won't know," he said.

In the bathroom Hand held the tape recorder against his stomach while I taped it on with the medical tape and then wrapped the bandage around his torso to keep it in place. The doctors who'd fucked up would go to jail. Or the paramedics. They'd be sued for billions. They'd be ruined. He wore the apparatus for the next six hours. The button on the top right side of the machine had to be pushed to record. He would pretend to sneeze, turn away and push the button. It would work.

But I didn't think it would work. The door was closed to the room where Jack was and I didn't know our next move. Every second we could have done something and we were waiting. We too were waiting. We were standing, blinking, waiting. We were thinking of things to do with our hands while we waited. Everyone was waiting. Only intermittently did the world give us tasks, in quick beautiful bursts, that we had to complete and feel electric and roaring while doing so. But here now we needed to act because only we could fix this. We couldn't do fucking anything. You come upon a store that's just closed. You see the lights on, you see the people still in there, putting things away, and you turn away, because a sign has told you to turn around. We're so easily thwarted. We're all weak and cowardly. But I want to pound the windows, to break the glass and thrust my hand in and turn the knob and let myself in—

Hand taped conversations with nurses and orderlies, getting closer to the doctors. When he filled one side of the tape, we went back into the bathroom and unwrapped him and switched the tape's side, and wrapped him back up. "You gotten anything good yet?" "Not quite, but I'm getting damned close. Everyone's scared. They're scared to death."

—Lord God, don't you think I could use these things against you? Don't you know that what *you* can do, *I* can do? Don't you know that I can summon your own winds, move the plates of this earth, just as you do? This earth is not yours; it's ours. Don't you fucking know this? Why do you play with us when you know I will do the same, and worse, to you? I will bring the winds of your world to bear against you. I will take your winds and twist them and throw them to you. I will mix them with your oceans, I will wrench them together and send them up to you and watch you drown in screaming waters of the blood and bones of your favorites. Look at you. Look at you! You all hairless and white with eyes burning black and red—what makes you so sure I won't hurt you the same way? What makes you so sure? I can take your skies and rip them in great swaths and crumple them, swallow them, turn them to fire. What makes you think I won't stalk you to the corners of the earth and make you pay for this? What makes you so sure that I won't bring it all back to you? I shall have waters of blood cast you away! I will sit upon the mount and send judgment down upon you. You shall cleave to *my* house! Therefore shall evil come upon thee; and mischief shall fall upon thee; thou shalt not be able to put it off: and desolation shall come upon thee suddenly, which thou shalt not know! And what shall ye say in the day of visitation, and in the desolation which shall come from below? To whom will ye flee for help? And where will ye have your glory?—

Oh Lord I am spinning and wet—I will forgive you everything before if you allow us this, if you allow us this. If you should allow us this, if you should invest us with the necessary strength and then clear our path, so shall I honor thee and praise thee across the earth. But if thee shall take him away I will know vengeance—

"I've got an idea," Hand said. "Get off the floor." Hand had been on the phone with a few of his medical acquaintances in St. Louis, and found a place in Mexico that did experimental spinal cord surgery.

"Where?"

"Chiapas."

"No."

"I swear."

The vertebrae would be replaced by ceramics made from molds of the originals, and the spinal cord would be frozen first—Hand said *hypothermal shock treatment*—making it more accepting of treatment, to peripheral nerve grafts—

"Insurance isn't going to pay for that kind of thing," I said. I was standing again now, and we were next to the blood orange painting. The painter of that orange was a lunatic.

"So? You have money," Hand said.

I did. I did! I was thrilled with the idea of using it now. *I'll use that godforsaken money!* I could use that money. The money had a purpose. I felt a divine order that I'd never known before. This was why I had been given the money. It all made sense. *Of course it makes sense! There is order!* A lightbulb, a windfall, now this.

—Lord God this is your last chance.

I was sure the Mexican treatment would cost exactly $80,000. This would work. It would be hard but it was possible. Sometimes there was work laid out before you and you had to thrust yourself into it and find your way out of it. I'd pay to fly Jack down there, however they did it. Was that some kind of helicopter? "A military plane," Jack said. That we'd hook onto a military jet already heading down that way. Or maybe the cargo hold of a regular jet. I'd never seen a gurney on a plane. "It'll cost more than $80,000," Hand said. "All in all, the whole treatment will end up costing more like half a million." "No, no," I said, so sure. "It'll be $80,000. It won't be more." There's a reason. This was when there would be a reason. He let it go.

It was only five o'clock in Hawaii so I called Cathy Wambat to make sure I could access all the money right away. It would take a day or two for the mutual funds, she said, and I'd be taxed. Fine, I said. How much in cash did I have? About twenty thousand, she said, in a money market. We hadn't invested it yet. Good, I said. $20,000 would be enough to get us started in Mexico, for sure. They'd know we could afford the procedure, they'd know we were serious. What about cash? I said. How would I get that in cash? I thought they'd prefer to have it in cash, to be able to prove it, clearly and without hesitation. She suggested a wire transfer. They could do one within an hour, she said. I said okay but wasn't sure. Would we have that hour? We'd know once we got to Mexico.

The payphone rang. It was my mom. Cathy had called her and given her the number. It was two in the morning. I didn't want to talk to her yet. Cathy hadn't known why I wanted the money but called Mom anyway. I'm driving up, she said. I told her we were bringing Jack to Mexico and we'd be gone by the time she made it here. I begged her not to ask questions—the plan was still in the works. It would be hard but it could be done. She could fly, she said. I told her to wait until the next day—maybe she should meet us in Mexico. How would she get to Mexico from Memphis? she asked. I don't know, I said. You're wasting our time. I made her promise she wouldn't tell Jack's parents about our plans. They wouldn't understand.

Now how to get to Mexico? We knew it was too far for a helicopter. But how to get the military plane? Hand thought he had a connection outside of Kansas City, at Whiteman Air Force Base. So a chopper to Kansas? Too far. Hand remembered a guy he knew at the base in Peoria—someone in the Air Guard there. Peoria was much closer. A chopper to Peoria, then to Kansas? Or maybe a plane from Great Lakes Naval Base? No, no, we had no connections there. We'd have to drive part of the way.

Fond du Lac to Peoria

Peoria to Whiteman

Whiteman to Mexico City

But why Whiteman at all? Maybe we could skip Whiteman. But did they have jets at Peoria, or were those all propeller planes? Hand was mulling. Hand made more calls. Soon we were sure the doctors were hiding something. We'd seen them talking among themselves, looking concerned, and one doctor raised his voice, angry at the rest of them, then was hushed. They avoided us. They avoided our stares! There was internal dissent. Someone had fucked up. Now it was too late for them to fix it. We had to leap in.

But the choppers and planes were falling through. Hand was calling his connections and getting no help. Regular people didn't get flown around on military planes, and we'd need to be family to get him on a commercial jet. Maybe bribe an agent at the airline? Too big a risk. We knew we might have to drive him all the way ourselves. We'd probably have to. We'd rent a minivan. The drive would take about thirty hours, we figured. Maybe more? Forty hours. We'd call his parents from the road. They'd know it was the best thing. They'd know they'd given up but we hadn't and that it was worth a shot. We had the money, we'd tell them. We had $80,000 and that would cover it completely. We'd have to be vague enough so they wouldn't try to find us, stop us. They'd have lost their minds by then and couldn't be trusted. They'd thank us in the end. We'd save Jack so they'd have to thank us. Would we get stopped at the border? We didn't know. We could hide him. He could be sleeping. We'd lower the gurney so it looked like a bed. We'd bring lots of pillows.

We asked again but they said it would be at least another twelve hours before we could go in and see him. "He'd want to see us," I told the doctor, and she nodded, and agreed but then said it would be twelve hours. We'd lock her in the closet. They were working on some of the lower vertebrae, then had to relieve some pressure on the brain stem, and then—

It's 3 A.M. We went to the parking lot again, to race. We were so wired we needed to run. We raced from one end to the other, dodging parked cars, under the lights that give us each six speeding shadows. The finish line was over a low hedge, rough, black— we had to jump it to win. There was work to be done but not yet; the time would come. When Mexico wakes up we'd call and let them know we're coming; when Jack stabilized we'd take him. But for now we'd have to fill the hours without sleeping and we ran around the parking lot and Hand imitated the way Jack runs, chest first, chin jutting out like he was forever at the finish line.

At 5 A.M. we were back inside and Jack's mom came in from the ICU. She said Jack's mental activity was minimal and was diminishing hourly. What does that mean? I asked. She said it meant that he didn't have any noticeable cranial activity—did she say cranial? that's not even right—that he was fading. She didn't say brain dead. She said his mental activity was receding, something like that. Hand wanted more details but she didn't have them. She and her husband weren't asking the right questions. We needed to be in charge. So they did an MRI? Hand asked. Of course, she said. He's not responding to any stimuli, she said. That doesn't mean anything, I said. You can't measure mental activity. You can't! I said. You're right, Hand said. Jack's mom left and Hand said he'd once read some journals to the same effect and that I was probably right. No one knew anything about mental activity. Can't measure it. Inexact science. Hand and I gave her words almost no thought.

Hand went to the Walgreen's again and got an atlas and plotted the best route down. We asked a nurse, our age, black and sturdy, how long each IV lasted. We'd need at least six of them, we figured. We'd bring ten. We asked if they had any portable respirators, respirators that could run on some kind of generator and into a car. Hand had been sure that they had portable kinds of every machine, and all had to be able to function in case of a power outage. She explained that the hospital had something that might be able to work if rigged properly. They had them in ambulances, after all. We'd go to the hardware store for wiring in the morning. When did everything open? Hardware was usually at six. The hours went quickly until five, then stopped. Between five and six we slapped ourselves to stay awake, alert. There was no news.

At 6 A.M. Hand went to the hardware store and came back with hundreds of dollars in extension cords, electrical wiring, copper cable—I didn't ask—and a small generator. At 7:30 I left to rent the minivan. We weren't that far from the Enterprise so they picked me up. It took too long. I waited in the parking lot for half an hour, cursing them, planning to ruin their van. A young bright cheerful guy with his polo shirt-collar turned up brought me to the office and twenty minutes later I was in the hospital lot, with a minivan the color of grape juice and we were removing the seats. The two back seats had to be taken out but to where? We left them on the sidewalk, planning to hide them in the woods across the street. So many other things had to be figured out. My car, which we'd driven up, would be found by the cops and they'd tow it and keep it once they knew we'd taken Jack. Did I care? I couldn't decide. No, I didn't care much. I moved it to the back of the lot, anyway, behind the building, near the dumpsters, still expecting to lose it. I grabbed what I could from the backseat and brought it to the minivan. The van was a strong car, and we could go fast. We could get a ticket in each state and still be fine. Just part of the trip. Wouldn't have to sleep or stop, with two of us driving. The terrain would get warmer as we got closer to where we'd bring Jack to have him saved, to have him wake up and say *Shit, guys, where the fuck am I?* and we'd tell him the story, and he'd be so amazed, but then not so surprised. As he recuperated everyone would come down and visit, and eventually we'd wonder if we should, hell, maybe stay down in Mexico after all, the three of us. Land down there would be so much cheaper than even Phelps, right? Damn right it would be cheaper. Maybe Jack would be fragile afterward. He'd be like Kennedy, where he'd be playing touch football and be fine that way, but also brittle, never quite robust again. Kennedy! Damn, that's who he looked like! Or was it just his hair, that neat part he wore? Or was it just the name they shared? I was trying to think, and was shielding my eyes from the new sun, low and screaming at me, watching as Hand was jogging back from the woods, where he'd hidden the seats. It was getting hot already, so early, when Jack's mom came out of the hospital doors and toward us with her hands clasped over her head—

"Not again," Hand said.
"I'm not, fucker."
"Don'twiththenewguyinthecar."
"I'm not."
Taavi said nothing.

The road bled into Pärnu, a small city of red squat brick buildings, and in its center the spires of a squat burgundy municipal building. This was where he was getting off, Taavi said.

"Here, stop please," he said. We stopped at a gas station. Hand gave him his address, and Taavi said he'd send Hand a tape, and we all said goodbye. Taavi got out and walked briskly across the parking lot, heading to the bus stop across the street. I pulled all the German marks out of my sock and gave them to Hand.

"Good," said Hand. "I was hoping you'd do that."

He ran after Taavi.

He caught up with him in the road and handed him the bills, about $850. "For the band," he said, "but not for vodka!" Taavi laughed and thanked him and jogged across the street. Hand walked back and closed the door and turned up the heat.

"That was good," said Hand.

I pulled out of the lot. We passed him, as he waited at the bus stop, but didn't want him to see us anymore, so we didn't wave.

"You still want to?" Hand asked.

I did.

At this point, the kids were definitely out of school. It was almost four and in the fading light—just a drop of yellow in a shallow pool of white—we saw them everywhere, the small people. Hand was driving now, and we passed the residential area off the main road, between the railroad tracks and the ocean. We knew where the kids were; now we had to bury the treasure.

We had at best an hour of daylight. We left town and after a few miles pulled off at some sort of forest preserve. We drove down a winding road, then over a set of train tracks, and immediately hit a three-pronged fork in the road. Hand stopped the car.

"This is as good as anyplace."

I agreed.

We got out and surveyed. I found a crooked tree about fifty feet from the base of the fork. Behind it there was already a kind of hole—home for chipmunks or snakes. It would do. I took a roll of bills from my left sock. With his feet Hand started gauging the distance from the fork to the tree, heel to toe, slowly, as if measuring a room. He was counting, concentrating, so I got a funny idea. Something funny I would say.

"Four six twelve ten one two six—"

This was good.

"Stop it, fucker."

"Nine eighty twelve four."

So good.

"Did that work?"

"Yeah, stupid."

"Whoa."

"What?"

"Whoa did I just pull some psy ops on you!"

He started over and when he finished it was twenty-three steps. He stood at the hole. The forest was soundless and still.

"What are you putting the treasure in?" he asked, without looking up.

"I don't know. Do we have a treasure chest?"

"No. But we do need something. You still have that thing you bought in Morocco?"

"The bracelet-vessel thing?"

"Yeah."

"No, that's for my mom. We can't use it," I said, knowing we would.

The forest was quiet.

I clawed through my backpack and found it. We stuffed the money into the case, silver and crude, bejeweled with colored glass. The bills didn't fit. I removed half the bills and folded those remaining, twice, and squeezed them in, their bulk straining under the lid. Inside was about 2,000 kroon, though we wanted it to be more. We were having an increasingly hard time getting rid of this goddamn money.

Hand dug behind the tree. "We bury it a foot or so down, then stick a knife from where it's buried."

"What knife?"

"The one you bought in Marrakesh."

"No way. I was giving that to Mo and Thor."

"We need it. It won't look right without the knife."

I had to agree that it would look cooler with the knife handle sticking out. I retrieved the knife and he stabbed it, blade-down, into the dirt, just above the treasure. It looked good, that knife, cheap but elaborately engraved, in this frozen Estonian forest, so quiet.

"What's the story we tell on the map?" Hand asked.

"What?"

"We need a story. To explain why it's here. Like, some Moroccan sailors were on the run from thieves and decided Pärnu was the safest place to hide their treasure."

After he said it, Hand decided that sounded just about right. "Yeah, that's the story," he said. I liked it, too. I would have loved it when I was nine. This would have sent my childhood in an entirely different direction. *Real buried treasure.* Even if the kid didn't believe in the Moroccan part, still it would be so expanding, would open their minds to such possibilities—this act alone could keep a child—and his or her friends, and theirs—from the grey low-slung sky of adolescence; whenever they would feel that they'd seen everything, or, conversely, that the extraordinary was not possible—and how funny that those two things, diametrically opposed, are always both found in the jaded brain—whenever that happened they'd remember the treasure, the Moroccans on the run, the fact that they'd found the money here, in this ragged forest by the tracks on the edge of their tiny town—

I wanted this so badly when I was young. With this my ceiling would have been higher.

I covered the knife with a long light branch covered in needles. Then, around the tree, we laid three long branches, in a loose triangle in a way, one that would be noticed by the eventual map-bearer but not the average passerby. On cue, a couple in jogging suits ran past, quickly glancing our way. Hand pretended to be examining some flora. I waved.

In the car, with the heat on, we drew the map. I wanted it to look weathered and authentically Moroccan, but feared that the ball-point pen betrayed its youth. I wanted it to be mysterious, with a cryptic and ancient aura, without implying the occult.

"Then why are you drawing the shiv?" Hand asked.

"Is that scary?"

"Of course it's scary."

"Too late now."

"At least make the knife shiny. Shiny knives are less scary."

I made the shiv shiny. Hand did the Moroccan-style writing—though Hand is not such a skilled speller—and made up the rules.

"Turn up the heat," Hand said. It was getting even colder. "Do you think the graph paper blows the mood?"

"It's the only paper we have," I said.

"What if we burn the edges?"

"No. Come on. That's so corny."

"It'll work," Hand said. "They'll believe it. We have to."

"I refuse."

"What kind of treasure map is drawn on neat graph paper with the spiral holes all frayed like that? It'll look like some idiot did it."

"You have matches?"

"In the first-aid kit," he said, lunging into the backseat for his backpack. He found the matches. I wanted to do the edge-burning myself.

"Give me those," I said. I got out and lit a match and set it upon the paper. It burned its liquid flame into the paper and I blew it out. My hands were so cold they were almost useless. I touched the flame to another part of the page, and extinguished it again. It did look better. I had one match left and applied it to the right edge of the map, here, and there, and there. I blew out all three small fires and then tried to blow out the match. I couldn't. I couldn't find the wind. My mouth opened but there was no wind. My head was light. I dropped the match. The upper half of my vision started darkening. I opened the door and sat inside.

"Close the door!" Hand said. "It's freezing."

I couldn't. I couldn't feel my hands. There was a vibration all the way through me, like my whole body was asleep, like a foot would be asleep. It shook my ribs and tickled them. It seemed to move my organs, switching their places, removing them, leaving cold cavities, then replacing them.

The air was so clear! Our breath so clear!

"Close it!" he yelled.

I found my hands again. I closed the door.

"Nice," he said, holding the map. "It looks much better."

I regained my vision and blinked slowly. Jesus.

"Freak," he said.

The map appears on the following page. You see how I made the knife shiny? I think it worked.

Hand turned the car around and we headed back into town. We had to find a boy or girl, alone, walking home, and then put the map, in a bottle, in their path. This seemed fine in theory but was instantly impossible to carry out. The streets were too crowded, and besides, if we chose one kid, he'd see us place the bottle in their path, ruining the mystery of its origin.

"We'll leave it in the bushes then," Hand said. "Some bushes on a well-traveled path."

"But what if a parent finds it?"

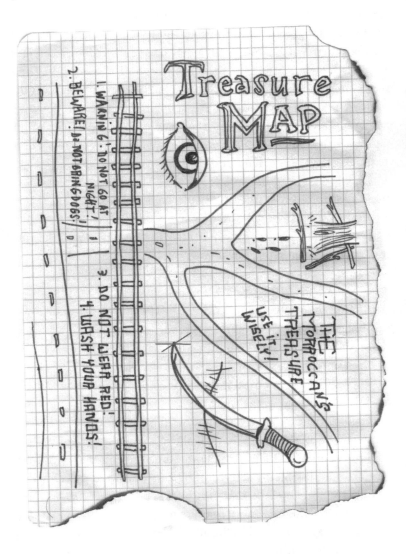

"Right. Forget it."

We decided to just give it to a kid. Just get out of the car and give it to him or her. No, a group of kids, so they felt safer—a kid alone would never take a map-holding bottle from a pair of strangers, right? But if the kids told their parents that a pair of Americans had given them this map, the parents, fearing some molestation trap, would definitely forbid their looking for it—

"We should just be straight-up about it." Hand sighed. "We'll just find a kid with his dad and give it to them together."

"No. No way. That isn't fun at all. What kid wants to look for treasure with his dad? No, no."

"Okay. I've got it. We find a bicycle in front of a house and stick it on the bike. Then we're sure it reaches the kid, he finds it himself—"

"Good. That's it." It was a good idea. And lent more romance to the project. Estonian bicycles! Maybe they were different. The spokes thinner—or *curved*.

We drove around the residential neighborhood, a mix of solid and ordinary suburban homes—not unlike those in our town, really—and shanties, sheds and empty lots. But after twenty minutes it was just about dark and we hadn't seen one bike. Hand scoffed.

"These kids don't ride bikes? What's wrong with them?"

"It's winter. It's too cold."

"*I* rode my bike in the winter."

"Course you did."

"I *did*. I had a fucking paper route!"

The ocean was now visible. Dunes just beyond the last row of houses. We turned the car.

We drove past the last houses and onto a narrow road that wound through tall grasses rising through ice and snow, great hairs from a white cold scalp. Over a small bridge and then almost to the beach and ah!—light! It was much brighter here. The sun was setting, or had recently set—it wasn't clear because the sky was only grey and pink and the cloud cover obscured the sun, if it was still at all with us. The ceiling was all mother-of-pearl, pink and blue and silver, tidepooling.

I jumped out and crunched through the snow. The wind shredded me. The beach was jagged ice-shards all the way to the water, scores of white dishes dropped and broken, the water frozen in its shallows. Off to the right and toward the shore was a swingset, two tires hanging and entwined. A simple silhouette alone against all the pinks and whites tangled in coarse yarn and smooth ribbons. It began to snow.

I ran back to the car and yelled as I did:

"This is it!

"This is it!

"Bring the bandanna!

"And the tape!"

Hand ducked into the car and came out and closed the door and, tripping over the white crooked ice, so like fragments of Sheetrock, he came to me.

"The swingset?"

"Yeah."

"Okay."

We would hide the map inside the tire on the swingset. It would be safe there, and would be discovered in the spring. We ran to it, our feet drawing groans from under sheets of ice. When we reached the swingset its supports were black thick-marker lines. Snow on the tires' tops and innards.

"We'll put it on the upper inside of this tire," I said. "It won't get snowed on there."

"How are you putting it together?"

"I'm gonna just put the money in the bandanna, and then tape it—God it's fucking cold! I can't feel my fingers already."

"Hurry!"

I put a roll of Moroccan money inside the blue bandanna and I folded the—

"Don't fold it," said Hand. "Roll it."

"You roll it. My hands are gone."

—map and he stuck it inside the bandanna.

"What's the money for?" he asked.

"So they know there's real money at stake. More where this came from, when they find the treasure—"

"Nice."

He closed the corners around the money and the scroll and I held it to the inside of the tire as Hand taped it there, looping the tape dispenser around and around. I couldn't feel my hands. I could feel my left thumb. My thumb was dimly attached. Otherwise, nothing.

"Is it stuck?" I asked.

"I think so."

"Let's go."

Back to the car and the thump-thump of the doors, and the heat on high. Snow covered the windshield in a thin gauzy skin. We hugged ourselves and shivered. Palms covered heaters. Fingers warming quickly, fingers that were brittle with cold now were melting, shrinking, becoming liquid. I thanked my fellow and previous humans for the miracle of heat and I started the car.

We drove in the dark to Latvia, past Häädemeeste, Jaagupi, Treimani, the snow coming at us like ghosts, an army of tiny ghosts with no leader. We debated the likelihood that someone would find the map. That someone would find it before spring. That someone would save the map, would actually obey its commands, would not throw it away.

"The money will prevent them from doing that," I said.

"Right. The teaser cash was good," Hand said. "But why did we put Moroccan money in the bandanna but Estonian money in the treasure?"

"Damn."

"We could go back."

"No, no. Let's go. We're almost at the border."

At the border town, Ainazi, a checkpoint. Part of me hoped for Soviets and Kalishnikovs. We stopped and Hand rolled down his window. A man in a full puffy snowsuit and a clipboard asked where we were coming from: Tallinn, we said; and where we were headed: Riga, we said. He asked to check the trunk; we complied. He had us get out—the air a cold that scrapes you everywhere, a credit card against an unshaven face—and then sent us to a window in a small building, where behind the window a woman, also in a snowsuit, asked us, in English, for our passports. We provided our passports and noticed she had a box of chocolates on her desk. The snowfall was thinning.

"I have a question," said Hand.

"Yes," she said, handing back his passport. It would be weird, I thought, to work at a desk, in a snowsuit. Hand:

"Are you going to offer us some of that chocolate or what?"

"These?" she said, pointing to her chocolates.

Hand rolled his eyes. "Yeah those. Are they all for you?"

She gave him a look, one of exasperation hiding great warmth, that said loudly that if he came back tomorrow they could be together and later married. She didn't seem to mind our filthy clothes and dirty faces. We'd vowed to get some new clothes, at least pants, in Riga. Our smell was now noticeable.

Smirking, she handed the box through the window. I took a round one. Hand grabbed three.

We said thank you and got back in the car.

"Latvians are great!" he said, pulling through the gate.

"Yeah," I said. "Latvians are the best!"

Twenty minutes later:

"These people are diseased!"

"They're fucking *wrong*."

"I don't understand," Hand said, "what the point is in acting that way."

"What the fuck did we do to that guy?" I said. We were back in the car, fuming, after stopping for gas and Pringles about twenty miles after the border. In the dark we'd pulled up to the gas station with a food mart and café attached, and the twelve people in the café inside had stared as if we were driving a hovercraft with bloody bodies strapped to the hood.

When we walked inside, the clerk, a square-shouldered man with a wide jaw squinted at us, but when we returned his stare he looked down. Everyone stared at us. Angrily, with visible suspicion, bald hatred, even menace. When we approached the counter Hand said hi to the burly man, with a little wave. The man did not return the greeting. We paid our money and the man slammed our change on the counter in a way that told us to leave, quickly, that we were not welcome. Now we were driving again through the frozen everything, on a two-lane road cut through a dark forest of straight thick unbending trees.

"They should like you," I said, pointing out that Hand, with his Aryan looks, his blond hair and dark eyes, at least seemed to belong here.

"But you're the Pole," he said.

"I'm a fourth Polish," I said. It might have been less. It was my father's name, which diminished my attachment to it, to its origin, to the ancestors whose genes gave way to that man.

"I know this comparison is going to sound weird," Hand was saying, "but I feel like we're black and in the Jim Crow south. Like they know they have to accept our money but they don't like it one bit. Like everyone here's just waiting for us to leave. I mean, do we look fucked up or something? Are we dressed funny?"

"You look like a snowboarder, I look like a junior explorer, and my face looks like something rotting."

—Why are you people the way you are?

—You cannot judge us.

—I know you.

—We have been overrun for centuries. The Swedes, the Germans, the Russians. Then the Germans again, the Russians again. In the last thousand years, we have known twenty years of peace. You have no place to judge. You know nothing.

—But I do!

—You can't ever guess at life, at pain. All pain is real, and all pain is personal. It's the most personal thing we have. It eats each of us differently. You cannot know—

—But I can! I can!

For a while we drove with our tongues. The road was empty and dry and I was behind the wheel and tried it first. I pushed my tongue down hard and got a sort of grip on the wheel. I could easily keep the car straight, but did not try turning. Then Hand, leaning over, licked the wheel to steer. It didn't work as well from the side. We kept veering. I wiped it down with one of Hand's shirts.

"That was fun," he said.

It wasn't all that much fun. For more fun we stopped for a second to practice rolling over the car like stuntmen, in case we got hit from the side while walking, or if we were chasing someone with a gun. We stopped and Hand got out. Then I drove, very slowly, and Hand ran from the side of the road, jumped, and rolled over the hood, regaining his feet on the right side. It was pretty smooth. Then we switched and I did it. For a moment, sliding over the hood, I knew I could have been a great cop. But being a cop requires you are forced to react only—your destiny daily is determined by the failings of the world—

We didn't have coats and after a few minutes couldn't feel our extremities. In the car we threw the heat on.

"I can't believe we never tried that before."

"I know," Hand said. "It's totally a skill you need."

Stopped in the road, our headlights were the only illumination for what seemed like hundreds of miles, though they, feeble and pointing down, made clear only the fifteen feet ahead of us.

"Let's run," Hand said.

"Where? The road?"

"Through the woods."

"Okay."

We ran down the embankment into the woods. It was absolute black. I knew one of us would hit a tree. I ran with my hands outstretched, like a blind sprinter. Hand hooted. We were running at full speed, dodging the trees, our footsteps skatching loudly under us on the thick crosshatched forest floor. My eyes were tearing up in the cold wind. The tears were leaving my eyes quickly and shimmying toward my ears. Hand was running with his arms out, too. I turned around briefly to see how far we'd gone. The car was visible but small. When Hand and I were young, before we knew Jack, we ran from the older kids. At high school football games, which were too boring to possibly watch, we'd throw acorns at their heads and run. We were never caught; we knew every hiding place, every gully and footbridge along the creek behind the field. Lord—just now I jumped over a circle of stones, the remnants of a fire in its center—what were we doing in Latvia?

Now there was snow again. It was black but the trees were slightly blacker, and the snow poked tiny holes into the surface of the night. My breathing was becoming louder, filling my head, and the leaves underfoot were hitting my feet harder—

I fell. The ground was soft and it was a relief to fall. It was warmer on the ground. Hand was ahead and still running. I turned onto my back and looked up through the black interlocking boughs, their edges silver. My breathing was so loud.

I had the fake star stickers on the ceiling of my room at home. The room had been Tommy's first, and he'd done it, and now they curled from the ceiling at their points. They didn't glow.

I would get up. I would walk the cold steps to my mom's room and as soon as her door was cracked her eyes would be open. She did not sleep the way people should sleep. She rested but never slept. *C'mere sweetie,* she would say and open her covers. The smell was sweat and lemon; her breath was so warm. It was so hot under that I wondered if I should go back, to my bed with its space, my cool blanket, my cool pillow. She would scratch my back softly for a few seconds and whisper

Oh Will

Oh William

Oh William honey

Oh Will my dearest one

Will, Will my son

then stop, falling back asleep, or wherever it was that she went. I would lie, staring at the painting on the wall, it appearing black and white in the dim foggy light. In the painting was a sailboat on sawhorses, tilted, with a green lake in the background. Or maybe a river. It was a boat being repaired—the picture was called "By Spring We Sail"—painted by my grandfather, she had explained once, hands on my shoulders as we looked at it. In her bed I would stare at this painting, its yellow greys and grey blues, its hollow whites, at the way the naked trees bent and the ground beneath them twisted and knotted.

Sometimes I wouldn't fall asleep and would slip out of the bed—from her hot face a breathy "Okay, sweetie, you go back to bed now"—and would slowly open her door, its bottom shushing over the carpet, slowly close it again, shushing again, and then would sit in the hallway, in front of the linen closet, sliding its two doors back and forth, slowly, first one open then the other. I would sleep in that closet often, on the floor, covered in towels. I would sleep anywhere; I would love to hear her looking for me in the mornings. I slept in the bathroom, head under toilet. I slept in the living room, under the glass coffee table, waking up to the white-ringed bottom of my milk glass from the night before; in the car I slept again and again, in the driver's seat, as she had so often done on long trips, after pulling over to rest on the heat-blurred high-way.

—Hand you're the one we never were sure about. When something had to be done, it wasn't you we went to. I went to Jack and Jack went to me. I trusted Jack. I trust you, too, but I knew, we knew, that you would not be there—not always. You were usually there but you have to always be present. Most of being a man is being there, Hand.

—You're talking about your father again.

—I am not!

—You are.

—I am. He was not there and that means you must! It means I know a man from a worm. And it means I have no patience for men who are worms. For men who are not there.

—But this whole trip, Will, is about you not being there. You're not anywhere. Where are you? Who are you there for? You're halfway across the world, driving at 100 mph through countries you know next to nothing about.

—There was a time when we planned to go into space.

—I did. That was me.

—When we all argued about whether we'd leave everything here to go into space. What we'd do if given the chance to see space on an exploratory mission, without possibility of return. Without possibility of ever seeing family or friends again. It was a choice between the world or your eyes.

—I said I'd go.

—That's why we worried about you, Hand.

—I won't go now.

—Now you wouldn't go.

—No.

We were lying in the forest and had to think of something to do. I had a vision and we would have to enact it. I told Hand that I would climb one of these trees and, once about twenty feet up, I'd jump from its branches to another tree, which I would catch and hang from.

"Can't be done," Hand said.

"Of course it can."

"Not by you. Look what happened to you in Morocco."

"That was different. It was a moving target."

"You'll die this time."

"We're doing it," I said.

"Now?"

"Give me a second."

I needed to rest first. It was still snowing. I needed to be sure.

—Jack.

—

—Jack I know you hate us for doing this. I know you think it's stupid. Everything we've done I know isn't your thing.

—

—Jack I have forced myself to dream of you. I have dreamt of you under ice, awake.

—

—Jack Lord God yesterday we traveled under a baking sun and in forests that looked like our forests. Jack I looked for you between those trees and I know it's stupid but in Saly while we watched a woman who would later be Annette, Hand talked about something called the multiverse and I wasn't really believing anything, wasn't convinced that what he said had any validity or basis in anything true but still then, as my fork ticked against my knife, I wondered over possibilities, and then today I found myself thinking that I would see you. Today it seemed not possible but maybe even probable. Probable here where the landscape was so similar to ours at home and—The multiverse explains dreaming, doesn't it? Fuck Jack I really thought we'd see you. But I don't even know if it's possible for you to live somewhere like this, another you, if you've died in Wisconsin. Is it many selves living at once, dying at once, or do all of our selves have their own path? I should have asked. Why didn't I ask?

—

—But Jack I've spent this day in Latvia thinking I would see you. The people here look like us, look like our neighbors, and the forests look like ours—there was a road today, one we followed looking for the Liv, that bent through pine so much like the road that takes us to Phelps and for a second I thought that yes something like this was possible and yes Hand and I would be delivered to you. I thought for a second that around the bend in the road there would be light and clarity and you'd be there and it would be like some kind of surprise party, you know what I mean?

—

—I just had a moment where I thought something like that was possible, that we would turn around a bend in the road and there would be an explanation, and an end, and we would say *Oh, right, there he is*. Or, *Of course, of course, it was leading up to this all the while*. Something like that, you know?

—

—Jack we have been above Marrakesh, to the top of the Atlas Mountains, we went there at midnight or something and we weren't even sure why but we outraced everyone chasing us and then we went up, and the whole while as we climbed I was sure there would be a reason. So often lately I have believed that if we put ourselves somewhere that we will be answered and there will be a reason. That if we see the Atlas Mountains in the dark and are compelled to drive to the top of the Atlas Mountains in the dark that once we've arrived at the top, after passing soldiers and over bridges, that a reason will be revealed to us. Because otherwise why have we come? Our own guidance systems . . . well, I just don't know if they're working so well at this point, we keep finding ourselves lost between the narrowest alleyways, men holding other men at knifepoint while others cheer and goad, and so many times I've thought that maybe that was the answer itself, that we were meant to stay there with them, that the car in front of us was meant to slow and the car behind us was meant to squeeze us and together they would keep us there, in those dark streets. But then the car chasing was gone, and maybe wasn't chasing us in the first place, and the car we followed we followed farther and he pointed us to the mountains. Everything opened up and we were free to go. We're there under the blank sky and we're free to go.

—

—So we went up to the mountain, as the air went cooler and colder, and we illuminated the treetops with our headlights, and all the while we were sure there would be a reason at the top, but then we were at the top, where we imagined the top to be, and we stopped and stepped out onto the road, and could feel that we were at the pinnacle of something, and there was silence. There was no sound of anything—no animals, no water, no birds, no insects, no people, not even the wind pushing through trees. We had come to the mountain, to its apex, and there was nothing. So many times this week Jack, Hand and I have found ourselves somewhere we thought would speak to us and when we got there no one was speaking to us. At the hospital, Jack, I was sure we were being spoken to, that we were being given a chance, that that wretched money would have a point and Hand and I would have a point but then your mom came out to the parking lot with her hands on her head.

—

—A few times out here, and on the savannah, people appeared and made gestures to us, and we gestured to them, but I don't know if we were understanding each other, ever. Sometimes we were. I don't know. We've chosen money as our language, and I don't know if it was the right one. Jack?

—

—You know, though, the worst thing was being on top of that mountain, and having the thought that I wanted to be back below, being chased through those streets. I don't want to tell you this because I'm not in a position to be wishing for these things, and I'm sure you find this offensive considering where you are and why but Jack while up on that mountain listening to nothing, waiting and hearing nothing, and getting cold, I wanted to be back down in those alleys. Jack I wanted to be pursued and wanted to pursue, I wanted to be closer to death than I did to be there in the silence at the top of the mountain. Jack I don't know if you know how quiet it was up there. It was so black! It was much lighter within those streets, and even the knife at the throat of the man being pressed against the wall of the alley seemed to promise so much comfort, the edge of the blade seemed to me to give such love, would be like a finger lightly stroking my neck, and I wanted then, on the roadside when Hand and I had gotten out and were waiting, to be back down there again, lost in that ghetto. There were rules down there, and there was a task at hand, and there were few options and with few options comes such great solace, Jack!

—

—Jack I never told you this but for so long I've wanted something like that, I wanted to have some kind of boundary, and this part you will hate but before you were gone and even after, I daydreamed about car crashes. I wanted so many times while driving to flip, to skid and flip and fall from the car and have something happen. I wanted to land on my head and lose half of it, or land on my legs and lose one or both—I wanted something to happen so my choices would be fewer, so my map would have a route straight through, in red. I wanted limitations, boundaries, to ease the burden, because the agony, Jack, when we were up there in the dark, was in the silence! All I ever wanted was to know what to do. In these last months I've had no clue, I've been paralyzed by the quiet, and for a moment something spoke to me, and we came here, or came to Africa, and intermittently there were answers, intermittently there was a chorus and they sang to us and pointing, and were watching and approving but just as often there was silence, and we stood blinking under the sun, or under the black sky, and we had to think of what to do next.

—

—Jesus, Jack, there would have to be a fucking reason that woman in London, that beautiful information woman, sent us here, right? When we were there it seemed random and we thought ha ha, we're in control, yes ha ha, we have a week and here we are why not—but then when we were on the plane, and landing in Tallinn, I had that feeling you always get when you've arrived somewhere unconscionable: you wonder what went wrong in the world to allow you to be there. You want to go back. You want to have never left home. You've made a mistake. Everyone's made a mistake. It's a nightmare. You want to have never left. You want to throw yourself back into your bed and then later spend the money on CDs. But you also hope that quickly you'll be told or reminded why you're there in the first place. At an airport I guess it would be if your relatives were waiting or something, your mother, your cousins, an aunt or uncle, nieces—you would see them, maybe your chubby little cousins, and they'd show you their homework or something and you'd know why you'd come. But I never had that kind of thing, you know that, and when we landed in Estonia, or any of those places, there was nothing, of course, no one waiting, and no one wanting us there, no one needing us. There wasn't one thread connecting us to anyone and we had to start threading, I guess, or else it would be just us, without any trail or web and if it was just us, ghosts, irrelevant and unbound, not people but only eyes, then there was something wrong. Something would feel wrong. I don't want it be just my eyes, do I, Jack?

—

—But I mean, $32,000? What kind of shit is that? What could that possibly mean? Jack at different times of my life I've wanted to be eyes only but I don't want to be eyes only. I want that knife at my throat, Jack, or holding the purses of the Moroccan girls so everyone can dance. And the $32,000—I know you would think I was a fucking jackass, I know you would stare at me for a full minute, cleaning your teeth with your tongue in a way that threw my stupidity back at me but I do think it's worked, is starting to work. Intermittently it works.

—

—Jack at the top of the mountain we heard nothing, and there was no order. There wasn't even a line in the middle of the road. There were no homes, no animals even. But within the streets below, chasing and being chased, following and being followed, there was such order! Brilliant order! Not a doubt about any one moment—all was scripted, all was action. Reason! Purpose! A love born of caring that we were there! Even if their intent was to rob or maim or kill, they cared enough to give chase! There was reason to the butchers pushing their bloody carts under the windows of the homes within which young boys heard the knives, still sharp after quartering so many calves, and they knew their future. There was reason! And I wanted to be that boy in that room. I wanted to be in that room, safe, enclosed, thinking of a girl in a burqa walking on the outer streets of Marrakesh with her mother, smiling at strangers in a car. Smiling at strangers in a car from behind her burqa good God can you imagine! That was it, Jack, holy fuck! I want to be in that room, Jack, thinking of one day knowing a Charlotte—Fuck, Jack, when we were young did you ever think we could know a Charlotte, a Charlotte with the hair to there and flesh abundant everywhere, a Charlotte who could kill us with one low meaningful laugh? In that room over the streets full of knives there would be life because you were never far from the touch of a blade or the hot breath of your mother, her breath on your back, half-asleep behind you as you watched the painting of the sailboat on sawhorses and dreamed of a home on Saturn—See, there was order there in those narrow streets! There was a task at hand! There were people to touch and fight! People to touch and fight! Fuck, even fighting is better than that quiet up there—I want only to speed more through that narrow path, feeling squeezed, chasing and chased—every turn was our only option and that felt so good!—but as we climbed up the mountains there was nothing like that—we couldn't even see where we were, how high, how far it would be to fall.

And so we came back down. And so soon we were back in the warmth of that labyrinth, looking for anything—for a cop to stop us, to ask us about Chicago, for people giving Hand notes of the gentlest affection after we taught them the shopping cart . . . Shit, Jack, I don't know what that was, all that dancing—what we're allowed to do when we're looking for things we're required to do. What are we allowed to do when we're looking for things we're required to do?

—

—Jack I'm sorry. But we're not going up there again, to that mountain, or maybe any mountain, again.

"Help me up here." Hand clasped his fingers together, making a stirrup, and hoisted my foot. I caught the lowest branch of a sturdy fir tree and pulled myself up. I stood on the branch, this one the thickness of my leg and extended perpendicularly from the trunk. I was about nine feet up.

"Just jump from there," Hand said, looking up at me. "I'll catch you here. It'll be great."

"I'm serious. I'm going up."

"Don't."

"You know you've always wanted to do this."

"So? I'm me, you're you. You're a wreck."

I took the next few branches quickly. They were spaced conveniently, and in a minute I was about eighteen feet above ground. It was brighter here, closer to the moon, but my visibility was still low. I wasn't really sure where I'd jump to. I had another vision, this one involving Hand jumping at the same time, to my tree. I shared the idea with him.

"No," he said.

"Yes," I said.

In a few minutes Hand was at eye level with me, about twelve feet away. I could make out his form, though not the details of his face. We were picking out branches on the opposite trees—him to mine, mine to his—to lunge toward and grab. The idea was to leap and, like a gymnast would an uneven bar, grab a branch, one below our present level, and once secure, purposely and carefully fall the last twelve or so feet.

"You got a branch?" I asked.

"I think so. The one right below you."

I hoped it was a strong branch. "Wait," I said, trying to inspect the limb below me. It was about twelve inches around. It looked strong. "Looks good," I said. "Is mine good?"

He did the same. "It looks strong," he said.

"Okay," I said. "I'm freezing. You ready?"

"No. Wait a sec," he said, blowing into his hands. "Okay."

"Okay."

"Shit," he said.

"I know."

"This is gonna hurt if we fall," he said.

"There's nothing sharp down there. All we can do is break bones."

"Don't land on your head, that'll be key."

"I know."

"You'll drag me out of here if I break something?" Hand asked.

"C'mon."

"Really."

"Sure."

"Good. Okay. Shit."

"Okay—"

"Man, this is like the helium," Hand said.

"What?"

"The helium. Didn't I tell you about that?"

"No. Let's go. Stop stalling."

"About Raymond and the helium and stuff?"

"No." He was maddening like this.

"We were in Senegal. I started telling you about it at one point. The day after."

"Can it wait? We should do this before our hands are too cold to grip."

"That's the point of the story."

"I know."

"No. I mean—Okay, forget it."

"On ten," I said, "we jump."

"We've wanted to do this since we were eight. You remember that?"

"That was from my roof to the tree, not tree to tree," I said. "Now shut up. Ten."

—Hand you need to do this.

"Nine."

—You fucking bastard this is for me.

"Eight," I said, my head humming. Could we get far enough across? We hadn't talked seriously about falling yet, the possibility of falling.

"Seven," I said.

—Hand: last chance.

"Six," he said.

Maybe it wasn't all that far. We felt safe.

"Five," I said.

—Hand if you jump I'll know I can leave.

"Four," he said.

It was an easy jump. It wasn't an easy jump. We were eighteen feet up and were jumping fourteen feet laterally. If we didn't hit or catch a branch to break our fall, we would break a leg or worse, for sure. *Can't land on your head.* I know, I know.

"Three," I said.

"Two," he said.

"One," I said. "Go."

"Now?"

"Go, Hand!"

He leapt toward me and I leapt toward him. We passed in the air. The air was black and all I saw were his eyes, his hands like huge white claws and then my own branch bisecting my vision, thrumming toward me. It hit my forearms and I fell until my hands caught it—I'd caught it!—and I stopped. My legs swung in front of me, and then back behind me, the weight straining my shoulders—but holy shit, I'd done it. I whooped. Hand whooped. I turned around and saw Hand's back to me, he too hanging by his arms, looking back at me, over his shoulder.

"Holy shit," he said.

"I know."

After a few seconds, we fell at the same time, the last twelve feet, collapsed on the loud dry forest floor.

"Oh man," Hand said.

"I know."

"I feel like I could catch anything."

"Yeah."

"I mean, any building. I could jump between any buildings. I always wanted to do that, too. How did we get to twenty-seven without ever trying that? Jumping between buildings? Everyone wants to do that."

It was not as cold on the floor, so low. My feet were bent below me, together and to the side, in a broken-looking way, but they were fine, and we were good.

Back in the car we warmed and picked sticks and leaves off our sweatshirts, out of our hair, while recounting the jump fifteen, twenty times, the best moments, the true feeling of flying while headed from one branch to the other, the incredible pull on our shoulders once we'd caught the branch, like a shark yanking our legs down from below—

"How much left? To Riga," I asked.

"About an hour."

"So the helium."

"Sure I never told you this?"

"Yes. Let's drive."

Hand pulled the car into drive and we left the forest.

"The Chilean helium thing, Raymond's story?"

"You didn't tell me," I said. "What story?"

"I thought I told you this. That last night after you fell asleep I went back to his room for the Scotch. We had a drink and he went into this long thing about his ancestors. We talked forever. I never told you any of this?"

"Shit."

"What?"

"Look."

Ahead of us, coming at us from the opposite direction, a police car fulminating. Soon it was stopped and the driver, arm out his window, was flagging us down. We stopped. The man in the passenger seat was out of the car and, in a ski suit, appeared at our window. He said something in Latvian. I lifted my hands and did a confused clown face. He barked through the window again and, guessing at his question, Hand passed me the rental car papers, which I handed through the window, with my license. He opened my door and beckoned me to follow. Hand opened his door and we were all standing. The officer, red-faced and with a blond crew cut, motioned Hand to get back inside. He did. I followed the officer to his car, where a larger officer, also in a ski suit, sat inside.

"Too fast," the first one said.

I told him I was sorry. I was, he said, going 123 in a 90 kph zone. I almost smiled.

"Oh," I said. We'd been going 135 a few minutes earlier.

"Too fast!" he yelled. He'd become suddenly angrier.

We hadn't really figured out the relationship between kilometers and miles per hour. Now I guessed I'd been speeding.

The cop was really angry.

"You pay fine," he said.

"Okay."

He didn't say how much.

"How much?" I asked.

He took out a calculator, just like the Moroccan two days before, and pressed 4-0-0.

"You take Estonian money?" I asked.

He sighed extravagantly. He didn't take Estonian money. He said something to his partner. They seemed flummoxed, then pissed off. They argued.

"That's all I have," I said. I showed him my wallet, full of Estonian money, with some marks and pounds mixed in. He returned to the calculator and tapped it. He and his cohort spoke quickly to each other. (*Ask for more!* How much? *Did you see that wad he had?* Grab it!)

He showed me the calculator. 2-0-0. I gave him 200 kroon and he waved me away.

Back in the car, Hand was playing with the stereo.

"I have a question," he said.

"Yeah."

"Is there any country where we haven't been stopped?"

"No."

"Not one."

"Wait. Estonia."

"We've been pulled over four times in five days."

This was true.

There is a corner of the sea that is deep but not so deep that it's black. It's the blue of a blueberry, violet in its heart, though this blue allows light through its million unseeable pores. The hue is evenly painted but electric, a klieg light pushing through a gel of cyan. But invading this blue are clouds of inky purple, billowing clouds curling in small waves, and they grow from below, splitting the sea between light above and dark growing from below.

Turn it upside down and this was the sky above Riga.

What did we expect of Riga? Something more drab, with less panache. But good God, this Riga, when we plowed through its suburbs and into the core of the place, was glittery and so alive. Full of stores still lit at 7 P.M., and hotels, casinos, restaurants, people going home in big coats and tall furry hats, the huge cable buses, whatever you call those things on tracks and attached from above, full of commuters rehashing in their heads easy but punishing mistakes and wondering about God and his gifts long-withheld.

We stopped at a clothing store, resembling a Gap and staffed by the same sorts of young and indifferent women. It was closed. We knocked on the window, watching the girls fold and carry hangers from the dressing rooms. We knocked again.

"Sorry," I said, as one, a short-haired girl with the face of a British boy, cracked the door. "We really need pants. Can we just run in and get something? We'll be easy."

We assumed they spoke English and were right. She smiled and let us in, locking the door behind us. I went to the shelf of pants, found my size in some green khaki kind of pants and brought them to the counter. There was another girl there, petite with black hair. Their skin, all of them, was so pale, petal-pink.

Hand asked them to dinner. They said no. They told us to come back the next day and then they would eat with us.

"We leave tomorrow," I said.

"But you said you just got here," the small one said.

"We did," I said. "Ten minutes ago."

I really wanted them to say yes. I wanted to talk, for once on this trip, to young women who were not for sale.

"We're buying," I said.

"You should come tomorrow," the taller one said. "Why not come back tomorrow? We eat tomorrow. Tonight we are busy."

We said we'd be back, knowing we wouldn't, and left and checked into a hotel in an ancient building the color of wet sand and next to a block-long McDonald's. We dropped our things and for a few minutes watched British news. They were covering the Paris to Dakar race—

"Holy shit."

"I can't believe it."

—though it seemed like weeks ago when we'd last seen news of it, but of course it had been one day, and two days before that the cars had been hurtling toward us, in Dakar, in person.

But now the race was over; someone had won, someone had died. A well-known driver had died, and this was big news, while the incidental deaths of seven pedestrians along the way was not.

We showered and dressed and had the concierge direct us to the restaurants. It was colder than before. It was so unreasonably cold. People hurried from amber-lighted door to amber-lighted door across the narrow cobblestone streets walled by ornate and tidy European storefronts, framed in ancient brown brick, offering food, compact discs, souvenirs, lingerie.

We got lost; we were hungry. Hand asked a young woman, with hands stuffed stiffly into her coat, if she spoke English. Without breaking stride she lied: "No."

We started jogging, looking for the place recommended. With help from a pair of middle-aged men who looked local but sounded Australian, we found the restaurant and inside everyone stared. The place looked medieval and knew it, with great tables of oak and long benches crowded with loud friends. We ate as people stared. We left as people stared. Was it my face? It was always my face. Everyone hated seeing a face like that. We wanted to be everyone's friend, wanted us all to sing hearty songs together, but instead they laughed privately and stared at us. We walked out and wanted to drink. The cobblestones soaked in our footsteps.

"Look at that." Hand was stopped and pointing to a small engraved sign above us. "The Jewish Museum."

"So?"

"I didn't think there were any left here. The Germans killed every Jew in the Baltics. I thought so at least."

We stood for a second. I breathed into my hands.

"That's got to be the grimmest place in Riga," he said.

"Yeah."

Hand shuddered. "I could never walk in that place. Can you

imagine coming back here? Being Jewish and coming back here? Fuck. No way."

We continued and when we couldn't stand the cold anymore, walked into a small bar and down a spiral staircase and stopped at a Lasertag labyrinth.

"Is this Lasertag?" Hand asked. The teenager at the counter stood up—

"It iz!"

—and led us into the room, painted in mid-eighties dayglo, like a retro disco built for bachelorette parties. The place was a half-bar, half-Lasertag outlet, which seemed to us like a plainly great idea. We went upstairs and ordered two beers. We watched people walk through the cold muttering, grimacing, planning.

"It's colder than Chicago," I said.

"The latitude must be similar. The air feels exactly the same."

"Everyone walks fast here."

"They all wear black."

"And fur."

"Right!" Hand said, "So much fur!"

"Almost all the women wear fur."

"Especially the over-forty women."

"But why all the black?"

"They are expressing their inner darkness. Their gloom. [Now in sociologist voice] The Latvians, many believe, cover themselves in large coats and furs because they want to *disappear*. They are ashamed of their bodies. And the hats. Notice the large hats, some also covered in fur. These they wear because they are ashamed of their heads—"

Two women near us, sitting at the bar, nodded hello. We said hello. Actually, only one spoke to us. She was about fifty, with short black hair, a masculine jaw and wide-set eyes, looking very much like someone's mom. She tipped her drink to us and asked questions—where from, having fun, where staying. We told her.

She moved from the bar to our table and sat down. Her name was Katya. Her friend, wearing a fuzzy blue fur coat that tickled her face like a feather boa, stayed at the bar, legs crossed on a high stool.

"How long are you stayingk een Riga?" she asked.

"We leave tomorrow," I said.

"Tomorrow! You come here for one drink!"

"Yes," said Hand, very seriously. "We heard the beer in Latvia was very good."

"Where in America do you live?"

Hand said Chicago.

"Chicago? Is it very dangerous?"

"Very!" he answered.

This comment somehow changed the tenor of the conversation, and prompted the advent of the furry woman. Her coat was green. She slid off her stool and descended to our table.

"She speaks no English," said Katya.

The second woman smiled, then held her thumb and forefinger an inch apart. "A little." She smiled again. Her eyes examined me and then, more closely, Hand. She squinted then opened them wide, in a way you'd have to call feline. She did it repeatedly. At some point some idiot must have told her that was sexy. Her name was Oksana.

"I am sorry we do not speak Latvian," Hand offered.

"We also don't speak Latvian," Katya said.

"What were you just using with your friend?"

"Russian. We are not Latvian. We are Russian."

"Oh. So you're visiting too?"

"No. We were born here."

"How are you Russian then?"

She said something to the green-fur friend and they both laughed—quick mean coughing laughs, laughs like the throwing of clenched fists.

"Half of Latvia is Russian," she said.

"Oh," we said. We had to accept this as true, until we could get back to our guidebook.

"But they treat us like [tongue out and hand waving away, dismissively, like brushing a cat off a tabletop]."

"They treat you not well? Why?"—Hand again. I wanted to beat him.

"Why? How do *I* know why? They are corrupt."

"Who?"

"The government. Run by the mafia. The people here, they are fine. But the government don't want us here and they make it hard. They are criminals, mafia."

"The government is the mafia?" Hand was really interested. The bartender, our age and goateed, was watching us.

"Of course. In Russia there is mafia too but they are not organized. They are broken and they [then gestures for stabbing through one's heart and the cutting of one's throat]. The mafia here is organized."

Here I knew what Hand was going to say—I saw it coming from miles away, a slow steamtrain chugging and hooting—and I could do nothing to stop it.

"So you might call it . . . organized crime?"

"Exactly," she said, nodding her head slowly, then pointing to Hand while taking a squinting sip of her drink. She didn't get the joke; Hand knew she wouldn't. He was such a prick.

A large man, bearded and ugly, the hooked face of a rooster, who was at the bar, was now standing behind the women and talking to me and Hand.

"Where are you from?" he asked.

We told him Montreal and gave him a bitter French-Canadian look, like he too was trying to oppress us.

"You like these women?" He swung his hand over their heads like a game show model would over a washer-dryer set.

We both nodded. We liked them fine.

The man scoffed. "A lot of people like these women. Real nice ladies!" A small woman slipped beside him, touched his shoulder and they started for the door.

"Have fun," he said to us over his shoulder.

Katya and Oksana glared. I glanced at Hand and we both knew. If we'd been smarter we'd have known sooner. But why are almost all of the women we meet in this line of work? *Because who else would talk to you?* I don't want to think that way. *And what line of work are you two in, if not the exhange of money for love?* Oh c'mon. *It's not that different, is it?* I want to think it's different.

"He is a stupid man," said Katya. "See how we are treated?"

The women talked about their rent, and the lack of work available, and about Katya's seven-year-old son. I asked if she had a picture of him, but she did not. Hand asked what kind of work they did. Katya paused for a few seconds, glanced at Oksana. They were unemployed, she said. Oksana did her catty eye thing again, to Hand.

"So," Katya said, to Hand, "do you like dancing?"

Hand said sure. Katya described a dance club, called The Pepsi—

"Like the drink?"

"I don't know."

"We have a drink called . . ."

"I know."

—where she assured us that there would be people, even tonight, very late on a weekday. Hand said maybe we'd meet her and her friend there. The lie was obvious to all.

"You will not come," the catwoman said to Hand, pouting.

"We will try," said Hand, holding her small hand between his two, still covered in marker from the Scorpions pouch he'd created in Senegal.

I stood up and indicated I was heading home. He stood, too.

"So you will meet us. You must," Katya said.

"Yes," he said.

—I would almost prefer if you just asked us for money.

"When? What time?" she said.

—You're playing us both ways. You'll offer Hand sex—you'll offer your friend—but if that doesn't work, you throw in the stuff about your kid. And we have no idea if you have a son at all.

—You have no right to judge.

—I think I can wonder. I can speculate.

—You can do neither. Just one day in my life would cripple you.

"Right after we change, we'll dance," said Hand, swinging his hand over his clothes like a security wand. "I don't want to wear this stuff to the disco."

"Okay, so half an hour?"

"Yes. Then we will meet."

"You will promise to come?"

"Yes."

"You promise?"

"Yes. We promise."

I was out the door and Hand followed.

The street was barren.

"You're not going to meet them?" I said.

"No."

"The one with the fur was kind of cute."

"I don't even know what to say," Hand said. "I feel so shitty for them. With Olga it was different, she was just between jobs or something. But these two—Why not give them the money?"

"We gave them some, didn't we?"

"No, we didn't. We paid for their drinks."

"Oh."

"You heard Katya talk about her kid, right? We should give her the money. Give her all of it. They need it, right? They've got the Estonians breathing down their ass. They need it."

"Who?" I said. "Breathing down their ass?"

"Yes. The Latvians. Sorry."

"I don't want to give it to them."

"Why? Because you don't like them."

"Right."

"But what does that mean? That makes no sense. You're going around rewarding what? Good manners? That's about control."

"Anytime you don't know your head from your browneye you say it's about control. *It's about control* has turned into the catch-phrase of you amateur psychologists."

We were heading toward the hotel, we thought, but were quickly losing our sense of direction.

"If you want, you can give them what I have in my shoe."

"How much?"

"About $200."

"I think we should."

"Fine."

We walked back in their direction. We started jogging again. I was jogging with my knees high, anything to keep warm.

"You never finished about the helium," I said, finding the words through pants. "Before we got stopped by the cops."

"Oh!" He stopped in his tracks. He liked that sort of drama. "I have to tell you this!"

"I think we're lost again."

"I know."

We asked an older man, heavy-lidded and angular. The man gave us a general sense of how far off we were. We thanked him and I thought of paying him for the directions, but his overcoat, of camel's hair, betrayed his wealth. We still didn't have jackets of any kind.

"Go on," I said, as we passed the Lasertag place again.

"Okay," Hand said. "I have to start back a ways. So first of all, I guess Raymond's ancestors were more or less native to Chile, on the Pacific—the southwestern part of the country. The something Archipelago. Chronos. Something like that. Chronos Archipelago. And these people had this theory, or maybe belief is the better word for it probably, that all people carry all of their relatives with them. Like in their blood, in their heads."

"That's not so—"

We were on a cobblestone side street. Riga was so tidy, everything reflecting the most delicate of European gestures, and yet I was—fuck—so stunningly cold.

"I know, it was how they put it," said Hand, "that made it different I guess. Their point was that not only are you of the same blood as those in your bloodline, but you carry all of their memories with you. All of their *souls*. You carry their dreams and their pains and their anger and everything. Raymond was talking a lot about the bad stuff you carry. Like if your relatives died in some wrong way."

"Jesus. Sounds terrifying."

We stopped at a shop selling cheese and electronics. We were the only people walking in Riga, it seemed. When we did see people, they were alone and walking briskly, shrouded in fur.

"No, they made it sound okay. It's like a density thing. Apparently they wanted that density of soul. The density is desirable. Apparently they see the soul the opposite as we do, where it's the lightest thing, this wispy ghost thing. They think of it like a mountain. Like a mountain each of us carries around, and you want your mountain strong and dense, because that means your family has lived lives of great experience. But the trick I guess is to find a way to move around."

"With your mountain."

"Yeah. This is where I got a little lost. I love the part about the blood and the voices of everyone in your head."

My feet were frozen. They felt like claws.

"You didn't do the voices part," I said.

"Sorry. Well, I guess you can hear from these people, the dead and the people who share your blood, your parents first and everyone else, aunts and uncles, on and on—on some level you share it all. In varying degrees, depending. Thousands of voices, millions maybe. This endless chorus. And it's all there in the blood! I love that idea. I was thinking of fiber-optic cables, the way they can hold all that information—"

"Oh come on."

"Let's go this way."

"Good."

"Well so the point is, these are the people you're responsible to. You're literally carrying them with you at all times. You're you but you're also *them*, in a way that's much more, you know, tangible than any Judeo-Christian way. And it's not a reincarnation kind of thing—you'll never really be you again, directing some body with any sort of control. You die and become of a chorus, a voice in a chorus. The way Raymond explained it, it sounded so beautiful. And so when we talk, you and I, we're speaking on some level with the voices of thousands. And part of the challenge is to remember this, or I guess the point of their ceremonies and teachings is putting themselves in better touch with the chorus, searching for them and recognizing them, speaking with them."

"Like channeling?"

"No, no. It's more like *listening*. It's considering. What was the word he used? It wasn't an English word, it was Spanish, I think, and he couldn't find a word for it in English or French. It meant speaking with the dreams of thousands, the judgment of a blood-line. Which I took it meant acting in a way taking into account this chorus."

"Right."

"I think that was it."

"But—Wait, is that the hotel? The spire there?"

"No. We face the square, remember?"

"Right."

"So . . ."

"Well, it sounds so limiting. It's like having your whole family second-guessing every action."

We were nowhere near the bar, or the Pepsi disco, but we did see the McDonald's, which meant we were close.

"Let's go in and ask the concierge," Hand said.

We passed through the revolving door and were warmed in the tall white marble lobby.

"Were you high?" I asked.

"What does that have to do with anything?"

"Go on."

The concierge was gone. We were at the desk. There were small maps of the city center. Hand took one. On the back were ads for restaurants and clubs. He located The Pepsi. We would go again and find them. We stood in the lobby, warming ourselves.

"We weren't high," Hand said.

"Fine. Go on. All the voices in the head."

"Maybe I'm not explaining it right. The way Raymond put it—it was so perfect—it just seemed so rich, their being alive. They carried their blood and their voices with such grace, you know?"

I didn't. "I don't."

"It's just this illusion we live with, the illusion that we want to for*get* things. That we need to forget so we can live, because everything is too *much*, our burdens are so great we need to self-lobotomize, at least partially, chemically or whatever, right?"

"Sure," I said.

"But these people *want* to carry around everything and everyone. They walk with thousands in each step, speaking with thousands with every word. They forget nothing, you know—they recognize the weight of these mountains, everyone walking around with these mountains, or trying to walk around. Man, these guys were amazing."

"I believe you. So is this a God-based religion? Did they have a main mountain-god entity guiding the rest, the mini-mountains?"

"No, no. That wouldn't fit. Why would you need a central over-seeing god when everyone has the wisdom of thousands inside? The accumulation makes all people have the wisdom of gods, the experience of immortals. Potentially at least."

"They worship themselves."

"No. No worship at all. It's just these people carrying around their mountains, knowing the weight of their souls."

"This is where the helium fits in?"

"Let's go find the ladies."

We braced ourselves and pushed through the door again and the cold punched us everywhere.

"So apparently," Hand continued, "ages ago these people, a thousand years ago or whatever, were bird-worshippers."

"Oh come on."

"They were totally fascinated by flight, more than most ancient tribes, and of course they wanted to fly themselves—"

"But there's a catch: they're mountains."

"Right, right. They were mountains, and so heavy. They knew this. So this was the primary problem of their civilization after a while. How to fly? How to fly with this weight? They would jump from small cliffs and try to fly, but would fall. Hundreds died that way, and they assumed it was because their souls were too heavy."

"Jesus."

"Yeah, they would just jump and fall. It was horrible. They lost about a third of every generation. So many died. So they started studying what the birds ate and did, and sort of applied what they could to emulate the birds."

"They made wings of feathers."

"No. They weren't allowed to harm the birds, their faith wouldn't allow it, so they couldn't get enough feathers. The main thing they figured out, I guess, was the concept of—"

He stopped.

"Didn't we see that cheese shop before?"

"Can't remember."

He checked the map. He chose a way.

"So what did they say about the birds? They studied them for about a hundred years and came up with something. Something about air. Sucking in air."

"I'm surprised you've remembered this much."

"Oh I remember everything. But I can't believe I'm not remembering their name. There was an Indian name and an English nickname—Oh!"

"What?"

"I remember the air thing. So they watched and studied the birds, and came to the conclusion that the birds ate air to stay afloat. They see the birds fly with their mouths open, like I guess whales eating plankton or whatever, and because their village was so high on this ridge, the birds they saw, hawks and falcons I guess, were gliding, using upward currents. So to these people the wings weren't seen as crucial."

"The wings weren't crucial."

"To them it was about air intake. They figured—you know, come to think of it, their science was pretty naïve, but it was ambitious in a way. They were really trying to figure things out. So they theorized that the birds were taking something from the air that they weren't, or processing it differently, or something. They saw these birds as vessels for gases, like balloons, with the wings just guidance tools. So they figured that they could be vessels for gas, too. Lighter than air. So they started jumping."

"They're lunatics."

"Well, they see the birds gliding around their valley, and gliding down and then up again, and they start thinking it has something to do with the angle of intake. They're really just experimenting, and they've already been jumping off the cliffs to their death, so now they just jump from lower levels, trying to get themselves full of this special air. They're jumping like crazy. They're jumping, and they're running, and it becomes just part of their daily routine, leaping around and darting from place to place."

"They're trying to what? Build up their helium content?"

"Something like that. They start mythologizing it all, claiming that some day their tribe will fly. They figure with enough jumping and the proper special air intake, maybe three generations away, there'll be enough helium in their mountains to fly."

"Jesus."

"Yeah, but of course it doesn't really work, and they start realizing, deep down, like Christians have with the Second Coming, that maybe it's not going to happen after all. But that doesn't mean the lessons aren't valuable. The one goal has all these nice by-products. In this case they started liking all the jumping around, I guess. It was part of their culture. They saw a hill, they started leaping down. They saw a green valley, they'd run like mad to the other side. And they had sex like mad, but I take it that was just some clever cleric's idea. Anyway, I guess it all looked pretty goofy to the Spaniards, all these people running and hopping around with their mouths wide open, like they were completely surprised or in awe all the time, so these people were always considered a little flaky."

"So they would just—"

"The Jumping People!"

"What?"

"That's what they called them. The Spanish found these people and they were jumping around all the time, going up hills and crests and jumping all the time, so they called them the Jumping People."

"The Jumping People."

"The Jumping People, yeah. They really liked to jump. It became a rite of passage, a big jump from the ridge, and they incorporated the whole custom with their mountains. They held onto the helium notion, or maybe it was hydrogen, but instead of flying they saw it as a way to lighten one's load, to leaven one's mountain. So they'd do all this leaping and running and swimming and stuff, just running and running around sometimes, to lighten the weight of their mountains. It became essential to their functioning at all. They figured in the need for not only food kind of nourishment, but also a helium kind of nourishment."

"And so they still live there?"

"In Chile? No. They were chased around by the Spaniards, I think. They were dispersed all over the place. But they were relatively nomadic in the first place, so it wasn't a huge deal. I think most ended up assimilating, though. Raymond thinks he's descended from them but there's almost no way to prove it."

"Oh."

"But get this. This is the best part. Or one of the best things. The conquistadors at some point are mounting a siege on their main village, high on a jagged ridge. It's Masada, basically. There's about three thousand Jumping People there, and maybe fifteen hundred Spanish, but the Spanish have the artillery, so the Jumping People know it's a lost cause."

"So they killed themselves."

"No! No, no. They don't do that. Never."

"Oh."

"Never!"

"So?"

"So they ran!"

"They ran."

"These guys think they're the fastest people on Earth! They think they can outrun anyone, barefoot. So they're going to wait for a while, see if the Spanish go away, and then they're gonna haul ass. They're going to fly, basically. Take their mountains and go."

"So they just left?"

"There wasn't anything there worth fighting about, from their perspective. I mean, they're just sitting there one day, and the next second there're these people who want to kill them or whatever. They just had no way of processing that."

"So they ran."

"The other thing they believed, which goes way back into their history and philosophy, is the impermanence of place. They didn't ever stay anywhere all that long. They weren't constantly nomadic, like moving every other week or whatever like Indian buffalo hunters or anything, but they had a curiosity about place, knew there were other places to go, and so when these guys are after their land, they're not thrilled about it, but they also don't feel like they own it or anything either, so—"

"They left."

"They moved on. They kept moving. There was a lot to see."

"And the conquistadors got the land or money or whatever."

"Yeah. But the Jumping People left this one message on the cliff above their village, carved it in for the conquistadors. This basically turned into the motto of the Jumping People, even though I don't think it makes all that much sense. I mean, it does and it doesn't. Raymond admitted that this has been translated from the original Jumping People tongue, into Spanish, and back again, and then into English, so who knows how accurate it is. There was another American scholar who polished the words, I guess, a guy at the University of Chicago, so at least it sounds like something you'd carve on a cliff over a village under siege, so your invaders would see it after you've left."

"Give me the fucking message."

Hand took a breath and opened his palms, as if accepting the gift of rain. "YOU SHALL KNOW OUR VELOCITY!" he bellowed into the cold exhausted city.

Ten minutes later we found it: The Pepsi was about a hundred yards in front of us.

"Good," said Hand. "I'm numb everywhere."

There was no one at the door and we descended a wide staircase into a low-ceilinged club, with red lights and barstools of dull copper. It looked like someone's basement, converted for good times at home. In the first booth, Oksana and Katya. Katya, facing the door, brightened when we finished the stairs and strode toward them.

"I am shocked!" she said as we slid into the booth, Hand next to Oksana and me next to Katya. "Never the men come!"

"We would not," said Hand, with a drama he relished, "have missed this for the world." Then he kissed her hand.

We drank some whiskey drink they were having and Hand danced with Oksana. I didn't want to dance with Katya. It would be, I thought, like dancing with one of the parents at a wedding.

"You do not like me," she said, looking at my forehead.

"I do," I said.

"Come home with me. You are tired."

I didn't want to go home with her. But I didn't want to wait for Hand. Hand was teaching Oksana the Charleston.

"I should wait for Hand," I said.

"Hand will be fine."

"Okay."

I had no interest in Katya sexually, and she had no charm. She was coarse and made no attempt to be pleasant. I didn't know why

I was going with her. I wanted to see her home, I guess, and see what she thought she'd do with me there. I signalled to Hand, now slow dancing with Oksana and her coat—she had not taken it off and it looked at first glance like Hand was dancing with it, the coat—to Cyndi Lauper, that I was leaving. He gave me a concerned look that softened into a shrug.

Outside we found a taxi and in the back I knew Katya's strong perfume, a sharp and liquid smell like apricots but alcoholic.

"What is your job?" she asked.

"I work for a contractor," I said.

"What is this?"

"A builder. Houses, offices. We build stuff."

"I see. You are tough man."

"Right," I said. "Tough man."

"And this is how you hurt your face," she said, reaching for my ear and then moving a hair from my eyes. "While building."

"Yes," I said.

"This will go away," she said, and waved the cuts from my head like she'd earlier waved off the Russians and their crimes.

She lived in a brick box, on the second floor, after a black-dark staircase up which she held my hand as we stepped over an animal, probably a dog but smelling worse, about ten minutes from The Pepsi. The coffee table was crowded with plates and glasses and what looked like schoolbooks. Above, a photograph of a man in uniform, circa 1970, mounted on posterboard and wrapped in plastic. On the couch, a huge blanket with a British flag as its pattern. There was a person under it. The son?

"My niece," Katya said. I peered around the blanket and saw the head of a young woman. I wondered where her son was, if she had a son. "Come this way," Katya told me.

She led me through a dim hallway, the color of wet sand, and into her room. A queen-sized bed, unmade. On the wall over the bed, a Hawaiian landscape, waterfalls bursting through the most optimistic green. She left the light off.

"Sit," she said.

I sat on the bed.

"Take off your clothes," she said.

"It's cold."

"Take off," she said, indicating my shirt.

I took off my shirt. When my face resurfaced she was gone. I heard running water in the hallway and it made me colder, and I thought about putting my shirt back on. Instead I took off my pants and boxers. I sat naked on the bed, wondering if my testicles were resting on something unsanitary.

She came through the door again and stood in front of me.

"What do you want here?" she said.

"Excuse me?" I spoke into her stomach.

"What do I do for you now?"

I had no idea. There had been the fleeting thought half an hour ago that at some point between the disco and here I would find myself attracted to her, or to the idea of consummating with this older tired woman. But now that I was here I felt like I was visiting my pediatrician. I shrugged.

"Lie down," she said.

I let myself fall back onto the bed. The mattress was thin and soft, styrofoam. My toes were cold and I could feel a draft, narrow but strong, come over my shins from the window to my right.

"Turn over," she said.

I did. I was warmer with my stomach on the flannel sheets. I closed my eyes and felt immediately that I would sleep here. Thirty seconds passed while I heard the whisper of clothing behind me. The thump of boots.

I felt the bed pull at the edge and then knew her heat above me. Her knee grazed the back of my left thigh, and her right hand sunk into the mattress near my right shoulder. Her pelvis landed on me first, on the upper part of my rear, then her stomach on my lower back, then her ribs and chest met my back. Her arms mirrored and rested on mine and she laced my fingers in hers.

"Are you warmer now?" she whispered into my neck.

"Yes," I said. I was so warm.

"Just lie here," she said.

"Okay."

And we did. I expected to feel her breathing on my spine, her chest heaving, but instead knew it through her pelvis, as it pushed into the small of my back each time she inhaled. Her midriff contracted with each breath and her pelvic bone pushed into me as her breathing, audible near my ear, set the beat of my heart. Her weight was the ideal weight and I was warm and wanted her to be warm.

I woke up at 4:30 alone in the bed. I found Katya in the living room, watching TV on the floor, with her back against the couch and sunk into her niece's rounded form. She was watching men in Michigan perform elaborate waterskiing tricks at high speeds.

"And that is it?" she said.

"I have to go," I said.

"Where?"

I wanted to tell her so badly. Cairo. Cairo!

"Back to the hotel. We drive back to Tallinn tomorrow."

"Is it nice?"

"What? Tallinn?" She hadn't been there—it was like someone from Green Bay never having been to Milwaukee.

She nodded.

"It's beautiful," I said. "We didn't see much."

"Will you help us?" she said, and held out her palm.

I looked at her for a moment. Her eyes did not blink.

"Of course," I said, and began exploring my pockets. I found a packet of traveler's checks. I wondered if I could sign them over to her but guessed I could not. In my side thigh pocket there was about 5,000 kroon. I gave it to her and looked for more, checking and rechecking pockets. How much was her lying on top of me worth? You couldn't measure it. You could say it was worth nothing—that it should have been free—or you could say millions and both would make sense. Nothing was quantifiable—or rather, at some point things were so, and numbers could be spoken with confidence, but no longer.

I found an American fifty in another pocket and gave it to her. She put the kroon aside to unfold and inspect the U.S. bill. That was all I had. I kept some Latvian coins in my left front pocket, worth about $12.

She noted my mild discomfort at having given away all that I had with me. "You will get more," she said.

"I know," I said.

"There is always more for people like you," she said, and pointed to the waterskiers, two of them, hitting a jump and soaring over a group of people, twelve and cowering, in a dinghy the color of new blood in an overhead sun.

I took a taxi through the black city to the Esplanäde Park and ran across it and burst into the hotel. In the elevator I dared myself to attach my head to the elevator wall. Then did it. I dared myself to walk around the elevator with my head attached to the wall, and did that, too, trying to make with my body the most oblique angle possible. The wall, the floor and I—as one we were isosceles.

Hand was awake and calling about flights to Cairo. We had forty-two hours before Hand had to be back in St. Louis and I had to be at the wedding in Cuernevaca, so we did the math, backward:

Three hours from New York to St. Louis

Two for the hours lost = five hours gone
Eleven between New York and Cairo
Eight hours in time-zone loss
Twenty-four hours right there
Eight to get from Riga to Cairo
Thirty-two hours, at least, in travel time.
I was deflated. Hand was excited.
"That's a solid ten hours in Cairo! Perfect!"
"But that's if we leave this second. It's midnight, Hand. We lose another eight sleeping tonight, here."

He watched me blankly, as if waiting to see if I'd take back what I said.

"Oh God," he said. He threw himself on the bed and cursed Latvia. Whose idea was Latvia? he wanted to know. I couldn't remember whose idea it had been. We'd picked it out of a big grey book. How could we trade Cairo for Riga? He was pacing. He turned the heater on then off. He tried to open the window but the window wasn't that kind of window. He brushed his teeth then opened a beer from the minibar.

We called the airport anyway. We learned we could get to Cairo the next day, but only via Prague. It would take ten hours in the air. We'd get to Egypt at 2 A.M. Hand was chipper again.

"That's perfect. We get off the plane, get a cab to Giza, climb Cheops at five, ready for the sunrise. We're there when it comes up, and then we shimmy down and have plenty of time to get back."

It did sound good. We called the airline again. But then learned that to get Hand back to St. Louis, we'd have to leave Egypt at 6 A.M. It was the only way he could make it. The limits were dawning on him.

"So we'd have about two hours at the pyramids."

"Right."

"In the middle of the night."

I nodded.

"Fuck!" He couldn't believe it. He turned on the TV, to a porn channel. Two American women had pulled up to a beachside house and asked directions from two long-haired men. Hand walked around the room, doing math in the air, carrying ones with his index finger, testing scenarios, asking the same questions: *Why isn't there a redeye? Are you sure the sunrise isn't till six . . .*

"We should go now," he said.

"Where?"

Now the women and men were having sex, the two pairs parallel and moving in unison, then perfectly alternating, like pistons. It was impressive.

"What happened with Katya?" he asked.

"Not much."

"You get naked?"

I nodded.

"You use something?"

"We didn't have sex."

"Still. If she was touching you—"

"It didn't happen that way," I said.

"Well, we have to get out of here," he said. "I hate it here. Riga sucks." He was watching for movement in the square below. I agreed it didn't make sense to be here.

"You know Cairo won't work," I said.

"But Cairo was the main place I wanted to be."

"Listen—"

"That's the main fucking place!"

The two women were now putting makeup on the men, and then were sitting on their laps, everyone naked and gyrating, and they were doing so while keeping time with the soundtrack.

"Fuck!" he yelled.

"Shut the fuck up!" I said.

"I can't believe we're not going to Cairo. Goddamn!" He kicked the TV, knocking off a faux-wood panel that obscured its fine-tuning dials.

"Get a little perspective, Hand," I said.

He was sitting now, on the heater, looking out at frozen Riga, then was yelling into his pillow about the unfairness of it all, how we had a week and were in Riga and would not make it to Cairo for the sunrise. How could everything else have gone so right, even the treasure map was so good, and now this?

I fell into sleep and Hand stayed up watching for hours, periodically calling airlines and whispering urgently to them, in tones alternately pleading and accusatory. I was afraid, vaguely, that he'd find a good fare and wake me up, insisting we leave immediately.

But in the morning we were still in Latvia and had until 2 P.M. to catch a flight to Copenhagen, the hub on the way to New York and then St. Louis for Hand and Mexico City for me. We decided to drive an hour northwest, along the coast, to look for the Liv village. They were indigent and dying and only five spoke their language. We'd find them, unload everything we had left, leave Latvia and the continent, and head home.

We were done. No Cairo. No sunrise at Cheops. And from now on, there would never be options, never like this again. Lord this was obscene. We should have saved the money, most of it, invested it, so there would always be more. I could have done this every year if I had planned it better. I planned nothing well. I dreaded being back in Chicago, or Memphis, wherever—the stasis, the slow suffocation of accumulation.

We needed more money, and another week somewhere, and we needed more Senegalese men residing in resorts-to-be, more children yelling bonjour!, more Moroccan discos and soft kisses goodbye, chocolates from a woman in a checkpoint parka.

TUESDAY

Morning in the hotel restaurant was all suits, continental breakfasts and tinkling silver. I felt dizzy. The silverware was so heavy.
"You have to drive today," I said.
"Fine. I'll drive. I want to drive."
We read an English-speaking newspaper commemorating the anniversary of the liberation of Riga. Citizen after citizen, their breath blurring their faces in the small snapshots of each, recounted where they were, how they felt, and all admired those who had defended the radio tower. We loved the Latvians again. They were tough as nails and they used the available light. They made their light into fire.

Hand drove and we went north from the city up the western coast of the Gulf of Riga, looking for the Liv. It was 10 A.M. when we started, and we had to make a flight from Riga at two. We hadn't thought it through. We couldn't make it there—it was 90 miles at least—and back in time to make the flight. But we didn't know that yet. The landscape was unchanging, was Wisconsin, the sky milky and suffocating.

I decided we had to send Mo and Thor a letter from Latvia. I'd been feeling guilty since we did the treasure map, knowing I'd never done one for them. I dug out the graph paper and started, though my hand was unsure and I felt dazed or drunk. I planned to send it to Stu and make him promise not to show it to Melinda.

Mo! Thor!

(Did you know that in Scandinavia they always use the exclamation mark in greeting? I think this is true, even though Hand told me this. Remember Hand? He took you to the aquarium and argued with the tour guide.) So I have advice for you guys. I don't want you to actually use it. I just want you to hear it, have it, sometime after the fact—after it's useful. Don't listen to me. Advice so rarely finds its intended audience. It's like the sword in the stone—you leave it there, maybe someday someone finds it

useful. Sorry, people—we're driving through Latvia and I can't vouch for my state of mind. 1. Thoughts are made of water and water always finds a way. 2. If you can't dodge the water, run.

"What are you writing?"

"A note to the twins."

"You can't write now. You're missing everything."

"But this looks like Michigan. I'm missing nothing."

"You'll never be here again. How can you not soak it in. Think about it—you will *never see* this again, *ever!*"

"I'm almost done. Let me finish."

"You're like the people that sleep on the plane. They're going over the Rockies or something and they're asleep, heads against the window."

"You slept on the plane, Hand. On the way to Dakar."

"That was at night."

He was right.

"Just shut the fuck up and let me finish."

3. There are bears and there are small dogs. Be strong like bear! If they take out your teeth, sit on the dogs. Bears always forget they can just sit on the dogs. Sit on the dogs!

4. If your house is haunted bring in your friends and start tearing the walls down. How can they haunt a house that you take apart? Aha!

We drove close to the water, the ocean to our right, through a rough-edged pine countryside, intermittent communities of that strange combination of vacation beachhouses and slump-shouldered shacks. We were ogled and squinted at by the pedestrians and motorists alike. We could not see why. At another gas station we were hated. I gave up on the postcard. I folded this one, too, and threw it into the backseat. I was out of postcards and hadn't gotten it right. We drove on, the sun melting the ice on our windshield.

"Here's a guy."

A man stood on the side of the road, leaning on a twisted cane.

In peasant garb, feet wrapped in cloth. A scrunched face, a knapsack by his feet, a wooden cart.

"We'll ask him directions to Riga."

Hand stopped.

We pulled up next to him and Hand got out. I could see him motioning inquisitively at the man. The man, extending a thick bent finger, pointed the way we were going. Hand used his arm, in a straight semaphore motion, to confirm. The man nodded, bewildered. For a full twenty seconds they alternated in pointing the same way down the same road. We all knew the way. It was ludicrous. The way was always obvious when you're right there and the road's straight and cold. Hand pulled out a wad of bills and gestured them toward the man. The man waved them off. Hand pushed them closer. The man took them as if accepting something more personal—a lock of hair or a handmade card. Then the man turned around and stood, watching the road in the direction we came.

After an hour we'd gone only about a quarter of an inch on the map and we knew we wouldn't make it to the Liv in time. We turned around.

As a kind of consolation, I turned off the main road and drove down a path to the ocean. It was less frozen than Estonia's side, but the beach was a melting smattering of ice and pools. I figured we should try to walk out to the water, and maybe swim. Swimming here would be spontaneous and would never be forgotten, if we survived.

Hand stayed close to the car as I made my way toward the water. There was an old cannon on the beach, stuffed with ice cream wrappers. I crunched toward the shore again. It was ice, though it wasn't clear how far below sat the sand.

I walked out toward the water, grey and studded with ice the size of softballs. A great slide of ice sloped out from the beach over the water. I rested my stomach against the ice and leaned down to touch the water. I'd done this on Phelps Lake. The water in winter was homelier and more affectionate.

The sun was gone. I had missed its final few seconds. Time had become elastic. I'd forgotten about Hand.

I rested my palm on the water. The water, undulating slightly with the waves unformed, rose to kiss my palm.

The water was not God. The water undulating slightly with the waves unformed was not spiritual. It was jagged cold water, and it felt perfect when we put our hand into it, and it kissed our palms again and again, would never stop kissing our palms—and why wasn't that enough?

Then I fell through. The ice under my legs gave way and I fell through three feet of ice and was knee-deep in the grey frigid water. I'd fallen through ice before, maybe a dozen times, but never on a beach like this, with a volume of water limitless. I gasped. For a second I knew something. I knew a grip that felt assured and felt right. It felt right. It felt right. It felt right. Maybe this was the way. There was a reason for this, I thought. This would be the way. When it happened, it would be something like this. I wondered if—

I turned quickly to Hand, expecting him to be running toward me, panicked. But he hadn't moved. He was laughing.

He was about a hundred feet away and was really enjoying himself. I thought I was in real trouble—I thought I would keep falling—but Hand saw it all, saw the depth, and laughed.

"You fucker," I said.

"You are way too entertaining," he said.

He lumbered over and helped me out.

We walked back to the car and turned the heat on my feet. My toes were cold rocks glued together. I took the shoes off and my feet melted like plastic.

We left. Hand continued to laugh, but I told him the water was kissing my palms again and again, and he knew what I was talking about.

Hundred and twenty kph through the forests of pine and birch, speeding toward the airport. We had an hour for a drive that should take two. We were headed straight into the sun, which was low already, the road slathered in mercury.

"We can go over the North Pole," Hand said. He was driving and had just pounded the steering wheel. The idea had him going. "We're pretty close, right?"

"No, I—"

"Of course we are. We're like two hours by plane. We get back home over the north pole. That'll be even better than Cairo. That's all I want."

"And you think there'll be flights over the North Pole, leaving today from Riga?"

"I do," he said. "I have a feeling."

I said nothing.

"I'm actually pretty excited to be home," Hand said. "I'll sleep through work tomorrow, though. It'll take a week, I bet, to get back in the flow. When do you get back from the wedding?"

—I don't, Hand.

"Will."

"I don't know, actually," I said. "I think I'm staying down there for a while."

—I'm going to keep going, Hand.

"How long?" he asked.

"I don't know."

He was staring at me.

"Drive," I said. "Watch the road."

—You understand me, Hand.

—Now I do.

* * *

Close to Riga, we stopped at a bus stop for directions to the airport, Hand dumping a wad of deutsch marks into the plastic shopping bag of an old woman. Off the highway we sped on the frontage road, passing through an uninterrupted string of shuttered factories and abandoned equipment. There were no signs for any airport, let alone the main airport leaving Riga, though on our map we were already upon it. To our left was a wide open field, covered in long yellow grass.

"That couldn't be it," I said.

"Dammit," Hand said.

We wound through light woods and between backyards, as the road potholed and split in widening tendrils. Finally it opened into a large parking lot before a handsome and completely dilapidated building resembling a great brown-brick midwestern train station.

There was one other vehicle in the lot, driving out as we were driving in. We waved it down.

"Excuse me!" Hand said.

The man, in the small weathered truck and wearing a painter's cap, shook his head.

"Airport?" Hand tried.

He shook his head and drove on.

This was a decommissioned Soviet airfield.

"Damn," I said. "We're missing our flight."

We drove the way we came. The airfield, as we ran along its perimeter, was now on fire. Flames five or six feet high, a swath fifty feet long. We hoped it was intentional. I thought maybe we should alert someone. But there was a truck on the field, and two men within. They had it under control. We kept going, toward the other airport on the map. We'd passed it on the way here.

We stopped again at the same bus stop, to confirm our direction, and found the same group still there, the same woman. She approached the car rapidly and started jabbering.

"Let's go," I said. "We don't have time."

We were back on the highway, heading back over the river and about twenty minutes from the airport. After suburbs and scenes of abandoned industry, we passed a mile of tiny shanties, stuck together it seemed, all low to the ground, built with scraps of lumber and corrugated steel.

"We still have too much," I said.

We would get rid of everything else here, everything we could find, though we didn't have time to stop and personally hand any of the money to the shanty-dwellers. I pulled my backpack from the backseat and grabbed most the Estonian money inside. I left a few bills, as souvenirs for Mo and Thor.

"How much is it?"

"All of it," I said. "We're leaving."

I crumpled it into a series of small orbs. About $3,000 worth.

"Do it," Hand said.

I heaved it out the window, toward the shacks, as we sped by doing 50 mph. It landed in the shrubbery between the road and the buildings.

I took all of the British pounds from my sock. Every window was open. I crumpled again and threw. The wind was everywhere and the bills swirled into the car and slapped our faces. I threw again.

"This is the —!" Hand yelled something.

"What?" I yelled. My head was out the window, watching the money loop and leap. I threw again. This time the wad undid itself midflight, bursting like a piñata, the money swirling in our wake. The truck behind us swerved to avoid it.

I found a stack of Moroccan bills and threw them. And Estonian money—everything. And in a minute it was gone, and it was so small, and at the real Riga airport, we careened past the security guys, again in their orange snowsuits, and slept en route to Denmark.

* * *

We had an hour in the Copenhagen airport. There had been no flights over the North Pole and Hand had taken it hard. In the Danish airport, customs: "Is this your first time in Denmark?" "Yes." "Well then I welcome you!" I found a phone and called Mom. As I dialed, a Japanese man walked by with a Hello Kitty bandage on his eyebrow.

"So who got the cash today?" Mom asked.

"An old peasant man."

"Oh good. Peasants are good."

"And we threw some out the window of the car."

"To more peasants?"

"We didn't see the people. We were passing a shantytown near the airport. It was endless. It looked fake almost."

—Mom I'll take you with me. You'll meet me down here and we'll go. We'll keep going south. I have some money left and we'll get rid of it.

"And you threw the money out the window."

"Right. British money, mostly. It was cold."

"That reminds me. Someone left the windows open here."

"What?"

"I came home from the market and the house was almost flying with wind. Everything was moving! This was Dorothy's house, Will. And I thought to myself, *Who would have come and left all the windows open?* And my brain gave me one person, a certain Will H.—"

"Mom."

—You'll meet me and we'll go.

"Well, I guess we'll leave this one a mystery, won't we?"

—It's so hard to listen to you, Mom. You don't even know. Can't you hear me catching my breath? You haven't even seen me since. Mom, you don't know what they did to me.

———

—I haven't given you anything of substance ever, my mother. I will give you something. I will take you in this world, the fourth world, whatever the hell it is. You don't know how close I've felt so many times this week. My heart's been shaking and popping, Mom. It's so strange. But I feel good. I've got a good running start now. It'll be so good. I'm going to get you and take you and we'll go fast.

Hand's face appeared next to me, anxious.

"I have to go," I told her.

—We're flying over the ocean. Mom: over the ocean!

I hung up. The airport was full of glorious clean-smelling people. This had to be the richest and most magnificent airport in the world. Hand and I got in the security line.

In front of us a family, or some sort of large group, was saying goodbye to a man of about thirty, they doting and sad and he excruciatingly handsome. First a man, older and balding, hugged him and whispered something. Maybe the uncle. Then a young girl, sixteen, reached up—the handsome man was tall—and hugged him and kissed him. Then a boy, about thirteen, reached up and hugged him and kissed him. There were four women about his age there, too, and they each stepped in and held him tightly, then stepped back again. Then they all did it again, in order, this time with more kissing. Finally, there was his mother, it seemed, who I hadn't seen at first but who now threw her arms around him, kissing his neck and whispering in his ear. It was, the whole scene with all of them, almost lewd—such affection!—but then wasn't lewd at all.

Hand and I had to get on different planes.

"I'm glad we did that," he said.

"It was a good week," I said.

We shook hands and said good-bye.

* * *

There was a vacant seat between my seat, 13C, and a grandfather's, by the window, and we both stretched our legs. When we dozed we knew our feet were touching but neither bothered to shift. I forgot my Churchill on the plane and I don't remember being at Heathrow; I was there, wandered around and sat waiting for three hours. I connected and slept sitting upright in my aisle seat and landed in Mexico City in the morning, with a spinning and newly risen sun.

WEDNESDAY

I needed cash and looked for traveler's checks. None in my backpack, none in my pockets. I checked again. Nothing. I had given too much away. I was an idiot. I had no money. I knew there was nothing in my ATM card for three more days. Jesus.

In one pocket I found 2,000 dirham. I brought it to the Mexican currency exchange desk.

"We don't take second-tier currency," the man said. I could have said something about the peso but said nothing.

I remembered my shoes. I sat down on a bench and took them off. Under one sole was an American hundred-dollar bill. Under the other sole was an envelope, folded twice, with $1,000 in traveler's checks. Deliverance.

But it was soaking wet. My traveler's checks, now in Mexico, were still soaked from the Baltic Sea, from when I'd fallen through the Latvian ice. On the bench's small side-table I laid them out to dry, all ten checks.

As I waited, porters and travelers glanced at me and my setup. I was, it seemed, playing solitaire, or that memory-concentration game, with my money. I smiled weakly.

A group stood watching me. It was a family maybe. There was

a young girl, twelve maybe and molded quickly from baby fat, and she had a plan. She approached me, followed by the rest.

"Hello," she said, in English. "How are you?"

I told her I was fine.

"Good," she said. "Can I . . . can I ask you questions?" She had a notebook at her chest. Behind her were five huge smiles. A father, mother, little brother (also a pudgy one), and maybe an aunt and uncle? They were all watching, a few steps back.

I asked her if this was for school. "*Para escuela?*" I said.

She smiled and nodded. Her brother, who was now right behind her, nodded, too. He looked like a kid I knew when I was little, a tubby tan boy named Carter.

"Is this your first time to Mexico?" she asked.

"Yes," I said.

She checked a box in her notebook.

"What is . . . your name?"

"My full name?"

She wrote something down. She continued.

"Have you ever had Mexican food?"

"Yes. Many times."

She thought my name was My Full Name. I almost laughed. You could see her outy belly button through her too-small shirt, hippos dancing across her stomach.

"Have you bought any Mexican . . . andicraff?" she asked.

"Handicrafts? No, not yet."

She checked a box.

"Do you like Mexico?"

"Yes," I said. "Very much. I love Mexico." I wanted to say so much more. I wanted to say, first and foremost, that I loved her. And that I loved her brother, and only partly because he looked like my first friend. And also I loved her family—what kind of perfect, astounding family would travel, en masse, to the airport to help with their daughter's social studies project? She would never know anything but abundant and unceasing love. I wanted to be part of her family, to move in with them. I would pull my weight.

I was grinning at her and they were grinning at me.

"Thank you very much," she said. "Can we take picture now?"

I said sure. I was still sitting as the father came forward with a camera and the brother came to my side. I grabbed the brother's waist, all that chub, with his sister on my right.

"*Como te llamas?*" I asked him.

"Gabriel," he said.

"*Y tú?*" I asked the girl.

"Tiffany," she said.

I said nothing.

"Tiffany María Cervantes," she said.

I laughed. She smiled.

These two would always love each other. Dad took the picture and thanked me. I wanted a hug from the girl but decided it might seem strange. She would do it, give me the hug, but then they'd feel sorry for me and wonder what was wrong, why it was that I needed affection from strangers twelve years old.

It hit me then that her teacher would know she'd messed up the part about my name. I had to correct it on her paper.

"*Por favor,*" I said. "*Mi nombre es . . . no es . . .* "

She looked confused. I thought about just taking her pen and fixing it in her notebook but now the family was watching as if something was wrong.

"*Por favor,*" I said again, then took one of the checks, still soggy on the edges, and held it to her, with my finger underlining my name in the middle. "*Mi . . .*" I said.

The implications swirled. My name was my name—was comprehensible and complete—only while watched by the centurion, only on the line upper-center of the check, and I hated this name, hated it there. But Tiffany María understood. She began copying my name into her book, front teeth biting lower lip, determined to get it right. She finished and showed it to me. I smiled.

I patted her on the back. She waved goodbye. Her family, behind her, waved too and she joined them and they walked down the corridor, where light burst through the doors and threw itself across the floor in thick white stripes.

I was writing quickly. First I wrote my name, signed each check on the bottom line, matching my signature again. I signed nine checks, knowing each time I came one step closer to being done with that godawful name of mine. *Swik, swoop, swik swoop*—each dotted *i* a stab at that wretched man. And then I started over, and in the middle of each check wrote her name, with more clarity and flourish each time:

Tiffany María Cervantes
Tiffany María Cervantes
Tiffany María Cervantes
Tiffany María Cervantes
Tiffany María Cervantes
Tiffany María Cervantes
Tiffany María Cervantes
Tiffany María Cervantes
Tiffany María Cervantes

And I put the checks back into their wet envelope and was ready to go after her—they were still visible, the whole family, five white doors down—but could they cash these things? Nine hundred dollars made out to a twelve-year-old?

I wrote a note of explanation. I took the checks out again—I could still see them; they'd stopped to interview another traveler—and I put my driver's license number on the back of each. I stuffed the checks back in. That would prove it. I was free and I took off after them, running like an idiot, chest puffing, chin leading my way.

*　*　*

They were still chasing me, laughing but confused, when I got on the bus to Cuernavaca. It was pretty great. I had no baggage to throw in that storage compartment underneath so I just leaped on and the bus drove away, pulled away as they came after me, all six of them, Tiffany's dad first, and I waved from my tinted window as we pushed off.

The bus was crowded and smelled of someone's spaghetti lunch. There were TVs above us and a romantic comedy flickered on just as the bus's babies began to wail and just before I fell into a perfect swirling leaden blue-black sleep. For three hours I was out cold, drool pooling on my shoulder, my crown resting on the cool dark window.

My room was in a huge old yellow mansion, where much of the wedding would be held, on the tip-top of a hill, overlooking all of the twisted and unnavigable, plainly beautiful pastel patchwork city, with stables next door and lilies everywhere. I arrived late, after 2 A.M., and everyone was asleep. While they slept I ran through the cool empty halls. I flew down the stairs and into the courtyard. On the grounds, black and wet with dew, there were peacocks—blue peacocks and also three white peacocks, magnificent, so pure they shocked, and with their tails extending four feet behind them, each levitating perfectly and horizontally, like a magician's assistant sleeping and unconcerned. I slept in the biggest bed I'd ever seen, high off the ground and so soft, a bed atop a thousand beds, surrounded by a small close-knit group of books, hovering in mahogany, about the miracles of the saints.

The next day there was a lunch where everyone, really just about almost everyone, maybe a hundred of the wedding's guests, gave a toast, some in both Spanish and English, everyone brilliant and wiping away tears with fingers and palms and it was all so gorgeous, the sun lighting the umbrellas like lanterns—on that green lawn everywhere people wept. The bride and groom mentioned how many children they hoped to have—between six and twelve—and that no matter where they chose to live—and frankly they had no idea just yet—the babies would be born in Mexico, so their systems would be tougher, not so fragile, not like the babies born in America.

And there was a girl there I knew in high school, Frances, now pregnant and married to a huge blond man from Mexico City, who worked on the Sacramento River, taking pictures of whitewater rafters as they passed the bend, and I almost cried when I saw her—I never thought I'd see her again!—she was so big, and with cheeks so red, her husband so proud—such a good-looking baby that would be—and the ceremony itself, in an ancient church a mile away from the estate, wore moaning music by a bowlegged band of plum-clad mariachis above us and when the bride and groom walked out we threw pink and yellow and white flower petals, all still moist with life, and the neighborhood children scrambled to pick them up and throw them again.

At the reception that night, outdoors under a strong-mooned sky, amid the whitest of tablecloths, amid the white chairs and so many lilies, we ate and bought cigars from the waiters on the sly and then everyone moved for the dance floor and I didn't know if I could dance too but my pregnant friend pulled me out and, sober, I jumped around with her, as she laughed and laughed. My back felt good and my head was clear! When she left with her husband I stayed, and I danced with the bride, and with the groom, and with the tiny flower girls, and with the wild-haired bridesmaid whose hand at the small of my back was the grip of great strength and utter determination—

And soon there were only twenty of us left—the parents and children had gone home—and we danced until two and then three to Slade and Quiet Riot and Cyndi Lauper, her voice tearing through us with its bloody wailing grieving hope—the deejay, from Cuernevaca, knew everything and knew joy and how to maintain and even elevate joy—and when at five we were all soaked in sweat and bewildered by how blessed we were, after the last bus left, for the hotels, leaving us to get home via foot or taxi or sleep under a table on the high soft grass, people started jumping in the pool and when they jumped in I jumped in too. I took off my pants and my shoes which still held currency from a cold and suspicious land and I jumped in—it took so long to land and in the air I saw all the faces!—I jumped with my mouth so open, taking it all in, and the air was cold and the water was so cold but I jumped all the way in, all at once, and my heart froze. Man, I thought that was the end, right there. It stopped for a minute I swear, but then the sound and pictures came back on and for two more interminable months we lived.

Acknowledgments

Thank you Flagg, Marny, Sam, Jenny, Chris, Brie, John, Cressida, Andrew, Michael and Eli. Thank you Sarah, Barb, Julie, Scott, Yosh and everyone at McSwys and 826 Valencia. Thank you Toph and Bill. This book owes a tremendous debt to Brent Hoff.